Advance Reviews of *House of Clouds*

"KI Thompson's historical romance, *House of Clouds*, envelops the reader in the drama of the Civil War and the intense passion of a woman's love story…Thompson shares her gift for vivid description with fascinating detail to make her characters and their struggles come alive. This novel offers the reader an opportunity to enjoy a good story that is both well-written and captivating." – Diane S. Isaacs, PhD in African American Studies; Professor, George Washington University Honors Program

"In her first novel, writer KI Thompson has ventured into well-trodden ground—the American Civil War—and made it fresh and fascinating all over again…If you think you've heard it all before, you haven't. This isn't just the Blue Coats vs. Johnny Reb, the drum-and-bugle-corps history we are so familiar with. This is the consequences of war as played out in the disrupted and chaotic lives of the women of that era…This is a lovely romance. It has the inevitability of a well-structured novel and the emotional delight of a troubadour's tale one wants to hear again and again. With her first novel, KI Thompson has entered the community of 'ink-stained wretches' who enchant us all with stories well-told. Welcome, Ms. Thompson, to the ranks of the writers. I look forward to your next book." – Ann Bannon, *The Beebo Brinker Chronicles*

House of Clouds

by

KI Thompson

2007

HOUSE OF CLOUDS

ISBN 10: 1-933110-94-5
ISBN 13: 978-1-933110-94-3

This Trade Paperback Original Is Published By
Bold Strokes Books, Inc.,
New York, USA

First Edition: October 2007.

Library of Congress Control Number: 2007933422

Credits
Editors: Jennifer Knight and Stacia Seaman
Production Design: Stacia Seaman
Cover Art: Barb Kiwak (WWW.KIWAK.COM)
Cover Design By Sheri (GRAPHICARTIST2020@HOTMAIL.COM)

Acknowledgments

There are not enough words to express my gratitude and admiration for Radclyffe. Thank you for your vision and dedication to publishing as well as the craft of writing.

My editor, Jennifer Knight, richly deserves the accolades for the breadth and depth of her genius. Thank you for your hard work helping to make this story what it has become.

The beautiful painting on the front of the book is due to the talented artist Barb Kiwak, and the graphic design work of Sheri. I could not have imagined a better cover.

I am indebted to the invaluable research assistance of Marty Corson, who gave freely of her time and did so enthusiastically.

My deep appreciation also goes to Toni and Tarsha for their helpful comments and support.

To Kathi, the best beta reader and supporter ever, without whom this book would never have been written.

And finally, to readers everywhere who still love the feel of a book in their hands. Thank you.

Dedication

I have never studied the art of paying compliments to women; but I must say that if all that has been said by orators and poets since the creation of the world in praise of women were applied to the women of America, it would not do them justice for their conduct during this war. I will close by saying, God Bless the women of America!

> Abraham Lincoln, Closing of the Sanitary Fair in Washington, DC, March 18, 1864

For all the women throughout history whose stories we'll never know. And for Kathi, whose history and future are my own. You are my heart.

Prologue

April 1871

A light mist collected on dense foliage and dogwood blossoms as a lone figure meandered along the path leading into the woods. The sound of receding thunder whispered to her that the storm had dissipated and was moving on. As she approached her destination, the tangle of brush and overhanging vines nearly suffocated what had once been a well-kept garden. And with each step her sadness deepened, clutching at her heart and summoning memories of a childhood blithely spent in the shadow of cataclysmic change to come.

The clearing she sought was recognizable only by a familiar stand of oak trees and the opening of the canopy overhead. She stood still, staring into the knotted overgrowth until she saw the ivy-covered stone. Brushing away dead leaves, she laid a bundle of white lilies on the damp ground at its base. Almost ten years had passed since she had stood over her brother's grave that muggy summer morning in 1861. Laura traced a finger over the letters etched in the stone marker. *Ransom Barrett St. Clair*. She was still stunned, still devastated, that in an instant a life could be snuffed out, a future snatched away. Such hope, such endeavor, was housed in the fragile flesh of fathers, sons, and brothers. So many of Virginia's young men would no longer walk the land, hunt in her woods, or grow old to see their grandchildren thrive.

The Civil War, the War Between the States, the War of Northern Aggression, whatever one's point of view, had stretched its gnarled fingers across the land of her childhood, leaving no household untouched. Four years of fighting had produced nearly one million casualties, three percent of the population. Over six hundred thousand men had died, appallingly many more from disease than in battle. At Gettysburg alone, more than fifty thousand men had been killed or wounded, or had gone missing during the three-day battle. The statistics were incomprehensible to Laura, even ten years later.

The war had come home to the St. Clair family almost immediately, with the First Battle of Manassas, the bloody fray that abruptly ended illusions of romantic heroism. The battle took place on the hills overlooking Bull Run, in Virginia, and began badly, with the Union forces descending in an attempt to flank the Confederate left. Outnumbered, the men in gray had crumbled at first, but as reinforcements arrived, the South retaliated and forced the Federals to retreat in confusion. Somehow, during this retreat and the capture of Union prisoners, Ransom was killed.

Laura could still recall every detail of that day in late July when her life changed forever. An officer in gray rode up to the St. Clair home on a bay gelding and dismounted in one swift motion. He was fair haired and not a tall man, but wore his yellow sash and braid of the Confederate Cavalry with distinction. He delivered his news in an emotionless tone, perhaps not so much for their sake as for his own. His face gave little away, but Laura could see his hands shaking very slightly. Her mother asked if he was present at the battle himself, and if he had known Ransom. He admitted to being at Manassas but with a regiment on the other side of the field. Regrettably, he had not made her son's acquaintance, but he'd heard from other officers that Ransom had acquitted himself heroically.

Laura had received the news as though standing outside her own body, hearing but not believing. Ransom had seemed an indestructible constant in her life, the brother she could rely on in the worst of times. For days afterward, she moved numbly from room to room in the house, too restless to remain in one place, unable to occupy herself with Bible readings or needlework. That he had been taken in the first major battle of the war made his loss all the more difficult to believe and to bear. The newspapers gave accounts of the battle, but in glorious and triumphant praise. The South had expected a victory, but not at such a high price, and none of the Northern spectators who gathered on the slopes with their picnic baskets had anticipated ten hours of human butchery and a panic-stricken stampede back to Washington.

The details of the dead and dying were left to the women to ascertain as best they could. Many traveled to the field of battle to prowl among the carnage in search of their sons and husbands, while others kept watch outside post offices, awaiting the casualty lists that were posted on the doors each day.

In the years that followed, Laura read every account she could find and listened to stories from the lips of wounded soldiers and veterans who had somehow survived four years of fighting. She desperately wanted an eyewitness, someone who could tell her exactly how Ransom died, if he had managed to say anything to anyone, if he suffered. Now, long after the collapse of the Confederacy, she had given up hope of ever discovering the circumstances, and she wondered why an explanation mattered so much. The facts would change nothing of the larger truth she lived with, that he was gone, and all she had left were the shifting sands of memory and a future that would never be.

Already, with time, her memories of Ransom had begun to fade and their precious moments together seemed further into the past. Their relationship had withstood all that life had thrown their way, from dark secrets about their parents to a war they both believed in, yet had not understood. Laura often wondered if Ransom had shared her private misgivings about their way of life and the cause that would eventually be vanquished. Would it have made a difference for him? Would he have done as so many other young men did, and simply chosen to fight on the opposite side? Would he still be alive if he had traded honor for victory?

A slight breeze drifted through the clearing, bringing relief from the humidity that weighed upon her almost as heavily as her thoughts. She lingered at the graveside, delaying her return to Charles City. The locals looked upon her with undisguised hatred. To them, she was a traitor to her country and an embarrassment to her family, especially her brother, a hero of the Confederacy. She avoided their angry stares and concealed her hurt over the insults and petty humiliations she had to endure on her daily rides from town to Barrett Hall. For a long while she had not been able to face coming back, but she was no longer afraid or ashamed. She felt sad, appalled by the impoverished homes, and shocked by the wailing bitterness that flowed like a ghost river through the South.

Had the war really changed anything? If not, for what purpose this devastation, for what the sacrifice of so many? Tears stung the corners of Laura's eyes and she dabbed at them lightly. She had walked through cemeteries, along the orderly rows, reading the names aloud. She had prayed in church for the souls of the dead, and she had begged God to give her answers. But even God had turned His face away from the country. He had no answers to give.

Perhaps it was true what they said, that He was punishing the South for the sin of slavery. Little seemed to have changed. White people still treated their colored neighbors with contempt and resented those who could find paid work. Even living up North where so many former slaves had fled, Laura could see that relations between the races were far from cordial. But at least she felt safe, far removed from the lawlessness and desperation of the South. Sometimes she thought about the modest comforts of her life and felt guilty that she was the one who had survived.

Coming back, standing over her brother's grave, she had made herself remember all she wanted to forget, because that much was owed to those whose blood and bones decayed beneath the earth, whose eyes saw no glory, whose nation was lost to them. *Good-bye, Ransom.*

Laura returned the same way she had come, avoiding the briars and rocks strewn along the path. After a short distance, she stopped and faced what remained of her childhood home, a crumbling red brick chimney. Unlike the slave quarters made of brick and still standing near the fields, the abandoned house had escaped burning by the Yankees, only to be destroyed by locals. Any wood that had not been carried off for fuel had long ago rotted and dissolved into the earth. While these ruins had once been the beautiful house where she was born and raised, Barrett Hall had never really felt like home to her, not like the home she had now.

She had always known that someday she would leave the plantation, as it merely provided shelter and the requisite nourishment for that eventuality. Looking back, she realized all that had really mattered to her were the people in her life. At first, home and family had sustained her. Her father, Edward, whom she adored and idolized; her mother, Rachel, who, although they were never close, had earned Laura's respect for surviving all that had happened to her; Ransom, whom she loved more than life itself; and even her younger sister Meg who, despite everything, Laura knew she would always love. And then there was Martha, the St. Clair cook who had been a slave long before Laura was born and now lived free somewhere. Laura had confided in Martha all her hopes and dreams, not realizing that Martha had her own dreams to fulfill and, like so many others, bided her time until God and the Yankees set her free. Her daughter, Ruby, would not be so fortunate.

They were all gone now. Like characters in a novel whom she'd grown fond of in the reading, they had been placed on a shelf in her heart to be revisited often. She had begun a new life in a small, unfamiliar town among strangers who knew nothing of her past, nothing of her family, her childhood friends and acquaintances, and nothing about the experiences that had made her the woman she was. She had formed new friendships and created new memories, but though Chambersburg, Pennsylvania, had been her home for ten years, Barrett Hall beckoned from a past that would always remain a part of her. It called to her in her dreams and in the dark of night, when she sought escape from the insistent drumbeat of memory. She had not been ready to answer that call until now.

Chapter One

Ten years earlier
November 1860

Laura St. Clair wrestled with her hoop skirts as she rushed out the front door. Her father's carriage rolled up Barrett Hall's broad entrance road and came to a clattering halt before the house.

"Papa?" she cried, barely waiting for the slaves to still the horses. "Who is President?"

Edward St. Clair stepped down from his place alongside their coachman, John. His face was grim and although he opened his arms in a great bear hug, Laura could see that the news was not auspicious. She sighed deeply as she was enveloped and held close. She was happy to see the parent she loved, but she was upset by the defeated expression he had swiftly concealed and the anxiety that creased his forehead. Her father was a robust, barrel-chested man with ruddy complexion and flowing silver hair matched by an equally flowing mustache of which he was very proud. He walked like a man accustomed to being obeyed, confident in his ability to manage his property and his family. However, this morning his posture sagged a little, hinting at a weariness that was more than physical.

"Who, Papa?" Laura begged once more as he released her.

Before he could answer, Rachel St. Clair stepped onto the porch. "Good morning, Edward. It is good to see you home."

"Rachel." He glanced up at her sadly. "I am afraid it is to be Mr. Lincoln. God help us all."

Laura's mother paled, her hand rising to her throat. Visibly gathering herself, she said, "Come to the dining room, my dear. I've been holding breakfast far too long and can only hope that it has not entirely gone to waste."

She reentered the house with Edward and Laura following behind. Out of the corner of her eye, Laura observed John and another house servant unloading the luggage. From their impassive expressions, it seemed neither man had heard the announcement. Typically when the master arrived home from an extended absence, they were animated, but now it was as though they were mute, unable to hear or understand the news that their world was about to change forever.

In the main hallway, Edward handed his coat, hat, and gloves to Henry, his trusted valet.

Leaning into her father, Laura whispered conspiratorially. "Is it war then, Papa?"

"No one knows what will happen, my dear, but I fear the possibility. Threats are being made every day, but so far nothing has changed."

"Margaret?" Rachel called up the stairs to Laura's younger sister. "Margaret, you hurry now, breakfast is on the table and you will get none of it if you are not here in one minute."

From a distance could be heard the reply, "Coming, Mamma!"

Laura followed her parents into the dining room, where the polished mahogany table was completely laid out with linen, china, silverware, and crystal. As they sat down at their regular places, with Edward St. Clair at the head, she heard the sound of footsteps on the stair and moments later, Meg flounced into the room and sat down hard upon her chair, folding her arms across her chest in the process.

Laura could almost hear her father sigh as they all waited to hear what complaint was in store this morning.

"Margaret St. Clair!" Rachel spoke sternly. "You have not yet welcomed your father home."

Dutifully, Meg arose and tossed her golden curls from her eyes. Putting on her most sincere smile, she skipped to her father's side and kissed him affectionately on the cheek. "I'm sorry, Papa. Welcome home. Did you bring me something from Richmond?"

As Rachel watched her younger daughter wheedle and flutter begging eyes, she reflected that Meg had the potential to be every bit as beautiful a young woman as her older sister were it not for the hard, thin-lipped expression carved indelibly upon her face. This suggested a harshness and experience well beyond her years, and a willful nature in sore need of correction. Rachel was confident that with time she could shape Meg into the very woman that she envisioned her to be. She was not so sure about Laura.

"Don't I always bring you something from my travels?" Edward laughed warmly. "Later, my dear. For now, you must eat and then we shall see what I have brought back from the city."

Sarah, the serving girl, entered the dining room, placed trays of ham and eggs on the sideboard, then went to fetch the biscuits and gravy. While they awaited her return, Laura begged her father for news of the latest events.

He stroked his mustache thoughtfully. "Well, it's too soon to tell, but I have been asked to return to Richmond as soon as possible. There are firebrands and compromisers, and all sorts in between in the legislature. Some are for secession, some against. Virginia, like all the other Southern states, must meet to decide what she shall do, if anything."

"If you must return, then you must." Rachel paused to command, "Sarah, be careful with that ladle. Don't rap it against the side of the dish so harshly. It is delicate china and breakable, do you understand me?"

"Yes'm." Sarah flinched slightly and scurried out of the room.

"Richmond is too close to Washington and quite vulnerable," Rachel said, returning her attention to the family. "Virginia must surely make preparations to defend herself."

"Will Ransom be in the fight, Papa?" Meg asked excitedly.

"I would venture to say that all the cadets at West Point will be making up their minds as to which side they will fight on, if there is a fight, little one. Let's hope it doesn't come to that."

"So, Papa, we will be staying in town then, won't we?" Laura was excited. When they resided in Richmond she could visit friends, attend the theatre, and shop in the stores where the newest fashions were available. Best of all, the latest developments would take place there, and her father's membership in the Virginia legislature meant she would receive her information firsthand.

"Yes, I will definitely be spending all my time there." Edward sliced a piece of ham with his knife. "You, however, may come and go as you please from Barrett Hall."

"Someone must remain here to take charge of the fields and the laborers," Rachel said. "I don't trust the overseer to attend to our affairs as he ought."

"Well," Edward reflected, "as soon as the crops are planted, there won't be much to do except wait until they are ready to be harvested, which won't be for some time to come. Richmond is not such a distance that I cannot be here whenever I am needed."

"Oh, Papa," Meg finally piped up, her earlier sulky mood forgotten, "am I to come to Richmond as well? May I, Papa?"

"Yes, my dear. Everyone can come, at least for now. I have missed you all these last weeks and am in no hurry to be away from you again so soon."

"When shall we leave?" Rachel asked.

Edward shrugged. "Within the month."

❖

Barrett Hall was more than a home, it was a way of life. The plantation extended northward from the tidewaters of the James River deep into the interior of Charles City County, Virginia. A tobacco-growing property, it had descended through the Barrett family for seven generations until it passed to the oldest surviving child in the line. Rachel Barrett was a girl of sixteen at the time.

Laura sometimes wondered how it must have been for her mother to lose a father to typhus after the deaths of all but one sibling through childhood. Her sister Ann, although only one year younger, had a delicate constitution and was almost as dependent on Rachel as their invalid mother. Single-handedly Rachel had taken on the running of the plantation, supervision of the slaves and crops, as well as the running of the household. She had done it all seemingly without effort, as though her destiny was written on the landscape. These responsibilities had shaped the steely, determined woman she would become. Rachel did not allow sentiment to dictate her decisions; life had given her no other choice. For her, the land was all that mattered, all that gave meaning to a life entirely shaped by the legacy that was Barrett Hall.

The plantation was not merely about its past, the accomplishments of its owners and the production of its main crop. Barrett Hall was a timeless, living and breathing sanctuary that spoke of blossoming love and tears yet to be shed, of the eternal cycle of life and the traditions that linked each successive generation. Rachel had chosen a husband she thought would be a capable master for the rich acres that sustained her, the children they would have, and the sixty slaves who depended on them for food and shelter. Over the past several years, she had spoken of her decision to Laura, making it plain that Laura, too, was expected to marry for duty. She seemed slighted by Laura's slowness to do so. Time was marching on, and with the prospect of strife between North and South a daughter should be a comfort to her mother, not an affliction.

The late fall of 1860 found the demand for quality flat chewing tobacco on the rise, with talk of war and secession boosting prices. The harvest that year had been bountiful, and an aura of wealth and promise enveloped the plantation's fertile valleys and verdant forests. Barrett Hall seemed to instill a sense of contentment and well-being into all who crossed her threshold. None could imagine a time when the gentility and serenity of the South did not exist. And none could conceive a future without it.

Laura knew she was supposed to share her mother's single-minded dedication to the plantation, but managing a household had never held her attention for long. The world contained in books had always transported her to a time and place far more interesting than the care and maintenance of tobacco. However, she was not so naïve as to deny that the lifestyle that she and her family enjoyed was that provided by the plantation and the slaves. Their way of life should have instilled the same deep contentment her mother felt, but of late, Laura was restless and irritable, plagued by the persistent feeling that life was passing her by. The events gathering momentum around her made the future suddenly less certain. Gazing out her window at the whirls and eddies in the river, she had a strange feeling that she was about to be swept up in a mighty current that would forever change the world she knew, and her along with it.

She watched the few boatmen on the James who still guided their bateaux upstream to the wharves at Richmond and she wondered about their hopes, dreams, and aspirations. She imagined herself on one of the boats, traveling to places unknown, meeting new people, and seeing cities she had only read about. While she loved her home and the beauty of the land, she yearned for something she could not name. Everything she needed, all that she could want, was hers for the asking at Barrett Hall, yet she sometimes felt that what she most truly desired was just beyond her reach.

A soft knock on the door interrupted her musings and a young chambermaid entered, a mulatto slave known as Ruby. Although the morning ritual had been virtually the same every day of Laura's life, she never felt entirely comfortable when the slave was in her presence.

She was an intensely private person, and having the watchful girl in her room made her feel exposed. All the same, Laura greeted her pleasantly and asked, "Is my mother awake?"

"She's waiting for you to get on downstairs, Miss Laura." Ruby poured water from a pitcher into a basin atop a chest of drawers, then left a towel, a soap cake, and a sponge next to the bowl. Moving to the windows, she drew aside the heavy curtains to let in the late morning sunlight.

Reluctantly Laura strolled to the chest and removed her nightdress. She bathed slowly, absently, despite the sounds she could hear outside her bedroom. The household was in a fit, preparing for the influx of guests for the celebration the next day. With family and friends, neighbors, and colleagues of her father's from the Virginia legislature expected, her cousin Charlotte's wedding to Robert Reynolds promised to be the social event of the year. Laura wanted to be excited, yet she couldn't help but dread the occasion. Of course she was happy for Charlotte, and she was looking forward to seeing her cousin in the lovely gown they'd chosen together. She and Charlotte had been close throughout childhood and maintained that strong bond even now. Charlotte was the one person Laura could bare her soul to. The thought that she would be leaving Virginia to live in Maryland with her new husband upset Laura, for she feared the distance would alter their bond irrevocably. What she dreaded most, though, about the wedding was the gossip that would inevitably circulate.

Already a current of tittle-tattle had swept the parlors of every lady in Virginia from Norfolk to Charleston, at least that's what her mother claimed. Why, even the slaves were embarrassed. It had long been predicted among family and friends Laura would be married well before Charlotte. Their mothers had always spoken as if this were a given. Older than Charlotte by one year, Laura was considered the beautiful one, accomplished at all she set her mind to. By contrast, Charlotte's plainness and lack of achievement in even the simplest of homemaking tasks made her hopes of a good marriage sadly misplaced, at least according to Rachel St. Clair.

The fact that the stellar marriage expected of Laura had not materialized and instead her mother would now have to feign delight over an "ill-favored" niece's happiness promised to add a special misery to the next few days. At the best of times, Laura's relationship with her mother was strained, but Charlotte's engagement had reduced their communication to perfunctory courtesies. Unless Laura produced a suitable fiancé of her own in the near future, she anticipated a further decline into utter silence. Perhaps this would be a blessing, all things considered. Laura had difficulty holding her tongue when her mother got started on her own catalog of personal sacrifices and the shortcomings of the man she'd married.

Laura had been closer to her father since she was a little girl. They shared the same curiosity about the world and sense of humor, and their like temperaments naturally drew them together, making them kindred spirits. Laura sensed that her mother resented their closeness and, as a result, distanced herself emotionally. It did not help matters that as Laura grew up, her mother constantly compared her with her cousin Charlotte, who was everything Laura was not. Dutiful. Considerate. Obedient. And now, about to be married. Charlotte's mother was forever harping on the close mother-daughter bond they enjoyed, needling her sister with hints about imagined maternal failings.

Laura thought her Aunt Ann was simply being spiteful because Rachel was the one who had inherited Barrett Hall. According to Charlotte, Rachel had also seen to it that Ann was married off as soon as the mourning period for their father was over; she had even chosen the groom. Now, with Charlotte's wedding imminent, Laura had detected a renewed vigor on her mother's part, aimed at securing a suitable husband. So determined was her focus and so frantic her dread of disappointment, that she'd even made Laura fear eternal spinsterhood if she did not marry soon. Several eligible bachelors had been pursuing her for the past six months, and she knew she must select one of them before they went elsewhere. But which one?

Miserable with indecision, she glanced at the gown Ruby had laid out for her to wear the next day. The dress had been made for her in Richmond by a fine seamstress, at a cost of nearly five hundred dollars. A deep gold crinoline, with the bodice cut low enough to reveal a modest amount of cleavage, it was the perfect gown to entice an offer of marriage. Laura only wished she could embrace the prospect with appropriate enthusiasm.

Despondently, she finished bathing, and then dressed, delaying the moment when she would have to go downstairs to face her mother. If she had to hear another disdainful reminder of her ultimate purpose in attending the wedding, she thought she might run away. Slaves went north, did they not? Laura had heard rumors of Northern women holding jobs like men, wearing men's clothing, and cussing too. Other horrors had been described to her but she refused to give them credence. In the face of such ignominy, running away to the North was not an option, and with no other possibilities open to her, Laura felt trapped. The only respectable way out was marriage. She knew it, but she still couldn't make herself do it.

Perhaps she would feel differently when she saw her cousin walk joyfully up the aisle. Charlotte was fortunate; she was marrying the man she loved. That must change everything, Laura thought with a small pang of envy. If she loved someone, she would not think twice about leaving Barrett Hall to make a new life. What a marvelous adventure that would be. She sighed, picturing the beaux vying for her hand. None of them made her heart beat faster, and she would be expected to dance and flirt with them at the wedding dance and end the evening with an announcement. The very thought made her ill.

The one silver lining in the ordeal would be the presence of many people she did not see on a regular basis. Too often, family and friends gathered only for more somber occasions. A wedding was a happy event, a time not only to celebrate the union of man and wife, but also for distant relatives to see newborn babies and appreciate the growth of older children, and for shared reminiscences about days gone by. Besides family, classmates from the Hollins Institute would be attending Charlotte's celebration. She and Laura had both been pupils at Virginia's first women's college and had boarded in Roanoke together. Laura was originally enrolled to attend a finishing school her mother chose in Richmond, but her father preferred the headmaster at Hollins. A progressive man, he believed in educating women in the classics. Thanks to her three years there, Laura could speak French fluently, carry a discourse on topics such as politics, philosophy, and music, as well as discuss the great literature of the past and present.

All of which, Laura thought wryly, would equip her most ably for marriage to a man who would expect her to think of little more than children and pretty dresses. With another loud sigh, she made her way to the dressing table and sat down, ready for her hair to be arranged in the catogan style she had adopted since her last visit to Richmond. As Ruby combed the heavy red-gold waves and began braiding, her mood began to lift and she admired herself in the full-length mirror. The bright blue morning dress she'd chosen for today enhanced the delicate paleness of her skin, and the way Ruby arranged her hair atop her head accentuated the perfection of her oval face. Laura pinched her cheeks sharply when the slave was done, drawing blood to the surface and causing her blue eyes to water. Satisfied with her appearance, she stood and shook her skirts out over the steel hoops under her crinoline, turning slowly to make sure no petticoat was showing. Before she left the room, she pinned a dainty gold brooch to her bodice, a birthday gift from her father.

"You have improved your hairstyling," she told Ruby, pleased that even if the girl often seemed sullen and brusque, she was working hard to acquire the skills of an acceptable lady's maid. No doubt she saw an opportunity. Even the slaves were aware that Laura must marry soon. Perhaps Ruby also wanted a way out of her Barrett Hall existence and thought if she made herself indispensable to Laura, she would be among the slaves chosen to accompany their mistress as a marriage gift from the St. Clairs. Offering a gracious little smile, she said, "When you've finished cleaning, you may choose a petticoat for yourself from the ones in the mending pile."

Ruby's strange greenish eyes glowed briefly, but her mouth did not budge. Bobbing her head, she mumbled, "Thank you, Miss Laura."

Once Laura had left the bedroom, Ruby leaned close to the door to make sure she heard her walk away. Satisfied the spoiled young missy would not be returning, she scanned the bedroom she knew best of any in the house. Her gaze fell upon the plush bedcovers, the maple writing desk, and the large pine chest that nearly reached the ceiling. The room was bright and cheerful and filled with the feminine finery rich young white ladies took for granted. Ruby loved spending time here, even if all she did was dust and polish and make the bed. As she worked, she often fantasized that this was her bedroom and she was the one who slept in comfort and awakened to breakfast in bed.

She strolled past the bed, trailing her hand across the fine linens and the polished wood of the four-poster. When she reached the writing desk, she picked up a leather-bound volume and opened it to a page Laura had written on. She peered curiously at the ink marks, wondering not for the first time what they meant and if she was ever mentioned inside. Placing the book back on the desk, she went to the padded bench where Laura's gold dress for the wedding was carefully laid out and lifted the heavy gown. Her hands shook but she held the gown up to her shoulders anyway and stepped in front of the long mirror. With a fearful glance toward the door, she made a small turn, amazed to see herself looking like the fanciest house slave she ever saw, Tillie from the Lewis plantation south of Barrett Hall.

Her mother said Tillie was Mississippi trash and ain't no one need to ask the reason why she so uppity. But Ruby thought she was beautiful, and Tillie could read and write. Her master had seen to her book-learning so she could make herself more useful to him. The last time she came to Barrett Hall, she read a newspaper out loud in the slave quarters, taking this great risk so that they would all know the truth about what was coming, the war that could change everything for Negroes. Ruby could not believe white folks would go to war with other white folks, but she supposed the men who lived in the North would want to own the lands that grew tobacco and cotton, so maybe it was not just a slave dream.

Ruby pulled away the handkerchief tied around her hair and stared at herself more closely. The gold dress made her light skin look like the coffee and cream her mother made for Marse Edward and also seemed to change the green of her eyes, making the gold flecks stand out. Clutching the dress to her with one hand, she lifted the other to pinch her cheeks as Laura did; then she picked up the ivory comb Laura would wear to the wedding and slid it into her soft brown waves. A bottle of perfume rested on a stand nearby and she set the dress carefully aside so she could remove the glass stopper and sniff the fragrant contents. She dared not dab a drop on herself since anyone would instantly know that she was wearing Laura's perfume. She could only imagine what the punishment for that would be.

Once again she returned to the four-poster and, listening for any sound of Laura's return, she threw herself onto the bed. Ruby bit her lip and giggled as she kicked her feet and wrapped her arms around the soft down pillow. Lying there, in the soft linen, staring around the room as if it was her own, was a dangerous thrill she allowed herself only when the family was occupied downstairs. She imagined staying in this bed until the sun was bright, instead of rising long before dawn. If their situations were reversed and she had been born into such a life, Ruby would treasure every moment. She would have her own servant to press her clothes and do her hair. She would be a kind mistress and not give away clothing from the mending pile. Her servant would be dressed in finery every bit as fancy as what she wore. Ruby despised being a slave. It was torture to be so close to such grandness but to share in none of it, and have to clean up after white folk who took everything for granted.

That brainless Laura didn't deserve half of what she had. She thought she was doing Ruby a big favor by giving her an old petticoat that had a tear in the hem and would soon be torn up for rags. Ruby had seen the expectant look on her face when she made the offer. That's how it was with white folks. They thought slaves should fall down in gratitude for the simplest acts of decency. They wanted praise and smiling faces and "Yes'm. You too good to Ruby. I's not fit to walk the same earth as you!" Ruby watched the other slaves put on this act every time a St. Clair bothered to offer them an unwanted item or gave a small gift. She refused to do so herself. To have no land or possessions, no hope of freedom, no hour of daylight to call her own was her life. But she would choose who she smiled at.

Sounds outside in the hall stirred Ruby from the bed. Sighing deeply, she slid her feet to the floor and picked up the dirty towel and nightdress the young missy had discarded. Tossing them onto a heap of other laundry, she began another day of cleaning.

❖

"Meg! It's nearly eleven o'clock." Laura peeked inside her younger sister's room. Meg was still asleep.

"Mother will be cross with you if you are not downstairs very soon. We are supposed to be helping, or have you forgotten our cousin is to be married here tomorrow."

An incoherent mumble made its way to the door but no movement was forthcoming. Laura stalked into the room, yanked the covers off the sleeping girl, and shook her awake.

"Stop!" Meg cried, tossing a pillow at her. "You horrid creature!"

"Get up, you lazy goat. Breakfast is ready, I'm sure, and yours will be cold."

Laura left her sister grumbling and proceeded out into the hall once again. As she descended the main staircase to the central passage, she paused to gaze at herself in the hall mirror. After making slight adjustments to her hair, she continued down and entered the parlor to her right. Her mother was on the settee, looking as elegant as she always did. Today she seemed almost regal in her morning dress of amber and cream tones. Her posture was rigidly erect and her hands moved with the swift assurance bestowed by many years of needlework. She was fashioning another finely embroidered handkerchief for Charlotte's wedding trousseau.

"Good morning, Mother." Laura kissed her briefly on the cheek.

"Good morning," Rachel responded without looking up from her work. "Cook says that breakfast will be ready shortly."

"Of course," Laura said. "I'll go see how things are coming along in the kitchen."

Her mother dropped her hands in her lap. "I cannot for the life of me understand your fascination with the culinary arts. It is unseemly to be spending your time in such pursuits, especially among the slaves. You are in grave danger of picking up language and habits unbecoming to a respectable young lady."

"Oh, Mother." Laura was all too familiar with this ongoing argument. "There is little else to do with my time other than read and sew, and I'm sure I have already done enough of both to last a lifetime. Besides, the fresh air will do me good."

"The air holds a chill to it. See that you put a cloak about you."

Her mother's words trailed after her as she left the parlor and walked smartly to the front door. Once outside, she scanned the road leading to the house for signs of her father, who had been up since dawn surveying the fields. A long dirt stretch, the road was lined on either side by oak and chestnut trees, and in the distance it wound into a forest mixed with oak and pine. Seeing and hearing nothing, Laura retraced her steps to the back of the house where a long walkway led to an outbuilding containing the kitchen. As she approached, the fragrant aroma of country ham and baking bread filled the air, and the rumble of her stomach was the first sign that she was hungry.

She entered quietly, not wanting to startle Martha, who was removing a kettle from the fire. The room was nicely warmed from the cooking and would stay that way all day long as Martha prepared the meals for the family. Laura enjoyed its cozy comfort once the heat of summer passed and fall advanced into winter; the spaciousness of the main house was never devoid of chilly drafts. Upstairs, where Martha lived, was Laura's favorite retreat during the coldest months of the year. She had been escaping up there ever since she was a small child.

"Good morning, Martha," she called out, once the kettle was safely resting on a bank of coals on the brick floor.

"Why, bless me, child, I didn't hear you come in." Martha looked up, smiling broadly. Still beautiful despite years in the tobacco fields when she was small, and then as a house servant, the cook was the most optimistic, outgoing, happy person Laura knew.

"Everything smells delicious," she said. Her stomach once again agreed loudly with the sentiment.

"Yes'm, I hear!" Martha laughed. "Well, come on now. Set yourself down. I don't know what your mamma will say, you here again."

She laid a thick slab of ham on a plate, along with a ladle of grits, a biscuit, and an egg. After pouring gravy over everything, she placed the meal in front of Laura.

"Miss Charlotte here?" Martha had turned her back on Laura to knead the dough for the many loaves of bread that would be needed over the next few days.

"She'll be arriving this afternoon along with her family," Laura said, devouring the food.

"I 'spect you's happy about that."

Indeed she was. Laura could hardly wait to talk to Charlotte and learn all the details of Robert's proposal.

"Soon enough you'll be the one getting married," Martha said with a trace of sympathy.

All Laura could manage was a weak smile in return. She had looked forward to this day for Charlotte, all the while knowing that it would remind her that she had yet to find someone of her own. Her inability in this regard served to fuel the tension that had settled in her stomach the day she had heard of Charlotte's engagement.

When Laura did not respond, Martha's brow furrowed with concern.

"You ain't worried none about Miss Charlotte, is you?"

"No, of course not." Laura reached for a pitcher of water and filled her glass. "All her letters convince me that she is truly in love. I couldn't be happier for her."

"But you's all quiet. Looks like you got something on your mind, Miss Laura." Martha dumped more flour on her bread board.

"No. Not at all."

It would do no good to complain to Martha about something neither of them had any control over. Laura would find a beau soon and that would be that. Besides, Martha was busy with preparations for the arrival of the guests and their servants. She would have to feed both groups, with the help of Ruby and the other house slaves. Her days would be quite long enough without the added burden of Laura's personal concerns. But it was times like these that Laura almost wished she could change places with Martha. She would gladly trade the strain of finding a suitable mate—one her mother approved of—for the hard work of cooking for the St. Clair family. If only her life were as uncomplicated as that of a slave.

❖

That evening, Laura retired to her room early, already planning what she would take to Richmond after the wedding. Ruby had helped arrange some of her belongings, putting them in order for packing in the large trunk set aside for her. After she left, Laura sat down at her writing desk situated under a south-facing window. The moon glowed intermittently bright and dull behind fast-moving clouds and was reflected off the water of the James. She opened a drawer and withdrew a leather-bound diary, the fifth volume of its kind, and found the page where she'd last left off. Taking up her pen and dipping it into the inkwell on her desk, she began to write:

8 November, 1860

So much is happening now that I don't know where to begin. I have recorded many interesting occasions in my journal over the years, but never before in my lifetime shall anything be as momentous as the election of Mr. Lincoln. Papa thinks there may be war, and certainly all the papers proclaim it is inevitable, but we hold out hope for better circumstances.

Cousin Charlotte's wedding is tomorrow and already several admirers have asked me to dance so that I'm sure I don't know which one I've agreed to dance with first! Mr. Taggert is nice enough, but his features leave much to be desired. Mr. Elliott is handsome, but so dull that I find myself dozing even while engaged in conversation with him. And Mr. Young has no personality whatsoever and all the money he possesses will not purchase him one. I fear that I must choose from among these decidedly wanting suitors. Why can I not find someone who encompasses all their positive qualities? When will I meet someone who makes me feel?

The sound of coughing from beyond the window gave her pause, and Laura set down her pen and lowered the kerosene lamp to barely a flicker. Rising, she peered down into the darkness, moving to one side so as not to be visible to anyone below. As her eyes adjusted, she made out the figure of her father moving silently in the shadows. He stopped under the bay laurel outside the kitchen garden and lit his pipe. The aromatic smoke drifted upward, curling among the branches of the tree. After what seemed like hesitation on his part, he strolled onto the walkway leading up to the kitchen building, opened the door, and went inside.

Laura drew back into the room, grateful for the wall that held her up. The first time she had seen her father steal away to the kitchen late at night was four years ago. She remembered it clearly because it was the night of her sixteenth birthday. However, that first night it had not occurred to her why he was going to see Martha so late. She had believed it was to discuss food supplies or menus. It wasn't until she had seen him go there time and again late at night over the years that realization dawned on her. There were reasons the master of the house might visit their female slaves after dark, reasons she heard whispered in parlors, where women gossiped about other women's husbands.

She placed her pen in the inkstand and closed her diary. Her emotions were in such turmoil that any attempt to write a pleasant entry seemed absurd. Disheartened, she turned off the lamp, trod heavily to her bed, and climbed in, drawing the covers snugly up to her chin. For a long while she lay awake, thinking about her parents. She wondered if they loved each other, if they had ever really loved each other. She thought at one time they must have, but she could never know for sure; they so rarely displayed their affection for one another in public. Did her mother know of this conduct? Did she care?

Laura pictured her mother waiting alone in the marriage bed for her husband to return and saying nothing at all because no decent woman could speak of such a matter. She wondered if Charlotte's father behaved similarly and whether other married men frequented their slaves' quarters. Was it something they were taught as young men? Did Ransom do such things? Worst of all, would the man she married expect to take these liberties himself? She resolved to ask her brother in her next letter, knowing he was the only one who might answer her questions honestly. She closed her eyes, but it would be well into the night before her restless mind drifted into peace.

Chapter Two

Ward Hill Lamon wondered for a moment if the new President had fallen asleep at his desk. The tall, gaunt figure was hunched over stacks of congratulatory letters and telegrams from those responsible for getting him elected. He wore a tattered wool shawl to keep off the chill, and his shoulders rose and fell in a steady rhythm. His long legs were still and his chin rested heavily on his chest.

"Sir?" Lamon prompted his close friend and former law partner. When no response was forthcoming, he called out more insistently. "Sir!"

Abraham Lincoln's head jerked upright and his eyes focused on his friend.

"Hmm?"

"I know it has been a long day, sir, but these papers need responding to. Once you are in Washington, there will be precious little time to deal with these matters."

Lincoln nodded weary agreement.

His rise to the Presidency had come as a surprise to no one more than himself. And though he wanted the position badly, his election served as a catalyst for Southern states to threaten secession, an event he firmly opposed.

"Here's a letter from a gentleman who thinks his brother should be the next President of the United States," Lamon muttered.

Lincoln smiled tiredly. "Send him this reply: 'Tell your brother that he cannot be the next President of the United States unless there shall *be* a United States to preside over.'"

Lamon spat and picked up the next letter on the pile. His expression darkened after a few moments. Abruptly he crumpled the paper into a tight ball and threw it in the corner of the room.

"Not from an admirer?" Lincoln surmised aloud.

"A Southerner who claims he does not consider you his President."

"Well, I can't say as I blame the man." Lincoln folded his hands in his lap and twirled his thumbs rapidly around each other. "My name wasn't even on the ballot in nine Southern states, and I won only two of nearly a thousand counties in the other Southern states. Hardly what our forefathers and the Constitution had envisioned."

"Nevertheless," Lamon continued, "you are the President-elect and you carried all the Northern states except New Jersey. Let's hope, as you say, that there will be a United States to preside over. President Buchanan is doing little enough to ensure the continuation of the Union."

Lincoln leaned back in his chair, his hand rubbing his chin. He was also worried that the current administration had buried its head in the sand and was determined to keep it there, leaving whatever mess lay ahead for him to unravel. He recalled years ago in his speeches, and in his beliefs as well, saying that there would be no civil war. Time and events had lessened this conviction, and he knew there would be more strife to come for which he would have no clear answers. But one thing he was certain of, the Constitution that he would swear to uphold and defend contained no clause for the cessation of the United States. For his country he would fight to the death. If that was what it would take, so be it.

"Then there is the other matter of those to whom promises have been made."

Lincoln's anger rose quickly to the surface, but he managed to control any regrettable outburst. In order to get him elected, his managers had made deals with delegates in Chicago, promising cabinet posts and patronage.

"I authorized no bargains and will be bound by none." He ground his teeth loudly together at the thought.

"And what about your cabinet?"

Lincoln had already been framing in his mind those he would make offers to, with others still held in abeyance. His efforts would be focused on harmonizing the fragmented Union, and his cabinet would reflect that.

"All in due time, Ward."

Frustrated at Lincoln's evasiveness, Lamon returned to the

possibility of secession. "The South is clamoring for war, Mr. Lincoln, and South Carolina is threatening once again to secede. The country wants to know what you will do if that occurs."

Lincoln stared thoughtfully at the man who had helped him win the election. The question had been raised many times during his campaign. "Physically speaking, we cannot separate. A husband and wife may be divorced, and go out of the presence and beyond the reach of each other, but the different parts of our country cannot do this. They cannot but remain face-to-face, and intercourse, either amicable or hostile, must continue between them. Suppose you go to war. You cannot fight always, and when, after much loss on both sides and no gain on either, you cease fighting, the identical old questions as to terms of intercourse are again upon you."

Lincoln rose from his chair and walked to the window, his long arms dangling from the shoulders, his hands sticking out from the sleeves.

"Ward," he said, the sadness in his voice almost too painful to hear, "I do not wish to see the country go to war, but neither can I allow it to be divided in half. It is in the hands of the South. We are not enemies, but friends, and I pray that calmer minds prevail."

Lamon understood the lengths to which his friend would go to prevent conflict. Many times they had sat in the office in Danville where Lincoln expressed his views on the subject. While not a friend to slavery, Lincoln would, if necessary, maintain slavery in the states where it existed in order to preserve the Union. The position found no favor with the abolitionists, but it offered a middle ground between two extreme points of view and, ultimately, by taking the more moderate stance, Lincoln had been elected President.

Despite his words, Lincoln gazed out at the barren trees and tried to imagine what his life would be like in Washington. Would he have the strength to hold the country together in the face of such animosity, or would he be known for all posterity as the last President of the "United States" of America?

❖

"May I have this dance, Miss Laura?" A handsome young man, his beard and mustache neatly trimmed, stood over Laura with his hand outstretched.

From her seat near the dance floor, she smiled up at him. "Why, yes, you may, Mr. Elliott."

She put her hand in his and they strolled toward the couples waltzing gracefully to the music. The front parlor at Barrett Hall had been cleared of all its furniture and the walls were decorated with colorful streamers and flowers. The room easily contained fifty people, along with a small quartet of musicians, and the entire house pulsed with the ebb and flow of laughter and song as people moved from one room to another to dance or dine. Servants hurried about, replenishing drinks and supervising a massive spread of turkeys, hams, fish, vegetables, and pastries. The St. Clairs were known for their hospitality, and all present freely ate and drank, enjoying the generous bounty of their host.

Laura scanned the dancers until she spotted her cousin with her new husband, sheer joy evident in her expression. Her insides churned with conflicting emotions. She wanted Charlotte to be happy, yet she resented the groom for taking away the one person in her life who was most like a dear sister. With Ransom off at West Point and Charlotte now a married woman with the responsibilities of a wife, Laura felt desolate and abandoned.

Glancing past her dance partner's shoulder, she caught her mother's eye and tried to look like she was enjoying the attentions of her handsome suitor. Thomas Jefferson Elliott was the consummate horseman; in fact, riding and hunting were the only two topics he could discuss with ease and authority. Any other conversation left him with a perpetually dazed expression and a nervous tic in his leg as though he wished to flee the room. Laura thought that perhaps with the sensational political events of late, he might be more inclined to new subject matter, so she attempted to engage him.

"So, Mr. Elliott, what do you think of the newly elected President?"

He shrugged dismissively. "The man is a baboon from all reports, and I hear he sits his horse accordingly."

Laura waited for more, but when none was forthcoming, she sighed in resignation. Mercifully, the dance was only of limited duration, so she would not have to endure his dull conversation for more than a few long minutes. Mindful of her posture, she followed his steps and allowed herself to enjoy the waltz. She could feel speculative eyes upon her, but shunned the idea that the stares were those of pitying mirth over her spinsterhood. No, she decided, she simply cast all the other marriageable girls into the pale, and her lovely figure was the envy of young matrons who had now seen their waistlines expand after their first child. She did not envy them, not one little bit. Not their married smugness. Not their boring, pompous husbands. Not the mistress-of-their-own-house airs they assumed around their single sisters, constantly remarking upon which lazy, careless slave they punished for breaking crockery, and which carriage they had *insisted* their dear husband purchase for town outings.

Laura lifted her head higher and made a point of smiling haughtily at anyone whose eye she caught. Indeed, the men were wishing they could swap places with her horse-mad dance partner, and the women were wishing she would twist an ankle so their own more plodding steps would appear to better advantage.

While her dance partner regaled her with his latest hunting exploits, Laura happened to see Mrs. Daniel Finch waltzing gracefully with her husband across the room. While older than Laura by almost fifteen years, she was every bit as breathtaking as any woman half her age and even more desirable. Laura held her in high regard not only for her beauty but for her grace and kindness as well. She carried herself with a confidence that distinguished her from most women Laura knew, and her good works with the poor were legendary. She was the model of womanhood that Laura most admired and tried to emulate, and she often found herself oddly wanting to be near her. She wanted so much to be like this woman, to feel that she had a place in society and a strong sense of herself among her peers. And though many people complimented Laura on her own beauty, she felt sometimes that she had little else to offer.

When she looked at Anna Finch, she saw a different possibility. Mrs. Finch had traveled abroad, and anyone fortunate enough to dine at her table was enchanted by her wit and charm. On the few occasions Laura engaged in conversation with her, she felt as though Anna treated her as an equal rather than a child. She appeared truly interested in what Laura was saying and seemed to think that what she said mattered. Her attention gave Laura a strangely giddy, pleasant sensation that left her flushed and happy.

Mr. Elliott wheeled her about with a flourish and as they glided past the refreshment table, she noted with satisfaction the appreciative glances of all the single men and even most of the married men standing nearby. Aware of their gaze, she adroitly tilted her head to something

Mr. Elliott was saying, knowing that by doing so she exposed to view the full length of her graceful neck and soft, pale shoulders. And while his comments were utterly devoid of interest, she laughed merrily, pretending to be enthralled by his every word. Once past the table, though, she let her smile fade. Sustaining such false emotions exhausted her and left her feeling empty. In truth, she was bored and depressed by this evening's event. Bored by Mr. Elliott and depressed at seeing in the married women a future she dreaded. Was this the life she was born to? Shouldn't there be more to it than managing a household and attending one party after another?

There were moments, alone in her room at night, when she could envision a life like her mother's, one in which she shared a home with a husband and adoring children of whom she'd be proud. But when she contemplated the thought of spending day after day doing precisely the kinds of dreary activities that her mother and other matrons did, she felt daunted. The waltz ended and Mr. Elliott guided her back to the refreshment table where he retrieved a glass of punch for each of them. Laura noted the looks of disdain on the faces of a few married women who tugged at the arms of their gawking husbands, and she smiled. Little did they realize that she could not have cared less about any of them. After a few moments' respite, the music began again and she reluctantly allowed Mr. Elliott to lead her back to the dance floor. After this evening, one thing was certain: her mother could have no complaints about her efforts to secure a husband.

❖

"They make a lovely couple," Ann Kendall said.

Rachel inclined her head politely toward her sister but kept her eyes on Laura and her beau.

Ann sank down on the chair next to her, sipping a glass of apple toddy. "I wish my Charlotte had married as handsome a man as that."

"Your Charlotte has married well," Rachel said. "She will want for nothing." In fact, the groom, Robert Reynolds, possessed an old Maryland name and vast land holdings, the thought of which took her breath away.

"Laura should be next to marry," Ann said with a self-satisfied air. "Why, she is more than a year older than my Charlotte. And she is such a beautiful young woman, I would think any young man would be desirous of her hand."

Rachel had already encountered pitying condescension far too often that day and was in no mood to put up with it from her younger sister. However, she retained her serene smile and said, with the very faintest hint of acid, "That is, perhaps, the problem. When a girl can take suitors for granted, she discards them like last year's bonnets. You are fortunate that Charlotte was never confused by such distractions and settled quickly when an offer was made."

Ann let the slight pass in favor of sprinkling salt on Rachel's wounds. "Has Laura not spoken to you of anyone who catches her fancy? Charlotte confided all in me from the very first."

"Laura has been busy living her life as she pleased, and thinking she can do without the advice of her mother. But that is about to end. She is getting too old to be so careless about her future prospects, and I've spoken to Edward about this. I have my eye on several eligible men, and she would do well to choose one of them. Hopefully this wedding will engage her mind and inspire her in that direction."

"Well, Laura is quite the headstrong girl, Rachel. She may not be ready to make such a decision."

Rachel merely smiled and watched Laura attempting to look interested in something her beau was saying. At least she was making an effort instead of offering her usual stubborn discouragement. Whenever Rachel saw her yawning, sulking, or rolling her eyes as a man tried to charm her, she wanted to shake her soundly. She had already made up her mind as to which of the prospects she preferred to see Laura marry, but she was a patient woman. If her daughter selected the wrong one, she would simply convince her that the young man would not do and then guide her toward the correct choice. She sighed deeply. If only her own mother had been as wise as she.

❖

When the interminable waltz came to an end, Laura seized the opportunity to excuse herself and escape into the library across the hall. It immediately occurred to her that she could not expect to hide in the first place—her mother would come looking for her, knowing her habits as she did—so she hurried down the central passage and out the back door to the kitchen. Slaves ran to and fro, from the main house with empty platters or from the kitchen with replenished ones. They greeted her quickly as she passed them. Laura stepped aside as a serving girl exited the kitchen, carrying a pitcher in each hand for the punch bowl. When the way was clear, she flattened her skirts as best she could and squeezed through the narrow door.

"Miss Laura, you know you got no business here." Ruby frowned, looking up from a cake that she was slicing. "Your mamma won't like it none."

"Ruby!" Martha admonished. "Don't you go tellin' Miss Laura what she should be doin'. You mind yourself and get that cake to the house before Miss Rachel comes looking for you!"

Ruby cast a reproachful glance at her mother and made a point of leaving the kitchen unhurriedly. As she passed Laura, she purposely brushed against her, as though the space they occupied was so small that contact was unavoidable. Laura recognized the intimidation for what it was, and yet she knew that if she drew attention to the discourtesy, Ruby would only apologize and say it was unintentional.

Laura sat at the big oak table in the center of the kitchen and moved food out of the way to make room for her arms. Folding them neatly on the table, she rested her head on them and began to cry. Martha laid a hand on her shoulder and Laura released all the tension she had been holding inside. When all her sobs had subsided, Martha stroked her hair and gently coaxed her to talk about what had distressed her so.

"Oh, Martha. Mother expects me to choose from among three men to marry, and I confess that I don't love any of them! I've tried, truly I have, but I feel nothing for any of them. I don't want to be alone, I want to find someone who loves me passionately, someone who makes me happy, but I fear I am destined to be in a loveless marriage." She burst into tears again. "I can't bear it, Martha, I shan't survive. I shall run away if I must."

"There, there. All's well. Give it time. Not many women marry for love. Men neither. Love grows with time when you gets to know the one you married in a way you can't know before. You'll see. And you'll survive, child, you'll survive."

Laura looked up at her and laughed derisively. "'To endure is greater than to dare.'" She sighed, drying her eyes on a napkin. "Thackeray knew whereof he spoke."

She rose from the table and, with a surge of emotion, threw her arms around Martha's neck and clung to her, not wanting to abandon the safety she felt there.

"You mustn't think of running away, Miss Laura. Where'd you go?"

Reluctantly, Laura let her arms fall to her sides. There was nowhere to go, no one to turn to who would help her avoid her fate. "Where would you go if you could leave, Martha?"

Martha's open expression instantly closed and her eyes grew dark and distant. "Why child, you know I can't leave. My life is here, with your papa and mamma."

Laura knew there was probably more that Martha would not tell her, no matter how close she thought they had become. But Martha was right, she could no more run away than Martha could. She was destined to marry someone, someday, and she would leave Barrett Hall only to move into the home of her husband. The sooner she got used to the idea, the better. Moving to the door, she glanced at Martha, who had returned to her work. "I should get back to the house before Mother comes looking for me."

Martha nodded but did not look up and, with a heavy heart, Laura left the kitchen and headed toward the main house. She didn't bother to scold Ruby when the girl rushed by without making way for her.

"What she want in here?" Ruby demanded as she lowered an empty platter to the counter. Placing more biscuits on it, she said, "She got no business bothering us colored folk when we working. She got that big old house up yonder and she come sassin' her way in here. It ain't right."

"You mind what you say, Ruby." Martha picked up a slice of beef and nibbled on it. "Your mouth is gonna get you in trouble one of these days."

"I don' care!" Ruby ran her finger on the edge of the bowl of lemon curd and stuck it in her mouth. "You treats her like she was your own kin. She's white and we's black and ain't never the two gonna live together in peace."

Martha gazed thoughtfully at her. "Ruby, you's my daughter an' I love you with all my heart, you know that. But it ain't Miss Laura's fault that she's born white. And it ain't your fault that you's born black. It just is. We is slaves to the Barretts and they our masters. It was that way for me, my momma, my granny, and my granny's momma. And it's that way for you too. It ain't never gonna change."

Ruby smiled slyly. “Ain’t what I heard,” she said softly. “I heard the white folks down here, they scared of they new President. Mr. Lincoln wants to set us slaves free.”

Martha slowly put down the piece of meat she was holding and her expression hardened. “Well, ain’t that something?”

The other slaves in the kitchen stopped what they were doing and glanced at each other uneasily. The talk of war had already made some slaves run away, but no one spoke openly about the idea of freedom except in the dark of night and only when in their cabins.

“You ain’t known nothing else, Momma,” Ruby said. “So you think you belong here with your white folk. But ain’t no one gonna worry about us no more, if they fighting. You wait and see. If that day come, I ain’t staying.”

“Lord Jesus, Ruby. Talk like that get you whipped, or worse. You stop talking like that right now or I’ll take the switch to you myself. Now put some more biscuits on that plate and get yourself in the big house before Mrs. St. Clair comes looking for you.”

Ruby averted her eyes, chastened by her momma’s harsh words. But she knew there were others in the slave quarters she could talk to secretly about the events they all knew were underway. She wasn’t the only slave making plans. Tillie said her master was going to send her south to friends in Montgomery if there was a war, but she wasn’t going to wait for that to happen. She had a brother who had run away a long time ago. He had his own business in the North, making boots for rich white folk. Ruby prayed Tillie would have a reason to come to Barrett Hall one day soon. She had an important question to ask her.

❖

With the passage of time and the liberal consumption of punch, some men always sought to escape the dancing and the conversation with ladies. They generally congregated in the small parlor near the rear of the house, smoking cigars and drinking brandy. Laura was not at all surprised to hear a group of them in heated debate as she crept in the back door. From the nature of the discussion, it seemed clear that members of the Virginia legislature were involved.

“Virginia was a leader in the first great struggle for independence,” one man insisted, amidst murmurs of agreement, “and she should take the lead now in disavowing Northern aggression.”

"Virginia's role in the Revolution is precisely why she should stay within the Union," another contradicted. "Our forefathers fought to form this country. Virginia must retain her position in keeping the country united."

"The North is weak." A garrulous voice entered the debate. "She does not stand a chance against the determination of the South. All she has is a token military presence and she will lose most of her officers with the departure of the Southern states."

"The Northern states' manufacturing ability far outweighs our own."

"But she won't have the time to employ it. Everyone knows that the North will be conquered in one quick, decisive battle."

The heated rhetoric continued for several minutes before Laura heard her father's deep and commanding tone.

"Gentlemen, gentlemen, whatever we decide, we must do so unanimously, as there can be no sign of weakness or disharmony on our part. I say that when we next convene, we should bring the secession debate to a vote. Whatever the outcome, we must all abide by the decision."

"Hear! Hear!" came the resounding reply.

"Why, here you are, Laura. I have been looking for you."

Laura glanced up to see her mother leading a balding, middle-aged man toward her.

"I believe Mr. Young has not yet had the pleasure of your company this evening." Her mother's glare announced her displeasure at Laura's departure from the party. She caught Laura's arm and tucked it in her own, as if in affection. "However, that is easily remedied. Laura loves to dance, Mr. Young, and I'm sure she would be delighted if you were to ask her."

Laura had to restrain herself from rolling her eyes. Her mother knew very well that the stout Mr. Young had two left feet.

"Why, yes, of course!" Mr. Young beamed as they proceeded along the hall to join the small crowd taking a respite outside the parlor. "Miss Laura, would you care to dance?"

"I would love to, Mr. Young, but at the moment my throat is so parched that I would prefer a glass of punch. Would you be so kind as to bring me refreshment?"

His sallow face lit up with the task before him. "I shan't be but a moment."

As he disappeared eagerly into the crowd on his quest, Rachel asked through clenched teeth, "Where have you been?"

"I needed some air after Mr. Elliott made me giddy fit for the vapors," Laura said pertly.

Her mother was not mollified by the reminder that Laura had been mindful of the need to encourage any eligible man who looked at her. "You know how important this evening is and what must be accomplished. Mr. Young is quite the eligible bachelor, and you would do well to encourage his affections instead of dancing with men of meager fortune."

"Preston Young is twice widowed, Mother, and has six children. You cannot possibly believe that I could fulfill the role of both wife and mother all at once. I would not know what to do with that sizable brood."

Her mother snorted. "Servants will take care of the children until they are of age to be sent to boarding schools. And then, once you have your own children, you may do as you please. Mr. Young's wealth will allow you the opportunity to have many choices you would not enjoy with Mr. Elliott or Mr. Taggert. Think, Laura, think what the possibilities are. You shall never want for anything and if you wish, you could travel the world and—"

"But, Mother, I don't love him!" Laura nearly shouted in frustration.

A harsh laugh escaped her mother's lips. "Love? Don't be ridiculous. I can see that you have once again been spending too much time in the library reading of fairy tales and fantasy. Marriage is not about love." At this, her voice turned bitter. "It's about work, and children, and ensuring that life continues long after we are gone. However, it is possible that love may occur eventually, and that is all well and good. But if you were to wait around until you fell in love with someone, you might just be waiting forever."

"Here we are, Miss Laura." Preston Young handed her a glass of punch and offered the other glass to her mother.

"How thoughtful, Mr. Young, but no thank you," Rachel said sweetly. "I should be returning to my guests. Besides, you and Laura should get better acquainted and there is no room for a silly old woman like me." With one last intent glare at Laura, she returned to the parlor.

Laura and Mr. Young stood awkwardly in the hall, listening to the music and exchanging occasional pleasantries with guests they recognized. Laura sipped her drink, trying to think of something to say, but was at a loss. Her mother's words haunting her, she once again felt the heavy weight of depression settle about her. She wanted nothing more at this moment than to retire upstairs to her room and bury herself in her bed.

"Miss Laura, are you all right?"

Startled, Laura had forgotten that the widower was still there. "Yes, Mr. Young, I'm fine. Why do you ask?"

"You seem so sad this evening. I don't recall you ever being this way before. Is there anything I can do?"

Laura had to struggle to keep the tears at bay. "No, you are very kind to inquire. It is nothing, really."

His brow creased in a frown that made him look even older than he was. He was silent for a long while, although his lips moved often enough that Laura assumed he was searching for words. She almost felt sorry for him. "Miss Laura," he finally ventured. "I know I'm not a handsome man—" When she began to interrupt him, he insisted. "No, please let me finish. And I'm not especially adept in the social graces. Quite frankly, I am always tongue-tied when women are around. I'm merely a farmer, a man with children I adore, the land my family has worked for generations, and a love of watching things grow and bear fruit. I have simple needs and simple wants, but one thing I do know, Miss Laura, and that is you would make me the happiest man on earth if you would consent to be my wife. I would care for you, never raise my voice or my hand to you, and love you until the end of my days. Miss Laura, would you marry me?"

Laura knew her jaw hung agape, but she was helpless to contain her surprise. She had expected an offer of courtship, a delicately worded request for the pleasure of her company in private, but Preston Young's offer was so plainly worded and direct, the breath was knocked from her lungs. His expression was raw and stripped of pretense, and she knew he awaited her response with no small degree of trepidation, yet she could not speak.

Laura could feel eyes boring into her and knew exactly why her mother was watching her. She would be thrilled to know that Mr. Young had proposed. All it would take was a nod from Laura and she would announce the engagement to all present. Laura thought back to when she was a little girl and had fantasized about this moment, picturing a romantic encounter with a dashing suitor who swept her off her feet. She had always imagined the breathless joy she would feel, the swooning yearning for a kiss. She had not imagined her mouth frozen with dismay and a sick feeling of dread.

Her mother's words came back to her like a restless wind rattling in the back of her mind. She was not getting any younger, and she still had not met anyone who made her feel what she thought she was supposed to feel when one falls in love. It was very likely that she never would.

"Mr. Young, I—"

"Laura!"

Laura jumped at the sound of her name. Marching purposefully to her side was her cousin, Charlotte, whose broad hoops kept getting caught in the press of those around her, compelling them to make way.

"Robert and I were about to leave and I could not depart without speaking to you on a matter of great import. Mr. Young, may I be so discourteous as to steal Miss Laura away from you? It is imperative that I speak with her immediately."

"Why…no, of course…"

"Thank you, sir." Charlotte grabbed Laura's arm and led her upstairs and along the walkway into the guest bedroom she and Aunt Ann were sharing. She closed the door quickly and grinned at Laura, placing her hands on her waist in apparent satisfaction. "Whew! I thought perhaps I was too late."

"Charlotte, whatever are you talking about?" Laura asked, nonplussed.

"Why, Mr. Young, of course! He was about to propose to you, was he not?"

"He did propose to me."

Charlotte gasped. "What did you say?"

"Nothing, you interrupted me and—"

"Thank God! Then I was just in time." At Laura's quizzical expression, she continued. "I was trying to save you from the possibility. Clearly you don't love him, and I'm sure Aunt Rachel has stated her opinion on the subject. She probably has given you the 'marriage is not about love' speech by now, am I right?"

Laura began to laugh despite her misery. "You certainly know my mother well."

Charlotte snorted. "And why shouldn't I? My mother had told me everything about her own marriage. She heard that very speech from Aunt Rachel when my father was introduced to her. Your mother chose him, as she has chosen Mr. Young for you."

"I thought Aunt Ann selected Robert for you," Laura said. Her mother had made a great deal of Charlotte's respect for her parent's decision.

Charlotte smiled. "She did indeed, and it so happened that we fell in love anyway."

"What if you had not?"

"I cannot say for certain. I do not possess your strength of mind, so I would probably have married him all the same. Fortunately, I did not have to consider the alternative."

Laura strolled over to the window and looked out into the night. "You are so lucky," she murmured, wiping tears from her cheeks. "Oh, Charlotte, what shall I do?"

Charlotte rushed to her side and held her tightly. "What we need is a delaying maneuver."

"I have delayed quite long enough. Mother will not tolerate any more procrastination."

"He has already proposed, and that is most unfortunate, but we shall think of something. Tell him you need time to think it over. You can stretch it out for however long you need to make a decision."

"My mother will never allow that." Laura sniffed. "If she had her way we would be married tomorrow."

"Then tell her that he proposed, so that she is satisfied. Tell her you understand the wisdom of the match, but you are overwhelmed and fear that you may not make a good wife for a man with children."

"I have already expressed doubts on that score," Laura said dryly. "She has no patience with such qualms."

"She will have to have patience if you ask Mr. Young to give you some time and he agrees," Charlotte said firmly.

Laura looked up at the moon, wishing she were anywhere else but where she was this evening. She was tired and her mind was overwhelmed with what was happening in her life. "Well, I suppose it is a start. I do not want to mislead him, but if I promise to think it over that will not be a lie. I will do exactly that." She kissed Charlotte on the cheek. "Thank you, Charlotte. Thank you for your friendship, I shall miss you so."

Charlotte began to tear up. "Now don't you make me start crying, not on my wedding day."

Laura smiled ruefully. "I'm only practicing…until my wedding day."

Chapter Three

It was high noon in Washington on a cold January day. Senator Jefferson Davis stood at his desk in the traditional oratorical posture, fist clutched behind his back, his chest puffed up like that of a proud bird. He wore a black coat with full skirts and a stiff white shirt with a black silk band tied at his throat. The dark attire made his face seem more pale and gaunt than his illness could account for, and Jordan Colfax felt almost sorry for him as he braced the knuckles of one hand against his desk.

"I rise, Mr. President, for the purpose of announcing to the Senate that I have satisfactory evidence that the state of Mississippi, by a solemn ordinance of her people in convention assembled, has declared her separation from the United States. Under these circumstances, of course, my functions terminate here."

As Jordan listened to him speak of a state's right to secede, she sat motionless, intently watching his every move, her fingers digging deeply into the armrests of her chair. She glanced at the faces around the packed Senate chamber, trying to ascertain whether every other man and woman present was as shocked and angry as she at this treasonous declaration. They were as still as statues bearing witness to history. Unable to discern from their intent expressions what their emotions were, she returned her attention to Davis.

He was a thin, hollow-cheeked man with a stern and foreboding expression. An aura of sadness clung to his pale countenance. His left eye, glazed over from the effects of neuralgia, added emphasis to a visage consistent with his tone of voice. He had not always supported secession and the idea of a Southern confederacy, but he now appeared to believe that the time for compromise was past and disunion was inevitable. Jordan could not agree, and she hated him and what he stood for. Anger boiled hotly within her, bubbling up from the depths of her patriotism and commanding her to action. If she thought she could get away with it, she would have leapt to the floor and throttled the man in black. It would have given her great satisfaction to alter the tide of events that was irrevocably altering her world. And a very large part of that world was sitting next to her in the form of her brother.

"Mr. President and Senators, having made the announcement which the occasion seemed to me to require, it remains only for me to bid you a final adieu."

Davis sat heavily in his chair and placed his head in his hands. He seemed shrunken in that moment, as though the magnitude of such an admission weighed heavily upon him.

Jordan was startled when thunderous applause broke the spell of the moment. Gentlemen stood shouting and ladies waved their handkerchiefs in silent approval. Turning to her brother, she had to shout his name to be heard above the din. She thrust her chin toward the exit and they slowly made their way through the sea of men in broadcloth and women in crinoline. The hoop skirts of the ladies commanded the space around them, and the gentlemen were obliged to give them room to maneuver. As they passed down the marble hallways toward the main exit, vendors hawking beer, apples, and nuts added to the clamor of the departing crowd. When finally they burst out into the cold afternoon, Jordan gulped the fresh air like a fish out of water.

"I cannot conceive such traitorous speech, and in the capital of our nation!" She angrily tugged at the edges of her black kid gloves, pulling them tightly over her wrists. "Are they fools? Do those people not see that they are tearing this country asunder?"

Tyler stood next to her, watching his sister perform a habit he had witnessed many times over the years. Removing her gloves was a precursor to a violent eruption of temper and one from which he very well knew to keep his distance.

"I must confess it comes as quite a shock to me as well." He spoke calmly, trying to soothe her mounting agitation.

Jordan observed her younger brother as he became lost in thought. He was handsome in his blue West Point uniform, the sun glinting off the highly polished buttons that ran down his chest. It dawned on her what Davis's announcement would mean for him personally, as well as for the country, and a lump formed in her throat. The maternal instincts she had always harbored for him rested just below the surface of her awareness, and now they came spilling up. She wanted to stop the madness, but she was powerless to do anything. She could not even cast a vote in the election Mr. Lincoln had recently won.

"What will you do?" A quiver in her voice betrayed the rush of emotion she felt.

Tyler smiled brightly at her. "I shall serve the Union I swore an oath to defend, of course. But I assure you, if war does come, it will not last long. It is in the interests of both sides to end it quickly."

"Tyler Colfax!" Another cadet pushed his way through the crowd on the portico. Broad-shouldered and powerfully built, his was the antithesis of Tyler's slender, more lanky frame.

"Ransom!" Tyler shouted back and waved. He met the larger man partway, hand extended in greeting, the other clasping his shoulder. Leading him back to where Jordan stood, he said, "I should like to introduce you to my sister. Jordan, this is my classmate, Ransom St. Clair of Virginia."

"My brother has spoken of you many times, Mr. St. Clair. It is a pleasure to finally make your acquaintance."

Hat in hand, Ransom bowed grandly. "The pleasure is all mine, Miss Colfax."

"Well, old boy, what do you make of it?" Tyler folded his arms over his chest, waiting to hear what his friend would say.

Ransom appeared to choose his words carefully. "It is a dark day indeed when our country should come to this. But I thought Mr. Davis's speech was superbly written and majestically presented."

At the predictable gasp from Jordan, Tyler took a step back. He knew what was coming and laid a hand on her arm to try to mute the ferocity of her words.

"Superb! Why, sir, the man is nothing more than a liar and a blackguard. He and his ilk shall soon regret this *crime* and suffer the consequences of such a rash decision."

Ransom put up his hands in self-defense. "I sincerely regret if I have offended you, Miss Colfax. It was not my intention to do so. Please, accept my apology."

Slightly mollified, and chagrined at her lack of manners, Jordan accepted the apology. "You must forgive me, Mr. St. Clair. I'm afraid the emotions I feel this day are entirely for my country. Please do not think unkindly of me."

"How could I?" He smiled warmly. "The day is only half over and already sentiments are quite strong on both sides. It is only natural for you to have your own opinion, Miss Colfax."

"Please." She made a small peace offering, knowing this man was close to her brother. "You must call me Jordan."

"And since the day is only half over," Tyler interrupted, "Ransom, what say you to lunch at the Willard? Your treat, of course!" He winked at his friend, already turning and heading down the steps.

Ransom St. Clair's laughter rang out over the crowd, and as Jordan walked between the two young men, she felt an odd tremor crawl from her neck to her waist. She was not entirely sure of the cause. Perhaps a seeping away of tension, perhaps a reaction to the thought of what was to become of the world she knew—she was not certain. Her nerves were a little on edge. Perhaps that could explain why, for most of the morning, she'd had a strange sense that someone was watching her.

❖

Kate Warne stood on the steps of the Capitol casually eating an apple. Throngs of people passed by, oblivious to her presence or her purpose. Occasionally her eye would fall upon an individual she recognized but who didn't know her. However, her focus remained on three people conversing a short distance away, two young soldiers and a statuesque auburn-haired woman who appeared to be doing most of the talking. Jordan Colfax was a well-known actress in Washington and barely seemed to notice the second glances she received from passersby. No doubt her striking beauty had made her the center of attention even before she appeared on the stage. In fact, most men, and even a few women, looked at her with undisguised lust. Her appeal was an attribute Kate was counting on.

When her boss Allan Pinkerton had first asked her to consider the actress as a possible recruit for the Union, she had been skeptical. As Pinkerton's Chief of Female Detectives, Kate was responsible for ensuring that the women she hired would withstand the rigors of the job. Grown men were known to crumble under the pressure, and there were plenty of agents who thought Pinkerton was a fool to hire women under any circumstances, let alone plan for female spies if war broke out. While Jordan's acting skills suited the requirements of a spy well, Kate was concerned about her youth and inexperience.

But as she eavesdropped on the party, she was not only glad to hear the girl's stance on the Union but was impressed by her vehement, well-reasoned arguments. Jordan had the strength of her convictions and sufficient knowledge to express herself cleverly. Time would tell if she would be suitable for the task at hand. The consequences if she was not could be dire for her as well as others.

As the crowd continued to surge out of the Capitol, Kate took a few steps closer to remain within earshot of the actress and her male companions. She observed Jordan with interest, noting that the actress certainly knew how to perform for her audience. From her hand gestures to her stiff-backed outrage to the fetching tilt of her head, her posturing seemed calculated for maximum effect. She really was a pleasure to watch, and Kate began to wonder if her initial concerns were misplaced.

Time was now working against Kate. Allan Pinkerton wanted to have people in place before the inevitable conflict, so she did not have the luxury to pick and choose potential agents. War was looming closer by the day, and Washington was already full of spies who were mostly sympathetic to the South. She could trust no one and had to be extremely careful about whom she approached.

Jordan could move freely in society, and her beauty would make important men lower their guard. Fortunately, her father seemed to support the Union, if one was to believe his newspaper accounts, so a parental view would not undermine her commitment. Would the actress be able to accomplish the dangerous mission that the government intended to place in her hands? Would she even accept the job?

As the threesome headed down Pennsylvania Avenue, Kate tossed her apple core over the railing to the dirt below and followed. Lunch at the Willard was definitely out of her price range, so she would make do with light fare so as not to appear suspicious. She hoped an opportune moment would present itself, so she could make contact with her target. If not during lunch, Jordan would be performing at Ford's Theatre tonight. In her field, the tasks she undertook seldom promised to be a pleasure. Kate intended to take full advantage of this rare prospect.

❖

The Willard was even more crowded than the Senate, and they had to struggle to make their way into the hotel restaurant.

"Tyler, look over there. It's Father."

Jordan pointed at a gentleman being led to a corner table. Joshua Colfax was a slender, serious-minded man in his late fifties, distinguished looking and clean-shaven except for thick side whiskers reaching all the way down to his chin.

Tyler pushed his way into the dining room and took his father by the elbow. They managed to get a larger table as it was being vacated, and the waiter quickly cleared it for them. After introductions were made, talk resumed of the states that had now seceded from the union.

"Did you hear the speeches, Father?" Tyler asked.

"Yes, I heard." Joshua Colfax adjusted his spectacles. "I suspect, Mr. St. Clair, that this new turn of events meets with your approval?" At this he lifted one eyebrow, the only sign of emotion he ever allowed.

Ransom shifted uncomfortably in his chair.

"Don't be alarmed," the senior Colfax urged. "I will not judge you. I simply ask if you have an opinion in the matter."

Ransom's jaw stiffened. "I believe, sir, that affairs have been heading in this direction for quite some time, and now the moment has arrived when the question must be decided once and for all."

"Hmph!" The elder gentleman sat back in his chair and the waiter took the opportunity to slip a plate of oysters in front of him. "You should have been a diplomat, Mr. St. Clair. Your answer was most decidedly no answer at all. The South will not acquiesce to Mr. Lincoln's desire to prevent their further departure from the Union. As of now, South Carolina and Mississippi have seceded, with Florida, Alabama, and Georgia close on their heels. And I have heard rumor that we should expect Louisiana to do the same at any moment. If she goes, Texas will go. All that remains to be seen is what Virginia will do. The South needs the home of presidents and would be hard-pressed if she remained in the Union."

A shadow passed over him as he looked at his son. He was proud of the man and soldier Tyler had become and wondered what would happen should the country devolve into civil war. Having lost his wife shortly after the birth of their son, he had raised his two children virtually by himself, with the aid of his housekeeper, Mrs. Johnson. He had taken the loss badly, succumbing to months of depression, emerging only to immerse himself in the newspaper he had founded nearly thirty years earlier. He loved his children dearly, but reserved his deepest affections for his late wife, his cherished Elizabeth.

"Mr. St. Clair." His voice was tired with the strain of impending events. "You are a Virginian. Will you follow your state if she elects to leave? And if you do, can you raise your sword against your country, against my son in battle? Tyler, can you slay your fellow classmate, friend, and countryman?"

The two younger men looked down at their laps, neither able to voice the thoughts that surely kept them awake night after night.

"*These*, gentlemen, are the questions that we face closer to home," Joshua Colfax continued. "*This* is the greater view, in my opinion."

The busy hotel clattered with the sounds of the midday meal hour. Silverware clinked against plates and people laughed, seemingly oblivious to the table of downcast diners. Jordan glanced at Ransom St. Clair, wondering at her father's speculation. It did not seem possible that either of the friends could strike the other in anger; their regard for each other was too obvious. Surely fate would not be so cruel as to place them in such circumstances. She refused to believe it and dismissed the thought outright. A war between the states was unthinkable and therefore impossible. She finished her meal confident in her own pronouncement.

"You'll have to excuse me." Jordan set her napkin aside and stood. "I have to rest before tonight's performance. Perhaps we can meet afterward for a late dinner?"

"Performance?" Ransom asked as the men stood with her.

"My sister is a thespian," Tyler clarified. "She is this evening performing at Ford's Theatre."

"How extraordinary!" Ransom looked astonished. "I suggest that we acquire tickets for the production. I for one would love to see Miss—rather, Jordan's," he bowed, "performance."

"I would be delighted if you came, and I'll ensure that tickets are left for you at the box office." Jordan turned to her brother. "And, Tyler, where shall we dine this evening?"

"Harry's, most definitely," Tyler replied as they departed the hotel.

Jordan kissed her father on the cheek and he crossed Fourteenth Street to Newspaper Row, where he would spend the afternoon writing the story that would appear on the front page of his *District Daily* the next morning.

"I shall meet you at the theatre at seven," Ransom said.

"And then to supper." Tyler led them up the street to Lafayette Square and the Colfax home.

"This time you buy!" Ransom said.

The men exchanged a few more words and Jordan looked back along the way they had come, wondering why she thought someone was walking behind them. She shrugged to herself. There were people everywhere. Naturally, some must be walking in their direction. Ransom gave a casual salute off the tip of his cap and Jordan wished him a pleasant afternoon.

"Of course, we would not fight each other," Tyler said as his friend strolled away. "It's unthinkable."

❖

After her final bow, Jordan exited stage right into the wings toward her dressing room.

"Great night, Jordan!"

"Thanks, John." She smiled broadly at the theatre owner, John Ford.

"When you get some time, I should like to speak with you about the upcoming production in Richmond."

"A little later, if you don't mind. I'm dining with my brother and his classmate this evening and am in a bit of a hurry. Perhaps tomorrow before the show?"

"Tomorrow it is. Don't stay out too late."

She approached her dressing room door and was surprised to find a slender, brown-haired woman waiting for her when she let herself in. Of average height, the stranger was dressed plainly, as though she did not want to draw attention to herself. At Jordan's startled greeting, a pair of sharp gray eyes instantly lifted to her face.

"Miss Colfax, you were simply brilliant this evening," the visitor said. "I don't believe I have ever witnessed a more engrossing performance."

Irritated to find this stranger in her room, and in a hurry to join Tyler and Ransom, Jordan said, "Thank you. May I help you, Miss…?" She waited at the entrance to signal her desire for the woman to leave.

"Warne, Kate Warne." The woman extended her hand.

Jordan took it briefly, wanting her to get to the point.

"I'm here at the request of Mr. Allan Pinkerton, who has been retained to protect the President-elect during these troubled times. He attended your performance the other night and wishes to make you a proposal."

"Allan Pinkerton?" Jordan had a feeling she had come across the name but she could not recall the man. "I do not believe I've had the pleasure of his acquaintance. What is this proposal?"

"Well, actually, he would like to offer you a job."

Jordan laughed. "Miss Warne, in case you haven't noticed, I already have a job, and one in which I'm most satisfied. Now if you'll excuse me…" She stepped aside, holding the door open for her visitor to exit.

"Please, Miss Colfax, hear me out." Miss Warne closed the door instead of leaving. "We believe you have the qualities necessary, as well as the unique opportunity, to perform a service to your country. Right now, the Union needs its daughters as well as its sons. She cannot afford to be at a disadvantage should hostilities progress into armed conflict. Miss Colfax, we need you to help us achieve this goal."

"Me?" Jordan laughed. "What can I do to help the country? I believe it is my brother you are seeking, Ms. Warne. He is a trained soldier."

"I am not referring to battle, though that too may prove inevitable. We were hoping to utilize your talents in other ways. Most specifically, we would like you to use your entrée into society and your ability to travel with the theatre troupe as an avenue for delivering messages."

"Travel? Why, I merely perform in local theatres for the most part, although I have on occasion traveled to New York and Philadelphia in various productions. For now, I'm contracted to perform in Mr. Ford's theatres, here, in Baltimore, and at the Marshall in Richmond."

"Precisely what we want." The woman's smile did not touch her eyes. "Mr. Ford will approach you soon regarding his production in Richmond. We hope that you will accept the role and, if needed, collect information from our contacts in that city."

Jordan recalled John's words earlier, and a chill made her tremble involuntarily. "Is Mr. Ford aware of this as well?"

"No, he knows nothing of us. We happen to know what his plans are and hoped to convince you to make this important contribution to the Union cause."

Taken by surprise, Jordan stalled for time. "This is so sudden."

She thought quickly about the implications of taking on such a role. She saw clearly the inherent dangers of transporting secret messages, but she also needed to consider the impact on her family as well as her career.

Miss Warne seemed to sense Jordan's hesitation. "Remember, this is for duty and country. Perhaps your efforts, along with our agents, can help forestall an all-out war, so that soldiers like your brother will not have to sacrifice themselves fighting against this 'crime.'" Smiling sweetly at the use of Jordan's own choice of word, she reached into her bag and pulled out a card. "My *carte de visite*. I will be in touch with you soon. And Miss Colfax." Her gray eyes turned black with determination. "I must ask you to keep this conversation in the strictest confidence."

"You have my word." Jordan fingered the edge of the card, then slipped it into her bag.

She sat in silence for several minutes after Miss Warne slipped out the door. *For duty and country.* Jordan could not help but weigh the offer very carefully.

❖

"I should be delighted to travel to Richmond with you, Jordan." Ransom sipped his wine. "When do you leave?"

"Next week." Jordan placed her napkin next to her plate. "But you really shouldn't trouble yourself. I have traveled many times on my own, and I'm quite familiar with the city."

"Nevertheless," Tyler signaled the waiter for the bill, "I know that I would feel more comfortable having Ransom escort you. There is too much excitement going on right now, and a traveling companion, particularly a native Virginian, would allay my fears."

"And I would love to show you the city," Ransom continued. "I'm quite certain you will enthrall Richmond society. They have few opportunities to rub shoulders with an actress of your renown, and there is nothing society matrons love better than fresh blood."

Jordan's thoughts immediately returned to her encounter earlier in the evening. It was almost as though Ransom had been privy to her conversation with Kate Warne, readily providing the convenient social entrée that the detective desired from her. She had to admit that the prospect of delivering a few important messages for her country intrigued her, the excitement and danger causing her pulse to beat a little faster and her mind to sharpen. She was willing to play any small role she could in keeping the Union intact, but she needed to know more details before she could accept. She thought of the card in her bag and determined that she would contact Miss Warne in the morning to resolve the situation as quickly as possible. She knew what she needed to do, and now she had to tie up the details.

"Jordan, are you ready?" Tyler stood at her side, his hands on the back of her chair.

"Yes." She nodded. "I'm ready."

❖

"Won't you have a seat, Miss Warne?" Jordan gestured to a chair in her dressing room and sat down at her dressing table.

"Thank you for inviting me to discuss my proposal in greater depth, Miss Colfax."

"Not at all. I only wonder if it's not all a waste of time."

Miss Warne's brow furrowed. "I beg your pardon?"

She was rather nondescript, Jordan observed, not anything like a real spy. Jordan imagined someone exotic looking, with an accent. But this innocuous woman looked like anyone she might see shopping at the market or sitting in the audience at a performance, almost invisible.

"Well, surely you don't think that anything will come of this," Jordan said. "All this saber rattling on the part of a few Southern states gone astray is not something our government should be overly concerned about. I would think after a few months of floundering that they will come scurrying back into the fold in short order."

Kate sat back in her chair, her face expressionless. "Miss Colfax, our government must be prepared for any circumstance regardless of its potential occurrence. Were we not constantly vigilant in protecting the country from all threats, we would be negligent in our duty. I sincerely hope that you are correct and that nothing will come of this, but we must prepare for the possibility. Your help is critical."

"What precisely is it that you want from me, Miss Warne?" Jordan poured them each a cup of tea and handed the cup and saucer to Kate.

"You possess skills that uniquely qualify you for the job we have in mind. You are an actress and presumably can hide your true feelings as well as display false ones convincingly. You also have access to both Washington and Richmond social circles and travel between the two cities without suspicion. Your first assignment will be to ingratiate yourself into Richmond society, paying particular attention to members of the local government or military. We have reason to believe that there are those in Richmond who wish to see Virginia join the other states in rebellion against the country, and this must be prevented at all costs."

"And how am I to accomplish this?" Jordan asked

"We want you to identify key political and military figures and ascertain their political persuasion and convictions. Record the important points. Who said what, who was present at these events, and so on. If possible, obtain any documents that seem relevant. Letters, telegrams, maps, anything that might give us clues as to the intent of these individuals."

Jordan was surprised by this new information. Somehow she had assumed she would merely be a conduit of messages, not the active information-seeker Kate Warne was suggesting. Could she copy, or steal, documents from a neighboring state? This had more far-reaching significance than she had first imagined, and far greater consequences.

"How am I to get these messages or documents to you, Miss Warne?"

Kate reached into her bag and pulled out a small, thin, leather-bound pamphlet and handed it to her. "This is a code book that you must not let fall into the wrong hands. Study it well, memorize it if you can. It shows you the alphabet and the corresponding representative code figures. When you write your messages, transpose them into the code, fold the paper in half once, and hide it behind the loose brick in the storage room at the Marshall."

"How do you know that there is a loose brick in the storage room at the Marshall?" Jordan asked.

Kate laughed. "Miss Colfax, we have prepared everything for you in advance. There are many other friends living in Richmond willing to help us. But none have access to what we need like you have."

"And who will retrieve these hidden messages?"

"I shall be your go-between in Richmond. I have an assignment of my own there and will be available if you need me. However, we must not be seen together in case one of us is caught. An agent will retrieve your messages and deliver them to me. If you need to get in touch with me, leave a message stating when and where, and I shall endeavor to meet you."

Jordan wondered what it meant to be "caught" doing what she was tasked to do. Since Virginia was still a part of the Union, would she have recourse through the government? Would she have legal rights in the courts for spying on another state?

"If I'm caught, Miss Warne, what shall I do? Whom shall I call upon?"

Miss Warne's eyebrow twitched, the first involuntary movement Jordan had seen her make. "If you are caught, Miss Colfax, you will be at the mercy of the state of Virginia. However, there are those you can turn to. Myself, if you can get a message to me in time. If not, and if you find you must flee without a moment's notice, there is a woman in Richmond, Elizabeth Van Lew. Commit her name to memory. She lives on Church Hill and is a good friend to the North. She is easily found but her opinions do not endear her to her neighbors, so be discreet if you need to seek her help."

Jordan fidgeted in her chair, weighing the consequences of accepting or rejecting the proposal before her. If she was caught, what would it do to her family, to her father's reputation as well as her own? Should she tell him or Tyler her intentions? Knowing them as she did, she already knew they would refuse to let her go. On the other hand, she despised what the South was doing and wanted nothing more than to see them put in their place. Tyler would give his life to support his country. Could she offer to do less, or nothing at all?

She regarded the woman who would be responsible for this life-altering change. Physically, Miss Warne did not instill confidence. She looked as though she might blow away with the next strong wind that rushed down Pennsylvania Avenue. And yet something in her eyes and the set of her jaw exhibited an inner strength, a sense of iron-willed determination Jordan came close to envying. She was a woman on a mission and woe to any who stood in her way.

"When do you wish me to begin?" Jordan asked.

Kate Warne smiled, and this time, it reached her eyes.

Chapter Four

The train to Richmond was packed. To Jordan it seemed that half the city must be fleeing south. Besides South Carolina and Mississippi, the weeks of January 1861 had seen the departure from the Union of Florida, Alabama, and Georgia. A mass exodus had ensued as citizens whose political sympathies were pro-Southern left Washington. Even sympathizers whose states still remained with the Union were leaving their homes, anticipating inevitable secession. The atmosphere aboard the train was both tense and celebratory as the passengers loudly discussed the latest news.

"There's going to be war, I say," an elderly gentleman sitting three rows in front of Jordan asserted to the man behind him.

"Nonsense," the other replied. "The North wouldn't dare invade Southern soil. She would outrage the nation, and friend and foe alike would come to our aid in defense of Southern independence."

"I have to agree with the old man," an officer sitting across the aisle said. "Mr. Lincoln has stated his intentions clearly. All that is left to determine is which side will fire the first shot."

"Give me a gun and I'll do it." The old man stood up and shook his fist at the ceiling.

Almost all the passengers in the car erupted in laughter, and Jordan noted only a few who remained absorbed in the passing landscape outside the window. Whether they were in support of the North or simply against the possibility of war she couldn't tell. Either way, they knew they were outnumbered and wisely kept their objections to themselves.

Jordan and Ransom sat in the rear of the car doing their best not to engage in conversation they both knew would lead to disagreement. Jordan pretended to be engrossed in her script and thus avoided any opportunity to quarrel with the young cadet. She liked Ransom St.

Clair well enough, especially since Tyler had such affection for him, and he was still a member of the United States Army. As long as he remained so, she had no reason to quarrel with him. She could not help but wonder what he would do if Virginia also rebelled.

As the train lumbered along its southerly route through the rolling fields of the Virginia countryside, the clickety-clack of its wheels lulled Jordan into a semiconscious state. Images of her final meeting with Kate Warne and the instructions she had imparted prior to Jordan's leaving, wove in and out of her awareness. She had sewn the mysterious code book Kate gave her into the inside fabric of her carpet bag, and clung to the bag so that it would never be out of her grasp. No one knew of her covert assignment, and for the first time since accepting Mr. Pinkerton's offer, she felt suddenly alone, her connection to home and the North tenuous at best. If anything went wrong, she could only turn to strangers. She wasn't even sure if she could trust Kate Warne.

Jordan rationalized that nothing grievous would befall her. Even if she was accused, who would believe that Jordan Colfax, the popular actress, was a spy? The idea was nonsensical. All the same, Jordan had never been able to take comfort in the unknown.

"Don't you agree, soldier?"

Jordan looked up from her script.

"I beg your pardon, sir?" Ransom asked.

"Don't you agree that the North doesn't stand a chance against us? That it'll take three Yankees for every Southern fighter we've got?"

Ransom opened his mouth to speak but Jordan did not give him a chance. "No, sir, I do not agree. What the South is doing is not only illegal, but immoral as well. If it should come to war, you would do well to get down on your knees and pray that God in His righteousness does not entirely smite the Southern states and render them incapable of future existence. For if He does not, the North shall surely rise up as one people and happily perform the service themselves."

The man stared at Jordan in shock and anger. Even Ransom raised his eyebrows at her.

"Why you…" the stranger began, but got no further.

Ransom rose from his seat, a polite expression on his face.

"Excuse me, sir, I believe you and the lady have both had the opportunity to state your opinion. Nothing further need be said."

Ransom towered above the small, squat man, and clearly realizing he was no match for the soldier, the angry Southerner quickly sought more like-minded compatriots.

Pleasantly surprised at Ransom's defense of her, Jordan said, "Well, I'm happy to see that there are still Southern gentlemen who are willing to stand up for what is right."

Ransom gazed humorlessly at her. "Do not mistake my feelings, Jordan. I happen to agree with the man, despite his lack of civility. And while I doubt it will take three Yankees to every one Southern soldier, I do believe that our cause is an honorable one and God help the North if she should invade us, for we shall surely do whatever it takes to defend ourselves."

Jordan did not reply. Ransom held his principles just as dearly as she did her own. The same was true for most people she would encounter from now on. No one who loved home and country could claim to be impartial. She would have to be more circumspect in whom she confided her opinions and how she behaved publicly. She could not afford to have anyone suspect her true intentions.

Jordan returned to reading her script but could not concentrate. It unsettled her that from now on she could not trust anyone. She was not accustomed to subterfuge or second-guessing. At home with family and friends, in her work and social activities, she had always been able simply to be herself. Her life was unique in that regard, a fact she appreciated when she compared her situation with that of other women. She had chosen a lifestyle unavailable to most, making her own choices and supporting herself comfortably from her own work. She could do and say as she pleased, come and go as she pleased, without a by-your-leave to anyone, not even her own family. She was an independent woman who spoke her mind, much as the suffragists demanded, and she wouldn't trade her way of life for anything or anyone.

Jordan supposed her independent streak was the consequence of having lost her mother at a young age. Despite her father's best intentions, she had, for the most part, raised herself and was in large measure responsible for raising Tyler as well. Together, the two of them had developed a bond greater than that of brother and sister. They treated each other as equals, and Jordan shared in almost all the activities available to Tyler.

Of course, she now found herself in a dangerous situation of her own making because of the very freedoms she enjoyed. While she was happy to play her own small role in putting down the secession fever running through the South, she once again questioned the sanity of her decision. She was risking her reputation and perhaps her life, but in the end would her sacrifice make a difference? She had to believe it would. If their roles were reversed, she knew Tyler would make the same choice; in fact, he had said as much to her in private.

Jordan shuddered and closed her script, abandoning all thought of refreshing the lines she'd memorized. If war broke out, Tyler would be fighting for the North. He would be risking his life. If Jordan truly believed herself the equal of any man, she should not hesitate to do the same.

❖

Richmond was a large Southern city with a population close to forty thousand people, still nearly fifteen thousand less than Washington. But of most significance to Jordan, it was one of the top five cities in the country for theatre productions, a profitable statistic not lost on theatre owner, John Ford. Stepping down from the Richmond, Fredericksburg, and Potomac Railroad car, she paused on the platform to wait for a porter to unload her luggage. Through the crowd, she searched for the familiar face of Bill O'Malley, who was to escort her to her hotel. Only two blocks from the station and the same distance from the theatre, the Broad Street Hotel would be her convenient home until the middle of April while she performed at the Marshall.

"Miss Colfax! Over here!"

Walking toward her was the short, stocky stage manager she'd worked with for the past two years. Bill O'Malley was amiable but gruff, and his teeth incessantly clenched the stub of a cigar which, despite its length, never seemed to be lit. Jordan had taken an instant liking to the older man, and he treated her much like a daughter, protecting her from the usual cadre of actors who tried to woo her both on- and offstage. What she liked most about Bill was his approachability, something she never found with her own father, who could be distant at times, absorbed in work or in memories of her departed mother.

"Hello, Bill." Jordan smiled. "How is the set coming along?"

"Still working on it, lass. But it'll be ready by and by."

"Jordan, I'll be on my way, then," Ransom said.

"Oh, Ransom, I would like to introduce our stage manager, Bill O'Malley. Bill, this is Ransom St. Clair, my brother's classmate."

"A pleasure to make your acquaintance." Ransom extended his hand.

Shaking it, Bill replied, "Likewise, sir."

"Ransom, thank you so much for escorting me to Richmond," Jordan said. "And for defending my honor."

His eyes sparkled at her playful tone. "You're most welcome. And please," he withdrew a card from his coat pocket and handed it to her, "may I extend an invitation to dine this Saturday with my family at our home on Church Hill."

"Only if they don't tar and feather me and run me out of town on a rail for being a Yankee." Jordan was jesting, but she could hear the tiny serious note that strayed into her voice.

"I'm certain we will manage, at least through one meal."

"Truly," Jordan let a hand rest on Ransom's arm, "I'm very grateful. For your friendship with my brother and for your integrity. Despite our differences, you are a good friend indeed." On an impulse, she kissed him on the cheek, wanting to demonstrate her sincerity.

Blushing profusely, Ransom stepped back. "We shall see you at eight o'clock, then?"

"Eight it is, and thank you."

She watched him as he headed up Broad Street, his posture erect and soldierly, his youth evident in the spritely gait of his step. An overwhelming feeling of sadness enveloped her as he vanished into the crowd, and she wondered what would become of him. If Virginia also rebelled, he would be pitted against her brother, as her father predicted, and he would also become her mortal enemy. There would be no going back and no sympathy for him if he chose the wrong side. This absurd possibility was incomprehensible, and the very thought made her physically ill. She breathed deeply to calm her nerves.

She turned to Bill, who had picked up both her trunk and carpetbag, wincing as he hefted the weight to achieve a walking balance.

"God almighty, Jordan." He chomped on the stub of his cigar. "Are you carrying every damn script you ever read in these bags o' yourn?"

She laughed warmly and fell in alongside him as they left the station and walked up Broad Street toward the hotel. She felt exhilarated being in Richmond once again. The day was chilly but not too cold, and the prospect of a new production in a different locale lifted her spirits. In the back of her mind, but never forgotten, was her mandate from Kate Warne. The tasks that lay before her made her heart beat rapidly, but fear was not the only emotion tugging at Jordan. She was also excited.

"Rehearsal's at two, and don't be late." Bill took his leave after she'd checked into the hotel.

Jordan saluted him as he strode away, then followed the hotel boy with her luggage up the stairs to the second floor.

Her room overlooked the street, and she stood at the window watching people, carriages, and horse traffic wind their way down Broad. The bustle of activity was magnified from the last time she had been here, with a large increase in the number of soldiers marching hurriedly to and fro. She made a mental note to ascertain which regiments were in town, their numbers, and where they were bivouacked. After unpacking, she refreshed herself by washing at the basin in her room. She then changed her traveling clothes for more comfortable attire and stood before the mirror to brush her hair.

The soft, fawn-colored cotton dress she'd chosen accentuated her chestnut hair and forest green eyes. The cameo brooch she wore at her throat had belonged to her mother, and she rarely went anywhere without it. She treasured the few memories it brought to mind. The only attention she paid to her appearance was to put up her hair and wash her face. She spent so much time in stage makeup that once it was removed she had no desire to put anything on her skin again. Her features were strong, and not particularly feminine. But they were suitable for the stage, enabling her to play both feminine and masculine roles with complete believability. Her face served her well, in both her private and public lives. She could not change it if she wanted to, and she did not.

❖

The Marshall Theatre was a two-block stroll from the hotel. Even though it was early February, the sun was warm on her face and she needed only her light wrap to keep her warm. The busy street was cluttered with small businesses displaying their wares, and shoppers argued with shopkeepers about prices and quality. In the opposite direction she could hear the sound of the two o'clock train departing for Fredericksburg. Jordan had visited Richmond on several occasions in the past and had enjoyed the city's hospitality and enthusiastic theatre-going crowds. For the most part, she found Virginians to be more rational than their fiery Southern neighbors. The difference was due in no small measure to the fact that cotton was not "king" in Virginia. Tobacco, the main crop, required slaves; however, planting and harvesting were not as labor intensive as with cotton.

Turning down a small alleyway, she approached the rear stage entrance and noticed Bill O'Malley speaking with a young Negro male. As soon as the man saw her, he nodded briefly to Bill and then hurried off down the street.

"Who was that?" Jordan asked as she stepped up onto the platform leading into the theatre.

"Just a messenger," Bill said dismissively. "Everyone's inside waiting for you."

Upon entering the cool, darkened interior, Jordan walked down the center aisle to the dimly lit stage. The other actors were already present, and stage workers throughout the theatre were preparing it for opening night. Sounds of hammering and the smell of fresh paint alerted her to sets still in progress.

The director, Richard Harwell, was seated at a table downstage, along with Bill O'Malley and the actors for the Marshall's stage production of *Macbeth*. Charles Taylor, playing Duncan, was an actor with whom she had worked frequently and knew well. But the actor playing Macbeth to her Lady Macbeth, George Lamont, was someone whose path she had tried to avoid. He was a narrow-minded, foul man who did not believe women should work at all, let alone be in the theatre. She despised him and knew he felt the same toward her.

"Jordan, good to see you again." Charles stood and moved the chair out next to him. "How goes the scene in Washington? I haven't been back in ages but hear our politicians are in even more chaos than usual."

Jordan sat and removed her gloves, putting them aside to pick up her script. "Well, everyone is placing bets as to which state will secede next. And of course they are awaiting the arrival of the new President to see what he is made of. From all accounts so far, he seems to be keeping a calm and steady demeanor. Something quite lacking in the previous administration."

Sitting across the table from her, George Lamont snorted in

derision. "Lincoln is nothing more than a clown. He's an inexperienced, backwoods Western lawyer whose command of the language is at best questionable. He is hardly qualified to lead his country."

Jordan seethed at the insult to her President. While it was true that he lacked the sophisticated grammar more commonly found among the higher echelons of government, he had an ability to speak to the broad diversity of the common people with forthrightness and clarity. This talent endeared him to the masses like no other President before him.

"I imagine the people who elected him felt quite the contrary, George," Jordan retorted. "From all I have read, he seems to have been the one candidate who has a solid grasp on the issues involved."

"Bah! His election is why Southern states are leaving the Union now."

"Silly me." Jordan could not contain herself. "And here I thought it was because of your last performance in Philadelphia."

A round of laughter at the table interrupted the discussion.

"That will be enough." Richard Harwell said. "I will have no political discussions during the production of this play. I've had about all I can take of this nonsense and am sick to death of it. We've got quite a lot of work to do before this show is ready, and we need every minute to whip it into shape. So, let's get started. Bill, where are those witches?"

Bill removed the cigar stump from between his lips. "Most like with the stable boys drinking a bit too much of their own witches' brew." He stood, roughly pushing back his chair. "I'll get them."

Richard smiled a welcome to Jordan. "Good day to you, Romeo. I hear you have accepted the upcoming role at Ford's in May."

Jordan nodded, accepting his outstretched hand in congratulations. "Yes, it seems there is not a Romeo to be had in all of Washington."

The director laughed.

George Lamont gave her a disingenuous smile. "Jordan, I am sure playing a man will suit your disposition satisfactorily. It seems a shame, though, that you could not put it to better use and enlist in the ranks of the army."

Jordan returned George's hypocritical smirk. "The war has not yet begun, George. Speaking of which, I see you are still in civilian attire. Maybe it is due to some deficiency on your part, a certain lack of the male anatomy perhaps?"

Several loud guffaws and even outright laughter greeted Jordan's comments. Richard Harwell put his hand over his mouth and glanced down at his script, as though concentrating on some detail of stage direction. The smile left George's eyes in an instant, replaced by a cold glare. Jordan turned her back on him and glanced around the stage approvingly.

"It looks as though all is ready for tonight," she commented to the director.

"Yes, very good indeed," he replied, "thanks to Bill's efforts. I think we should all retire and meet back here at least an hour before the curtain rises. Are you ready, Jordan?"

Jordan was indeed ready, although a bit more nervous than usual. This would be her first time playing Lady Macbeth, a role she found extremely challenging. She had once seen the great actress Charlotte Cushman play the role in New York and had been impressed with her wit and the energy that captivated her audience. While Jordan preferred to approach a role fresh and without influence, she certainly found Miss Cushman's interpretation similar to her own. Jordan dismissed those actresses who moaned and groaned and flung themselves across the stage in great fits of overacting. There were those in the audience who believed that was how actors should be—the more bombastic the better. But Jordan most definitely preferred understatement. To her, it made a performance all the more believable.

She was also nervous at having received flowers from the woman who would be playing Juliet opposite her in the May production. Nell Tabor, a Baltimore actress, had never had the makings of a great performer. The woman had married into wealth and used her deceased husband's mining fortune to influence theatres and directors alike. In fact, when Nell found out that Jordan was to play Romeo, she had pressured Mr. Ford into casting her in the role of Juliet. Normally Jordan would have refused to play opposite someone whose craft was weak, as it only meant she would have to work harder to overcome their shortcomings. However, she was flattered by Nell's attentions and certainly enjoyed the gay parties and interesting people she met through her. It occurred to her, now, that the role would offer yet another opportunity for her to spy on behalf of the cause.

Still, she was uneasy as she thought about Nell. Whenever Jordan was in her presence, she felt a spark between them that could easily be mistaken for attraction if such a thought were not absurd. She did not read too much into her own responses. Nell's sophistication and influence lent her an undeniable charisma; Jordan was not the only person drawn to her. Among Nell's friends were actors, writers, and artists, many of whom paid little regard to convention.

Jordan's work in the theatre exposed her to the same crowd, some of whom were men she could only refer to as "dandies," since she knew of no other word to describe them. They were the sort of men others whispered about, and Jordan had initially been shocked to learn of their proclivities. But with time and the opportunity to know them as people as well as actors, she had found them kind and amusing companions. Indeed, she felt more comfortable in their presence than that of certain lecherous actors. Her thoughts returned to Nell and her stomach fluttered not unpleasantly. Playing Romeo to her Juliet would not be such a hardship. Nell, she was sure, would make the experience memorable.

Taking one last look around the theatre, Jordan gathered her wrap and exited through the main lobby. Heading to her hotel, she focused on tonight's performance and in particular the scenes that most fully encapsulated Lady Macbeth. She had rehearsed them endlessly and with variety, attempting to understand as much as possible not only Shakespeare's intent, but also what a woman would feel in those circumstances. When she entered her hotel, she asked to have a bath drawn so she could relax and immerse herself in the role. After a nap, she would return to the theatre refreshed and ready to prove her reputation well earned.

CHAPTER FIVE

"I cannot believe I am to spend my evening watching a woman perform at the theatre," Laura said, tying the long, pale green satin ribbons from her opera bonnet around her chin and angling her head in the mirror.

"You could have said no," Ransom observed.

"I could do no such thing!" Laura adjusted the bonnet to the most flattering angle. "I have a new evening dress. And besides, Cousin Charlotte recently saw Miss Colfax act in a play in Washington City. She said it is very fashionable there for women to perform on the stage, even if some find the idea in lamentable taste. Evidently Miss Colfax has appeared in Richmond before, but I must have been at Barrett Hall at the time."

Ransom sighed loudly. "No one is twisting your arm to attend, sister, if it's your reputation you are worried about."

"Don't be stuffy. Of course I shall attend. Where did you say you met this…lady?"

"Miss Colfax is the sister of my dear friend Tyler and from all accounts a most accomplished young lady. Apparently there is not a book she hasn't read."

"She sounds exceedingly pompous." Laura gave him a stern glare. "And you have invited her to dinner tomorrow evening also? I cannot imagine what you were thinking. What will Mother say?"

"She seemed perfectly delighted with the idea when I told her." Ransom's eyes flashed mischief. "Come, come, Laura. We are in Richmond. Why not enjoy more diverse company?"

Secretly, Laura was thrilled with her first big night out since arriving with her family last week. The theatre offered an excellent opportunity to see and be seen, and she wondered at the latest fashions she would encounter there. Additionally, she was intrigued that they would be hosting a notable female actress in their town home for dinner the next evening. What scandalous things the woman must have seen and heard. Laura could only hope Miss Colfax would be willing to share her wicked stories. They would make for interesting gossip in her next letter to Charlotte.

Meg flounced into the parlor as they were preparing to leave. "It's not fair that I cannot attend the theatre with you."

"Don't be silly, Meg." Laura put on her gloves. "You are much too young and the play far too disturbing for someone as impressionable as you."

"I am not impressionable!" Meg pouted. "I can read Shakespeare. I merely have trouble understanding what they're saying."

"Well, when you understand what they're saying, then you will be able to attend."

"Let's go or we'll be late." Ransom pointed to the clock on the mantel and advanced toward the doorway.

He helped Laura into the carriage and their driver, John, pulled slowly away from the front of their home. Laura squashed her hooped skirts so she could face her brother. Ransom looked so handsome in his immaculately pressed blue uniform. She was terribly proud of him and happy to be seen in public on his arm.

"So tell me what this woman is like, Ransom. I wish to know everything."

Ransom tilted his head in thought. "Let me see. She has three heads and blows steam out of her nose, ears, and mouth. A most extraordinary sight."

Laura slapped his arm playfully.

"Honestly? She's extremely attractive. Tall, auburn hair, and very smart." He chuckled softly. "I must confess that when Tyler first introduced us, I was a bit intimidated by her. But she has a soft side, I assure you. Besides, she's my best friend's sister and she'll be in Richmond for several weeks. I thought it only proper to make her feel at home here and invite her to dinner. You would do well to befriend her and introduce her to your social set."

Laura gasped. "Oh, Ransom! I couldn't! What would people think of me, being acquainted with a stage actress?"

"They would think you worldly and resent their own provincial existence."

Laura thought about that for a moment. An acquaintanceship with Miss Colfax would make her appear sophisticated. Still…

"Please, Laura? For my sake?"

Whenever Ransom asked anything of her, Laura could not deny him. She so infrequently spent time with him these days that she wanted to please him while he was at home.

"Well, let me at least see what she is like. If she is in the least bit presentable to my friends, I may invite her to afternoon tea."

❖

"Laura, I declare. Where have you been hiding that brother of yours?" A belle in blue taffeta swished across the lobby.

Emma Harper flicked a costly fan. She had removed her gloves, making certain the engagement ring on her left hand was visible to anyone unaware of her recent engagement. The news had reached Laura in a letter from Charlotte, and she couldn't help but feel the tension as several mutual friends gravitated over and began chattering about the upcoming wedding and the Georgia plantation owned by Emma's future father-in-law.

The prospect of her nuptials did not prevent Emma from flirting with Ransom and any other gentleman who could sit upright on a horse. Tapping his arm with her fan, she said, "Your own offer of marriage was so tardy, what choice did I have but to accept David's?" Casting a generous smile at her friends, she added, "However, none of these ladies is spoken for."

"And all so beautiful," Ransom said gallantly.

"What about you, Laura?" Emma made her point. "I am quite holding my breath for an invitation."

Ransom chuckled. "Do not wager your next breath upon my sister's announcement, Miss Harper."

Laura joined the laughter as if she, too, was amused, but when the call came for the ticket holders to take their seats, she could hardly wait to escape the pitying stares. Everyone, Ransom included, knew she was fast becoming the prettiest old maid in Virginia.

As the gaslights lowered, the thrill of excitement she always got when she attended a play settled over her. To Laura, the stage was the place where a book came alive. The characters and events she had fantasized while reading were made manifest in the performance of the actors. While *Macbeth* was not a play in which she wished she could live, many productions she had been to were so romantic and beautiful that she thought her heart must break. Tales of love and passion the likes of which she could only dream about, but never believe they were meant for her.

As she watched the play, she found that the actor playing Macbeth was far too histrionic for her tastes, although she noticed several women down front swoon over his looks. George Lamont was a well-known actor, and she had met him at several social functions in Richmond but had managed to avoid his overly solicitous attentions. She did not care for the way he had leered at her and felt uncomfortable whenever he was near. Perhaps her feelings toward him affected her impression of his performance, but she didn't think so.

When Jordan Colfax made her appearance, Laura heard a slight murmur arise from a few members of the audience, shocked at the idea of a woman onstage. She almost giggled out loud at the thought that she would be entertaining this very woman in her home the next evening. If only her friends and the patrons of the theatre knew. They might even whisper behind her back. She was determined not to care. She would show them that she was above such snobbery and could appreciate the refined tastes exhibited in places like Washington and New York. She might have been raised on a plantation, but she refused to live as though she had no culture whatsoever.

Laura marveled through her opera glasses as Miss Colfax performed effortlessly on the stage. The actress's self-assurance called to mind Anna Finch, the most handsome woman at Charlotte's wedding. Both were not only beautiful but had the poise and carriage Laura longed to display herself. Jordan Colfax's presence was electrifying; her personality radiated all the way up to the second floor, making Laura hang forward ever so slightly, trying to identify the essence of what she was seeing. Miss Colfax conveyed strength and confidence, two qualities Laura respected, in part because they were traits she felt lacking in herself. She traced a strong jaw line back to small, well-shaped ears. From these dangled multitiered black crystal earrings that reflected the gaslights glowing from the proscenium walls. The actress's face was open, her expression conveying complete honesty and warmth. The high cheekbones and aquiline nose were in perfect proportion with the full lips and the hint of dimples in each cheek.

Laura felt—she wasn't sure what—mixed emotions, but overall, she admired her. *That's silly. I don't even know her.*

She wondered at this realization and continued to observe Jordan, trying to understand what it was that both attracted and repelled her. She adored the costume and admired the thick chestnut hair elegantly coiffed atop the actress's head, accentuating the long graceful neck. Yet this woman was making a spectacle of herself, demonstrating a lack of concern with public opinion that appalled Laura. At the same time she was secretly envious of this complete disregard for gossip. Being on the receiving end of unkind gossip herself, Laura understood how painful it could be. She wished she could dismiss the opinions of others as easily as this woman, but her mother would never let her failings go without comment.

"Come, you spirits that tend on mortal thoughts, unsex me here, and fill me, from the crown to the toe, top-full of direst cruelty!"

Laura shivered as Jordan spoke. Jordan was completely believable and Laura felt the beginnings of fear stir within her. She knew it was silly, it was make-believe, but the look of hatred in Jordan's eyes unsettled her. The actress's voice was also deep and hate-filled, and Laura could feel the sound sear through to her soul. As the play continued, Laura found herself distracted whenever Jordan was not onstage. She felt foolish waiting anxiously for her reappearance, but at least she was not alone. She couldn't help but notice that whenever Jordan was present, a sense of excitement infused the actors and the entire temperature of the scene increased. Audience members leaned forward in their seats at her every word, apparently transfixed.

By the end of the second act, Laura desperately needed fresh air and something to drink. Her throat was parched and the air was cloying with the heavy mixture of women's perfume. They made their way into the lobby where Ransom procured a glass of water for her.

"I have never seen anything so outrageous in my life," an elderly matron exclaimed to her party.

"But you must admit, she is the main attraction," a whiskered gentleman replied. "She is intriguing to behold, and I am not just speaking of her beauty, although there is that."

Laura had to agree. Jordan would soon be the talk of Richmond, and Ransom was her friend. Laura wondered what that would mean for her should she agree to shepherd Jordan around to tea and parties. Would she also become infamous by association? Anything, even the snubs she might receive for acquiring a scandalous reputation, would prove to be more interesting than the dull life she now endured. Laura decided Emma Harper and her mother would be among the first hostesses she would delight in shocking. She could hardly wait.

They returned to their seats for the third act, and as the lights lowered, Laura felt the exquisite tension grip her once again. She could not recall the last time she had been so excited about anything or anyone. She was looking forward to getting to know this strange woman and finding out more about her. What kind of life must she lead? Miss Colfax traveled between Washington and Richmond, and had no doubt journeyed much farther. She could come and go as she pleased, meeting new people and seeing far-off places. Her life seemed impossibly exotic in comparison to Laura's, and she envied her freedom.

When the play ended, each actor approached the edge of the stage to take a bow, and Laura noted with no little satisfaction that the greatest applause was bestowed upon Jordan. She had to admit, Jordan was the best part of the show. They rose from their seats and found their way to the stairs along with the rest of the balcony audience to the lobby below. The descent was slowed by the massing of people at the foot of the stairs, and the clamor of the crowd was so loud that Ransom had to shout to be heard.

"Jordan asked us to meet her," he yelled.

Laura nodded and clung to his arm to avoid being separated. Eventually they entered a side aisle, and as they approached the front of the stage the crowd had completely emptied the theatre. Ransom led her behind the curtain and she peered curiously at the people and objects on display.

They had to wait a while as a large crowd of admirers had gathered outside Jordan's dressing room, some with gifts to offer her. Laura suddenly wished she had thought of some small token to bring, as well. She blushed at the thought and was glad of her gloves, for her palms were quite clammy. It would be mortifying if Jordan knew she was nervous to meet her.

When Jordan finally emerged from her dressing room, Ransom congratulated her. "You were wonderful, Jordan."

"Thank you. I'm so happy you could come. Opening night is always such a special performance."

"Jordan, may I introduce my sister, Laura."

"Delighted to make your acquaintance, Miss St. Clair."

Jordan smiled. She had already been struck by the fair beauty of Ransom's sister, having noticed her among the audience during George Lamont's soliloquy. Jordan tried to appear interested in George's performance, but his physical theatrics had distracted her from the speech and her gaze wandered toward the audience. A flash of light from the balcony caught her eye, beaming off the button of a soldier's uniform. It was Ransom, and next to him the sister he had mentioned. Jordan would have missed her cue had it not been for the resounding sneeze from a member of the audience. Up close Laura's eyes were even more remarkable than they had appeared in the poor light of the balcony. They brought to mind an aquamarine necklace Jordan had admired on a patron at Ford's Theatre one evening.

Intrigued, she took Laura's proffered hand and held it briefly. "Our brothers are great friends, it seems. And please, call me Jordan."

Laura trembled involuntarily at the fleeting contact. "Why, yes indeed, Jordan. I declare, I'm quite certain Ransom would trade either of his sisters for Tyler!" Laura giggled, then felt embarrassed, aware that she was speaking too quickly and that Ransom was staring at her with a bemused expression.

A little awkwardly, he said, "Don't you think Jordan was simply marvelous, Laura?"

Laura cast him a warning look. She did not need any help remembering her manners. She had intended to compliment Jordan on her acting with the very next breath she drew. "Yes, simply marvelous," she echoed. "I have never seen anything so compelling as that moment when you remarked upon the blood on your hands. Behind me a lady actually fainted. I suppose that must happen frequently during such dramatic moments when you perform."

Something warm flickered in Jordan's eyes and she replied softly, "While I would like to take the credit for making the ladies among my audience short of breath, I suspect tight lacing and warm theatres are the more likely culprit."

"You are too modest, Jordan darling." The words were spoken in a dulcet drawl that came from directly behind Laura.

Half turning, Laura came face-to-face with a woman so beautiful and so scandalously clad, her garments were certainly Parisian. The cut of the lavender gown left nothing to the imagination, baring an expanse of the woman's bosom for all to see. Ransom's gaze momentarily froze at the sight until she nudged him to look away. The stranger's hair was flaxen and contrasted sharply with the bloodred rouge dotted on her lips. Were it not for the fact that she was a stunning woman of obvious wealth, the garish color would have caused derision. She moved haughtily through the crowd, carrying herself with the expectation that others would clear a path. If Laura hadn't known better, she would have suspected her of being a woman of the town plying her avocation.

"Nell!" Jordan looked delighted. "What are you doing here?"

The woman wrapped her arms around Jordan in a close embrace, drawing back just enough to kiss her squarely on the lips. Laura was shocked at the intimate contact, never before having seen one woman kiss another in such manner. She supposed it was a common greeting among those in the acting profession and tried to pretend she was accustomed to such behavior, but she could not help but stare.

"I'm sorry, please let me introduce you to my friends." Jordan broke the contact and turned her attention to Ransom and Laura, announcing Miss Nell Tabor, an actress from Baltimore.

Miss Tabor's murky blue eyes scanned Laura with blatant appreciation, and Laura blushed despite herself. When the actress was introduced to Ransom, he was so entranced that he could not speak and merely bowed clumsily.

Miss Tabor had yet to release her arm from around Jordan's waist. "You are invited to my hotel for a party I'm having this evening." She gestured grandly, one hand dramatically flung into the air. "And you must bring your delightful friends," she added, gazing longingly at Laura.

"I would love to," Jordan said, "but I have plans tonight."

Resenting Miss Tabor's intrusion, Laura caught Ransom as he was about to open his mouth and elbowed him in the side. She was positive he was about to invite the woman to dinner tomorrow evening and she absolutely would not allow it. She watched Miss Tabor's hand drift up and down Jordan's back, lazily finding its way to her side.

"Another time, perhaps." She smiled warmly. "I shall call upon you at your hotel, Jordan. I simply must catch up on all you've been doing since we were last together."

Laura detected a deeper meaning in the way Miss Tabor emphasized "last together," yet she could not quite grasp the significance. She decided she did not like this painted woman at all and was horrified that Jordan was acquainted with her. Trying not to show her disdain, she smiled weakly as the actress kissed Jordan good-bye and she, along with her entourage, departed in a flurry.

Ransom finally found his voice. "John is waiting with the carriage out front, so we shall be on our way."

Jordan followed them back through the theatre and out into the brisk evening air. The carriage sat across the street from the theatre, but the coachman was nowhere to be found.

"That's odd," Ransom puzzled. "He can't be far. I'll go see where he is."

He assisted Laura and Jordan into the carriage and then walked back to the theatre. The women sat in silence, staring out into the evening. After a few moments, Laura began to feel guilty that she was not being a good hostess and forced herself to say something polite. "So, Jordan, what made you decide to become an actress?"

Jordan glanced at Laura's profile in the dark. She hadn't expected the question and hadn't thought about her usual response for quite some time. "I remember as a little girl my father taking my brother and me on a trip to Philadelphia. We stopped at an inn along the way where a traveling troupe of actors performed for the patrons. It was there I saw a woman perform for the first time. I don't recall what the play was or what it was about. But I remember how graceful she was, and how I believed everything she said. I knew then that I wanted to be able to affect people that way. I guess after the loss of my mother, I was looking for something, or someone, to pay attention to me." She laughed.

The street lamps cast enough light for Laura to see the pained expression on her face. She suspected that if Jordan knew how she had revealed herself, she would be more guarded. "I'm so sorry, Jordan. I did not know about your mother."

"It was a very long time ago. I don't even remember what she looked like, except for a portrait that my father keeps of her." Jordan had spent hours as a child looking at the portrait, imagining how kind and loving her mother must have been. She even spoke to the portrait, telling her mother what she did from day to day, whom she met, what she was learning in school.

Laura shivered, partly from the cold but also because she felt the loss of her own mother, although in a different way. Still, at least she had a mother. Poor Jordan.

The carriage jostled as Ransom swung up into the cab. "I have looked everywhere and asked people in the area. No one has seen him, and he should have been back long ago. Quite frankly, I am concerned that he may have run away."

Laura blanched. "No, Ransom, that cannot be. Not John. He has been with father half his life. Why would he do such a thing?"

"Recent political events may have stirred him to action. I have heard from other planters that the abolitionists have increased their efforts in enticing slaves northward. I'll drive you ladies home and tell Father. He will probably want to report John as a runaway to the authorities. I wish we were home at Barrett Hall. At least we'd have the dogs to help search." He climbed down from the cab and jumped up into the driver's seat.

Appalled, Jordan could not keep silent. "Dogs? My God, he is after all a human being. All he is searching for is what any human being yearns for. Freedom. If he wishes to be gone, why force him to return? Why not let him be?"

"John's life is not his own, Jordan," Laura explained patiently. "He has been bought for quite a sum of money and, in exchange, he does the work required of him. He in turn is fed, clothed, housed, and cared for when ill."

"But don't you think that owning another human being is wrong?" Jordan asked. Her question was not accusatory; she really wanted to understand Laura's thinking.

"I myself could not leave my father's house without his permission," Laura said. "I too have obligations to fulfill and have no independent means of support. I rely completely on my father's care until I marry, and then I will come under the care of my husband." Her voice faltered and she felt her eyes begin to burn with the thought of her fate. She cleared her throat. "Without either of them I should surely perish, for I cannot earn an income with which to feed and house myself."

Jordan stared at Laura, shocked by her admission. She felt sorry for her, trapped in a life from which she would never be able to extricate herself. It was a shame, really, for Laura was a beautiful, seemingly educated woman. If she could learn a useful skill, she had the intelligence to start a business for herself where she could be independent from the care of a man. Sadly, the possibility would probably never occur to her.

They drove to Jordan's hotel in silence and Ransom helped Jordan down from the carriage. After bidding the St. Clairs good night, she climbed the stairs to her room, unable to clear from her mind the image of Laura as a plantation mistress. The mere thought of the dull, morally questionable existence depressed her, but she supposed it was what was expected of a woman in Laura's situation. Thank God Laura wasn't her responsibility.

Chapter Six

The carriage arrived at the St. Clair home on Church Hill precisely at eight o'clock. As the driver assisted Jordan to the ground, she glanced up at the imposing Georgian structure, admiring the elegant simplicity of the architecture. She approached the front door and knocked. Within moments, an elderly Negro man responded.

"Good evening, miss." He opened the door wide to allow her entry.

"I believe I'm expected," Jordan replied. "My name is Jordan Colfax."

"Yes, miss. I'll tell Marse Ransom you here."

Taking her coat, he bowed his way out of the room, leaving her standing in the entryway, which gave Jordan the opportunity to examine her surroundings. She stared around, in awe of the ornate, finely adorned foyer. A curving oak staircase to her right led up to the second story, while a marble-topped mahogany table stood in the center of the hallway containing a large vase of pink hothouse roses that brightly colored the room. A painting on the wall to her left drew her attention. A hunting scene of riders on horseback and fox hounds on the chase was very detailed and realistic, but she could not read the artist's signature in the lower right-hand corner. As she scrutinized the painting, she heard someone approach from the room to her left.

"Jordan! How good of you to come." Ransom embraced her affectionately.

He led her into the parlor where a cheerful fire warmed the room nicely, and she took her place on a large settee against a far wall.

"My parents send their regrets as they had an important political function to attend this evening. So it will be my sisters and me," he said, pouring sherry from a crystal decanter.

"Another time, then." Taking the glass from his hand, Jordan wondered what the political function might be.

Rapid steps on the stair could be heard, followed by the entrance of a young girl into the parlor. After being introduced, Ransom's younger sister, Meg, immediately took command of the seat next to Jordan.

"Ransom says that you are an actress, but I don't believe him. Is it true?"

Jordan laughed. "Yes, it's true."

Meg stared as if Jordan was a circus act. "How scandalous!"

"Meg!" Ransom said.

"It's all right," Jordan soothed. "It's not the first time I've heard that comment. I have learned to accept that some people have a difficult time seeing a woman on the stage."

"Mother says it is unladylike and that men think they may have their way with such women."

"Meg, that is quite enough, and *unladylike* of you to make such pronouncements." Ransom drew a chair closer to the fire.

"Well, I think I should like to see what it's all about." Meg sniffed. "I have never been to a play, but perhaps you will take me to see Miss Colfax, Ransom."

"He shall do no such thing."

Jordan turned in her seat to see Laura standing in the doorway to the parlor. Although petite in stature, she had a fire in her eyes that betrayed a strong inner disposition of one accustomed to being obeyed. But there was something else, a translucence that spoke of physical frailty. Jordan could not help but think that if not for her inner strength, Laura St. Clair might be too delicate to withstand the rigors of life. Still, her ethereal beauty was riveting to behold, and Jordan felt an odd sensation not unlike the nervous flutter she always experienced in Nell Tabor's presence.

"Laura." Ransom rose from his chair. "You look well, sister."

Laura smiled. She took her time sweeping Jordan with an appraising stare. "Miss Colfax, it's a pleasure to see you again." She signaled a house servant standing near the door.

A slave, Jordan concluded, instantly affronted. While fully aware of slavery, seeing it every day of her life on the streets of Washington, she had never really spent time in the company of those who actually owned other beings. Her father's political as well as moral beliefs would not allow it, and as Jordan grew older, she and Tyler embraced the same values. She knew she would have to call upon her most skillful acting to hide her contempt from the St. Clairs. She was, after all, a guest in their home.

Jordan took a sip of her sherry, and after giving some instructions to the slave, Laura took a chair near Ransom.

"My brother tells me you are to be in town for the next few weeks. Have you spent time in our fair city before, Jordan?"

"I've been to Richmond several times and have seen some of her attributes, but only within walking distance of my hotel."

"Well, we must rectify that immediately," Laura declared. "Is there anything in particular that interests you? Besides the theatre, of course."

Jordan thought for a moment, remembering her real purpose. "I must confess that given the latest political events, I should like to visit your legislature to hear the debate as to Virginia's position in the matter."

Laura was nonplussed. People often attended the legislature for varying political as well as business reasons, but she was at a loss as to why Jordan would be interested. She could think of so many other destinations of greater interest in Richmond, yet she did not want to disregard her guest's wishes.

Jordan watched the play of emotions cross Laura's face and wondered if perhaps she had exposed her hand too quickly. She did not wish to draw suspicion upon herself, especially this early in the game. Responding to Laura's hesitation, she said, "I understand your father is a member of the legislature, and I would so like to hear his view on the subject. Unless of course politics are of no interest to you?"

Laura's initial confusion was instantly replaced with determined conviction. "I'm a devout loyalist to the Southern cause, Jordan. I read the papers daily and am well aware of Mr. Lincoln's position. The issue at hand is the arrogance of the North imposing her will on the sovereign states of the South."

"So then, you are also a supporter of slavery?" Jordan asked.

Laura was tired of having slavery as an ongoing issue in the debate about Southern rights. Slavery had nothing to do with the fact that the Southern states merely wanted to be able to govern themselves as they saw fit without being forced to accept the North's ideas of what was right and wrong. Northerners had no concept of what it took to keep the plantations going with the cotton that clothed them and the tobacco they craved. She wished slavery had never existed so that the real issues could be properly addressed.

The North had become more powerful than the South, its economy based upon industry, mining, commerce, and transportation. The much larger cities in the North also provided the labor essential to these growing industries. The booming Northern economy was further fueled by immigration, with most new Americans choosing to live where they could obtain work. These differences, both economic and political, had created two quite separate cultures within the same country. Southerners, with their plantation way of life, would never see eye to eye with their industrialized Northern neighbors, and with the balance of power shifting in the North's favor, resentment was inevitable. Laura wished there were some way to bring the country back together, but it seemed too late.

"First of all, Jordan, *your* President-elect said he has no intention of freeing any of the slaves anywhere they exist. Be that as it may, slavery is dying even as we speak and will disappear of its own accord in time."

"Someone had better tell President Lincoln that," Jordan muttered under her breath.

Laura ignored the sarcasm. "Mr. Lincoln's true aim is to see the South subjugated and her freedoms dismantled. You may inform the North upon your return that Southern women will do their part in defending our country from Northern invasion."

Jordan was incredulous that Laura failed to grasp the North's abhorrence of slavery. Regrettably, while many Northerners did not care about the slaves, a growing number wished to see the evil institution come to an end. Jordan counted herself among them.

"Mr. Lincoln has every right to protect and defend the Constitution of these *United* States. There are no legal grounds for dissolution of the country, contrary to what your politicians mistakenly claim in their speeches. And as for subjugation, Miss St. Clair, it surprises me that you speak of such a thing when the South enslaves four million of her people." *This woman is simply too much!*

"Slavery is a device that Northerners use to inflame public opinion against the South," Laura continued. "The real issue is liberty, *Miss* Colfax, and the North's single-minded desire to see the South adhere to its values and to dissolve the Southern way of life. Our agrarian way of life has been the foundation of this country for hundreds of years. Northerners have chosen the manufacturing way of life, which, if I may say, enslaves a population in grueling work in dangerous conditions and at low wages. The cotton *we* grow is processed by *your* workers while the profits line the pockets of their wealthy overseers. Let's remove slavery from the discussion, and return instead to the matter of self-government. As I understand our forefathers' Declaration, it is the right of the people to alter or abolish their form of government if that government deprives its people of life, liberty, and the pursuit of happiness."

Jordan's temper began to flare. "Through the ballot, Miss St. Clair, through the ballot! Not through suicide!"

Not in the least bit intimidated, Laura stood her ground and looked hard into Jordan's hazel irises. "I assure you, Miss Colfax, if Southern women had the vote, you would hear most clearly our desire to separate from our Yankee masters."

Jordan was momentarily speechless. Women's suffrage had long been a cause dear to her heart, and to have it thrown back in her face, albeit unknowingly, by her adversary was a neat little argument indeed. She allowed a hint of amusement to infuse her glare, intending to soften any harshness. She could not help but feel a grudging respect for Laura; there was more to this fragile Southern woman than met the eye.

"Why, Miss St. Clair, is it possible I have found a kindred spirit, for surely you are a suffragist."

Barely able to speak, Laura spluttered indignantly, "I am no such thing—"

"Be that as it may, the South cannot secede," Jordan retorted. "Mr. Lincoln has declared that he will do all in his power to maintain the Union at all costs. Those who have already departed are well advised to reconsider their hasty decision. Virginia must think of her proximity to the North. Her Southern sisters are well protected, being so far from the nation's capital, yet she will surely receive the brunt of the blows if this impasse should come to war."

"Do you think it will come to that, Miss Colfax?" Meg could no longer keep silent.

Brought up short by the realization that there was a younger person in the room whose sensibilities might be affected by such talk, Jordan apologized. "I'm afraid I've momentarily lost my manners, Miss Meg.

Surely representatives on both sides get carried away with posturing and war-mongering rhetoric. I think war a remote possibility at this stage."

"Well, I think I should like to see it come to war," Meg replied with a toss of her curls.

"Meg, you cannot possibly think such an awful thing," Laura exclaimed.

"But I do, Laura. It would serve the Yankees right for being such beasts. We are ever so much happier the way things are. Our slaves love us and we treat them so well."

Laura cast her eyes to her lap. She did not want to think about the slaves and what they thought about her and the rest of the St. Clair family. She recalled a time when she had entered the barn to retrieve her horse and had come across their overseer, Mr. Humphreys, whipping the stable boy. Evidently the boy had not done the tasks he was assigned and had, according to her father, rightfully incurred the punishment. At the time, Laura had thought the flogging unduly harsh, but her father had made his decision. A wayward thought of her father and Martha leapt into mind once again, and she quickly dismissed it. No doubt Northern men had their imperfections, also.

"Dinner is served," Sarah called from the entryway.

Relieved to end the uncomfortable discussion, Laura rose with the others and entered the dining room. She felt pleased with herself over the next hour, for she artfully diverted the conversation to less controversial topics. Ransom played his part, entertaining their small party with tales of life at West Point, and Jordan answered questions about her life as an actress until she noted the late hour and took her leave.

"Isn't the theatre closed tomorrow?" Ransom asked her.

"Yes, a day of rest for me."

"Oh, but then we must show you around Richmond, mustn't we, Laura," Meg said.

Laura forced a smile but avoided answering. She was beginning to think it would be a mistake to escort Jordan around Richmond. They had nothing in common, they disagreed completely with political events, and what was worse, the woman was insufferably arrogant. *Such a typical Yankee.* Northerners seemed to consider Southern women simpletons. Laura was insulted, but she also had a whim to prove to this dreadful woman that Southern women were every bit as intelligent and informed as their Northern counterparts. She allowed herself an evil smile.

"Why, Meg, I think that is a superb idea. We shall begin with the legislature then, Jordan, as you desire. We could meet for lunch and then attend the sessions afterward."

Jordan wanted nothing more than to wipe the insincere smile right off Laura's face. Suspecting her plantation life did not involve rising early, a thought came quickly to her mind. "How kind of you both. But I propose we get an early start. There is so much to do and see in Richmond, I think a full day is warranted, don't you? Let's meet for breakfast, say nine o'clock? Then we could attend the sessions in the morning and still have the afternoon free to really see the sights."

Laura's eyes narrowed perceptibly.

"Nine o'clock!" Meg squeaked. "Why—"

"That is so much better," Laura interrupted. "We shall meet you at your hotel and dine there, then it's a short walk to the capital."

"Perfect." Jordan smiled. "I shall see you at nine."

❖

Laura awoke to the feel of Ruby shaking her from her sleep. She groaned and opened one eye. The curtains had been thrust aside and the morning light shone brightly in the room.

"Wake up, Miss Laura. You said to wake you up now so you won't be late." Ruby pulled the covers down to the foot of the bed, exposing her to the chill of the morning.

"Oh, Ruby, it can't be time to get up, can it? What time is it?"

"It's eight o'clock. I've laid out your dress and poured you some warm water. You said you didn't want to be late, now."

Laura closed her eyes. Why did she agree to meet Jordan at nine? She knew it was because she didn't want to admit that she usually rose late in the morning. That Yankee woman was so rude and vile, she would not give her the satisfaction. At dinner Jordan had talked incessantly of her career and the notable people she had befriended. Hers was the kind of life Laura would have wished for, with all the excitement and travel, and Jordan's independence. Normally she would have encouraged Jordan's fascinating revelations, but she loathed the woman's air of superiority and refused to flatter her ego.

Laura was surprised at how she tried to belittle the significance of

Jordan's accomplishments. Why should she care what Jordan did with her life? Why should she be envious? She let her feet slowly drop to the side of the bed until she found herself standing. With a glance at the dress Ruby had readied, she said, "No, I think I'll wear the organdy muslin. And I want to do something different with my hair."

Ruby went to find the other gown and, with her back to Laura, rolled her eyes. She knew getting the young missy up this early in the morning was going to be a problem. And now she wanted her hair done different. This was going to be a very long day.

After several attempts at getting her new hair style exactly right, Laura finally gave up. Ruby was becoming frustrated and the sharp tugs on her hair were the result. Whenever Ruby made her feelings plain in this manner, it was all Laura could do to keep a civil tongue. She was uncomfortable in the girl's presence no matter what her mood, but more so on bad days.

As soon as she was presentable, Laura gathered her belongings and descended the stairs to the parlor where her mother sat reading.

"I tried to rouse Margaret from her bed," Rachel explained, "but she was not to be moved. I suppose you ought to go without her."

"It's just as well." Laura pulled on her silk gloves. "I'm sure she would be bored to tears visiting the legislature this morning." Rethinking what she said, she amended, "Of course, Father will be worth listening to."

Rachel merely nodded and returned to her reading. Bidding her good morning, Laura hurried to the street where the St. Clairs' new driver, Aaron, awaited her.

❖

Laura thought that the legislature would never break for lunch. After hours of listening to the debate between those who argued for secession and those who did not, she found herself nodding off only to be rudely awoken by the sound of the gavel on the speaker's desk. Jordan's amused expression at catching her asleep only strengthened her resolve to pay closer attention. Once or twice she also noticed Jordan gazing at her with another kind of look, one that made her feel rather warm, and wished she could loosen her corset.

As they departed the Capitol Building, Laura invited Jordan to walk with her across the square and a couple of blocks down Franklin Street to the Exchange Hotel for lunch. Laura loved this hotel, as the food was excellent and the clientele among Richmond's most respected citizens. She hoped that it would compare favorably with the establishments Jordan was used to in Washington and her travels. Finding a table near the window, they ordered tea and perused the menu while they waited.

"So, did you enjoy this morning's discussion?" Laura asked.

"Very interesting," Jordan said. "I think your father showed remarkable restraint when faced with some of the more impassioned members of your government. You must be very proud of him."

Laura smiled modestly. "Yes, very proud. He is held in high esteem by his peers and his opinions carry weight. You see, Miss Colfax, not all of us Southerners are warmongers."

"Laura." Jordan lowered her teacup, her voice dropping to its lowest register. "I thought we had decided on less formal titles for one another."

Laura blushed. She liked the sound of her name when Jordan spoke it. And she liked the implied intimacy of the more familiar address. "Yes, you're right…Jordan." Laura felt the heat rise to her face.

Jordan gazed at the delicate woman, entranced once again by the pools of crystal blue-green peering back at her.

The waiter returned and they ordered soup for the first course. While they waited, Jordan took in the décor of the hotel and the patrons in the restaurant. No one seemed to pay them any attention and she allowed her gaze to sweep the room until someone caught her eye. Kate Warne sat at a table alone, and when their eyes locked, Kate immediately looked away and resumed eating her lunch. Jordan thought about the real reason she had befriended Laura and determined to elicit as much information as she could about her father.

Laura spent the afternoon escorting Jordan around Richmond, proudly showing her all that the Virginia capital had to offer. From the commerce along the waterfront to the Tredegar Iron Works, Laura believed that Richmond compared favorably with any Northern city, including Washington. She had visited the nation's capital several times and found it woefully depressing in both appearance and style. But Richmond, in her mind, was physically a much more attractive town and the society equally so.

Occasionally Laura would glance sidelong at Jordan, trying to gauge her impressions. Rather than focusing on the shops and fashions about town, however, Jordan seemed mainly interested in the harbor and iron works, the business and manufacturing aspects of Richmond. The woman was certainly odd, Laura thought. She had never met anyone like her before, what with her involvement in the theatre on one hand and a fascination for business on the other. None of the more feminine enterprises seemed to appeal to her, and Laura was at a loss as to what to do with her next. Exhausted from having risen early and indecision testing her nerves, she suggested tea back at the St. Clair home on Church Hill.

"Thank you for the kind offer, Laura, but I have another engagement this evening and must return to my hotel."

"But I thought you had no performance this evening."

"You are right, the theatre is closed, but I am expecting Miss Tabor around six o'clock."

A twinge of jealousy crept into Laura's mind. She did not care for the brassy woman one bit and believed she had questionable designs on Jordan. What that meant exactly she wasn't sure, but she felt an overwhelming urge to insist that Jordan be on guard against Miss Tabor's machinations. It was not her place to do so, however, and Jordan had a friendship with the actress that preceded their acquaintance. Who was she to tell her what to do? Obviously Jordan lived her life as she saw fit, choosing those with whom she wished to spend her time and those she did not. It was an enviable life and if she made mistakes, well, it was her life to make them.

Aaron drove them to Jordan's hotel on Broad Street and helped her alight from the carriage. Glancing up at Laura, Jordan was struck once again by the otherworldly radiance that seemed to shimmer around Laura. Jordan thought it strange that Laura could be so silly one moment, yet gentle and softhearted the next. On more than one occasion as they went about town, stopping in various shops, Laura inquired as to the health of the shopkeepers or recalled sick relations. Many thanked her for her gifts of food, medicines, and prayers. Jordan couldn't quite make up her mind what to think of her. Laura was so different from someone like Nell. And yet Jordan felt drawn in a similar way to both women.

"Thank you again for showing me your lovely city." She placed her hand on Laura's, which rested on the side of the carriage.

Laura pretended not to notice the connection, but she felt it nevertheless. What was it about Jordan that made her blood run hot and cold? "I'm glad you found the outing enjoyable. Thank you for your company."

Jordan smiled and allowed her hand to linger on Laura's. "The pleasure was all mine, Laura."

Laura again felt the slight prickling sensation of her skin when Jordan spoke her name. She liked to hear her say it. "Perhaps you will allow me to call upon you again to continue your education?"

"I shall look forward to it."

"Until next time, then." Laura signaled to Aaron and the carriage pulled out into the street.

Jordan watched as it traveled down Broad until it turned the corner and disappeared. She could still feel the impression of Laura's hand in the palm of her own, and she rubbed her hands together to dispel the feeling. But try as she might, it would not go away.

❖

Jefferson Davis held back a particularly thorny stem so that his wife Varina could prune the dying branch within the bush. Caring for their garden, and in particular the roses, was a favorite joint pastime, and he was pleased with their progress. They would soon enjoy the fine spring blooms that were admired by all their neighbors. As she trimmed the plant, he gazed up at the crisp blue sky where not a cloud could be seen. The cool air and warm sun felt good on his face and he closed his eyes in appreciation.

"General, if you would be so kind as to pay attention to the task at hand, we may both escape the treachery of this bush."

He blushed slightly, knowing that his mind was elsewhere and that Varina had been aware of his distraction for some time. He smiled inwardly at her use of the title "General." Upon his return to Brierfield after his speech in Washington, Governor Pettus had met him and offered him the job he most coveted, Major General of Volunteers for Mississippi. He knew deep in his bones that the country would soon be at war, and he had advised the governor of his home state to prepare with all the vigor and resources available. His former experience as Secretary of War made him the obvious choice for overall command of the army of Mississippi, and he was content to let the politicians meeting in convention in Alabama form the new government. This was going to be a soldier's fight, not a politician's, and he was well aware that with glory would come advancement.

Varina finished removing the dead branches and leaves, and they had moved on to the next bush when they heard the sound of horse's hooves. Jefferson glanced up and saw a young man on horseback dismount and approach.

"Good day to you, sir." The rider bowed slightly. "I have a dispatch for your attention."

He extended the message to Jefferson, who received it with a sense of foreboding. The telegram was short, only three sentences, but his hand shook as he read it, and his wife placed a steadying hand on his arm. He read it to her aloud.

Montgomery, Alabama

Sir:

We are directed to inform you that you are this day unanimously elected President of the Provisional Government of the Confederate States of America, and to request you to come to Montgomery immediately. We send also a special messenger. Do not wait for him.

R. Toombs,
R. Barnwell Rhett

He noted the names of his fellow senators from Georgia and South Carolina and was not surprised. They were both firebrands, anxious for war, and it made sense that they would wish to be the first to notify him of the convention's decision.

"I'll pack your bags," Varina said softly.

He could not speak and merely nodded his agreement. He would leave for Montgomery in the morning. The convention had decided his fate, and his only option was to obey. It was not what he would have wished, but his country was calling him to service and he could not refuse. The eyes of the world would now be upon him, and he must do all that he could to present a dignified visage.

He tried to imagine what it would be like to be President of a newly forming country and what history might say of its first leader. But all he could think about was all the work that lay ahead. A new constitution and laws would have to be written, and a mighty army would need to be assembled to defend against Northern aggression. His counterpart, Mr. Lincoln, had made clear his intentions. Now he would need to make clear his own.

CHAPTER SEVEN

The main story in the *Richmond Dispatch* was the election of Jefferson Davis as provisional President of the Confederate States of America. But Jordan had only skimmed that piece. She was much more dismayed by an advertisement several pages later.

$100 Reward!

Runaway from the subscriber, a Negro man named ***John****, about 24 years of age, 5 feet 9, will weigh 150 to 160 lbs. He has a smooth skin and good countenance; he took with him a gray frock coat of wool and a pair of dark brown pants—other clothing not recollected. No doubt but that he will try to get to some one of the free states. John left me on the 8th instant. The above reward will be given for the apprehension of said boy and his confinement.*

Edward St. Clair
11 February, 1861

Jordan tossed the paper aside, thoroughly disgusted with the St. Clair family and the South in general. How could these people believe in a right to own human property? They seemingly had no moral compunction in this regard, and she marveled that intelligent people like Ransom and Laura could not see things her way.

After breakfast, she headed back to the theatre to check on her costume. During the performance, the hem had caught and she had heard a distinct tearing sound. She wanted to examine the damage and repair it if she could. The dress had to last for several more performances, and she had hoped to use it again for a future production.

The theatre was quiet. Most of the actors slept late after a performance and the stage workers wouldn't be coming until the afternoon. She found the dress where she had left it, located a needle and thread, and sat down to begin her mending. After a while, she was surprised to hear voices coming from somewhere beyond her dressing room.

She ignored the sounds at first, but after she'd completed the repairs, she walked softly through the rear corridors listening until she heard a man speak directly overhead. She gazed up through the rafters and recognized Bill O'Malley and the escaped St. Clair slave, John.

"It's only for a couple more days," Bill said. "Then when the show's over, we get you outta here in a trunk used for equipment. Nobody's gonna know the difference. You get loaded on the train with all the other equipment, and I let you out when we get to Washington. Then someone will take you from Washington farther north, through Pennsylvania and Ohio."

"I don't know them places," John whispered. "I don't know if I want to go there."

"Well, you can't stay here," Bill said. "It's gonna be okay. They's lots o' colored folks up there that run away from down here. You'll see. Now eat that food I brought you 'cause you won't find much when you get out in the country."

Jordan had heard enough. Eager to get away before she was noticed and the men felt compromised, she stepped back but somehow made a board creak loudly. Both men peered down and saw her standing there. John started to bolt, but Bill grabbed his arm. His eyes pleaded with Jordan.

"You don't need to worry about her, she ain't gonna say nothing."

Jordan knew she could never bring herself to return the runaway to slavery, not even if he belonged to the St. Clairs. With a quick nod of reassurance to Bill, she hurried back to her dressing room to collect her bag before leaving the theatre.

Strolling down Broad, Jordan recalled Laura's comment about John and how his life was not his own. His subjugation first as a slave, and now as a runaway, dependent upon those who determined his fate, bewildered her. It seemed incomprehensible that any human being should have no control over his own life. Her mind wandered to Laura and her inability to make the choices an independent person took for granted. She had grown up belonging to her father, who dictated what her life was and what it would become, and would soon feel compelled to enter a loveless marriage where her husband would most certainly do the same.

Laura was clearly aware of her situation, but felt helpless to do anything but accept the life she was expected to lead. Yet the woman that Jordan saw was certainly intelligent, possessing great fortitude of mind and spirit. How could she accept her condition so placidly? Why could she not see that she had choices available to her, most importantly, that of her marriage and prospective husband?

A carriage rattled past, interrupting Jordan's musings. Glancing about, she watched as people hurried by, their slaves following obediently behind as second shadows to their masters. She observed the slaves' faces with interest, detecting a mixture of emptiness and fear in their eyes, perhaps the only two emotions they were allowed to feel. As she neared the hotel, it occurred to her that there were millions of slaves in this country who found themselves in the same hopeless predicament. If someday they all were freed, what would become of them? Was it possible for them to live side by side with their former masters? Jordan did not think it likely. If not, where would they go and what would they do?

The solutions to these problems eluded her and she feared that it would take more than political posturing to resolve them. As Mr. Lincoln said, a house divided against itself cannot stand. If that led to war, it would involve more than the slaves. The country would erupt into a conflict that would touch the lives of Northerners and Southerners alike. She could not conceive what that would portend for those she loved most.

Upon entering her hotel, she found a letter waiting for her, slipped under the door of her room. She opened it and removed an invitation to a levee to be held at the governor's home honoring the election of President Davis. At the bottom of the card was handwritten a brief note from Ransom: *I hope you can make it.*

She was amused that Laura had not added a comment of her own. Impulsively, she reached under the bed and withdrew her carpet bag.

She felt through the lining the little code book Kate Warne had given her and smiled inwardly. It looked as though she would be using the secret language after all.

❖

The Governor's House, lit up like a beacon on a hill, was decorated grandly and the social, political, and military elite of Virginia were in attendance. The atmosphere was electric and the celebration well underway when Jordan arrived. Every face she saw beamed with an ecstatic smile. Laughter and punch were in endless supply, women preened in their finest dresses, casting flirtatious glances at men in uniform. Jordan had the distinct impression that she was the lone dissenter in attendance and had best keep her own counsel. She left her wrap with a servant, and with Ransom at her side, entered the reception line to pay her respects to Governor Letcher and his wife.

As they filed along, she spied Laura chatting with a bevy of handsome young men attired in both civilian and military apparel. She was clearly the object of every young man's desires, and even Jordan had to admit she was a stunning young woman. Tonight she wore a blue crinoline in a delicate shade that served to emphasize her pale blue eyes and luminescent cream complexion. The only one among her admirers that looked out of place was a middle-aged man of about forty who stood awkwardly nearby, clearly unsure as to what to do with himself.

As Jordan and Ransom waited to enter the reception area, Meg joined them.

"It's a pleasure to see you again, Miss Meg. Are you enjoying yourself this evening?" Jordan inquired.

"Oh, very much, Miss Colfax. Of course I have met the governor before, but this is my first levee, and it's so very exciting. I think every one of our soldiers is the handsomest, don't you agree?"

Before Jordan could comment, Laura approached from the adjacent parlor with her parents following closely behind and a few hopeful beaux staring after her. Spying Jordan with Ransom, she led Mr. and Mrs. St. Clair over and made the introductions.

"It is an honor to meet you both," Jordan said.

"The pleasure is all ours, I assure you, Miss Colfax." Mr. St. Clair eyed her curiously. "It is odd, Miss Colfax, but is it possible we have met before?"

"Jordan is an actress, Father," Laura remarked. "She's currently performing at the Marshall in *Macbeth*. Perhaps you've seen her there."

"Of course," he exclaimed. "I saw you the other evening. A very compelling performance I must say. Bravo!"

Jordan smiled. "Thank you, sir. I'm so glad you enjoyed yourself."

"Will you be performing here in Richmond again when this production is over?" he inquired.

"Not until June." Jordan glanced along the line. It was taking forever to reach the governor. "This production ends in April, after which I shall be in Washington rehearsing for *Romeo and Juliet*." She also planned to travel to Washington for Lincoln's inauguration in March, but it did not seem wise to mention that in her present company.

"You seem rather…tall for Juliet?" Rachel St. Clair remarked. "Somehow I always envision a sweet, delicate girl in the role."

"No, I am to play Romeo, Mrs. St. Clair."

"I see. A breeches actress."

Jordan caught the quick look of disdain in Mrs. St. Clair's eyes. She was no stranger to condescension from women, having tolerated varying degrees of disapproval ever since she accepted her first acting role. Men, on the other hand, had a tendency to become a little more forward in their attentions when they discovered her profession.

"Well, shall we go and pay our respects?" Mrs. St. Clair turned her back on Jordan, took her husband's arm, and swept off into the reception area.

Oblivious to the slight, Ransom escorted Jordan and Laura, and they followed suit. The room was noisy and gaily lit, and a great many military uniforms could be seen throughout. The ladies were colorfully arrayed and did their utmost to attract the attention of several of the more senior officers.

After the governor had greeted Ransom, whom he seemed to know, Jordan was presented.

Governor Letcher bowed. "Miss Colfax, it is an honor."

"The honor is mine, sir." Jordan knew from the papers that the governor had recently been to the peace convention in Washington in an effort to avoid the impending crisis. He was against secession, but she wondered how long he would be able to withstand the avalanche of feeling for the idea in Virginia.

"Mrs. St. Clair tells me you are an actress at the Marshall," he remarked. "I believe I saw you in a production there last year, although as of late, my time has been taken by more pressing matters. It was *A Midsummer Night's Dream*, and I enjoyed myself thoroughly."

"Thank you, sir," Jordan replied. "I enjoyed myself as well, as it was my first time performing in Richmond. I will always cherish the memory of the warm reception with which the audience received me. You must be very proud to live in such a beautiful place."

Mrs. Letcher welcomed Laura warmly and immediately declared, "We are having a going-away luncheon for several ladies who are departing for Montgomery with their husbands. Laura, I have asked your mother to attend, and, Miss Colfax, we should be delighted to have you join us."

Jordan could not think of anything she would rather not do. She was never comfortable in gatherings with ladies, Northern or Southern, for they all talked about the same mindless topics.

"Well, that's a most kind invitation." Jordan knew she could not decline outright, but an excuse to avoid the purgatory eluded her.

Sensing Jordan's hesitation, Laura saw the perfect opportunity to expose her to the Southern women's perspective on the latest political events. "We would be delighted, Mrs. Letcher."

They thanked the governor again and Ransom led them to a huge silver punch bowl where a servant poured champagne punch from a crystal ladle. After they enjoyed a few cooling sips, the awkward middle-aged man from earlier sidled over to them.

"I have not had the opportunity to tell you how lovely you look this evening, Miss St. Clair." He took Laura's gloved hand and kissed it gently.

Jordan immediately noticed an uncomfortable expression on Laura's face that she quickly tried to hide.

"Why, thank you, Mr. Young. May I introduce you to my friend, Miss Jordan Colfax of Washington?"

Bowing a second time, he replied, "An honor to meet you, Miss Colfax. Hello, Ransom." His unease was as tangible as Laura's. Without entering into small talk, he said, "I hope you will honor me later with your hand for the Grand March, Miss St. Clair."

With a vapid smile, Laura replied, "Why, yes."

Jordan intercepted a look that passed between Laura and her

mother. Mrs. St. Clair raised her eyebrows and Laura gave a defeated nod.

A soldier standing nearby clapped Ransom jovially on the back. "Well, if it isn't Ransom St. Clair. How goes the academy these days?"

Meg immediately appeared at Laura's side, eyeing the soldier with unabashed interest. She curtsied and blushed when Laura introduced them. "Lieutenant Kincaid graduated last year from West Point," Ransom told Jordan. "Are you still with Major Jackson, Lieutenant?"

"Yes, unless things should change. It's very uncertain right now. What about you, old boy? Do you plan to finish or will you join us and get some real experience under your belt?"

"And what experience would that be?" Ransom chided. "Standing around and doing daily drills? I can get that back at the academy."

"So where is the rest of your troop, Lieutenant?" Jordan interrupted. "They must be nearby for you to be able to attend this gathering."

Laura glanced at Jordan. She thought it a rather odd comment and had not previously noted any interest in military affairs before from Jordan. She only hoped that she would not get into an argument with him in front of her parents, the governor, and the other soldiers in the room. She could hear now Jordan's lengthy diatribe on the merits of maintaining the Union while all of Virginia listened in.

"Regiment, ma'am, and they're near enough. But I spend a good deal of my time between here and the Shenandoah Valley. That's where my people are from, so it's nice to be able to see them once in a while." He returned to his conversation with Ransom. "Major Jackson is a tough old bird, but I think you would do well under his command. Have you thought about what you want to do after you graduate?"

"The cavalry is most certainly my first choice, but I know that others more senior than I also wish for the same thing." At this, Ransom glanced around the room.

Following his gaze, Jordan recognized several familiar faces from newspaper accounts, most notably Colonel Robert E. Lee, who had put down the rebellion led by John Brown and who, it was rumored, would take command of the forces in Virginia should war break out. He stood talking with the governor, and Jordan thought she could gain valuable information by listening in on their conversation. Troop locations and soldier allegiances would be of great interest to Kate. She was about to wander over when she barely caught faint whispering between Laura and Mr. Young.

"I know, I know." Laura smiled weakly. "But with all that has been happening, it seems so strange to be thinking of such a thing."

"I understand, but I have not had word from you in months," he whispered softly. "I do not wish to press you on the subject, but I should rest more easily if you could give me some insight as to your affections."

Laura had dared not mention the proposal to her mother and had begged Mr. Young to delay any formal conversation with her father. She would have been married off at least a month ago if only they knew. Laura's throat closed and her palms grew sweaty. She felt trapped in this room full of people and desperately wished Charlotte was there to rescue her. Mr. Young could not be making his intentions more obvious. Already she felt wretched for misleading an honorable man who had made her an offer. How could she continue to fob him off under her mother's sharp eyes?

Jordan watched Laura's agitation increase and her eyes dart about the room as if seeking an escape route. Recognizing an unwanted suitor when she saw one, Jordan interceded on her behalf.

"Why, Laura, you have not yet introduced me to your parents as promised. I'm beginning to think you've forgotten me entirely." She affected a hurt expression.

Laura was plainly puzzled by the comment at first, then the clouds parted and the dawn of understanding spread swiftly across her face.

"My parents! Why, yes, forgive me," and turning to her suitor, "and forgive me, Mr. Young. I shall return as quickly as I can."

Taking Jordan by the arm, she led her into the entryway and then into the library off the dining room. "Oh, Jordan, thank you. How ever did you guess?" She fidgeted nervously, rubbing her palms together.

"Well, I suppose one has to have gone through the experience oneself in order to appreciate that particular kind of misery." Jordan laughed, trying to soothe Laura's anxiety.

She was surprised when Laura placed a palm to her forehead and the other to her stomach, as though attempting to quell an oncoming headache or illness. Jordan took her arm and sat her in a chair near the fireplace.

"What is it, Laura? Are you ill?"

"It is of no consequence. I don't wish to burden you with my troubles."

"Nonsense. If Mr. Young is being presumptuous, you must tell him that you wish for him to leave you alone."

Laura sighed. "It's not that simple. Mr. Young has asked me to marry him."

Speechless, Jordan stared at her. Not knowing all the particulars, she approached the topic cautiously. "I take it that you do not return his affections."

Laura nodded, appalled to feel the tears once again rising in the corners of her eyes. She was embarrassed to let Jordan see her this way, so she rose and stood next to the fireplace, staring into the flames as though searching for the answers to her dilemma within their flickering depths.

Jordan gazed at the carpet, not quite knowing what to say.

"Does your family know?"

"No! And you mustn't say a word."

"You needn't worry," Jordan said. "But why can't you tell him that you do not share his feelings and that he should seek another?"

"Oh, if only it were as easy as all that." Laura gave a halfhearted laugh.

Puzzled, Jordan asked, "Why isn't it?"

Laura picked up the fireplace poker, adjusting a log until it fit nicely between the others and the fire leapt back to life. She did not think Jordan would understand her situation, given her uncomplicated life as an actress. She could not know what it was like to have a mother who determined the outcome of your life, whether you wanted it that way or not. It was all too much to go into now and, besides, this was neither the time nor the place.

The moment was decided for her when Meg interrupted them. "There you are, Laura, Mother is looking for you."

"Do not concern yourself with all this, Jordan," Laura said as she walked away with her sister. "Everything will turn out for the better, sooner or later."

Jordan wasn't convinced. After spending a day with Laura, she was beginning to get an inkling of what lay beneath. Did she oppose Laura's position on secession and slavery with every fiber of her being? Most decidedly. But she had glimpsed another side of Laura. The care and concern for others that she exhibited belied her otherwise superficial, self-centered exterior. Alone in the library, Jordan looked about with interest. Her heart rate picked up at the realization that she could search the room to see if she could discover anything of value. What had Kate said? Documents, maps, anything that might prove significant.

Noticing the large desk on the opposite wall, she strode over and perused its surface, but saw nothing but blank paper and a book of poetry. She tried the drawers but they were locked. This might be her only opportunity to search within the governor's own home, and she knew if anything truly important were to be had, this would be the place to find it.

"Jordan, darling, I thought I'd never get you alone." Nell stood casually in the doorway, her eyes dancing over Jordan's body.

Recovering her surprise, Jordan relaxed when several matrons entered the library investigating the governor's home. She was glad that it had been Nell to walk in on her rather than someone she didn't know.

"Come." Nell stretched out her hand. "Let's take a walk outdoors. I should think some fresh air after all this stuffy socializing would do us good."

Jordan approached the door and Nell slid her hand inside Jordan's arm. The heat from her hand was noticeable even in an already warm room, and Jordan felt her own temperature rise in response. Nell led her out through the doors off the library and onto a balcony, from which they descended steps into the chilly garden. They strolled among the barren rose bushes, their buds having not yet formed.

"I cannot begin to tell you how happy I am to see you and how excited I am by the prospect of playing Juliet to your Romeo." Nell's breath was a mere inches from Jordan's ear.

"Yes," Jordan replied, her mind still back in the library, "as am I."

Nell faced her. "Are you really?"

Jordan blinked, not understanding the question. "I beg your pardon?"

"I believe your thoughts are elsewhere this evening." Nell smiled. "And when I'm with someone I'd like to get to know better, I prefer to have their full attention. It is one of my many weaknesses. You may call me vain, but just as onstage, I enjoy the limelight."

Jordan felt a slight tremor pass through her body as Nell stepped even closer and rested a hand on her upper arm. Seemingly with a will of its own, it slowly descended, tracing circular patterns on its way down. Entranced, she remained where she was, ignoring the instinct that urged her to leave.

"I like you, Jordan." Nell stepped in so that their bodies were almost touching. "I like you very much. And I would love to get to know you even better, so I promised myself that I would do all in my power to make that happen."

A split second before their lips connected, Jordan knew that Nell was going to kiss her. Paralyzed, she let it happen. She wasn't sure she wanted to stop Nell. She was curious, had been for quite some time, since Nell had obviously been pursuing her for over a year. Nell's lips were soft and warm and Jordan's body involuntarily responded. The kiss was nothing like she might have expected. When Nell's mouth opened and her tongue sought entrance into Jordan's mouth, she invited her inside. A shudder passed through her that had nothing to do with the weather.

From the balcony, Laura was shocked, unable to watch and yet at the same time unable to look away. Her gaze remained locked on the two women standing in the garden, kissing as a man and woman might. This was not the kiss one friend might bestow on another. This was a kiss of passion, of lovers in the night, the kind she had read about in books. Fascinated and horrified, Laura was at once angry that Jordan would engage in such behavior with this clearly disreputable woman. It was scandalous, and she tried to run away, back inside where everything was as it should be. But her body would not let her. She felt strange, and a hot flush infused her as she broke into a sweat.

Only when the two women separated was Laura able to collect herself. Pressing a palm to her cheek, she tried to soothe her fevered brow with the cool fabric of her glove, but it provided no relief. A deep sadness enveloped her and she reluctantly reentered the house, wishing she had never witnessed the private moment.

Too overwhelmed to speak, Jordan could only stare at Nell's lips, amazed that she had actually kissed her in that way. What did it all mean? She wasn't sure, but she had the desire to do it again.

"That was everything I imagined it would be." Nell's eyes flashed.

"There you are, Miss Nell." A handsome gentleman descended the balcony steps. "You promised me that the dances were all mine this evening, and I mean to collect on the promise."

His arm found its way around Nell's waist in a possessive gesture not lost on Jordan.

"Yes, Mr. Crowley, and I *always* keep my promises." Her eyes held Jordan's briefly. "I shall call upon you very soon, Jordan. Until then."

Jordan remained where she was as the man led Nell back into the house. Within moments she saw them dancing out onto the balcony off the main parlor, and she could not help notice how Nell pressed herself to him. When she tossed her head back and laughed at something he whispered in her ear, a pang of envy stole through Jordan and she was briefly tempted to follow the couple and extract Nell from her companion's arms. Forcing herself out of her inertia, she strode toward the crowd once more. She reminded herself of her real purpose in coming this evening. Until she had something she could transmit to Kate, she would not allow herself to leave.

❖

The evening wore on, and whenever Jordan was able to listen in on the conversations of politicians and military officers, she did so. At one point, she stood next to the governor himself, deep in conversation with a group of men she did not know. As the comments became heated as to troop dispositions and strategy, a rough tap on her shoulder interrupted her concentration. Turning quickly, she found herself confronted by George Lamont, and her heart leaped in her chest.

"Well, Jordan, what an unexpected surprise seeing you here to honor our President. I would have thought you would be more interested in what Mr. Lincoln has to say about the events of late. I suspect though that you are as much a thorn in his side as you seem to be everywhere you go." Lamont sneered, exposing yellowed, tobacco-stained teeth, his breath overpowering her with the stench of alcohol.

Guiding Lamont out of hearing range of the group, Jordan led him over to an alcove. "Why, George, whatever brings you out on a night such as this? I did not think you left the taverns until well after midnight."

"I come and go as I please," he scoffed. "I'll have you know that I am often at these society parties. There are many here who know me as a fine actor and invite me to their soirées whenever I'm in town."

"Good for you, George, and what is it that brings you here this evening? Ah, I know, the free punch, and the debt you hold at each of the drinking establishments in town, isn't that it?"

George's face grew ugly, and he whispered harshly, "You best mind your manners, Jordan. You're a Yankee woman in a Southern town. You may be accepted into this society now, but watch your step. It won't be long until those who don't know you well discover what a murderous bitch you really are."

"Miss Colfax, is this man bothering you?" Lieutenant Kincaid gallantly interposed himself between the two of them.

Placing a hand on the officer's arm, Jordan shook her head and smiled sweetly at him.

"No, thank you, Lieutenant. I believe Mr. Lamont has merely imbibed a little too much this evening. George, perhaps you should go home while you can still walk. I'm sure someone can see you to a carriage." She raised an eyebrow to the lieutenant.

"You best mind what I say," Lamont warned.

"I should be happy to assist the gentleman," the officer replied, taking Lamont by the arm and leading him away from the party. Tossing one last glare her way, Lamont stumbled out of the room.

Jordan leaned against the window, trying to calm her rapidly beating heart.

"Miss Colfax?"

Jordan nearly leapt from the wall. "Oh, hello, Meg, you startled me. What is it, dear?"

"Ransom was trying to find you. Father has received an urgent telegram, so we are leaving." Meg smiled sweetly.

"Actually, I too think it's getting late. Let me get my wrap and I shall meet you all at the front door. Thank you, Meg." Jordan had gathered quite a bit of information this evening, and she wanted to get back to her room and encode everything before she forgot half of what she had learned. When she exited to the main hall and inquired after her wrap, a servant went to retrieve it and she stood in the hallway. As she waited, a young Negro woman appeared near an entryway, holding Jordan's wrap and motioning to her. At Jordan's approach, she held it out to her.

"Thank you," Jordan said.

"You're welcome, Miss Colfax." More softly, she said, "Miss Warne sends her regards."

Shocked by the name she thought only she knew, Jordan stood mute, staring at the woman as though she were seeing a ghost. Reaching into her pocket, the woman withdrew a piece of paper, folded over many times, and pressed it into Jordan's palm.

"You must get this to her as soon as you can," she whispered. "Tell her Mary sends it. Mary Bowser."

A rotund man came limping down the hallway. The woman nodded to Jordan, then disappeared through another door. Placing the note in her bag, Jordan glanced about her, then headed to the entryway. Laura and her family were already at the door putting their coats and wraps on.

"There you are." Ransom smiled. "My family is about to leave, but we can stay longer if you wish."

"No, thank you, Ransom." Jordan put her own shawl around her shoulders. "I've had about all I can manage in one evening."

"I should think so," Laura said acidly.

Jordan's head snapped around at Laura's caustic voice. She was puzzled by the comment but didn't have the opportunity to question Laura.

"Let us drop you at your hotel, then," Edward St. Clair offered.

"I don't want to trouble you, sir. It's only a few blocks to walk."

"Don't be foolish," Mrs. St. Clair huffed. "The hour is late and there may be ruffians about. There are so many soldiers and strangers in the city that an unescorted lady cannot be entirely safe."

Not wanting to argue with her, Jordan agreed, then glanced at Laura, who studiously avoided her gaze. Jordan wondered what she had done to merit her displeasure.

"Father, are you going to tell us what was in the telegram?" Meg asked as she settled in the seat of their carriage. Jordan glanced over at Edward St. Clair, noting the grim look on his face.

"It's a telegram from President Davis," he said flatly.

Jordan tried not to look too interested in the announcement.

"What does it say, Edward?" Rachel St. Clair inquired.

"He wants me to come to Montgomery with all due haste. He is forming his cabinet and wishes me to advise him on military matters."

Ransom saw the look of surprise on Jordan's face and explained.

"Jordan, my father was a classmate and friend of Mr. Davis's at West Point. They fought together at Buena Vista in the Mexican War, so I imagine he wishes his counsel in that regard."

"Oh, Edward," Rachel groaned, "not Montgomery. What a dreadful place, absolutely nothing of value to offer socially."

"Nevertheless, to Montgomery I must go." He sighed. "It is my duty, but you may stay here if you wish, Rachel."

"I will do nothing of the sort." She held on to the side of the carriage as it bounced sharply on the street. "The wives of the other politicians would make me the object of their gossip and I should never live that down."

"But Virginia has not yet joined her sister states in withdrawing from the Union," Laura said. "What about your place in the legislature? There are those who rely on your sagacity to prevent Virginia from making a rash decision."

"It is only temporary, my dear," he replied. "I shall offer whatever assistance President Davis may need and then return as quickly as possible. I'm sure once his cabinet is formed, those duly elected officials will replace me. Ransom, if need be, I will need you to attend to matters at home. Mr. Humphreys will handle the slaves, but if anything arises, I need someone there I can depend on."

"Yes, Father." Ransom looked unhappy.

When they arrived at Jordan's hotel, she waved good-bye and their new driver slapped the reins on the horse's flanks and clattered away down the street.

"Apples, Miss? Or perhaps some other fruit may interest you?"

Jordan looked up to see an old woman standing near the alleyway of her hotel. "No, thank you."

She was about to enter her hotel when the woman called to her again. "I think you will find the fruit most delicious, Miss Colfax."

At this Jordan stopped in her tracks. Peering closer, she saw the old woman hidden in shadows, seemingly avoiding the street lamp. She approached her slowly.

"How did you know my name?"

"Because we have met before," the woman said, drawing back even farther into the dark alley. When Jordan was close enough and away from prying eyes, the woman revealed herself to her.

"Do not fear, Miss Colfax. It's Kate Warne."

Surprised at this unexpected visit, Jordan was impressed at the clever disguise that Kate wore; she had been so readily deceived. "Miss Warne! What are you doing here?"

"Shh, please keep your voice down. We do not want to draw attention to ourselves."

Reaching into her bag, Jordan quickly withdrew the note that had been given to her. "This is for you. Mary Bowser asked me to give it to you."

"Ah, yes, excellent. Thank you very much."

"And I have much to tell you of what I have learned this evening," Jordan said.

"And I wish to hear it as well," Kate replied, "but not here, not now. All that you learn while here in Richmond I want you to write down using the code I showed you."

"How will I get the message to you?"

"Remember our conversation? Place it behind the brick in the storage room at the theatre. Place the lamp in your hotel room in front of the window, and it will be checked immediately. Do you understand?"

"Yes." Jordan nodded again. "You should know that I have been invited to a ladies' luncheon at the governor's house tomorrow."

Kate's eyes lit up. "That is good news. With the men absent, you have a perfect opportunity to see if you can find anything of interest. But you must be careful. Perhaps you could simply wander away from the lunch and maybe…get lost in the house and find your way into the governor's office?"

"I can try," Jordan said. "And if I need to contact you?"

"You can't. We cannot safely be seen together, as it could draw suspicion. If you need something specific, communicate it through code and the brick hiding place. I will find a way to get it to you."

Laughter erupted from the hotel and then footsteps could be heard along the walkway as two gentlemen headed in their direction. Jordan watched as they crossed the street and rambled toward the capital. Realizing she was holding her breath, Jordan released it and tried to calm her beating heart and rattled nerves. When she turned to face Kate again, she was alone in the alley.

CHAPTER EIGHT

Laura awoke abruptly, uncertain as to what had roused her. Within moments, however, the sound of her mother's voice, angry and insistent, made its way up the stairs to her bedroom. Laura sighed heavily and closed her eyes against the onslaught. Early preparations were being made for her parents' departure, so the servants were hurrying to pack. Obviously someone had broken something and incurred her mother's wrath. She recalled her dream, a fleeting, ephemeral memory that involved Jordan and Nell Tabor. But the scene shifted and it was she who was kissing Jordan.

Her pulse quickened at the thought. Unable to fall back asleep, she rose and dressed quickly, descending to the first floor after the debris had been swept up and all had returned to packing.

"Laura, please watch Sarah and Ruby in the dining room. I cannot be everywhere at once," her mother complained. "I must see to the packing upstairs. We may not have enough appropriate clothing to take with us, but I suppose I shall have you send us more or I'll have to solve that problem when we arrive in Montgomery."

Laura did as she was told and went into the dining room. While Sarah and Ruby wrapped dishes and cutlery, she glanced out the window to see her father and Ransom engaged in a heated discussion out in the garden. Curious and far more interested in what they were saying than her domestic duties, she walked outside to see what was going on.

"It's an opportunity that may not come along again, Father," Ransom pleaded.

"The opportunity or another like it will present itself in the future." Edward waved dismissively. "Right now, you must finish your schooling, and after that I'm sure you'll be in ever greater demand."

"But by then all the best commissions will have been handed out. I'll be lucky to be assigned to some lowly colonel's staff."

"Virginia has yet to make up her mind, but if she does secede and there is war, we will need you to join her army to defend your native soil. Richmond is directly in the Union path and you shall see your fill of battle then."

"But Father—"

"Enough! I have much to do before we leave, and this discussion is ended. You shall do as I say and return to school."

"But I can't return to school and finish if I am to attend to matters at home."

Edward St. Clair paused abruptly. Ransom's inability to be in two places at the same time had obviously created an unforeseen conflict. "Well, I suppose I shall have to think about this situation."

Ransom's eyes lit up with hope, which his father dashed immediately.

"Not about you going to South Carolina—you shall not go there under any circumstances. I am speaking of Barrett Hall."

Ransom looked instantly crestfallen.

"I must speak with your mother. I'll let you know my decision before we leave. For now I must return to my work." With that he strode back to the house, brushing past Laura on his way in.

Ransom thrust his hands into his pockets and kicked a leafless bush, his breath coming in puffs of white cloud on the morning air.

Laura descended the steps and stood hesitantly nearby. She had rarely seen her brother argue with either of their parents before, so she knew he must have a very good reason to do so now. "What is it, Ransom, what has happened?"

"Oh, nothing much, simply an offer to serve on General Beauregard's staff, that's all." He kicked the bush again, then pleaded, "Laura, he'll listen to you. You must speak to him on my behalf. Explain how very important this is to me."

His plea reminded her of when they were children. She had always been so frail then, and he had taken it upon himself to be her protector. Ransom had always defended her to her mother and even at times took the blame for something Laura had done so that she would avoid being punished. It seemed so odd now for him to be asking her to promote his cause to their father. She knew she would do anything he asked, because he never asked her for anything.

"I will see what I can do, but he seems very determined that you should finish school," she cautioned.

"At least speak to him, that's all I ask."

"Of course, but let's wait until after dinner when he has had his sherry and is in a more receptive frame of mind."

He smiled. "Thank you, Laura."

She returned the smile, but had something else on her mind. She wasn't sure if now was the time, but the question had been burning in her, and she had determined to ask him when he was next at home. "Ransom, may I ask you a question?"

"Anything."

"Well…have you ever…" She didn't quite know where or how to begin. Although she had thought about this subject for so long, now that the time had come to talk about it with someone else, she faltered.

"What is it, Laura?"

"I wanted to talk with you about Father." She took a deep breath and let her question tumble out as quickly as possible. "Are you aware that he's having relations with Martha?"

Ransom looked puzzled. "Martha who?"

"Martha the cook! What other Martha would he have relations with?"

He blushed profusely. "Oh, that."

"What do you mean, 'oh, that'? You mean you knew about this all along and never told me? Ransom, how could you?" She folded her arms across her chest and turned her back on him, angry that he had not confided in her.

"How could I tell you something like that? What could I say?" He gestured in frustration.

She spun around to face him again. "You could have at least told me. I thought we told each other everything."

Laura was hurt deeply. If she had been able to talk with Ransom about her suspicions from the beginning, she might have been able to come to terms with her father's conduct. Now it seemed that her brother had somehow taken their father's side, protecting him by saying nothing.

"I'm sorry, Laura. I couldn't talk to you about it. I guess I was ashamed." He sat down on a bench and put his head in his hands.

She felt remorseful over her outburst, and the anger she'd built up dissipated quickly. She knew she was taking out her frustration with her father on Ransom and felt a little guilty. He was as innocent of their father's behavior as she, but still she wanted to know about his involvement.

"Ransom, have you ever…?"

His head snapped up at the implication. "Are you mad! Of course not. How could you think such a thing of me?"

"I had to know, Ransom. I didn't know what to believe."

"So do you believe me now?"

"Yes, I do." After a moment's hesitation, she realized she had to know all of it. "Does Mother know?"

He shook his head. "I surely hope not."

Laura wondered. She thought she would never know the answer to the question anyway, so there was no use pondering the matter further. What would her mother do if she did know? Loss of trust would explain the distance Laura sensed between her parents. Then again, she couldn't ever recall a time when they were close. The ideal relationship between a man and a woman was supposed to be romantic and filled with happiness and joy. Her parents' fell far short of this perfection, as far as Laura could see, and her mother never pretended otherwise. Laura could not imagine being in a loveless marriage. Surely it must be miserable for both husband and wife. The thought reminded her of her own predicament.

"Laura!" Rachel called from the back door, and Laura felt her brother jump slightly, just as she did.

"Yes, Mother?" Laura responded.

"You had best come in from the cold before you catch your death. Besides, you must change before we go to the governor's house for lunch. We will be leaving soon." She closed the back door, leaving them alone once again.

Laura smiled weakly at Ransom. "I guess I'd better get ready."

"You'll speak with him tonight?" he pleaded.

"Yes. But don't be surprised if he refuses."

She went inside and found Ruby in her room. The glare in her eyes put Laura on notice that all was not well.

"Miss Laura." Ruby thrust a dress out for inspection. "You done gone and got a stain on this dress. Now what you gonna wear to the lunch today? And at the governor's house too."

"What stain?" Laura squeaked. The gray silk dress with three narrow pinked flounces at the bottom was her favorite visiting dress, and she could not recall making any such stain the last time she wore it.

Ruby showed where something green and splotchy marred the dove gray fabric on the back of the gown. An angry scowl clouded her expression. "You sat in something. You wasn't looking where you sat and now the dress is ruined. I tried, but I can't get it out."

She snatched the dress from Laura and tossed it onto a chair in the bedroom. She was so tired with her mistress's carelessness. It was Ruby's favorite dress too and now it was useless. She could not repair it and it was a waste to throw it away. All it would be good for now was the scrap heap.

Laura felt her own temper rise. It was her dress, after all. Ruby had no right to take her to task on it. "I can't watch everything all the time," she argued defensively. Feeling a little guilty about ruining such a good dress, and knowing that Ruby was right, Laura gathered it in her arms and held it out as a gesture of goodwill. "Here, Ruby, you take it. I know how much you like it. You can wear it for a special occasion, perhaps when you jump the broom?"

Ruby was appalled. Not only would she not wear a damaged dress in public, she would never wear it to her wedding. She grabbed the dress from Laura and threw it to the floor. "I ain't gonna wear no piece-of-trash dress."

A gasp at the bedroom door caused them both to turn. Rachel St. Clair marched into the room and slapped Ruby hard across the face. Laura quickly looked away, unable to see Ruby treated that way.

"How dare you speak to your mistress that way!" Rachel's face turned bloodred and a single blue vein on her forehead stood out in sharp relief. "Pick up that dress and take it to Sarah. Perhaps she can fix it and wear it herself. If I ever hear you speak with such insolence again I shall have you horse-whipped. Do I make myself clear?"

"Yes'm." Ruby curtsied deeply, scooping the dress off the floor. She scampered out of the room as quickly as she could, softly closing the door behind her.

"You have five visiting dresses." Rachel went to the pine chest and started pulling garments out. "Choose another. The dark blue taffeta always looks well on you."

Laura stared at the gowns piled on the chair, astonished that her mother could switch from one emotional extreme to the other so rapidly.

It was as though the incident with Ruby had never happened. Laura shuddered to think what it must have cost her mother to achieve that level of control. Reluctantly she lifted the blue dress she would now wear to the governor's luncheon and sat down on the bed to exchange her house slippers for shoes.

❖

Laura spotted Emma Harper too late to avoid her, and she forced a smile along with her polite greeting.

"How lovely you look this afternoon, Laura. I'm sure that if there were eligible men in the room, they would literally flock to your side."

"Thank you, Emma," Laura murmured.

"And what a pretty dress you're wearing. Why, I envy you so, being bold enough to wear that shade of blue. It makes skin seem so sallow, don't you think?"

Laura felt her color rise. She wanted to snap a hoop in Emma's crinoline, but she refused to let her annoyance show. "I'm sure you need not worry about that, my dear Emma. You have been in the sun, have you not? Your complexion is far from pale."

Emma's small eyes glittered and she made a show of smiling at a well-known matron who swept by. "More's the pity that it's only a lady's lunch," she sighed. "But don't you worry, I'm sure someday someone will come along and sweep you off your feet. There are still some men who pay no attention to a woman's age."

Laura cringed inwardly but was saved when Emma's attentions were drawn elsewhere. Taking advantage of the lapse in their conversation, Laura escaped toward the crowded parlor. Upon entering the bustle of the hallway, Jordan glimpsed Laura's rapid progress and wondered at its haste. She did not attempt to rush after her, but waited as a servant took her shawl and led her to join the party. About thirty women were already seated, drinking tea and chatting noisily. Jordan made her way to an empty chair next to Laura and her mother.

"I'm so pleased you could make it, Jordan." Laura smiled sweetly at her.

"I'm sure you are." Jordan smiled just as sweetly.

"Miss St. Clair tells us you are an actress, Miss Colfax," a matron spoke up. She had ample bosoms that defied the corset she wore. They seemed to quiver with outrage at the very idea of a woman on the stage.

"Yes, that is true." Jordan braced herself for the usual looks of shock and disdain.

"Well, I suppose that is what Yankee women do." Her interrogator sniffed. "I have heard that Northern women are accustomed to working in public and think nothing of it."

"It is those suffragettes," a needle-thin woman with a hawk nose interrupted. "Lord knows what is to become of womanhood when they want to be like a man."

Outspoken disapproval was not exactly what Laura had in mind in having Jordan attend the luncheon, but she was enjoying Jordan's discomfort nevertheless. She observed Jordan covertly, wondering if she had changed since those moments in the garden the night before. Laura didn't see anything different about her, but she was curious as to what Jordan must be thinking. *Have she and the actress kissed before? Have they done more than kiss?* Laura blushed hotly at the thought.

"Suffragists do not want to be like men," Jordan said. "They merely wish to have their rights recognized equally. And if a woman needs to work, why should she not be able to find a job like a man?"

"A woman has her husband to take care of her."

"What about women who are not married, or widowed?" Jordan responded. "What about the children of widows? Must they starve?"

"I've heard that many of the Yankee suffragettes are also abolitionists," Rachel St. Clair said. "I think it all a ruse to find equality for the inferior races. The Bible is quite clear that women are subject to their husbands and that the slaves must obey their masters. All this talk about equal rights is sure to lead to trouble, and no respectable woman I know would think of involving herself in such nonsense."

"Quite right, Rachel," one of the other guests agreed. "The decline in morality is yet another example of the North imposing its values on Southerners. Yankees have no idea what it is like to live in the South, yet they insist that we make their values our own. Well, we shall have none of it, I say. Virginia should do as so many of her neighbors have done and remove herself from a government that uses coercion to rule its people."

Jordan glanced at Laura and could see she was amused. Allowing herself a faint smile, she thought, *You are a wretched woman and I shall return the favor someday.*

"Lunch is served, ladies," Mrs. Letcher called out and they all rose as one to enter the dining room where several large round tables had been set up for the occasion.

"Excuse me, but I need to freshen up." Jordan retreated to the hallway.

The only people she encountered there were servants running to and fro, carrying serving trays laden with food. No one paid her any attention and she made her way toward the back of the house where she knew from the previous evening the governor's office was located. She entered the room quietly, closing the door behind her.

It was an elegant room, perhaps the finest in the house, with walnut paneling and solid oak furniture. The aroma of stale cigars clung to the fabric and the sun shone in muted slits through the curtained windows. A large desk was situated near a window, and she hurried to it and sat in the black leather chair. She began by examining the paperwork on the desk, but finding nothing of interest there, she started opening desk drawers. Working quickly, she scanned several documents, trying to find something relevant and worthwhile to pass to Kate Warne. The search proved fruitless until she reached the last drawer and discovered it was locked.

After tugging at it in case it was simply stuck, she sat back in the chair, frustrated. Intuition told her that if she could get inside, she would find something of real value. Jordan wondered if perhaps the governor carried the key with him at all times or if he kept it hidden somewhere near the desk. A sound at the door made her heart leap and she ducked behind the massive desk. After a few moments when no one had entered, she went back to work.

She attacked the drawers with greater fervor, seeing if she had missed a key in her previous search. Still finding nothing, she picked up objects on the desk and examined underneath them: a cigar box, a paperweight, a kerosene lamp. Nothing. She had little time left and, desperate to get into the drawer, she ran her hand along the bottom of the middle drawer of the desk and was thrilled to discover a small wooden box attached to the underside. She removed it and opened the box to find the key. She unlocked the drawer and found several files containing correspondence from Jefferson Davis, Senators Mason and Hunter, Robert E. Lee, and various other officials of Virginia and bordering states. Selecting the first document she came to, she began to read about the Virginia Assembly having recently authorized the development of coastal, river, and harbor defenses. Delighted, she realized she had struck gold. She was about to go through the other documents when she suddenly heard her name being called. Laura had come looking for her.

She slammed the drawer closed and locked it, putting the key back in its place. Just then the door to the office opened and she leapt up from behind the desk.

"Jordan?"

"Laura. Hello…uh, I guess I, that is to say, I was looking for…" Jordan could not think of an excuse quickly enough, and her heart hammered in her chest.

Laura stared in surprise. Seeing Jordan utterly flustered was a rare spectacle she would not soon forget. Knowing what she was up to made the sight even more amusing. "Jordan Colfax! I know full well what you are doing, and shame on you."

Jordan hung her head. Would Laura give her away?

"If you think for one moment that you can escape the scrutiny of the ladies of Richmond, you are sadly mistaken. You will return at once to your seat and at least have the courtesy to dine on the food prepared for the occasion." Laura was shaking her finger.

Jordan's heart decelerated its pace so abruptly that she felt faint from the sudden swing of emotion. She laughed out loud in relief. "I should have known not to try to pull the wool over your eyes, Laura." She swept a strand of hair that had fallen forward in her haste and stepped lightly toward the door. "But if that woman looks down at me one more time with those pinched spectacles on her nose and regales me with her narrow-minded opinions, I promise you I shall not be held accountable for my actions."

Laura followed Jordan out into the hallway, struggling to suppress a giggle. Jordan annoyed her, it was true, but she could not help but laugh, recalling Jordan's pink-faced guilt at being caught cowering in the governor's office.

❖

That night at the dinner table, the St. Clair family discussed the imminent departure of Edward and Rachel, and Ransom's return to

West Point to finish his education. The dilemma that preoccupied the family concerned Barrett Hall. Who would take charge if Edward and Rachel were delayed in Montgomery longer than anticipated?

"Father, I am quite capable of handling our affairs at home until your return," Laura insisted. "Mr. Humphreys knows what to do with the slaves and the tobacco crops. After all, you are often absent in Richmond when there is planting or harvesting to be done."

Ransom gave her a grateful look.

"In Richmond I'm still close at hand," Edward said. "Montgomery is too far away if I'm needed quickly."

"Besides," Rachel added, "a girl of your age should not be left entirely alone."

"You were younger than I when you took full charge of the house," Laura reminded her.

"Times were different then," Rachel huffed. "We did not have the threat of slave uprisings like we do now, let alone the interference of the abolitionists. It is simply too dangerous to leave a young white woman alone amongst the slaves."

"What if we asked Aunt Ann to come, then? Perhaps Charlotte might come along and we could make a visit out of it. Why, I haven't seen them in months, and I know Charlotte is bored to tears, what with Robert away in England on business."

Rachel frowned. "We would not have to worry about this if you were married."

Laura stifled a sigh. She had hoped Mr. Young might be forgotten now that so much else was occupying her mother's attention. "Mr. Underwood's farm is only five miles away, and I'm sure he would be willing to help in a pinch," she said. "And if anything particularly urgent occurs, I will send a telegram."

Edward St. Clair glanced at Rachel. He always deferred to her when it came to issues involving the family. Ransom looked hopefully at his mother. If he could not get an early commission, at least he would be back at school where he would know what was going on.

"I suppose if Aunt Ann agrees I would consider it," Rachel said.

"Does that mean I can come with you, Mama?" Meg was not looking forward to returning to schoolwork and the boredom of life on the plantation.

"I suppose so, since all you would do is get into mischief while I am away."

"All right then." Edward stood, placing his napkin on his empty plate. "In the morning I shall send a telegram to your aunt, and if she agrees to come, that will be satisfactory."

❖

The night before the St. Clairs were to leave for Montgomery, a freezing rain fell, coating trees and causing branches to snap throughout Richmond as well as the outlying areas. Roads were almost impassable and even the trains were brought to a standstill. The wonderland of ice and snow would have been beautiful to look upon if they did not have to travel. They arrived at the station on time, but the train was delayed until the tracks were cleared and the freight and people loaded on board. When they had finally departed, and Ransom had caught his train heading north, Laura returned to the house on Church Hill to await Aunt Ann's arrival the next day.

She was sitting near the fire in the parlor reading a book when there was a knock at the door. Before she could even rise from her chair, Sarah had showed Jordan into the hallway.

Laura got to her feet in surprise and hurried out to greet her. Her visitor was heavily attired to ward off the falling temperatures and the looming storm clouds that threatened once again to unleash their icy fury. Laura let out an undignified sneeze, destroying her attempt to greet Jordan with disinterest. "Bless you. Am I too late?" Jordan removed her gloves.

Jordan's nose and cheeks were a blustery shade of crimson and Laura marveled at the picture of health she presented.

"Ransom's train left an hour ago," Laura said, "and I am returning to Barrett Hall once Aunt Ann arrives."

Jordan noticed a distinct pallor to Laura's already pale complexion, and her eyes were slightly watery. "Are you ill?"

"No, not at all," Laura replied, wiping her nose with her handkerchief. "It's merely a cold. I'm sorry you missed Ransom, but he said he would include a note in the next letter that your brother sends you."

"Well, I've also come to say good-bye and to thank you for your hospitality. I will be returning to Washington in a few days, and I was uncertain as to whether we would meet again before June. When will you be leaving?"

An unexpected pang of regret struck Laura and she shook it off. It was of no consequence to her that Jordan was leaving; in fact, she was glad to see her go. Jordan's scandalous behavior with Nell Tabor had been a rude awakening. She had foolishly supposed Jordan to be of a higher moral fiber and had dismissed her mother's criticisms of the sort of behavior actresses engaged in. But now, having seen for herself precisely what that behavior entailed, she was forced to think again.

Jordan had been an interesting interlude in her otherwise dull routine, but her Northern ways were rather too forward for Laura's tastes. Still, she had feelings about Jordan's departure that she could not explain away so easily. The kiss she'd observed between Jordan and Nell left her feeling dazed. While shocked by it, she was also fascinated. A part of her was inexplicably drawn to the vision of two women embracing in such a manner. Her body had reacted strangely, although not unpleasantly, while her mind attempted to reject what it beheld. She was shaken to admit that she wished she were the one kissing Jordan.

Laura drew a shallow breath and wished she could loosen her corset. The very idea was simply too confusing and too much to think about. Her cold must have affected her thinking. She sneezed again and coughed to clear her throat.

"If the weather holds, Aunt Ann should be arriving sometime tomorrow afternoon, and we will move on to Barrett Hall the day after."

Jordan eyed her warily. The fragility she'd seen in Laura since they first met seemed magnified as she dabbed her nose and eyes. A protective impulse rose within her. "Laura, I don't think you should be standing here in the drafty hall. Let's get you into the parlor by the fire and put a blanket around you."

"Don't be silly, I'm perfectly fine. You needn't concern yourself with me."

But Jordan asked Sarah to bring a pot of tea, and when Laura returned to her chair, Jordan placed a quilt around her lap.

"I'm fine," she admonished again, provoked. The dull headache she had since that morning didn't improve her mood. "Will you quit being a mother hen? Now, you are planning to travel back to Washington shortly, are you not?"

"Yes, I'll probably be on the next train heading north. Quite a few of us are taking advantage of the break Mr. Ford has allowed for the inauguration period." Jordan's thoughts turned to the runaway slave being placed in a trunk to be loaded on the train going with them. As far as she knew, Bill had kept the slave up in the attic of the theatre for quite some time now. She hoped nothing would go amiss at the station.

"Well then, you shall just have to come to dinner tomorrow night and allow me to give you a proper sendoff," Laura offered halfheartedly. Good manners dictated that she extend the invitation, but she did so with mixed feelings. It would be best if they parted company before Jordan did something truly indecent and people began to gossip, perhaps ruining Laura's reputation. So why did she yearn to keep Jordan close?

Jordan considered the invitation. She hoped the lack of enthusiasm she'd sensed was a consequence of Laura's illness. It might be a good idea to check in on Laura one last time anyway to ensure she was well enough to travel. Without her family to care for her, anything could happen, and who would be there to help? Under the circumstances, Jordan did not feel comfortable leaving her alone. That thought gave her pause. Why should she feel responsible for this haughty, insufferable woman? *Because she is the sister of my brother's best friend. Lord, help me from becoming a Good Samaritan.*

Chapter Nine

The sleet that fell two days earlier had turned into a heavy snowstorm, and by the time Jordan and the rest of the cast and crew arrived at the train station, light flurries fell continuously. As the crew lifted large crates and trunks into the freight cars at the back of the train, Jordan noted Bill O'Malley's interest in a black trunk that was also being loaded. Once it was aboard, he glanced her way and, with a faint nod, confirmed her suspicions. Hoping that no one would observe anything odd about the large trunk, Jordan searched the platform for signs of anyone monitoring their group too closely. She could discern nothing out of the ordinary, and hoped none of the theatre workers were secretly suspicious. The $100 reward on offer for John's return to his "master" was worth nearly six months' wages. For such a sum, most of the crew would ignore any prickles of conscience.

Even when John reached the free states, he still wouldn't be completely safe. Slave catchers and Federal marshals worked in the North and would continue to hunt runaways as far as the Canadian border. They had even been known to abduct free men and women and sell them into slavery.

"Are you joining us this afternoon?" Bill asked, approaching her.

"No, I'm taking the morning train tomorrow instead. I have to attend a dinner this evening." Jordan drew her scarf higher around her face. "Take care of yourself, and good luck."

Bill thanked her, shook her hand, and boarded the train. Jordan didn't walk away immediately. She wanted to see the train leave and know that, for now, John was undiscovered. She hoped she would see Bill in Washington before her next role so she could obtain an update on the former slave's fortunes. Between now and the start of rehearsals for *Romeo and Juliet*, she planned to take a break and help her father with his paper.

As the whistle sounded and a cloud of steam burst from the brightly painted locomotive, Jordan hugged her coat close and walked along the platform. She only hurried her steps once the wheels were turning. By the time she found her hired carriage and provided the driver with the St. Clairs' address on Church Hill, the train had disappeared.

❖

"Forgive me for not welcoming you properly, Jordan," Laura croaked. She was embarrassed to discover her voice had not improved despite the hot slippery elm tea.

Her visitor sat down on a chair opposite her. "Has your aunt arrived?"

"I received a telegram from her this morning. She is ill herself and cannot travel. Fortunately, she has her daughter and husband there to care for her."

Laura elbowed herself more upright on the settee, feeling at a disadvantage lounging back like an invalid. She was surprised to find herself relieved at Jordan's arrival. The bravado she'd felt before her parents' departure had fled as her cold became worse, and while Jordan wasn't her first choice at a time like this, Laura was glad of the company.

"What are you going to do?" Jordan asked. "Shall I go to the telegraph office for you and send a telegram to your parents in Montgomery?"

Laura started to speak but a fit of coughing overtook her. When she was able, she sipped more tea and spoke in a near whisper to avoid irritating her throat. "I leave in the morning for Barrett Hall."

Jordan was appalled. "You can't be serious."

"Why? I have Sarah and Ruby to help me, and we have plenty of furs to keep us warm. Aaron will drive us in the brougham. I think we shall do nicely, assuming the roads are clear."

"Laura, you're ill. You have no business traveling in this weather. You must stay here and have a doctor tend to you."

"No, Jordan. I must see to Barrett Hall. The plantation cannot be left entirely in the hands of our overseer. As a matter of fact, it has been without a St. Clair for far too long now, and every moment I delay means decisions are not being made. I must also see to the health of our slaves. It may surprise you, but we do care for them, and if they are sick, I will need to send for a doctor."

"Won't your overseer do that?"

Laura regretted her laugh immediately when it became another coughing fit. "Mr. Humphreys has his own opinions on how best to tend to the welfare of our slaves. If he is not taking his instructions from a family member, I am not confident he will make the right decisions. That's why I need to be at Barrett Hall. It could mean the difference between life and death for any slave who has fallen ill."

"It could mean the difference between *your* life and death, Laura. Surely you can delay a little while longer until the weather turns warmer."

"I cannot afford to wait that long."

Laura knew she had sounded sharp and impatient, but she was irritated by Jordan's interference, and her resolve to make the journey only intensified in the face of opposition. Jordan knew nothing of the St. Clairs and could not be expected to understand her commitment to their land and their slaves. Laura had been brought up to take these responsibilities seriously and to assume them just as her mother had, if ever the occasion arose. Until now, she had never realized how much a part of her were the traditions and duties that came with her name.

Jordan took in the defiant tilt of Laura's chin and the challenge in her gaze with a sense of helpless frustration. The woman was incredibly stubborn, and so irrational about this trip that Jordan had to conclude her illness had affected her common sense or she was slightly crazy to begin with. Jordan could live forever and still not understand how Laura could, without conscience, keep fellow human beings enslaved and yet care enough about them to take foolhardy risks with her own health. Perhaps her real concern was the monetary value the slaves represented. Jordan had heard that a male slave in his prime cost about $1,800, almost the price of a small country cottage. It only made sense for plantation owners to keep their valuable labor force in good health.

Yet she had the sense that Laura was worried less about the financial consequences of a slave's death and more about the well-being of the people who depended on her family. Although she'd worded her concerns about their overseer cautiously, her meaning was clear. "Mr. Humphreys" could not be trusted to do the right thing. The very thought made Jordan angry. Tales of cruelty and neglect of slaves were widespread in the North. Many involved the tyranny of overseers who faced no consequences under the law or from plantation owners for their conduct.

Jordan was disgusted that Laura's family would continue to employ a man if they knew he would care nothing for a sick slave. In what other ways did this man display his contempt for fellow human beings? Did he indulge his base instincts as he pleased, plying the whip and abusing those without the power to protest their mistreatment?

Disgusted by the thought, and by the ugly institution in which Laura and her family participated, Jordan said, "Well then, I suppose I shall have to come along and see that you don't die on the way."

The words came out like a shotgun blast, arresting Laura's handkerchief in mid-wipe. "What?" she asked.

"You heard me. I cannot allow you to travel nearly thirty miles in this weather and in your condition. Obviously it is necessary for you to be in attendance at the plantation, since your family sees fit to hire a neglectful overseer; however, I will not have it on my conscience if you should sink into a dire illness and I had merely returned home with not a care in the world. My brother would never forgive me."

Laura's mutinous glare intensified the greenish blue of her eyes, and two small patches of pink glowed from the pallor of her cheeks. Her mouth trembled, a sight Jordan found distracting. She supposed it made her feel like a bully, browbeating a poor, fragile woman who lacked her own force of character.

Fighting an irrational impulse to stroke Laura's hair and comfort her, Jordan softened her tone. "I don't need to be back in Washington for rehearsals until the end of April, and I know you won't be ill that long. So I'll accompany you and take a later train when I can. If your aunt arrives soon, I may yet get there in time for the inauguration festivities."

Laura could not decide whether it was luck or misfortune smiling down on her. She knew she should graciously accept the offer; that would be the sensible response. But the thought of spending more time, alone, in the company of this unspeakably rude Yankee was intolerable. The insult over Humphreys stung, too, all the more so because she detested the man and thought her father should dismiss him.

"I have told you before not to concern yourself with my well-being," she said coldly. "I appreciate your offer, but I can manage perfectly well, thank you. There is no necessity for you to feel obligated just because our brothers are friends."

"This is not about our brothers, although certainly mine would chide me if I allowed you to be so foolhardy. I simply intend to make sure you arrive safely at your destination. I'll remain until you are well or your aunt arrives."

"You will do no such thing." Laura had reached the end of her patience, and it took all her self-control to keep a civil tongue. "Aunt Ann will be delayed no more than a few days, I'm sure. Besides, as you say, I shall be quite recovered soon. In fact, I feel better already."

She wanted to add more, but a violent coughing fit took hold of her and she dropped her teacup.

Jordan immediately retrieved it and took a napkin from the serving tray nearby. Dabbing the spilled tea from Laura's lap, she said, "Don't tell me you feel better. Do you mistake me for a fool?"

Exhausted from the strain of talking and the constant pain in her chest, Laura allowed herself to slide down the cushions until she was almost reclining. Wearily, she said, "Very well. Do as you wish. We leave early in the morning. Why don't you come for breakfast?"

"I have a better idea," Jordan said. "Your man can drive me back to my hotel now and I shall collect my luggage. When I return, I shall expect to see you in your bed."

❖

"Auntie Quince has got herbs and poultices and such what will fix up Miss Laura in no time," Sarah said. "She's the one what takes care of folks at home."

Ruby gave the younger Sarah a sidelong glance, then peered at Laura, whose head was resting on Jordan's shoulder. They had left the house at ten o'clock with Laura on the backseat, buried under a pile of blankets and furs, and Jordan next to her. On the facing seat, Sarah and Ruby shared a blanket and supplied food and water from the hamper they had packed for the trip.

"Miss Laura always been the sickly kind," Ruby observed. "She ain't never gone through a year without getting some kind of sickness—whooping cough, fevers, and one time malaria. But Mr. St. Clair, he rode all the way to Richmond and back in one day to fetch quinine. Fixed Miss Laura right up."

"Is there a doctor in Charles City?" Jordan asked.

"Yes'm," Sarah confirmed. "Ole Doc Wheelwright comes when there's babies that ain't coming out right or something real bad that can't be fixed. But Auntie Quince, she mostly does the healing for fevers and such and delivering babies. She's even better'n the doctor for that."

Jordan knew quite well that most doctors caused more problems than they solved. She would have to get Laura to Barrett Hall as soon as possible and see what could be done. She shifted slightly in her seat and felt Laura move with her. She was fast asleep and that was the best thing for her right now. Jordan slid along the seat so that Laura's head could rest in her lap, pulled the furs up to Laura's chin, and wrapped a scarf around her head to keep her warm.

"Sarah, hand me that damp cloth again," she requested and the two young women poured some water.

The heat continued to emanate from Laura even as Jordan sponged her brow and cheeks. Despite the cold, she began to perspire herself after a while and even contemplated halting the carriage so she could take some fresh air by riding up front with Aaron. She was reluctant to leave Laura, however, and she also had a feeling Sarah and Ruby were relieved not to bear sole responsibility for the health of their mistress.

They followed the Old Turnpike out of town and then settled onto New Market Road for most of the trip to Barrett Hall. The temperature was bitterly cold, but the roads had been continuously traveled, so for the most part were passable. Aaron drove the horses at a leisurely pace, as there were patches of ice interspersed along the way and, like any competent driver, he would not risk injury to animals or people. The trip would take longer, but they would arrive safely.

Jordan held on to Laura tightly so that she would not fall onto the floor as they ran over a bumpy stretch. Ruby and Sarah dozed, each propped against a carriage wall, and even Jordan found it difficult to keep her eyes open. Eventually, when the road leveled out, she slept as well.

Laura floated in and out of awareness, conscious of being held and occasionally hearing the others talk. She was too drowsy to participate in her waking moments and had little idea how long she slept in between. Her body ached and her throat hurt and she yearned to be in her own bed. She peeked up at Jordan, who seemed to be sleeping. If she had any strength, she would have forced herself upright instead of lying in her companion's lap. Jordan was too accommodating by far. She should have swapped places with Ruby so that she did not have to be inconvenienced on the long, uncomfortable journey.

Laura felt guilty that Jordan had delayed her travel to Washington to accompany her out of a misguided sense of obligation. Whatever would she find to do at Barrett Hall while they waited for Aunt Ann to arrive? Jordan could be at home with her family and friends, relaxing between one play and the next. Laura simply did not understand her, yet she was grateful that Jordan had been so insistent. She supposed that she was now in her debt. The thought made her head hurt even more.

"Where are we?" she asked when a jolt woke Jordan.

"I don't know." Jordan smoothed wisps of auburn hair back into the knot at her nape and withdrew her timepiece from her bag. "It's after twelve o'clock, so we've been traveling for two hours." She knocked on the roof of the cab and asked Aaron their location.

"We's almost to Turkey Island Bend, ma'am," he shouted above the clatter of the horses and wheels.

Laura sighed. It was still a long way home, and there was nothing she could do but sleep. She looked up into Jordan's dark jade eyes and her heart gave an odd little jump. The tenderness she glimpsed in her gaze was tempered with concern, but something else was present, too. Laura concentrated for a moment, trying to identify the emotion she saw, then gave up. Deciding her imagination was playing tricks on her, she snuggled down into the warmth of Jordan and felt safe.

❖

The train's shrill whistle alerted passengers of its impending departure from Philadelphia. Its destination: Baltimore. Kate Warne stood anxiously on the platform when a porter approached. He glanced at the three men she was with.

"Are you ill, sir?" he asked the tallest of them, who was huddled beneath a shawl, his hat pulled closely over his brow.

"My brother is convalescing," Kate replied, handing him the ticket. "I have reserved a private berth for him and his traveling companions. Everything should be in order."

Examining their tickets, the porter nodded and motioned them onto the train.

"Have a safe trip, brother." She hugged him briefly. "I shall see you soon."

"Thank you, Miss Warne," the tall man whispered.

She stepped back and waved good-bye as the three men climbed aboard.

Once inside their berth, Allan Pinkerton drew the curtains on the door, locked it, and pulled the shades down on the windows.

"You can relax now, sir," he said.

Abraham Lincoln removed his hat and shawl and grimaced. "I don't think I will relax, Mr. Pinkerton, until we reach Washington. And, Ward, will you not flash those pistols about? You're making me nervous."

"These pistols are not leaving my side tonight. If anyone tries to come through that door, they'll get both barrels." Ward Lamon sat on the seat nearest the door, both pistols resting in his lap.

"Let's hope it isn't someone who voted for me," Lincoln said. "Mr. Pinkerton, was this really necessary?"

"Sir, we have credible evidence that someone or some group is planning to assassinate you at some point along your travel route. That's why the decision was made to change your schedule and get you aboard this night train into Baltimore. No one else knows of the change, and I feel reasonably assured that you will arrive in one piece."

"That's comforting." Lincoln's expression was wry.

"Congressman Washburn will meet us at the station in Washington in the morning," Ward informed him. "I think you should try to get some sleep, sir."

"And what about the two of you?" Lincoln asked.

Ward exchanged a glance with Pinkerton. There would be no sleep for them this night. The most dangerous part of the trip was yet to come, the arrival in Baltimore and the change of tracks into Washington. If anything was going to happen, it would be in that hostile city on the Chesapeake.

❖

Jordan was intrigued to discover what a plantation looked like. It was dusk by the time they turned down the road leading to Barrett Hall, and all she could see clearly was the large main house and a few outbuildings, including stables, a kitchen, and what appeared to be a smokehouse. She presumed the slaves lived some distance away from the house in their own quarters.

By the time the carriage stopped, several house servants had assembled out front of the St. Clair's pillared home, one holding a lantern in the waning light.

"Welcome home, Marse Edward," one called out.

"Ain't no Marse Edward." Ruby jumped down from the carriage. "Master and Miss Rachel done gone to Montgomery." She called out to a timid servant. "Prissie, run go get Auntie Quince. Miss Laura is sick."

Leaving the servants to bring in the luggage, Jordan helped Laura indoors. Ruby led the way upstairs to Laura's bedroom and immediately set about starting a fire. As Jordan began to undress Laura, she became aware of a disapproving stare from the slave. Not for the first time, she noticed the strange green of her eyes. The girl was obviously of mixed race, no doubt the unacknowledged progeny of a white man who had taken advantage of her mother.

Ruby shook out a nightdress and said, "I's the one takes care of Miss Laura." She all but elbowed Jordan out of the way so she could finish getting Laura prepared for bed.

Jordan didn't fuss. This was not her home and she had obviously trodden on Ruby's toes by trying to assume responsibilities that belonged to her. She could imagine that being a house servant was a matter of prestige, and perhaps better food and living conditions, for a slave. The last thing she wanted to do was come into this house as a guest and conduct herself with as much arrogance as any Southern "Missy."

Within moments, the door opened and Sarah led a large woman to the bedside, introducing her as Auntie Quince.

"Can you do something for her?" Jordan gestured toward Laura.

Auntie Quince put her hand on Laura's face. "Coughing and fever?"

"Both," Jordan replied.

Auntie Quince shook her head. "She don't got enough strength to keep a mosquito wing flapping."

Mumbling a little more, she placed a small bag on the bed and began removing jars and little packets wrapped in paper or bits of fabric. Sarah brought her a bowl of water and some rags, then a teapot. She opened various packets and went to work.

After she'd infused a tea from an assortment of roots and powders, she said, "Ain't nothing gonna happen here for a long while, miss. Go get something to eat and change outta them clothes."

Jordan hesitated. She was tired and hungry from the journey but the thought of leaving Laura alone made her uneasy. "Do you think we should send for the doctor?"

"Ain't no doctor close by," Auntie Quince said. "And Miss Laura, she don't need no castor oil and asafetida."

Jordan shuddered.

"Prissie done dressed up your room, Miss Jordan." Ruby signaled for her to follow. "I'll show you."

As they walked along the hall, Jordan asked, "Were you born here at Barrett Hall, Ruby?"

"I's here all my life."

Jordan glanced at her sideways, unsettled by something in her demeanor.

Ruby opened the door to a pleasantly appointed guest room and said, "Just holler if you need anything, Miss Jordan."

❖

A short while later, Jordan descended the staircase and found the dining room lit with candles and a fire. It was a large, imposing room with a long table that made dining alone very uncomfortable despite the enticing food. The meal that was brought to her was delicious, however, and she ate hungrily despite her uneasiness over Laura. After her meal, she entered the parlor and wandered about the room, examining the furniture and the paintings of family members. From there she found a library and was impressed with the number of books in the St. Clairs' collection. But what drew her attention was a desk in the center of the room where Mr. St. Clair evidently did his work.

Knowing he was a member of the Virginia legislature, Jordan sat down at the desk and began to peruse the documents on display. She felt somewhat ashamed spying in Laura's house, but the pull of finding out information kept her where she was. As she reached up to draw the lamp closer to a document she was reading, she heard a soft sound and glanced up to see Ruby standing in the doorway, watching her. Jordan froze, her hand still resting on the lamp.

"Is Laura all right?" she stuttered, not really knowing what else to say.

Ruby approached her slowly and stared down at the paper she'd been reading. The silence was unbearable, and Jordan came up with the only excuse she could think of.

"I was looking for something to read tonight, while I sat with Laura."

"Auntie Quince was asking for you," was all Ruby said, and she turned and left the room.

Jordan let out a deep breath and realized that her hands were shaking. She put the paper back on the desk where she'd found it. She didn't know whether Ruby would keep silent or not, and there was nothing she could do to stop her from talking. All she had to do was come up with an explanation, but what that would be she did not know.

"You wished to see me?" Jordan stepped into Laura's bedroom and quickly crossed to the end of the bed.

Laura had a thick cloth wrapped around her neck. The pungent smell made Jordan pause.

"That there is mostly mustard leaves, hickory leaves, pepper, and such," Auntie Quince said, noticing Jordan's reaction. "And I made her drink some snakeroot tea. Miss Laura is mighty sick and needs to be watched day and night. I hope I's done enough to help her. It's in the Lord's hands now." She finished tucking the blankets around Laura and stood to face Jordan.

"I'll come back tomorrow morning and make some more of my tea. Now she needs sleep."

Jordan was nervous about being left alone with Laura. She wouldn't know what to do if anything happened. "How long will it take?"

Auntie Quince shrugged. "Lord knows, not me. Might be days afore she gets well. All's we can do is keep watch and pray." She gathered up her herbs and jars of mysterious ingredients, put them back in her bag, and prepared to leave. "Sarah knows where to fetch me."

After the door closed behind the healer, Jordan took a clean cloth and dipped it in the bowl of water and washed Laura's face. She wished there was more she could do than this simple act. Laura was alternately hot, then clammy as fever laid claim to her body. She was deathly pale, her skin so translucent that Jordan could see fine blue veins beneath the surface. Damp hair clung to her forehead and cheeks, framing the delicate structure of her face. She was beautiful, Jordan thought. Whatever she felt about Laura's family and the ideas formed by her upbringing, the thought of waking tomorrow and finding her gone filled Jordan with despair.

She was so young and willful, it seemed impossible that an illness could take her. Jordan hated the idea. She wanted the chance to get to know Laura better. The more time she spent with her the more she liked her, regardless of the differences between them. She couldn't help but be drawn to Laura's spirit and candor. It would have been easy to dismiss her as shallow, selfish, and unthinking, but Jordan had found she couldn't. Puzzled, she took Laura's hand between her own and stared down at her. A desperate tenderness stole her breath away, and tears stung her eyes.

"Don't go," she murmured. "There's so much to stay for."

She struggled to find the right words to inspire Laura to fight for her life. Marriage, the hope of children? Jordan couldn't envision her marrying the man she'd met at the governor's house. Laura had seemed halfhearted about her suitor and her fate, resigned to doing as her family expected. She was an intelligent woman, although her politics left much to be desired, and deserved a companion who could appreciate her and whose love she could return with equal measure. Perhaps she might meet such a person in Washington, moving among a wider circle of acquaintances.

Sensing that this idea would have some appeal, Jordan pressed Laura's hand and said, "When you are well, I shall take you to Washington with me. You'll love it there."

Laura stirred and opened glassy, unseeing eyes. She whispered something, and Jordan leaned very close to hear her.

"Washington?"

"Yes, Washington. We'll go to the theatre and I'll show you the best shops in town. Whatever you wish to do."

She wasn't certain if Laura understood, but her breathing seemed to slow down slightly and when she closed her eyes, a faint smile lifted the corners of her mouth. Jordan released her hand and placed it on the covers. The fire was low and a chill draft seeped from around the windows and beneath the door. Jordan rose and added more wood to the fire in the fireplace, stoking the embers into a final rush of heat. Then she went to the window and looked out.

A light snow fell, casting a veil of fine white specks across the darkness. At least it wasn't a driving, icy rain, Jordan thought. Perhaps tomorrow the sun would come out and she could explore the plantation while Laura was resting. She glanced back toward the bed and, yet again, felt a mix of emotions she was not used to. She had thought she would be more despondent about her change of plans, but she was oddly contented. She had expected to feel impatient with Laura and eager to leave once Laura was settled and receiving the care she needed. Instead, she was afraid to leave her side, even afraid to sleep. It was as if by watching over Laura, she could sustain her; as if by holding her hand some of her own strength would flood through Laura and keep her safe.

Jordan returned to the chair next to Laura's bedside and picked up a book lying on the table nearby. It was a book of Mrs. Browning's poems, one of her favorites. Lifting the quilt left on the chair, she sat down once more and began to read aloud. Whenever she saw Laura move in the bed she would pause and wait until she was still again before resuming. The sound of the clock in the hall kept its steady rhythm and Jordan was vaguely aware that she was losing her way, the words dancing on the page before her. When she could no longer concentrate, she closed the book and let it drop gently onto her lap. Five minutes, she thought as she succumbed to the tension of the day and caught herself falling asleep. If she just closed her eyes for five minutes, surely nothing could go wrong.

Ruby sat eating her supper in the cabin of her friend Jonas, along with several other field slaves. She had the place closest to the fire, due to her status as house servant and the daughter of Martha. The other slaves deferred to her in conversation since she had access to the latest news going on in the world, and she made the most of their regard.

"My friend, Tillie, she says Mr. Lincoln's getting an army and Yankees going to be fighting white folks in the South."

"They gonna free us?" Jonas asked.

"They ain't said, but they ain't happy 'bout folks down here 'cause of something called sessionitis. That means our white folks don't wanna be part of the United States of America no more. Could be them abolitionists is part of the problem."

"Abolitionists wanna free us slaves," an old man with gray hair said. "They'll help us."

"Maybe. But they ain't got no say now," Ruby said. "We can't wait for them. Tillie says when the fighting starts us slaves has got to run north. The soldiers'll take care of us."

"John done gone north without the Yankees," a field hand said.

"Maybe he with Harriet Tubman," some fool whispered.

"Don't say that name in here." Jonas warned. "You want to get us all whipped?"

"John was in Richmond when he run away." Ruby said. "That's closer to the North than we is. But y'all wouldn't never get to Richmond even if you's to try and run. Dogs would get you quick as you can say Yankee doodle."

"I ain't heard nothing 'bout him," one of the house servants said. "Maybe he in Canada now."

"What we gonna do?" Jonas stoked the fire.

"There's a lady up at the big house, a Yankee lady tending to Miss Laura. I might ask her what's going on and she might tell me."

"You can't trust no white woman," Jonas insisted.

"Abolitionists is white folk," Ruby reminded him. "Sooner or later we's got to trust them, else there ain't no hope."

Everybody was silent. They couldn't ever talk about leaving their white folk. Colored couldn't go abroad without a pass from Marse Edward. If the paddy-rollers caught a slave on the road with no pass, he'd never get out from under that whipping.

Ruby stood up and smoothed her hands down the front of her house dress. "I's got to get back to the big house. When I knows something, I'll tell you."

She left the cabin and followed the trodden snow path back to the house. A flash of movement in the bush caught her eye, and she saw a fox trotting along the tree line. He paused to stare at her, a dead rabbit dangling from his mouth. She shivered and hurried on.

Chapter Ten

Jordan woke with a start, unsure whether her dreams had forced her to surface or if someone had spoken her name. She blinked several times, clearing her blurry vision, then placed the back of her hand against Laura's cheek. It was still very hot. Perspiration stood out on her face and her breathing sounded thin and laborious. Careful not to disturb the poultice Auntie Quince had placed on her chest, Jordan rinsed the cloth and sponged her face and neck. Dark circles shadowed Laura's eyes. She seemed so delicate that Jordan worried about bruising her merely through her gentle touch.

At the sound of logs being added to the fire, she glanced over her shoulder, embarrassed she'd allowed the flames to die down. Since bringing Laura home, she'd felt incompetent to perform even the simplest tasks. Was that what happened when one was surrounded by slaves? She watched Ruby stoke the fire, positioning logs with the casual expertise of a person who had carried out the chore a thousand times.

"Good morning, Ruby," she said.

The young woman seemed surprised to be interrupted with a greeting. Her green eyes flicked toward Jordan and just as quickly shifted away. "Morning, Miss Jordan."

"You were right. I should have slept in the guest room." Jordan rose stiffly, her neck and back aching from her long night on the chair.

"Ain't nothing for you to do," Ruby said. "Prissie done unpacked your clothes. If you want to sleep for a while, I's here to take care of Miss Laura."

Before Jordan could thank her for the offer, Auntie Quince bustled into the room. Without a word to either of them, she marched to the bed and leaned over, inclining her head as she listened to Laura's breathing. After a moment she stood upright and opened her bag.

"She sleep through the night?"

"She seemed very cold and the cough woke her fairly often. Can you give her something for that, Auntie?"

"No, ma'am." She shook her head. "Don't wanna give her nothing for that cough now. We's got to get the fever down. I'll make some more of the snakeroot tea."

"I think we should send someone for this Doctor Wheelwright," Jordan said uneasily. "I don't feel right about letting this continue without at least having a doctor look at her. Hopefully he can get here later this morning."

Auntie Quince paused in making her tea. "Doc Wheelwright? Why, that ole man don't know what he's about. Seem like everywhere he go they got a funeral."

"Them doctors, they thinks they know all 'bout fixing people up, but they don't know nothing," Ruby said grimly. "We be lucky he don't kill Miss Laura with his white folks' medicine. What's Marse Edward gonna say about that?"

Auntie Quince continued her mumbling while she made the tea. "Now me, I know's what I'm doing. Don't nobody know more than Auntie Quince about making folks right."

Jordan didn't want to seem ungrateful, but she had to do all she could think of. "I'm sure you both only want what's best for Miss Laura, but I suspect Mr. and Mrs. St. Clair would be angry if we didn't call the doctor as well."

"If you want the doctor, you done got to write a pass," Ruby said. "I can't send no boy without a pass."

"A pass?" Jordan noticed the two women exchange a quick look. She was almost certain they stifled laughter.

"You's a Yankee woman, ain't you, Miss Jordan?" Auntie Quince said.

Startled by her directness, Jordan laughed for the first time since she'd left Richmond. "Yes, I'm from Washington."

"Don't need to feel no shame 'bout that," Auntie Quince consoled her. "Folks can see you is quality."

Jordan thanked her for the compliment and said, "What exactly do you mean by a 'pass'?"

"You don't think they let us colored folk leave and just go walking down the road?" Ruby said with a trace of bold mockery. "We not free like you. If white folk sees colored on the road, they think we done run off."

"You could be stopped by…someone."

"Paddy-rollers." Ruby shuddered. "Lord, they poor white trash and awful mean."

"Yes, I see." Jordan recalled a group of horsemen who'd passed their carriage as they drew closer to Barrett Hall. Sarah and Ruby had shrunk down in their seats, heads lowered.

At the time, Jordan had attributed their fear to concerns about robbery. She could not imagine living in the knowledge that she couldn't choose to walk along a road, or simply to leave and live elsewhere. Freedom was only a word until it was taken away, she reflected, shocked by the simple reality that an entire group of people was held captive by another and terrorized into compliance. How could Laura take this way of life for granted, and even defend it?

Containing her anger, she said, "I'll write the pass."

While Ruby and Auntie Quince sat Laura up and helped her sip the tea, Jordan found a piece of paper and a quill at the writing desk near the windows. She wasn't sure exactly what these "paddy-rollers" needed to see, but she wrote: *The man bearing this pass is instructed to fetch Dr. Wheelwright urgently to attend to Miss Laura St. Clair of Barrett Hall. Kindly refrain from delaying him.* She wanted to add that they should be ashamed of themselves for their vile activities, but that wouldn't bring the doctor here any sooner.

Folding the note, she returned to the bedside as Laura dutifully sipped the tea. "How are you?" she asked.

Laura winced as she swallowed. Pushing the cup away, she whispered, "Jordan, see to the slaves."

"I will."

"Auntie Quince, take her with you."

"Yes, Miss Laura. Now don't you start agitating yourself." Auntie Quince lowered Laura back down onto her pillows and inspected the poultice. "I's got to freshen that up."

When Auntie Quince had left the room, Jordan took Laura's hand. "I have to go change my clothes. I'll wake you when I get back from visiting your slaves."

Laura nodded weakly.

"Stay with her," Jordan told Ruby, who had dragged a pallet to the side of the bed.

As she made it up with a blanket, Ruby said, "I sleeps here when Miss Laura gets sick."

"Well, I'll sleep there tonight," Jordan said. "It'll be better than that chair."

"That ain't right, Miss Jordan. Oh, no ma'am. Missy Rachel, she be powerful mad if she knowed I lets a white lady sleep on the floor."

"I think she would make an exception in this case, Ruby. Now, if you would be so kind as to ask one of the servants to bring up some breakfast, I'd like to eat and speak with Dr. Wheelwright before I go out with Auntie Quince."

Ruby went to the door and yelled for Prissie, tapping a foot while she waited for her to dawdle along the hall. That girl was the laziest house servant Marse Edward ever bought off the block. Ruby glanced back at the Yankee. Miss Jordan sure seemed fond of Miss Laura. She was fussing over her with the wet cloth and fixing the covers. Ruby almost laughed. Miss Laura didn't care about anyone excepting herself. She'd never stand by her Yankee friend, especially not if the war came.

❖

The slave quarters shocked Jordan. In contrast to the grand opulence of the main house with its fine linens and crystal, the row upon row of about twenty small brick dwellings with dirt floors were at odds with Laura's contention that the slaves were well cared for. Each cabin was approximately ten by fifteen feet, with a fireplace for cooking and warmth. Occasionally a piece of rough-hewn wooden furniture, a table, chair, or bench could be seen, and aside from a few pieces of functional cooking utensils, they were the sole possessions in view. Entire families occupied each dwelling, sleeping in the open loft above or on pallets on the floor down below. Nearly every hut had a sick person in it, in varying stages of illness, and Auntie Quince started with the worst among them. The occupants, including children, stood at attention when Jordan entered until Auntie Quince explained her presence. With each patient, Jordan admired the woman's attentiveness and encouragement, tending to all with the same care she would members of her own family.

When they reached the fourth patient, an elderly man, it was too late. His body, laid out on the floor, was being prepared for burial. Jordan learned that he'd been ill for quite some time and had passed on that morning. His widow sat on the floor next to him, tears streaming down a face that showed no other emotion. It chilled Jordan to see her that way, and she wished she had hurried out here sooner instead of waiting for Dr. Wheelwright to arrive. She gave her condolences and quickly stepped outside.

"Who are you?" a thick, deep male voice demanded.

Spinning around, Jordan faced a white man of indeterminable age with a long, black beard reaching to his chest. He leaned sideways, one hand resting on the wall of one of the huts.

"Miss Jordan Colfax, a guest of Laura St. Clair. And who, precisely, are you?"

"Albert Humphreys. I'm the overseer. I heard Miss Laura was home and ailing. Is she better today?"

"Not yet, but hopefully soon."

"Can I ask what you're doing, miss?"

"Miss Laura asked me to attend to any of the sick down here. She'll be extremely disappointed when I inform her there has already been a needless death."

Humphreys shrugged. "An old nigger like him wouldn't fetch three hundred dollars. They're not worth the price of their rations at his age."

Jordan kept her temper with difficulty. Speaking a language he could understand, she said, "A number of younger workers are also ill, and I'm sure your employer won't be happy if they also succumb. Unfortunately Dr. Wheelwright has come and gone, for had I known about these poor sick people I would have delayed his departure. However, he'll return to check on Miss Laura soon and I shall send him to treat these people as soon as he arrives."

He frowned, shifting his weight from one foot to the other. "Well, miss, I don't reckon there's call for him to be stopping by to see the niggers. They're used to Auntie's doctoring. And besides, she's free." He grinned knowingly at her.

Disgusted by his callousness, Jordan said, "Nevertheless, Mr.

Humphreys, when the doctor returns, I shall have him visit *all* of the sick at the St. Clair home." She gathered up her skirt and headed back toward the main house, tossing over her shoulder. "If need be, I shall pay him for his services."

She felt his cold, lifeless eyes burning into her back as she strode away. Passing by a larger brick building in back of the house, Jordan paused to inhale the wonderful aromas emanating from inside. On an impulse, she knocked and was startled when a strikingly beautiful Negro woman answered the door. She looked familiar but Jordan couldn't quite place where she might have seen her before.

"Yes, ma'am?" The woman looked just as surprised to see Jordan.

"Are you Martha?" Jordan surmised this was the kitchen Laura had mentioned during the day they'd spent together in Richmond.

"Yes, ma'am, I'm Martha. Come on in." She opened the door wider and Jordan stepped into a very cozy room.

A fire in the large fireplace was burning brightly, and a work surface was covered with dishes in various stages of completion.

"I'm sorry to interrupt you," Jordan said. "I'm Miss Jordan Colfax, a guest here. I wanted to tell you I've never eaten a finer meal than the one provided when I first arrived."

Martha beamed. "Thank you, ma'am. I heard Miss Laura arrived with company."

"That's right. And I must confess that I could not pass by without stopping. The delightful smells coming from here are impossible to ignore."

"Why, set yourself down and I'll fix you up with something to eat right now." Martha indicated a chair at the table. "I made up some more chicken broth for Miss Laura. Is she still bad sick?"

"It seems so." Jordan sat down and tried to sound optimistic. "But Dr. Wheelwright thinks Auntie Quince's remedies are helping."

While she watched Martha move about the room, she could not shake the feeling that she had met her before. And yet, she knew that was unlikely. Eventually Martha noticed her close scrutiny and became obviously affected by it when she uncharacteristically dropped several items on the floor.

"Lord, I don' know when I've been so clumsy."

"No, I'm sorry for staring, Martha. You seem so familiar to me. Have we met before?"

Martha settled her gaze on Jordan for a few moments, an anxious look clouding her face. "No, miss. I was born here at Barrett Hall and never gone so much as ten miles in either direction."

"My mistake, then. Perhaps it is that you remind me of someone else that I know. Is the rest of your family here as well?"

Martha set a plate in front of Jordan. "My mammy is here, and that's my Ruby what's working in the main house. My boy was sold to the Porters some five years ago, but I see him once in a while. Two more is in Alabama somewheres."

"Your father passed on, then?"

Martha gave a stiff nod. She looked distinctly uncomfortable and began cleaning up the kitchen. Jordan had heard that the families of slaves were often broken up and children lost touch with their parents. She wondered if that was why Martha seemed so unsettled by her questions. Or perhaps she simply wasn't used to any white person taking an interest in her.

"Did you know him?" she asked sympathetically. "Did he work here too, along with you and your mother?"

Her head lowered, Martha gave a flustered, "Yes, miss."

Jordan fell silent. She had only wanted to make conversation since the cook had been so kind, but Martha obviously preferred not to discuss her father. Maybe she wasn't close to him, or maybe he'd abandoned them or was sold off later on. "Oh!"

Jordan smothered her involuntary gasp and lowered her knife and fork to the table. It wasn't that she and Martha had met before, rather that she recalled a very similar face, a white face. Martha's father and Rachel St. Clair's father were one and the same, the two women were half sisters. It was a connection that Jordan wished she'd never made.

She knew Martha had seen the recognition on her face, and burned red hot with shame on the woman's behalf. If Martha and Mrs. St. Clair were half sisters, then Ruby and Laura were cousins. Losing her appetite, Jordan got to her feet and thanked Martha for the food. She wondered if Laura had the faintest notion that she'd been sitting in the kitchen all these years with her own aunt, and that the same family blood ran through their veins.

In shock, she slipped back outside and let the brutal chill of the day sting her cheeks. This was all terribly wrong, she thought as she trudged the rest of the way to the house. And if she, a complete stranger, had drawn these conclusions in a matter of moments, how could Laura and her mother not know the St. Clairs had enslaved their own relatives?

❖

The open carriage was surrounded by soldiers on horseback as they led the way down Pennsylvania Avenue to the Capitol. Crowds lined the street and alternately cheered or stood solemnly as the outgoing and incoming Presidents passed by. As they alighted from the carriage, Lincoln glanced up at the clear, sunny sky and breathed deeply of the crisp, cold air. Sharpshooters lined the roof of the Capitol, leaning against scaffolding as construction on the dome continued. Also, cannon were placed directly in the path of every road leading in and out of the city. It was not the sort of day he would wish for his inauguration, and he hoped his address would ameliorate some of the nervousness that all in attendance felt. What he said would be heard by both Northerners and Southerners alike. But he would most definitely direct his speech to the South in an effort to prevent the further spread of secession.

After watching Vice President Hannibal Hamlin sworn in within the Senate Chamber, he and President Buchanan arrived at the East Portico where he waited patiently until it was his turn to speak. When the time came, he approached the ailing Chief Justice Roger B. Taney to take the oath of office. This chief justice had, just a few years ago, delivered the majority opinion against Dred Scott, the slave who had sued for his freedom. A staunch supporter of slavery, like most of his colleagues on the Supreme Court, Taney had ensured that Scott lost. The court had declared any person descended from black Africans, whether slave or free, could never be a citizen of the United States, according to the Constitution.

The decision, deplored by many, had certainly helped Lincoln obtain the nomination. Ward Lamon noted the irony of Taney administering the oath to the man who intended to undo the institution the chief justice had propped up. After Taney resumed his seat, Lincoln began his address. Part of the way through his speech, a loud crack sounded, and many in the audience jumped. A young man sitting on a tree branch for a better view of the scene tumbled to the ground when the limb gave way, fraying the nerves of soldiers in the immediate area.

"In *your* hands, my dissatisfied fellow countrymen, and not in *mine*, is the momentous issue of civil war," Lincoln declared. "The Government will not assail *you*. You can have no conflict without being yourselves the aggressors. *You* have no oath registered in heaven to destroy the Government, while *I* shall have the most solemn one to 'preserve, protect, and defend it.'

"I am loath to close. We are not enemies, but friends. We must not be enemies. Though passion may have strained, it must not break our bond of affection. The mystic chords of memory, stretching from every battlefield and patriot grave to every living heart and hearthstone all over this broad land, will yet swell the chorus of the Union, when again touched, as surely they will be, by the better angels of our nature."

Taking his seat again, Lincoln gazed out at the crowd. His address had met only with polite applause, and he frowned slightly in disappointment. If this crowd did not receive the President enthusiastically, Ward wondered at the response of the man who had now been appointed to head the Rebel government.

❖

Jefferson Davis was pleased that his call for 100,000 men had met with such overwhelming success that some volunteers had to be told to return home. There simply were not enough arms, ammunition, or clothing, or the wherewithal to feed that many men and horses. It looked as though each state belonging to the Confederacy so far would meet its quota, and Davis now had the task of appointing generals who would lead the men into battle, if it came to war.

Sitting at his desk in Montgomery, Alabama, he had compiled a list of names. However, the most pressing problem facing him was more than just soldiers and the formation of the new government. A small fort, still under construction in Charleston Harbor, was at the center of a diplomatic and military crisis that had to be resolved soon. When the Confederate states departed, they insisted that the Federal properties located on Southern soil, particularly those of military value, belonged to the newly forming country. South Carolina wanted the fort in its harbor for the same reason, but the Federal soldiers occupying it would not surrender it, causing the crisis Davis now faced.

Brigadier General PGT Beauregard's repeated calls for the surrender of Fort Sumter remained unheeded, and Union attempts at resupply and reinforcement had more than once been turned away. At the moment it was a stalemate, but Davis could not let it remain that way for much longer. Already word had reached him that the Union soldiers inside were starving, and he could well imagine what Northern newspapers would make of that. And yet, if he took stronger action, he might well be seen as the aggressor in the situation and could lose support of the border states whose allegiance hung in the balance.

Rising from his desk, he strolled to the window, his hands clasped behind his back. His thoughts wandered to Abraham Lincoln, the man he would face in the oncoming conflict. He had yet to gain a firm sense of him, other than what he read in the newspapers or heard through the widespread gossip. Accounts of the inaugural address had reached Montgomery, inviting avid speculation about Lincoln's assertion that he would not interfere with the institution of slavery in the states where it existed, nor would he invade a state or territory by armed force. It was any man's guess how much of that was mere rhetoric. One thing Davis had learned over the years was that events could quickly overtake the very men responsible for controlling them. And if ever there was a situation that could lead to the unthinkable, he had a feeling it was Fort Sumter.

Chapter Eleven

Laura woke to filtered sunlight streaming through the curtains. Tiny dust motes danced brightly in the shaft of light that struck the foot of the bed, and she watched them absently, allowing herself time to adjust to her surroundings. The sun felt warm on her feet, and a glance out the window told her that all evidence of snow had melted away. She felt so weak that she could barely lift her arms, but for the first time in many days she felt wonderfully warm. With all the energy she possessed, she rolled to the side of her bed to ask Ruby for some water and was shocked to see Jordan lying on the pallet instead. It took her several moments to recall that Jordan had insisted on accompanying her to Barrett Hall, but she could not remember the journey itself or how long she had been at home since.

She gazed at Jordan for a long while, trying to fathom this strange woman. Eventually, Jordan stirred and looked up.

"Good morning." Laura was dismayed by the rasping sound of her voice. It was rough from lack of use.

Relief flooded Jordan's body so rapidly that she felt weak. Surprisingly, she felt hot tears rush quickly to her eyes and she blinked them back, unprepared to show Laura how afraid for her she had been. "Good morning indeed. How do you feel?"

"Tired, but better. And terribly thirsty."

Jordan crawled up from the pallet and poured her a glass of water from the pitcher near her bedside. After Laura had consumed the contents, she grasped Jordan's hand.

"How long have I been ill?"

"Weeks," Jordan replied.

"You've been here throughout?"

"I've been back and forth from Richmond for performances. Your aunt was here for a week, but I don't think you noticed."

"I don't remember very much," Laura said. "The slaves?"

"All is well." Jordan decided the bad news could wait. She wanted to speak with Laura about the unpleasant Mr. Humphreys, too, but only when she was stronger.

Laura sagged back on her pillows, her strength exhausted by the short conversation. "Thank you. It was very kind of you to change your plans. I'm sorry for the inconvenience."

"You need to sleep now," Jordan commanded, pulling the covers back up to Laura's shoulders.

Feeling perilously close to tears of relief and gratitude, she went to her room to wash and change clothes, and as she splashed warm water onto her face, the tears spilled freely.

❖

"I've saved the newspapers so you can catch up on the latest events." Jordan selected a stack of recent papers and flipped through them casually. "I see your father gets all the local news—the *Richmond Whig*, *Examiner*, *Enquirer.* This last one is rather anxious to have Virginia join the traitors stampeding out of the Union."

"Then I should like to read that one first." Laura grinned.

"Yes, I'm sure you would." Jordan tossed it on the bed in disgust.

Laura laughed. It felt good to be well again, to feel the strength coming back to her frail body. She'd devoured a breakfast of eggs and biscuits with orange preserves, hot tea with milk, and rice pudding. The last Martha had obviously added to tempt her appetite, knowing it was her favorite.

"So what has been going on in the country?" Laura asked. "Have you heard from Father?"

"There are a few letters next to you on the table, I believe from your parents and from Ransom." Jordan continued flipping through the papers, the full sunlight striking her from behind, highlighting the deep reds and browns of her hair.

A flush of feeling stirred within Laura, and she yearned to touch Jordan, to run her hands through the thick tresses.

"Here's another one." Jordan held up a newspaper. "This story is particularly deplorable, quoting the Rebel Vice President Stephens in Savannah on March twenty-first. He says that the foundations are laid for this new so-called government, and that, I quote, 'its cornerstone rests upon the great truth that the Negro is not equal to the white man, and that slavery, subordination to the superior race, is his natural and normal condition.'" She flung the offending paper aside. "I cannot believe an educated man could spout such hogwash."

Anxious to avoid the kinds of arguments they'd had in Richmond, Laura picked up the letters that had arrived during her illness. Opening the one from her father first, she read about the dilemma surrounding Fort Sumter, which had been occupied since the day after Christmas. When President Buchanan had attempted to reinforce the fort, the ship bearing supplies and men was fired upon and turned back. The small garrison in control of the fort had not been allowed to buy food at local markets since then and was slowly being starved out. The dilemma now was what Mr. Lincoln would do. Rumor had it that he was planning to evacuate the fort altogether, but so far, the soldiers were still there.

"I must write to my parents before they become worried," Laura murmured.

Ruby entered the bedroom and gathered up the breakfast tray. "Miss Laura, I think it's done time you bathed and we changed the bed linens and got you in something fresh."

"I couldn't agree with you more, Ruby." Jordan placed the papers back on the table. "Laura, when you're ready, I think it might behoove you to come downstairs and enjoy more sociable companionship."

"Yes, I think I would enjoy that very much."

Ensconced on the settee in the parlor with a large quilt over her lap, Laura was thrilled to be out of bed and in another room. She and Jordan sat playing chess and Laura found her to be exceedingly accomplished at the game, a discovery that led to a very challenging encounter. She was thoroughly enjoying both the game and the company when there was a loud knock at the front door and Sarah entered the parlor a moment later.

"Mr. Young is calling, Miss Laura."

Laura froze for several seconds before she could force the appropriate words from her lips. "Show him in."

She met Jordan's eyes, and the expression that flashed there did nothing for her composure. Laura felt certain she detected annoyance, even resentment. Disconcerted, she held out her hand as Sarah led her patient suitor into the room. "Why, Mr. Young, what a pleasant surprise to see you."

He greeted Jordan, then bowed in front of Laura and kissed her hand briefly. "I heard of your illness and came as quickly as I could. Are you much improved?"

Laura glanced down at her lap, unable to meet his eyes. "I'm recovering slowly, but most assuredly I am much better, thanks to Miss Colfax."

"Then I am indebted to you, Miss Colfax." Preston inclined his head toward Jordan.

Jordan nodded, feeling uncomfortable in the presence of a man who so obviously adored Laura despite knowing his affections were one-sided.

"Would you care for some tea, Mr. Young?" Laura asked. "Martha has baked a spice cake which we were about to enjoy. Won't you join us?"

"If only I could spare the time, I can think of nothing I would rather do," he replied. "But I merely wished to see with my own eyes that you were recovering satisfactorily and to let you know that I will be returning to Richmond in the morning. Business opportunities have quickly asserted themselves and I must attend to them immediately." He paused, struggling for the words he wished to say next. "Before I go, however, I wanted to speak with you on the matter we have discussed previously."

Laura began to panic, feeling the tension build in her chest that never seemed to completely disappear when it came to her future. She had put his marriage proposal off as long as she could and it was only right that she give him an answer. If she said yes, she would be miserable for the rest of her life. Preston Young was a kind man and a devoted father, but she felt nothing for him. However, if she said no, the other two choices of husband were even less desirable and her prospects were dwindling, particularly with the crisis looming over the land. She dreaded to think of her mother's reaction when she learned that Laura had turned down the best suitor she had. The consequences could be dire. Perhaps over time she could learn to love him. Such a change of heart was commonplace according to many of her friends.

"Perhaps I should see how things are coming with the cake." Jordan rose to take her leave, unable to bear watching Laura's unhappiness.

She went out the back door and into the sunlight. The weather had made a dramatic turn three days earlier, melting all evidence of the ice and snow that had struck so rapidly and powerfully. The air was still cool, but the sun was intense and the blossoms on the trees and bushes were already recovering from the shock of the storm.

Cautiously she knocked on the kitchen door. She had not seen Martha since that awkward lunch and hoped she would not be unwelcome. Entering the kitchen, she found Martha removing the cake from the Dutch oven, the fragrant aroma of cinnamon and allspice infusing the warm space. Jordan sat at the table.

"Why, Miss Colfax, you have the saddest look on your face," Martha said. "Is Miss Laura feeling poorly again?"

Jordan shook her head. "No, Mr. Young has made an unexpected visit and I suspect he intends to ask Laura for an answer to his marriage proposal."

Martha did not seem surprised. "I sure wish she could find someone she loves, but maybe she'll grow to like him some."

Jordan was angry with the turn of events. Just when Laura seemed to be returning to her old self and her sense of humor making an appearance, this had to happen. She was especially angry that Mr. Young seemed to have arrived at a time when he could most take advantage of her weakness. Laura was a beautiful, vibrant, young woman. It was a waste for her to be married off to someone who neither appreciated her humor nor her intellect, and for her to spend her days tending to children and mindless household tasks.

Jordan felt as though all her nursing and anguishing during the past weeks had gone for naught. But why should she care so much what Laura did? What was Laura to her? She admitted that she was growing quite fond of her. Something about Laura made Jordan feel unsettled in a pleasant way. She wanted to be near her and loathed the idea that she could simply be dismissed as a mere social acquaintance the moment a prospective husband arrived on the scene.

Astonished by the strength of her feelings, Jordan paced over to the kitchen window and stared out across the clearing and into the woods beyond the house. After a while, she saw Mr. Young on horseback riding toward the woods. With a quick word to Martha, she all but ran out of the kitchen and back to the main house, where she burst open the parlor door before Sarah could scuttle to open it for her.

She found Laura lying across the settee, her face buried in her arm and her shoulders heaving convulsively. Jordan went to her side, gathered her in her arms, and held her tightly while she cried. She kissed Laura's cheek, tasting the salty tears, and wanted so badly to kiss them all away.

"Shh, all will be well," she soothed, knowing that it would not be.

"Oh, Jordan, whatever shall I do now?" Laura sobbed.

Jordan could not answer, her own eyes filling with tears at the thought of Laura's unhappiness.

"Have you never found yourself in this position?" Laura sniffed. Surely she was not the only one to have experienced this mortifying dilemma before.

"No, I haven't," Jordan admitted, "but then, I don't have a mother to look after such things. My father has left all such notions up to me to decide for myself, and I have determined that I shall never marry. The life of a married woman holds no appeal for me, and besides, I enjoy too much the demands of the theatre."

Laura absorbed Jordan's statements, unable to comprehend that a woman could decide for herself what she would do with her own life. Oh, how she wished she could be more like her, not a care in the world, an exciting job with her own income and the ability to go where she wanted whenever she wanted.

"So, have you decided on a wedding date, then?" Jordan asked hesitantly.

"I beg your pardon?" Laura pulled away.

"Your wedding to Mr. Young. When shall you marry?"

It dawned on Laura what Jordan was implying. "Oh, no, you misunderstand. I did not accept Mr. Young's proposal. I turned him down."

Jordan was taken aback. A fierce joy filled her and she could not help but smile. "Why, that is wonderful news! I am so proud of you for having the courage of your convictions." She kissed Laura on her forehead, embracing her once again.

Laura could not recall hearing anyone ever say they were proud of her. It did not occur to her until that moment that Jordan's opinion of her mattered so much, and warmth filled her heart at Jordan's praise. Enveloped in Jordan's arms, she felt safe and, oddly, loved. Of course she felt loved by her family and by Charlotte, but to be recognized for having achieved something on her own merit was new to her, and she relished the moment.

Jordan held Laura tightly, not quite ready to let her go. It felt right holding her, and a feeling of peace descended on her until she remembered what had led up to this. "But then why were you crying?"

Laura wiped away the last of her tears. "I don't love Mr. Young, and I don't love anyone else. There are two other gentlemen vying for my affections. However, my mother doesn't approve of them. It would seem that I'm doomed to remain a spinster, and now, with the possibility of war approaching, my chances of finding love are even more remote." An idea began to take shape in her mind and the more she thought of it, the more excited she became. "Perhaps you could teach me to become an actress. Then I wouldn't have to choose among men I do not love. I could be like you."

"Well, I'm not sure I particularly care for the implication in your suggestion, but I think I understand what you mean." Jordan smiled.

"Oh, I didn't mean that you would not find a husband yourself one day."

"I know, but you must think long and hard. It is not something to decide lightly. If you determine it is what you wish to do, I shall help you."

A thrill coursed through Laura and her world no longer seemed as dark as it once had.

Sarah entered with the cake and they resumed their game of chess. Laura felt better than she had in weeks, both physically and mentally. She knew she had Jordan to thank for that. She studied Jordan's face as she deliberated over her next move. Lines of concentration furrowed her brow and she stroked a fingertip absently over her bottom lip every so often. Laura loved the sharp intelligence in Jordan's eyes and the strength in her chin and jaw. She admired the determination with which Jordan seemed to approach everything she did. Even in the carriage ride home, Laura had vague memories of Jordan gazing down at her, a mixture of concern and resolve in her eyes, along with something Laura couldn't place. Whatever it was, Laura recalled feeling safe. Her worries about being ill and alone had simply disappeared. Being with Jordan now, as then, made her happy and content. She wished she could stay like this forever.

❖

Brigadier General Pierre Gustave Toutant Beauregard, known as The Little Creole to his friends, read the telegram from Secretary of War Walker once more. He was still in shock over its directive.

> *You will at once demand its evacuation and, if this is refused, proceed, in such a manner as you may determine, to reduce it.*

Folding the paper neatly and placing it on his desk, he picked up the reply he'd received to his earlier demand for surrender. Major Robert Anderson, the officer in command of Fort Sumter, had refused, but he'd also passed along a comment to the two aides-de-camp who had delivered the ultimatum. If they were to be believed, Anderson said that if the Rebels did not batter the fort to pieces, he and his men would be starved out in a few days.

Beauregard reflected back upon Major Anderson, his artillery instructor at West Point, and recalled their close personal friendship. He was not looking forward to the task at hand, but determined to do his duty as instructed. Also weighing heavily on his mind was the fleet gathering beyond the bar, a sidewheel steamer and various sloops, tugs, and transport craft sent by the Federals to reinforce Anderson. He could not allow that to happen either, and he knew that very soon the time for talking would be over.

Out of respect for his former instructor, Beauregard put pen to paper one last time in the hopes that Anderson would agree to evacuate the fort. Perhaps, at least, bloodshed could be avoided and the return of Fort Sumter to the state of South Carolina could transpire peacefully.

❖

Mid-April was rapidly approaching and the weather had turned from cool to warm. The pink and red azaleas had opened fully and the dogwood trees imparted a lacy, fragile effect amongst the pines and great oaks. Bored with her indoor confinement, Laura had begged, argued, and cajoled until she convinced Jordan that a picnic out in the fresh air was in order. Giving in only when Laura agreed to dress warmly, Jordan strolled with her along the James, the sun shining brightly, causing sparkling reflections off the flowing river. On the riverbank they spread a blanket in the shade of a large pink dogwood, its lush blossoms occasionally cascading down to land on their picnic.

"What a sublime place," Jordan sighed.

She lay comfortably on the blanket, resting on her right side as she watched a few small boats make their way downstream. A mockingbird called from a tree nearby and she was lulled into a drowsy feeling of contentment. She glanced up at Laura, who sat beside her, and felt her heart race. Laura sat in patches of shadow and light, a canopy of pink surrounding her as though framing her in a picture. All the elements seemingly conspired to enhance every aspect of her beauty.

Laura felt the intensity of Jordan's gaze and blushed.

"I'm sorry." Jordan realized she had been caught staring, but she had no regrets. The color in Laura's cheeks put to shame the petals on the tree. "It's only that right now, you are so beautiful. Even nature pales in comparison."

Laura was slightly shocked at the declaration. But Jordan's earnestness and lack of guile made her realize there was nothing but sincerity in her words. Flustered, she reached for the picnic basket.

"We have fried chicken, fruit, cheese, bread, and wine. What would you like first? Are you hungry?"

Recognizing that Laura needed to change the subject, Jordan sat up quickly. "I'm famished. Shall I pour the wine?"

As Laura prepared the plates, Jordan filled their glasses. Surreptitiously she continued to observe Laura, wondering at her own lack of decorum and discretion. *Perhaps I was too direct, but it is true.* She enjoyed the time they spent together, not recalling when she had felt such pleasure with anyone, except perhaps Tyler. But this was different. She never would have believed even a short while ago that she could come to like Laura. She didn't quite understand, but attributed it to their ability to talk about anything. Even those things they disagreed hotly about contributed to Jordan's sense of well-being. At least Laura took her opinions seriously, something most men never did, thinking her merely a woman. In Laura's presence, she felt somehow whole, as though who she was and what she was mattered.

Hours passed as they discussed their childhood and life experiences. After the meal had been consumed and the last of the wine poured,

Jordan lay back on the blanket, her head propped up on another blanket, content to watch the river flow past. Laura withdrew a book from the basket and read in silence.

"What have you got there?" Jordan inquired.

"Mrs. Browning. Do you know her poetry?"

"Mmm, 'Aurora Leigh' is her finest."

"I think I have that. Would you like me to read it to you?"

"Actually, do you have 'The House of Clouds'?" Jordan asked. "It's my favorite."

"I'm not sure I know that one. I haven't yet read all of her works, but I think it's here."

Laura flipped through the pages until she found what she was looking for. As she read out loud, Jordan closed her eyes, blocking out everything but the words of the poem. The food, the wine, the weather, all combined to add to her feeling of happiness. But it was the soft, melodic sounds of Laura's voice that gave her the greatest feeling of bliss.

> "I would build a cloudy House
> For my thoughts to live in
> When for earth too fancy-loose,
> And too low for Heaven
> Hush! I talk my dream aloud
> I build it bright to see,
> I build it on the moonlit cloud
> To which I looked with thee."

Laura continued reading, pausing now and then to absorb the beauty of the poem. When she finished, they were both quiet for a very long time. Captivated, she scanned the words once more. They expressed her own thoughts with such clarity it was as though Mrs. Browning knew her intimately. Laura was instantly flustered that Jordan had heard her speak such revealing words. The poem exposed her somehow, laying bare feelings she could not yet acknowledge in herself. She was not even sure if the feelings were real and what they could mean, they were so new to her.

Jordan opened her eyes and caught an odd, unsettled expression on Laura's face. Something stirred inside her and for several heartbeats they gazed at one another. Jordan's pulse increased with every beat. Of its own volition, her hand found the still-pale but soft skin of Laura's cheek and stroked it gently. She leaned forward just a little, her gaze fixed on Laura's lips. Daring to glance up, she could see Laura's eyes riveted to her mouth. A strong gust of wind blew in from the east, causing blossoms to rain down on them, and as though awakening from a dream, Laura blinked rapidly and shivered.

"It's getting late," she observed. "Before long the sun will be completely down, and it's already cooling off."

"I hope you are not too fatigued." Jordan drew Laura's cloak closely about her.

Laura felt the graze of Jordan's warm hand against her neck as she helped fasten the garment. She shivered again, whether from the breeze or from the prickle of Jordan's skin on her own, she wasn't entirely sure. Once everything was packed, Jordan shook out the blanket and tossed it over one arm, then picked up the basket.

She studied Laura closely, noticing the shivering. "Come closer. I don't want you to stumble." She extended her free arm.

At first Laura thought to decline, but upon rising from the ground and feeling slightly dizzy, she linked their arms and immediately felt the warmth of the connection. They returned to the house in silence, Laura at a loss as to what to say in the aftermath of what had transpired. What were the strong emotions that quickly found their way to her heart? She was unsure whether her lack of balance was due to her health or to the rush of feeling the poem had inspired in her.

By the time they approached the house, she definitely felt the need to rest and excused herself. But after fifteen minutes of tossing and turning on her bed, she went to her desk to write.

13 April, 1861

I have been away from my diary far too long now, my illness making almost any activity impossible. I am happy to say, though, that I am recovering quite nicely and in a week or so should not feel in the least any ill effects. In this I must be grateful to Jordan, who has been so kind to me that I shan't know how to repay her.

Jordan...I don't exactly know what to make of her. She can be so obstinate and yet make perfect sense at the same time. How can that be? How can I detest her arguments and at once think her brilliant? Admittedly, she is clever and does not suffer fools gladly. But it is most unfortunate that she cannot see that her position is a false one and that the South is justified in her desire to separate from an unjust government. She is a mystery, and so beautiful. I was quite taken by surprise this afternoon when it occurred to me how beautiful she is. She distracts me with her dazzling smile, and even when she is most querulous I cannot help but want to be near her. She is my friend, but so much more. What that is I cannot say, for I do not know.

Early that evening, dark clouds rolled in over the James and the skies took on a menacing appearance that kept them indoors for the rest of the evening. Martha had prepared a simple meal, after which Jordan and Laura retired to the parlor, each with a book. Jordan, having perused the same paragraph for ten minutes and still not recalling what she had read, peered over the top of her book at Laura, who seemed engrossed in her own book. Jordan recalled their picnic earlier that day and replayed in her mind that odd feeling she experienced after Laura had finished the poem. She was baffled by the new emotion she felt toward Laura and confused by what was happening.

Laura sensed rather than saw Jordan's eyes on her. That familiar gaze felt like the hot sun and made her dress feel uncomfortably restrictive. An ache had been forming in the pit of her stomach, although not an unpleasant one, ever since that moment at the picnic when she was overcome with the urge to touch Jordan. She wanted…oh, she didn't know what she wanted. A yearning deep inside her could not be assuaged by anything she knew or understood. She was frustrated at not having the words to express these new emotions and did not know how to discuss them with Jordan.

A low rumble in the distance caused them to look up from their reading.

"I'd better check all the windows," Laura said, rising from her chair.

"I'll help you."

Jordan went upstairs as Laura walked around the first floor. While closing the windows would increase the temperature of the house, the storm would also cool things off, and hopefully at some point in the night they would be able to open them again. Once she had checked that they were all secure, Laura headed upstairs, where she found Jordan in the guest room trying to close an especially tight window. Together, they eventually shut it. Standing inches away, Laura glanced up into Jordan's eyes.

"Thank you for everything, Jordan. I don't know what I would have done without you." Laura touched Jordan's cheek. It was an innocent and sincere gesture, but she was fully unprepared for the shock that coursed down her arm and into her heart.

Jordan felt her own heart stop and the breath knocked clear out of her chest. Time stopped, and she didn't dare breathe.

A sudden pounding on the front door made them jump apart and they shared a nervous laugh. They descended to the first floor, where they were met in the entryway by the St. Clairs' nearest neighbor, Samuel Underwood.

"Why, Mr. Underwood, what brings you out so late on a night like this?" Laura inquired.

"Miss Laura, I rushed here as soon as I could because I knew you would want to know of the latest events."

"Whatever are you referring to? Is everyone well in your family?"

"Yes, of course." He waved her off. "I am referring to the latest political news. Have you not heard? Fort Sumter has been fired upon! I received news of it in a telegram a few hours ago." His face lit up with excitement.

Stunned, Laura could only look to Jordan, uncertain as to her reaction.

"That's all I know right now, although I suspect your father has much more information. Should you hear from him, Miss St. Clair, please send word to our house as quickly as you can. Mrs. Underwood's family is from Charleston and she has a nephew at the Citadel, the military academy there. She is anxious for news of him."

He left as abruptly as he arrived and Laura closed the door gently behind him. They stared at one another in disbelief.

"How could this have happened?" Jordan asked, not really expecting a reply.

"I don't know, but I suspect that Mr. Lincoln attempted to resupply the fort. Why else would it be fired upon?"

"For any number of reasons," Jordan replied. "It would not be unlike a Rebel hothead to fire wantonly into a fort solely to make a name for himself. They have been trying to force the President's hand for some time. He could not let those men starve, could he?"

"Whatever the reason," Laura soothed, not wanting to fight with Jordan, "there may be war after all. What that will mean frightens me more than anything else right now."

She wandered into the parlor, unsure what to do with herself. Jordan followed, and they sat watching the fire until it had burned down to cold gray ashes.

❖

President Lincoln's call on Monday, the fifteenth of April, for 75,000 men to serve ninety days was extended to all the states in the Union, including Virginia. Unable to bear arms against her Southern brethren, Virginia chose to secede two days later, followed by Arkansas, Tennessee, and North Carolina. Only through the strength of the President did Delaware and Maryland remain in the Union, although they would only supply troops for the defense of Washington. The Confederates seized the Federal arsenal at Harper's Ferry as well as the Norfolk Navy Yard, quickly adding to the mounting tension on both sides of the debate.

Those in Washington sympathetic to the Southern cause crowded the trains heading south, while Jordan found herself packing to head in the opposite direction in an almost empty car. It was a somber occasion, and she was torn between returning home and her desire to ensure the well-being of Laura. A letter from Laura's father indicated that they would be returning home on the next train, and she knew that Laura had fully recovered, but still, something kept tugging at her, causing her to delay her own departure. But knowing that she needed to return to Washington, she knew that her departure was imminent.

At the railway station, Jordan and Laura stood facing each other, both unsure what to say. Laura could find no words to express her thoughts about the events occurring in their country, let alone the strange feelings she was developing for her friend. At last, the train blew its final whistle for boarding, and the sound impelled Laura into Jordan's arms. Tears streamed down her face at the thought of Jordan's leaving and the not knowing when, if ever, they would meet again.

"I can't bear to see you go, and I fear what is happening to our country may keep us apart. Say you will return, and soon." Laura brushed her tears away with her glove.

"Of course I'll be back." Jordan could not seem to hold Laura closely enough. The heat of her body pressed into Laura's made her feel weak and strong all at once. Her body ached all over and she had the overwhelming desire to kiss Laura as Nell had kissed her. "Our next production will most assuredly travel to Richmond, they always do. Don't worry, everything will be fine."

Laura clung to Jordan, desperately wanting to believe her. Something had changed between them during her illness, something she could not explain, but it was something she did not want to let go of. She needed Jordan's strength, needed her friendship. She refused to believe that Jordan would cease to be a part of her life.

Jordan held Laura tightly, not wanting to let go, yet realizing that her life awaited her and that the war would quickly escalate. She had to go now, as she did not know when the next train would be available. Unable to bear another moment in their embrace, she stepped back and bade Laura a farewell that sounded polite and reserved to her ears, a piece of acting if ever there was one. Wrenched by the pleading in Laura's eyes, she forced herself to climb aboard the train. From the window seat she selected, she looked directly down at Laura's pale, upturned face. As the train pulled out of the station, she focused on that fading image until she was blinded by her own tears.

Chapter Twelve

Situated on high ground overlooking the Hudson River, the military academy at West Point was in a state of turmoil, the scenic beauty and pleasant April weather lost on the cadets within its walls. The startling news of Fort Sumter had sparked a frenzy of speculation among the young men whose sole purpose in attending the academy was to train for war. The dilemma facing each cadet in the class of 1861 was not whether they would finish their course of study and graduate, but rather which side of the fight they would choose. For many, the decision was one of simple loyalty to their home soil, but for some from both North and South, the choice was complicated by other factors.

Many of the soldiers' grandfathers and great-grandfathers had fought in the War of 1812 or the Revolution. They saw secession as treason against everything their ancestors had died for. More than that, they could not conceive of one country, one nation, no longer existing without containing both North and South. Still others had family living on the opposite side of the Mason-Dixon Line whom they would not fight against. Whatever an individual's choice was, no one seemed to doubt the gravity of his decision, or its long-term consequences.

Tyler Colfax and Ransom St. Clair had first heard the startling news during Captain Benton's Ordnance and Gunnery course. The captain was able to reassert control over the resulting pandemonium and finish his lecture on pyrotechnics. The participants had lost their ability to concentrate and he released them early. Once outside the classroom, Tyler and Ransom found their usual companions and formed one of the many tight clusters of cadets gathered on the grounds.

Each was making bold pronouncements as to his choice and his opinion of the outcome of the war. Tyler recognized a certain bravado in the posturing and rhetoric of his peers, but still felt a rush of pride at their strict adherence to duty. Each man would fight as he felt bound.

"It was only a matter of time," George Armstrong Custer of Ohio commented. "I'm merely glad that the waiting is finally over and this thing can be settled once and for all. I shall be glad to get on with it."

"I don't know about y'all," John Pelham of Alabama said, "but I'm leaving for home as quick as I can. Jeff Davis needs every soldier he can get."

"Have you decided what you will do?" Ransom asked.

"You know my feelings," Tyler replied. "I've sworn an oath, 'Duty, Honor, Country,' and I cannot waver from my devotion to the Union and Constitution. I shall serve the United States faithfully as my forefathers did before me. Quite frankly, I cannot see how you can choose differently. This is your country, for God's sake."

Ransom glanced at the friends he'd made over the past several years at West Point. They had already begun to argue as each took his stand on the issues that had divided their nation, and would soon turn one against the other on the battlefield. Some would join the South along with him, while others, like Tyler, would become his enemy. Echoes of Joshua Colfax's words haunted him.

"Virginia is my home," he said. "It's the home of my family, and where my ancestors are buried. I grew up there, and I hope someday to be married and have children there. And when the day comes, I too will be buried on Virginia soil. I would defend her with my life. *Virginia* is my country."

Tyler met Ransom's eyes and knew the profound sadness in their depths also shone from his own. A lump formed in his throat as he gripped Ransom's shoulder tightly. "Good luck, my friend, and God protect you."

Unable to speak, Ransom clasped Tyler's hand. He had dreaded this day ever since the possibility of war loomed darkly on the horizon. Thoughts of fighting in foreign wars with his classmates by his side faded quickly from his mind. Instead, the reality of firing upon his dearest friend had made the occasion a miserable one indeed.

Forcing such unhappy thoughts from his mind, he focused instead on completing the remaining days of study at the academy. Most of his friends were leaning toward finishing out their programs so as to graduate and obtain plum assignments on some general's staff. A few, however, planned to leave immediately, anxious to get in the fight before it was over. Ransom knew his father would insist on his finishing, so there was never any choice for him. He was not sure how he would be able to face his classmates day after day knowing he would eventually head south while some stayed to fight on the opposing side.

In silence, he strode along next to his friend, the two trailing behind many of their class, unconsciously heading toward the Cadet Chapel and the temporary comfort offered within.

❖

Jordan entered Ford's Theatre as she had on so many occasions, via the alleyway behind Tenth Street. She moved with an uncharacteristic lack of enthusiasm, a feeling so foreign it left her dazed. Since her acting debut two years earlier, she had felt nothing but happiness and energy on stage, and with a starring role in a Shakespeare play in Washington she had all the makings of a stellar career and a national reputation. Any actress with a thimbleful of ambition would be ecstatic, so she was puzzled by the apathy that consumed her.

She knew the outbreak of war and the building tensions between North and South had contributed to her cheerless disposition. Living in the nation's capital did nothing to ameliorate her tension. Washington was the heart of all the political events taking place in the country, and her father insisted on dissecting every unfolding event over the dining table each night. He was in constant touch with the White House so as to be up on current affairs before even the public was made aware through his newspaper. Increasingly, all Jordan wanted to do was escape the ceaseless talk of war and fighting. The theatre had always provided a respite from the outside world, a place where she felt fully at home and could lose herself in the substitute world of make-believe.

Yet ever since her return from Barrett Hall, she'd found her usual refuge unsatisfactory. Her concentration was disrupted by constant thoughts of Laura St. Clair. She should have kept the promise made during her illness and persuaded her to come to Washington. Did Laura even remember what was said? Jordan had been so afraid in that moment that Laura was slipping away from her that she would have promised almost anything, yet she had spoken her own true wish—that she could bring Laura home and keep her safe. Even then, she knew in a small corner of her heart that she wanted Laura at her side.

Jordan frowned. Her feelings for Laura confounded her. The

entire trip home, she had examined the strange sensations that had accompanied that moment at the picnic when Laura had read to her, then later during the storm at the house. What all this meant was incomprehensible, and a dull but constant headache had asserted itself upon her return. The more she tried to sort out and put into words what was happening to her, the more perplexed she became and the more her head ached.

To compound matters, a heavy weight had settled in her chest as she considered the future. She was bothered by the half-truths she'd told Laura about her reasons for being in Richmond. Of course her role at the Marshall was not an invention, but Jordan was unsure if she would have accepted the play had it not been for Kate Warne's proposal. She still felt a strong duty to support the Union, but her growing friendship with Laura had complicated matters and she no longer saw her objective as clearly as she once had. Nevertheless, she would return to Richmond in June as promised and continue the intelligence gathering that she had begun, only because it was her duty.

"Jordan, darlin', welcome home." Bill O'Malley stood at his desk, going over directions with a stage worker. "I thought we'd see you 'round here before now."

"Yes, I was detained somewhat." Jordan avoided going into detail. After the stage worker left, she lowered her voice. "I take it everything went well upon your return from Richmond?"

Bill chewed thoughtfully on his cigar. "Aye, indeed it did, lass. I had word the other day saying he was safe in Canada."

"That's good news." Jordan allowed herself the deep breath she had forgotten to take while her mind was on Laura. "How many have you helped?"

"Can't rightly say. I don't keep track, but I'd guess a couple dozen."

Jordan admired his nonchalance. Most people hesitated to break the law, and with the passing of the Fugitive Slave Act ten years ago, Northerners were obliged to return runaway slaves to their masters. Anyone caught helping or feeding a runaway was liable to spend six months in prison and pay a fine of $1,000. People who opposed slavery faced a moral dilemma: if they followed their consciences, they had to defy the law. Many Methodists and Quakers did just that, claiming the law was unjust and no one of Christian morals should be bound by it. Jordan didn't know if Bill was guided by religious beliefs or decent human values; whatever his reasons, she respected his courage.

"Well, if you ever need help to pay a fine, let me know," she said. "And if I can be of help, you know how to find me."

Bill laughed heartily. "Be careful. I may take advantage of an offer like that."

Jordan left him with a smile and retreated to her dressing room to change. The mood around the theatre seemed oddly sober. The seamstress fitting her costume wore a worried expression and dropped what few pins she didn't stick directly into Jordan's unhappy flesh. Jordan knew she had three boys, each of them expressing interest in joining the fight. The actor playing Mercutio had sent a note explaining that he had signed up to fight for the South. His family had a couple of fishing boats that he hoped would contribute to whatever navy the South might be able to construct. And two stage workers joined merely to collect on bounty money offered by wealthy men who hoped to avoid service. The loss of those she was used to seeing every day added to the pall that blanketed the theatre while they practiced.

Several hours into a lackluster rehearsal the director threw his hands up in the air and called an end to the day's work. He pronounced his vehement hopes that, come tomorrow, the actors would remember they were in a production of *Romeo and Juliet*, not *Henry VI*, and cast and stage workers dragged their feet next door to the Star Saloon for drinks.

Jordan was briefly tempted to join them in this unfeminine pursuit; however, the President had invited members of the press to dinner that evening, and her father had asked her to accompany him. She would not miss the opportunity for the world.

❖

"So, Mr. Lincoln, how are you enjoying the office?" a newsman asked.

Lincoln cocked his head and his eyes grew distant as her father's sometimes did when he had a story to tell. "I'm reminded," he began, "of a tarred and feathered man who, as he was being ridden out of town on a rail, was asked by someone in the crowd how he liked it. 'Well,' the man said, 'If it wasn't for the honor of the thing, I'd sooner walk.'"

Jordan laughed along with the others and found herself relaxing. Normally at ease in most any social situation, she was overwhelmed by the history and power of the White House and personally in awe of the man who currently occupied it. Feeling out of her depth among the more informed press, she hung back in the crowd, letting her father and the others do the talking. A group of men had arrived before them and stood closely around the President, who was in his glory recounting stories appropriate to the occasion. He seemed to enjoy answering their questions with anecdotes that either had a moral or in some way evaded a point he did not wish to address. The discussion at the moment revolved around the deluge of office seekers who hounded him day and night and clearly tried his patience.

The guests had gathered in the blue drawing room, which was shaped in an unusual ellipse. Broad mirrors lined the walls, set in massive frames, the floor was covered in blue and white velvet carpet, and a blue-tinted fresco adorned the high ceiling. The furniture was sumptuously outfitted in blue and silver satin damask, and seemed far too elegant to sit upon. But those in attendance relaxed comfortably wherever a chair was available as though they frequented the White House regularly. When a servant offered Jordan a glass of punch, she declined for fear of spilling it on the beautiful tapestries.

Before too long, dinner was announced and the guests were led into the East Room where a beautifully adorned table awaited them. As individuals were led to their seats, Jordan was dismayed to find herself seated to the President's right at the dinner table, with her father seated opposite her. Glancing around the room, Jordan noticed that she was the only woman there and presumed that explained her unfortunate location.

"Good evening again, Miss Colfax." Mr. Lincoln smiled, holding her chair out for her.

"Sir." She curtsied politely and took her place.

Fortunately, the dinner conversation reverted to the political situation and the President's attention was engaged with the questions the newsmen addressed to him. Jordan sat quietly, enjoying a meal of oysters and pheasant, when she noticed a slender, bearded man standing near the doorway. He wore a bowler hat and seemed to be watching her. When she returned his direct gaze, he nodded briefly and left the room. She had no idea who he was and was puzzled by his seeming recognition of her.

As the dinner dishes were cleared to make room for the dessert course, the President leaned toward her.

"Did you enjoy the meal this evening, Miss Colfax?"

"Very much, sir, it was delicious," she managed. "I'm sorry I missed meeting Mrs. Lincoln, though. I hope she is well."

"Quite well, thank you. She is visiting her sister and took the boys with her." His face glowed at the mere mention of his children, and Jordan found herself warming to him immediately.

Out of the corner of her eye, she once again noticed the bearded man, but this time he was speaking to a tall, powerfully built man who also glanced her way. Their open interest in her made Jordan acutely uneasy.

"I must confess, Miss Colfax," he continued, "that I have seen you before this evening. It was two years ago at Ford's. You played Meg Merriles in Walter Scott's *Guy Mannerling*. I remember thoroughly enjoying myself that night."

Jordan was delighted. "I am so happy to hear it, sir. Do you get to the theatre often?"

"Not as often as I would wish." His face assumed a decidedly wistful cast. "I fear that I will find even less time given the state of the Union."

Jordan took in the careworn expression that already rested heavily on his features even though he'd been in office only a short time. The dark circles under his eyes accentuated the thinness of his face, and the lines that formed across his brow were deeply pronounced. His mouth, however, was sensitive, almost delicate, and along with the lively spark in his eyes, it saved his face from being too austere. She was about to extend him an invitation to Ford's when the dessert course was placed in front of them. Throughout the meal, Jordan had noticed how little the President ate. But when the final course was served, his eyes lit up and his smile broadened.

"Well, this is an unexpected pleasure." He quickly picked up his fork. "My wife's white almond cake. You must taste it and let me know what you think of it, Miss Colfax." He scooped a large piece onto his fork and ate enthusiastically.

Jordan took a small bite and found it was indeed tasty.

"What roles have you performed lately?" he asked without looking up from his plate.

"I'm preparing now for my role in *Romeo and Juliet*, and I recently finished a tour as Kate in *Taming of the Shrew* and then *Lady Macbeth*. Were you able to see any of them?"

He shook his head. "Sadly, no. While I would have looked forward to seeing you as Kate, I try to avoid something as dramatic as *Macbeth*. It reminds me too much of recent events."

Jordan nodded. She wished she had not brought up the subject. Here she was a guest of his and she was only contributing to his cheerless thoughts. She decided to change the topic to lighter subjects when she saw the bearded man enter the room. She could no longer hold her discomfort inside.

"I beg your pardon, Mr. Lincoln, but can you tell me who the gentleman is who is making his way to the center of the room?"

Lincoln glanced in the direction. "Do not be alarmed by the gentlemen at the door. They are my security and have been with me since I arrived in Washington."

Jordan sighed in relief.

"The gentleman with the beard," Lincoln continued, "is my Chief of Security, Allan Pinkerton. Mr. Pinkerton has informed me of your contribution to the war effort, Miss Colfax. He tells me that in the short time that you have been in his employ, you have already managed to provide information valuable to our cause. May I say that the nation is indebted to you and that I am personally grateful for your courage and loyalty."

Jordan blushed, suddenly realizing that sitting next to the President had been no accident. "It is the least I can do for my country, sir."

"Nonsense, my dear. You give yourself little credit for such a dangerous enterprise. You have done more than most up to this time. I have great hopes that the army will be as successful in their endeavor as you have been in yours."

"I shall hope so as well, Mr. Lincoln, for my brother is finishing his last year at West Point and will most assuredly join the ranks of the Northern army."

"My goodness! Is the entire Colfax family engaged in single-handedly returning the Southern states to the Union?" Lincoln's dark gray eyes twinkled.

Jordan laughed, delighted and charmed by the President's compliment.

"Yes sir, and might I add that I know of other women who would be willing to do more for our government if asked."

"And I should be glad to have them on our side, for a woman is the only thing I'm afraid of that I know will not hurt me."

Jordan could not remember a meal where she had enjoyed herself so thoroughly, except perhaps for the last meal she'd shared with Laura prior to her departure. Recalling Laura, Jordan once again felt that odd queasy sensation in the pit of her stomach. It would be at least a month, the middle of June, before she would return to Richmond and thus be able to see her again. As soon as rehearsals were completed for *Romeo and Juliet,* they would open in Richmond before returning to Washington. What would transpire politically and militarily between now and then was anyone's guess, but Jordan was determined to go. She could not stay away. From Richmond or Laura, she could not tell.

The evening drew to a close as the clock in the hallway chimed the midnight hour. The guests were all paying their respects to the President and he joked and entertained them as they left. When Jordan and her father approached him, his face once again took on a heartfelt gratitude.

"Joshua, thank you again for your editorial in support of my handling of the Baltimore riots. Needless to say, the *Baltimore Sun* has not been as kind."

"You could do nothing less, sir," Joshua replied. "There are Southern sympathizers still existing within local, state, and even the Federal government. Spies are everywhere and they must be dealt with harshly."

At the mention of spies and their treatment, Lincoln glanced briefly at Jordan.

"Well, good night, sir, and thank you for your gracious hospitality." Joshua turned to accept his hat from a servant.

"I concur with my father's sentiments, Mr. Lincoln." Jordan shook the President's hand firmly. "I cannot recall a more delightful occasion."

Holding her hand in both of his, Lincoln looked so sad that Jordan felt her own heart lurch in sympathy.

"Miss Colfax," he whispered, "you must take great care of yourself.

And if there is anything you should need, you must not hesitate to call upon me."

Jordan was bewildered by his sentiment, but was thankful for his support. "I shall, sir, and if there is anything I can do for *you*, I am always at your service."

He shook his head. "You already have, Miss Colfax, you already have."

❖

Jordan headed for her dressing room, exhausted after a day of intense physical activity. Romeo required so much more from her than previous roles in terms of acting ability and physical duress, not to mention the need to remember she was playing a man. She was looking forward to a quiet meal at home and an early bedtime. Entering her dressing room, she was surprised to find Nell lounging casually on her settee, intently reading from her script.

"I thought you had left hours ago." Jordan removed her sword and laid it on the dressing table.

Nell dropped her script on the settee and stood. "Alas, my dear, I had nothing to go home to this evening."

She stepped to within inches of Jordan but did not touch her. Jordan's pulse quickened and she looked everywhere in the room but directly at Nell. She knew what Nell was doing, or about to do, and it excited her, yet she was oddly fearful as well. Each time she was around Nell, she felt a degree of insistence from her that she was unprepared for.

"I thought perhaps you might wish to join me in a quiet supper at my hotel." Nell wiped a smudge of rouge from Jordan's face with her thumb.

"Well, I'm rather tired this evening," Jordan said weakly. Her cheek tingled from the contact, and she could not help but imagine more. "I had planned to make an early night of it."

"As did I." Nell smiled.

Her voice had lowered measurably and her hand slid from Jordan's cheek, coming to rest on her shoulder. Her thumb rhythmically stroked the side of Jordan's neck as she drew even closer. Jordan struggled to keep an even breath, but her heart raced in anticipation. No longer tired, her body drummed a steady cadence.

"I am thoroughly enjoying our scenes together," Nell murmured. "Each time I see you in those breeches it inspires me to greater heights." Her eyes focused on Jordan's mouth and her hand slid from Jordan's shoulder to her waist. Slipping it around her, she drew Jordan to her so that their bodies pressed together. "In fact, I feel very inspired right now."

Jordan was spellbound as Nell's lips found hers, and just as before, the kiss left her legs weak and her skin damp. Taking a backward step, she leaned against her dressing table for support. Uncertain what to do with her hands, she placed them on Nell's hips. Nell responded by removing her hands from around Jordan's waist and trailing a deliberate path up Jordan's blouse to her breasts. Jordan let out an involuntary moan, but her body reacted violently to the touch and she immediately pushed away.

"I can't." She pressed a hand to her heart, trying to slow its beat.

"Oh, Jordan." Nell did not step away. "I know this is new for you, but believe me, in time you will understand how wonderful two women together can be."

"I…I'm sure, I don't know. But this is all too fast."

Nell smiled. "I understand, no need to feel embarrassed. There is a first time for everyone. When you're ready, I'll be waiting." She picked up her script from the settee and put her hand on the doorknob. "Don't make me wait too long, Jordan. I'm a very impatient woman."

Once the door had closed, Jordan collapsed onto the settee, unable to stand any longer. It frightened her that her body had reacted in ways she had never known. She now completely understood what it all meant, that she was somehow attracted to women, but there was something about Nell that did not seem right to her. Nell was a beautiful, desirable woman, a woman of the world who had known men and women intimately. The gossip in theatre circles implied sexual trysts in the United States as well as Europe. Jordan had even heard of a love affair with the wife of a Parisian physician who had committed suicide when Nell had ended their association. All of that intrigue left Jordan feeling dazed and uneasy.

Her mind conjured insistent memories of her time spent with Laura. Simply being around Laura made her feel happy and complete. She could spend hours in her company and never be bored; just being near her was enough. And that day at the picnic when they almost kissed, Jordan felt a passion ignite that was both exciting and tender.

She wanted to touch Laura, but also knew that she had to be gentle with her. Laura was so beautiful and fragile, Jordan wanted to protect her and care for her in a way that she did not feel with Nell. Jordan felt deeply and intensely about Laura, and she knew those feelings must be love.

There were just a few more weeks left of rehearsals before they opened the show in Richmond on the fifteenth of June.

Jordan could hardly wait to see Laura, but she was anxious as to how to proceed. What would she say to her? What did two women do together? She knew for certain how she felt about Laura, but did Laura love her as well? Just the thought that Laura would not feel the same way left a knot in Jordan's stomach.

❖

Jordan and her father left the New York Avenue Presbyterian Church on Sunday morning and walked out into the warm spring day. The fresh air brought welcome relief from the stuffy interior of the church, and they paused to greet acquaintances also exiting the building. Jordan caught a glimpse of the President and Mrs. Lincoln as they descended the stairs and upon seeing her, he smiled and waved. Mrs. Lincoln, having observed the exchange, gave Jordan a cool glance, then slipped her hand possessively in the crook of her husband's arm. They climbed into their carriage and the horses trotted briskly away.

"Well, my dear, would you care to join me for lunch?" Joshua Colfax asked. "I was thinking oysters at the Willard would be just the thing."

"All right," she replied, "but let's walk. It's such a lovely day, and after all that sitting I feel the need for a bit of exercise."

"Walking it is."

They headed down Fourteenth Street at a leisurely pace, without speaking, occasionally stopping to look at storefront displays or admiring the Sunday attire of passersby. Everywhere they looked, soldiers were hurrying to a particular destination or, like them, strolling through the city and appreciating the sights. Thousands had arrived in the city and taken over all the open spaces and parks in Washington so that one could scarcely go anywhere without seeing them drilling or marching. Howitzers too dominated the landscape, surrounding the

White House and the Washington Monument, and placed at all the main access roads leading in and out of the city. The brick ovens in the basement of the Capitol Building produced thousands of loaves of bread a day to feed them, and one could smell the aroma a mile away. Immediately following the bombardment of Fort Sumter, the city had been almost completely deserted in fear of the Rebel invasion; even the Willard had gone from a thousand guests to fifty. But now, with the military presence, confidence had been restored and the routine of daily and political life had begun to return to normal.

"I received a letter from Tyler yesterday," Joshua said.

"Oh?" Jordan sidestepped a puddle in her path. "What did he have to say?"

"He is coming home the end of this month after graduation. He has been offered a commission with the Second Cavalry."

"The cavalry," she murmured, "as he wished. I'm sure he is very happy. And I shall be glad to see him before I leave for Richmond."

Joshua frowned. "Why on earth are you planning to go there again? It could be very dangerous what with the predictions of an impending battle. If the two armies engage and the Rebels are routed, we should be in Richmond in quick order."

"Father, it is my work and I have signed a contract to be there. It is all perfectly safe, don't worry about me. If there is one thing I know, Southern gentlemen would not harm a lady."

"Speaking of Southern gentlemen," Joshua stopped walking in front of his newspaper office and glanced in, "Tyler said in his letter that Ransom St. Clair has decided to join the Southern cause."

Jordan froze, her heart tightening in her chest. She knew she should not be surprised by his decision, but it still caused her considerable pain knowing that the two men would be on opposite sides. The additional strain it placed on her friendship with Laura was indeterminate at the moment, but she knew its impact would be far-reaching. How much so she could only speculate.

"Did Tyler mention how he felt about that?"

"He said it was a personally heartbreaking moment for him in an already unspeakable time in our nation's history. Apparently Ransom was the worst shock for him, but other classmates of his also opted to go with the South." Joshua sighed. "What should have been a happy occasion for him has turned into a rather distressing event."

"I should think that if it comes to war and they face each other in battle, it will be an even more ghastly experience." Jordan continued walking. "I can only pray that they survive both the war and their friendship."

Chapter Thirteen

7 June, 1861

Dearest Laura,

Washington has become a veritable fortress since I arrived. Thousands of troops have poured into the city and completely taken it over. Everywhere one looks one sees the canvas tents and makeshift housing. Even the grounds surrounding the Washington Monument are covered with men and the cattle that go to feed them. The stench is unmistakable and is to be approached at one's peril!

General McDowell is collecting his multitude across the Potomac in Arlington in preparation for what may be the first major engagement of this conflict. So many of the young men I see in uniform are mere beardless boys, eager for their first fight but blissfully unaware that bullets also fly in the opposite direction. I take consolation from those wiser in military matters that this will be quick work and that these boys will be returning home when their 90-day enlistments are up, if not sooner. I get down on my knees each night and fervently pray that this is so.

I have been to a White House levee and was formally introduced to Mrs. Lincoln, having dined with Mr. Lincoln a few weeks ago. Mrs. Lincoln speaks fluent French, as I heard her speaking to the French Minister, and although I could not hear much that was said, he seemed quite taken with her. I wish you could have attended that night with me as the men and ladies, while elegantly attired, could not hold a candle to the officers resplendent in their uniforms, especially

General Scott, who is quite an imposing figure. You would have laughed at the other officers who preened and strutted in their efforts to curry favor with Mr. Lincoln or Secretary of War Cameron, but most likely General Scott. The young girls were all silly geese wishing the men would pay them as much attention as they did themselves.

I have missed your good counsel of late, even if I don't always agree. I truly desire to understand why the South wants to separate from the Union. Surely there must be an amicable solution. We want you to stay...I want you to stay. Leaving us is like cutting off our nose to spite our face. I hope if you have any influence over your father, you may convey one Yankee woman's feelings on the matter.

I hope you are well and that your health has improved steadily. I'm looking forward to returning to Richmond next week to begin rehearsals. We have had to replace some of our cast as so many men have left to join the army. I hope the stand-ins will be competent in their roles by the time we arrive.

Give my regards to Ransom and to the rest of your family as well.

With fondest affection,
Jordan

Laura reread the letter and happiness settled gently over her heart. Jordan would be returning in a few days and they would be able to enjoy each other's company once more, although with all that was going on in the city she hoped that they would find the time. The ladies of Richmond had formed sewing circles and other group activities in support of the war effort. Clothing, shoes, food, and supplies were being hurriedly manufactured and most women were engaged in making pies, bread, preserves, and all manner of food to feed the men already in the city. Some even opened their homes, inviting soldiers to join them at table on a regular basis. Additionally, they provided beds to soldiers who had succumbed to illness while away from home, the likely culprits being measles, chicken pox, mumps, and whooping cough. The lack of hospital facilities had led to overcrowding, and every building and many homes housed at least one soldier either ill or recuperating.

But the most significant news lately had been the announcement that the capital of the Confederacy would be relocated from Montgomery to Richmond, where it was anticipated the main thrust of the North would be focused. The Confederate Congress believed that the government could not operate effectively in directing military operations unless it was close to the main body of the army. Laura was thankful to have her parents back home and in control of Barrett Hall once more. While the tobacco had been successfully planted and was in fact already a foot high, Laura had grown weary of her responsibilities on the plantation and was glad to have returned to Richmond where all the excitement was. She could hardly wait for Jordan to arrive.

Putting the letter in her desk drawer, she descended the stairs and entered the parlor where her mother, Meg, and several Richmond ladies were engaged in sewing.

"It is good to see the Brockenbrough residence put to such use," Mrs. Wilson observed. "The President's home should be a splendid abode and have ample room for entertaining."

"I cannot tell you what a relief it is to have the capital located here in Richmond," Rachel St. Clair announced. "I should have perished to stay another day in Montgomery. I'm sure Mrs. President Davis will have the loveliest of parties in that house. She is a very smart woman and has excellent taste."

"I would think, Mother," Laura said as she sat down and resumed work on the shirt sleeve she had been working on, "that the parties will be held to a minimum in honor of the soldiers and people of the Confederacy who are making sacrifices to the cause. What would it say to them to have festive galas going on while the people were sending their sons off to war?"

"Why, Laura, are we not sitting here right now working very hard to contribute to that cause?" Mrs. Dunne inquired. "And if we are to be the center of a new government, then we should act like one. My husband says that we must impress the British representatives in town as much as possible so that they view us in a positive light if we are to win their support. And we all know how the British enjoy a splendidly given party."

A general murmur of agreement spread among the other ladies in the room.

"I have only been to one such party in my entire life," Meg chimed in. "I should like to go to many more, as that is where the young officers shall be. Now that all the men have gone off to join the army, there are no opportunities to socialize with them anymore."

"Now, Meg, your turn will come," Rachel scolded. "Do not be in such a hurry. After all, it is Laura who shall be next to marry, and hopefully that event will be occurring soon." She stared at Laura to indicate her desire that it be sooner and not later. "By the way, Laura, have you heard from Mr. Young lately?"

Laura wished she had remained upstairs in her room. "No, Mother. As you know, I was ill for a while, and I believe his business brought him here while I was at Barrett Hall. There was no occasion for us to speak." Seeing Ruby pass by and wanting to change the subject, she called, "Ruby, might we have more tea, please? I believe this has gone cold."

"Yes, I could use a bit more tea and more of those pastries with the cherries, if you have them," Mrs. Wilson directed Ruby. "I know I should not allow myself to have one more of those, but they are so tasty, Rachel. You are very lucky to have such a fine cook."

The other ladies in the room glanced uncomfortably at one another, knowing the St. Clair cook, Martha, was not a topic that Rachel enjoyed discussing.

Realizing her faux pas, Mrs. Wilson pressed on to another subject. "I understand that General Beauregard is here in town to direct the army. I must say that I feel quite safe having him here. As commander, he will make short work of the Yankees, as he did in Charleston. And you must admit he is quite handsome."

"My husband says he is a most sagacious and capable man," Mrs. Dunne stated. "Mr. Dunne is trying to obtain a staff position for our son and I do so hope he is successful. I cannot bear to see him serve on the front lines."

"Ransom is to arrive home next week," Rachel declared proudly. "He'll be joining the cavalry under Congressman Stuart's son, Jeb. He is most anxious to be where he can do the most good."

"Are you not afraid that he will be injured or maimed? Or, God forbid, killed?" Mrs. Dunne fanned herself lightly.

"Of course I am. But Ransom did not attend West Point to join a general's staff in order to avoid fighting. He is doing his duty and I am proud of him. I only regret that I have but one son to give to my country."

The front door opened and Edward St. Clair entered the house. Striding immediately into the parlor, he removed his hat and bowed to the ladies seated there. "Ladies, I have a most wonderful announcement to make. There has been a battle at Big Bethel and the Yankees have been soundly defeated."

The commotion of the ladies led quickly to spontaneous dancing in the parlor.

"Were there casualties?" Mrs. Wilson asked breathlessly.

"As far as I know of the reports so far, only one Confederate loss and a handful injured."

"Glory to God," Mrs. Dunne exclaimed, "for surely He watches over the Confederacy."

"That is such good news"—Rachel hugged him—"especially after the embarrassment at Philippi. It will go a long way to showing those Yankees that we are a force to be reckoned with."

"Oh, I wish I could see Ransom's face when he hears." Meg clapped her hands.

"Yes," Laura agreed, "I'm sure he wishes he were in the thick of things rather than the dull duty he has in the Shenandoah Valley."

Edward St. Clair laughed. "Can you imagine if he were with Beauregard now, up at Manassas Junction? He would be chafing at the bit, being so close and yet unable to participate."

Laura felt the same way as Mrs. Dunne. She was happy that Ransom was away in the Valley and safe from all the killing going on. According to rumor, the Yankees might soon be marching to engage Beauregard as well. She was thankful Ransom would be elsewhere if that occurred. The farther from bloodshed he was, the more soundly she could sleep at night.

❖

Jordan had just finished packing all she would need to take with her to Richmond when there was a knock on her door. "Come in!" she called out.

Joshua Colfax entered, his spectacles sitting atop his head and a newspaper dangling between his fingers. "So you still intend to go." He watched as she buckled her carpetbag.

"Yes, Mr. Ford has obtained the necessary passes to get us through the lines. I doubt we'll have any trouble from the Rebels since they are the ones to benefit from the production. And now with most of the cast made up of women, I should think they will be very happy to see us."

He gazed at her quizzically. "I can't quite understand why you so ardently wish to go south. I thought you hated them and all they stood for."

Jordan's face flushed hot. "I do hate them! I hope General McDowell trounces those traitors quickly and harshly and sends them reeling so deeply south that they never venture into Northern Virginia again."

"Then why do you wish to give comfort to them by performing in *Romeo and Juliet*? Why don't you stay home and entertain our soldiers?"

Jordan still felt uncomfortable at not having told her father about her true motivations for agreeing to go to Richmond. But she rationalized that he would needlessly worry about her when he should rightly reserve his concerns for Tyler.

"I've told you, Father, I am under contract and I always keep my promises."

He sighed and shook his head. "Well then, be careful, my dear. I will still be able to reach you at the Broad Street Hotel as usual?"

"As usual." She smiled affectionately, then kissed his cheek. "I'm off to the theatre to ensure all my things there are packed and loaded onto the train. Then let's have dinner at home tonight, shall we? I have asked Mrs. Johnson to prepare roast pork for Tyler's departure tomorrow."

"Excellent idea," he said. "After all, Tyler's last meal at home for a while should be something special. Camp food will not compare to what Mrs. Johnson makes. At least I won't worry about you. Once you're in Richmond, you should be perfectly safe."

Jordan smiled sadly. *If you only knew.*

❖

When Jordan arrived at the theatre, the last crate was being hammered closed and the trunk latches tightened for their journey south. Bill O'Malley was shouting and cursing at a team of mules that balked at the heavy load they bore, effectively blocking the alleyway. Jordan sidestepped the chaos and entered her dressing room. She had been in there only a short while when the door opened and Kate Warne entered, followed by the man President Lincoln had identified as Allan Pinkerton.

"Good afternoon, Jordan," Kate greeted. "I would like to introduce—"

"There is no need of formal introductions, Kate," Pinkerton said, a slight Scottish accent apparent in his speech, "Miss Colfax and I know who each other are. It is a pleasure, though, to finally make your acquaintance."

"And to what do I owe this pleasure, Mr. Pinkerton?"

He smiled. "You get right to the point, Miss Colfax. I like that. So then, I shan't delay you any more than possible. I see you are very busy. May we sit?"

Jordan gestured to the settee in her room, and she sat at her dressing table.

"First of all, Miss Colfax," he said, removing his bowler hat and sitting down, "I must emphasize that the information I'm about to impart to you must be held in the strictest of confidences. Given what you have done for us so far, I trust that it shall pose no problem for you."

Jordan smiled briefly.

"We, that is to say me and my associates, are investigating a suspected spy within this city who we believe is transmitting top-secret information to the Rebel government. This spy is well known within the highest social circles of Washington and has access to and influence over both military and political figures in every sector of government."

"Who is this cursed individual?" she asked angrily. "Tell me his name, perhaps my father knows of him."

"It is not a he, Jordan," Kate Warne interposed, "but a she."

Jordan was surprised. It hadn't occurred to her that another woman would be involved in such activity.

"We are observing her night and day." Pinkerton leaned forward in his seat. "What we do not know, Miss Colfax, is what information she has already passed along to the Rebels. It is well known that there is soon to be an engagement between the two armies. If she has given the enemy any succor, the results could be devastating for us."

"And what is it, Mr. Pinkerton, that you want from me?" Jordan asked.

He sat back in his seat, indicating Kate at his side. "I have received the intelligence from Miss Warne that you have collected in Richmond.

You have specifically gathered information from an aide to Jefferson Davis, Mr. Edward St. Clair, is that correct?"

Jordan nodded.

"I believe that it is possible, given what you have provided us, that Mr. St. Clair may be privy to this information. He is a military aide to Mr. Davis and thus perhaps aware of what this woman has provided their government. If they know what our army is up to, we need to know so that General McDowell can alter his plans. What I need, Miss Colfax, is for you to gain access once again to Mr. St. Clair's office to obtain whatever you can find with respect to this ill-gotten information, their military intentions, and anything else you might come across. Do you think you can do that?"

Jordan shifted uncomfortably. The only reason she was able to gather that information in the first place was by taking advantage of Laura's illness and thereby gaining almost unhindered access to her father's office and private files. To attempt to do so at the St. Clair home in Richmond, with the entire family present, would be almost impossible. She wasn't sure if she could duplicate her previous performance, but when she thought of Tyler facing the Rebel army at a disadvantage, she set her doubts aside.

"I'll do my best, Mr. Pinkerton."

"That is all we can ask of you, Miss Colfax."

As they rose to leave, Jordan stopped them one last time. "Mr. Pinkerton, may I ask what will happen to her, the spy, if you establish that she is in fact spying?"

His eyes turned hard and gray. "She will be taken to Capitol Prison. After that, it will be up to the government to decide her fate." He paused at the door. "Good luck, Miss Colfax."

❖

The train chugged slowly into Richmond after several delays along the route. Their luggage as well as their persons had been searched on several occasions by Rebel soldiers who inquired as to their business in the city. One particular search caused Bill O'Malley to become irate with the constant intrusions, and it was only when a captain recognized Jordan from one of her roles that they were allowed to continue on their way.

Jordan stepped down onto the platform and stretched, relieved to have finally arrived in the city, and glanced nervously about her. The platform was crowded with Rebel soldiers in all manner of uniform: blue, gray, and butternut, with a variety of insignias, hats, guns, and other paraphernalia. She recognized the cadet uniforms worn by West Point graduates as well as those from the Virginia Military Institute. It angered her that these very men could switch allegiance so readily while still adorned with uniforms of the schools that had so recently provided soldiers for the United States Army.

"Jordan, lass, me and the boys will be waiting for the wagons to haul the equipment to the theatre. Why don' you and the rest go to the hotel. We'll be getting an early start in the morning." Bill deftly shifted his cigar to the other side of his mouth.

"For once I won't argue with you, Bill." Jordan yawned.

The other actors stumbled one by one toward her, and they assembled and sorted through their luggage. Jordan was about to lead them toward the hotel when a voice from the not-too-distant past abruptly reintroduced itself.

"Well, now, if it isn't the Yankee she-devil."

Everyone in her group gazed over her shoulder, and Jordan whirled around to find George Lamont standing behind her.

"Hello, George." She forced herself not to take a step back. She was surprised to see him dressed in uniform, the rank of sergeant on his sleeve. "Why, it would appear that you possess the necessary faculties for the military after all, George. Are you on the way to the front even now?"

He sneered in her face. "I'm here to pick up a few Yankee scum who were stupid enough to get themselves caught up at Big Bethel. Then I'm taking them to Belle Isle, where they'll spend the rest of the war."

"A prison guard," Jordan spat. "I might have known. It suits your temperament perfectly, George, and keeps you away from the fighting, too. I'm sure you feel very courageous wearing the colors of a brave man."

A line of bedraggled soldiers led by a guard carrying a shotgun shuffled their way along the platform. They stopped in front of the theatre party while the guard and George Lamont spoke to each other. One of the prisoners, a young man with a bandage wrapped around his head, glanced pitifully at Jordan. When she returned his gaze, he quickly looked away, seemingly embarrassed by his predicament.

Jordan wanted to comfort the man and tell him not to give up hope. But after a few moments, the guard shouted for them to move on and George Lamont fell in step behind them.

As he passed her, George's stare became sly. In an insinuating tone, he said, "I'll be seeing you."

"Not if I have anything to say about it," Jordan replied. But a chill ran through her despite the warm day, and she watched as they marched away down Broad Street.

Chapter Fourteen

Laura sat in the back of the darkened theatre observing the rehearsal. Despite the closeness of the air in the warmth of mid-June, she found herself lost in the performances, especially Jordan's as Romeo. In her scenes with Juliet, played by that horrid Nell Tabor, an odd feeling crept over Laura, and she was annoyed when the director constantly interrupted them to give instructions. She had never seen a woman dressed as a man before, let alone performing the role of a man. Jordan looked remarkably at ease in her costume, carrying herself with a lithe confidence that seemed effortless. Laura supposed she must have studied the demeanor of men so that she would be convincing in her role. It was strange to see her wearing male attire as if she was born to it, and that she could see Jordan's legs so plainly was a shock. The breeches that ended just above her knees accentuated her slender figure and the shapeliness of her calves. And the draping silk blouse that fell open at her throat exposed Jordan's graceful neck and pale skin.

Laura took a deep breath as Romeo and Juliet shared a tender look. Nell's flirtation with Jordan infuriated her, but she tried to attribute their behavior to the demands of the play. Thankfully, she hadn't had to endure more than a few such scenes in this rehearsal. Nell's conduct after rehearsals was much more difficult to bear. Her hands were always on Jordan, her bosom was always catching Jordan's eye, and she seemed to dismiss Laura's presence as inconsequential. Nell spoke to her as though she were a child, and sometimes it seemed that Jordan did the same. Her voice softened and her tone was mild and tender. She reserved her sharp, playful banter for the woman who kissed her.

Laura caught at her bottom lip with her teeth. She didn't want to think about that incident ever again, yet the kiss played over and over in her mind as she watched the "lovers" in Shakespeare's tragedy. She almost wept with relief when the director finally called a halt and announced rehearsal times for the next day. The actors wandered off the stage, and the workers swarmed on to finish constructing the sets.

Stepping down off the stage into the theatre, Jordan was surprised to see Laura sitting in a row midway down the aisle, her hand propping up her cheek as she leaned into the chair in front of her. A powerful surge of happiness swept through her and, stopping in front of Laura, she bowed.

"See how she leans her cheek upon her hand! O, that I were a glove upon that hand, that I might touch that cheek!"

Laura blushed and, without thinking, replied, "My bounty is as boundless as the sea, my love as deep; the more I give to thee, the more I have, for both are infinite."

Jordan was momentarily speechless, her heart fluttering. "Had I but known," she said, lowering her voice, "I should have recommended you to the director. I fear Miss Tabor does no small injustice to the part of Juliet." Glancing quickly over her shoulder, she leaned into Laura and whispered, "But don't tell her I said so."

Laura laughed. Being near Jordan blanketed her with contentment, and the small slight to Miss Tabor's skill pleased her immensely.

"You have the makings of an actress, Laura. A natural ability."

"You think so?" Laura was thrilled by the compliment. From Jordan, it meant a lot. Laura felt certain she was too honest to indulge in cheap flattery.

"Yes, I do." With a reflective expression, Jordan said, "Perhaps I can help you after all."

"Oh, Jordan, if you only would."

"Let me go change, and then would you care to join me for an early dinner?"

Laura could not help but glance down at Jordan's legs.

Jordan caught her glance and for the first time since donning the outfit, she felt strangely shy. "Would you like to see what goes on behind the curtain?" she asked, trying to shift the conversation in another direction.

"I would love to." Laura smiled. "It must take a lot of work to create the fantasy that goes on in a play."

They threaded their way around furniture and costumes while Jordan informed her of the purposes of each. Running into the theatre manager, she introduced Laura, then left her with him and excused herself.

"I'll be in my dressing room," she said, indicating a darkly painted door along a narrow hallway.

For several minutes Laura conversed with Mr. O'Malley about his job and Mr. Ford's theatre, but she found her attention wandering to the painted door. When an opportune moment arose, she said, "How very fascinating it must be. Do please excuse me, Mr. O'Malley. There's something I must mention to Miss Colfax before it slips my mind."

Jordan barely had a chance to react when she heard the slight tap at her door, and Laura entered. Hugging the silk blouse she'd just removed to her chest, she flushed hotly.

"Oh. I'm sorry. Forgive me." Laura's gaze darted everywhere but to Jordan's half-naked torso.

A tingling sensation crawled beneath Jordan's skin, making her body prickle all over. She reached for the dressing gown hanging from a hook next to her mirror and quickly slipped it on, then gathered the rest of her clothes and stepped behind her screen. She usually changed behind the small decorative barrier just in case she was intruded upon.

Laura apologized again, mortified at her own lack of discretion. She had not expected to find Jordan removing her garments in plain sight in a place so very public. The door was not locked, as Laura would have expected under the circumstances. She supposed people in the theatre business were more casual about matters of decorum. Perhaps they waited at a closed door after knocking, and did not rush into a dressing room without permission.

"Make yourself at home," Jordan called to her in a voice that seemed strained. "Tell me what you think of the play so far."

"Thank you." Laura stared at the screen. Jordan should have been changing her clothes behind it since she was here without a maid, then Laura would not have seen her partially undressed, embarrassing both of them so dreadfully. Unsettled, she sat at Jordan's dressing table and occupied her nervous hands by examining various makeup containers, wigs, and other articles of interest.

Making a determined effort to dispel the tension between them, she said, "I think you are a most dashing Romeo. Where did you learn your swordplay? It looks terribly dangerous. You could easily injure yourself." She picked up a bottle, removed its top, and sniffed it hesitantly.

"Actually, I had Tyler teach me," Jordan said. "As children we were forever entertaining ourselves, sometimes even pretending to be soldiers. Then when he went to West Point and actually learned how to use his sword, I had him show me." She removed her breeches and stepped into her petticoat.

"I've watched Ransom practice his swordplay, and it all seems terribly complicated." Laura realized she held a bottle of Jordan's perfume and she dabbed a tiny amount on the inside of her wrist. She inhaled deeply, closing her eyes at the warm sensation it gave her.

"I certainly did not learn all the steps required of a West Point cadet, just enough for the stage so as to be believable." Jordan tied her corset as best she could, knowing that she would never look as tiny at the waist as Laura. Just the thought of Laura's delicate features made her pulse race.

"Well, you make it all look utterly believable to me," Laura insisted. "And not just the swordplay. I, for one, believe that you are indeed Romeo."

Realizing what she had said, Laura was glad that Jordan could not see the deep blush that rose to her face. If Jordan were a man, she would never be in the dressing room right now, in fact would never be alone with him at all. And in contrast to her shyness around men, Laura felt completely at ease with Jordan. With the exception of Ransom and Charlotte, she could not recall when she had felt so at ease with another person. She never had to pretend to be anyone but herself. And yet she felt the stirrings of something deep inside that she had only read about in books, the sort of feelings that writers described as the feelings a woman in love would have for a man. Surprised at the realization, Laura breathed deeply to keep herself from fainting dead away. How was it possible that this could be so? How could she ever tell Jordan such a thing? Recalling the emotions she'd felt at the picnic, Laura knew that Jordan felt something for her as well. But how they would ever come to terms with it was beyond her.

Jordan stepped from behind the screen and smiled at Laura. "Shall we?"

❖

They strolled down Broad toward the Capitol and cut across the grounds on their way to the Exchange Hotel. It was a warm evening and the sun was beginning to set, casting long shadows on the grass and streets. They were content simply walking side by side without speaking, enjoying the slight breeze. After a while, Laura linked her arm in Jordan's. Jordan glanced down and smiled at her and Laura could not help but feel...*safe*. She could not think of another word to describe the comfortable familiarity she felt when they were together. Despite their differences, she felt closer to Jordan than she did even to Charlotte. There was no other friend she would rather be with.

Entering the hotel, they made their way into the dining room and were seated at a table in the corner. The waiter immediately arrived and, recognizing Jordan, fawned over them throughout the meal.

"So how is your family, are they well?" Jordan asked over coffee.

"Very well, thank you, and how is your father?"

"He's very busy. There is so much going on that he struggles with what to leave out of his paper." Jordan paused, hesitating to discuss more sensitive issues. "And Ransom?"

Laura lowered her gaze and picked at the remains of her dessert with her fork.

"He is fine. Happy, of course, to be in the cavalry, but frustrated to be in the Valley and removed from all the excitement up north." She placed her fork on the plate. "Everyone believes that if there is to be a major battle, it will occur soon, somewhere between here and Washington. Tyler is with McDowell's army, is he not?"

Jordan swallowed. She tried not to think of Tyler's involvement in what most likely would be the great conflict that would decide the fate of the Union. "Yes," she whispered, and then her anger flared at the helplessness she felt at stopping the inevitable. "If anything should happen to him, though, I shall hold Jeff Davis personally accountable for his murder."

Laura paled, and they fell silent.

As the seconds passed, Laura could not think what to say. The pleasantness of the evening faded as a tight knot formed in her stomach. She hated their disagreements and dearly wished that they were not of opposite minds on this sensitive subject. She was about to defend the Southern position, but realized that when it came to Tyler's life, there would be no justification in Jordan's mind. Ransom's life was equally precious to Laura, and she knew that if anything happened to him, she would not know what to do. The thought of that possibility made her eyes fill, and a single, heavy teardrop plummeted down her cheek.

Chastened by the sight of Laura's tears, Jordan felt her anger dissipate rapidly. She covered Laura's hand with her own, gently caressing it with her thumb. "I'm sorry," she murmured, mentally kicking herself for inflicting such pain on someone she cared for so deeply. "Please, forgive me?"

Laura gazed into Jordan's eyes, instantly remorseful at having caused the anguish evident there. Her heart ached with the need to hold her and comfort her. She turned her palm upward, interlocking their fingers and placing her other hand over them both.

"It's all right," she whispered. "I pray that God will watch over them both and protect them from harm, but if something should happen to either one of them, I know that I could not bear to lose you, for surely my heart would break."

Jordan could not look away. Despite her efforts to the contrary, her feelings for Laura had only grown stronger since she left Barrett Hall. When they were apart, she found herself thinking of her, wishing that she could talk to Laura about her thoughts and desires, counting the days until they were together again. Her mind turned to the important task before her, finding out what the Rebels knew of McDowell's army. How could she betray Laura's trust? She had no choice if she was to acquire the secrets locked away in her father's office. Perhaps if she confided in her, convinced her of the rightness of her own cause and the hopelessness of the Southern cause, Laura might work with her to prevent what would surely be a bloody and successful repulse of the Rebel army.

"Laura, I—"

"Why, Laura, and Miss Colfax, how glad I am to find you here."

Startled, relinquishing their handhold, they glanced up to find Rachel St. Clair standing beside their table, accompanied by Preston Young. Jordan noted the angry glare Laura's mother cast on her daughter, and her protective instincts came to bear as she watched Laura physically cringe at the withering appraisal.

"Good evening, Mrs. St. Clair, Mr. Young. We were just finishing our meal, but you are more than welcome to join us for coffee."

Rachel held up her hand. "Thank you, Miss Colfax, but Mr. Young and I would like to speak with Laura, alone, if you don't mind."

Jordan cast a glance toward Laura, letting her know that she was perfectly willing to stay and defend her.

Laura gave her a feeble smile. "Jordan, I very much enjoyed our dinner this evening. Perhaps I will see you later in the week?"

The hopeful tremor in her voice shook Jordan's resolve to leave politely. She struggled with an urge to sweep Laura from her chair and tell Rachel they had other plans and she would have to make do without her daughter. But that would not do. Forcing a calm she did not feel, she said, "I would be happy to call on you Thursday afternoon for tea."

"Unfortunately, Miss Colfax, Laura has a prior engagement then," Rachel interrupted. "I think it best if she calls on you at some future date. And don't worry about the meal. I'll be happy to take care of it."

Jordan glanced from Laura to her mother and back again, reluctant to leave Laura alone with what would most likely be a very unpleasant encounter. But Laura decided for her.

"Good night, Jordan. I shall call on you soon."

Hesitating briefly, Jordan rose from the table and stepped away. Mrs. St. Clair claimed her seat and Preston Young selected a chair next to Laura. When Mrs. St. Clair began talking, clearly ignoring her presence, Jordan exited the dining room, sick at heart for what Laura would endure.

❖

The days dragged by and Jordan heard nothing from Laura. Her performances at rehearsal had been flat and the director admonished her for the lackluster display. To make matters worse, she had received a coded message in her dressing room from Kate Warne, pressing her on the need for all due haste in obtaining badly needed intelligence about the Rebels. When news of the death of Elizabeth Barrett Browning reached her on the twenty-third of June, her first thought was for Laura. She was consumed with worry for her and made a call on Church Hill, but she was turned away by a servant who claimed Laura was not at home. Leaving her calling card on a previous occasion had resulted in no return visit on Laura's part, so Jordan was frustrated as she returned to her carriage.

On the drive back to her hotel, she tried to think of a way to get into the St. Clair home. She needed to see how Laura was faring. It almost mattered nothing to her that she was also supposed to gain entry to Edward St. Clair's study. She stopped at the front desk on her way through the hotel, asking for a bath to be drawn for her in her room. If she could only relax and clear her mind, perhaps she would devise a plan to succeed on both counts. She climbed the stairs to her room and, opening the door, was shocked to discover Laura seated at the small writing desk in her room.

"Jordan!" Laura ran to her and threw her arms around Jordan's neck.

Stunned, Jordan held her tightly. At the press of Laura's body against her own, a warmth and a trembling sensation made her want to hold Laura in her arms forever. An emotion gripped her that she hadn't experienced before. When she felt the tremors course through Laura's body and felt the hot tears on her neck, she clung to her even more, soothing her with soft whispers and caresses. And when the tremors turned to sobs, Jordan kissed Laura's temple, her cheek, her eyes, and then, desperately, she sought her lips.

Instantly Laura quieted. At first, they both ceased moving, their eyes open, but unseeing. Then, ever so imperceptibly, their lips moved against each other's, softly, tentatively, inquisitively, their eyes fluttering closed. There was no sound or thought, only the feel of supple, slightly moist lips exploring and questioning. Jordan tasted the salty tears on Laura's mouth and ached at the thought of the pain that caused them. She increased the pressure on Laura's lips, wanting her to feel how much she wanted to take that pain away. But when she did, Laura stopped her and pushed her away.

They stared at one another. Laura's heart pounded and the blood rushed through her ears so loudly she could hear nothing else. She felt dizzy and scared and excited simultaneously. She was confused and could not collect herself to think clearly about what had happened. Part of her wanted to run from the room, the other wanted to continue kissing Jordan. Her entire body shook violently and she thought she might faint where she stood. Grabbing hold of the bedpost to prevent herself from collapsing, she sat on the edge of the bed. Deep, slow breaths helped to calm her nerves and eventually her heart rate returned to normal. Jordan had not moved from her spot on the floor and continued to stare at her with an expression she could not plainly decipher.

"Laura..." Jordan began, her voice barely audible. Unable to think of anything to say after that, she let the word hang in the air, a plea awaiting response.

Laura opened her mouth but nothing came out. She could find no words to string together to form a coherent sentence. Visions of Jordan and Nell Tabor kissing in the gardens of the President's house crowded her thoughts.

Jordan was the first to recover. "What happened? With your mother and Mr. Young, I mean." She hoped she could get Laura to talk by steering the conversation toward a topic that did not involve the two of them.

Recalling why she had come to Jordan's room in the first place, Laura felt her eyes fill to overflowing. "I am engaged to Mr. Young after all," she choked. "Oh, Jordan, everything is so hopeless. I simply cannot go on."

"What?" Jordan's legs felt weak. "How can that be?"

"My mother convinced him that I had temporarily taken leave of my senses, that my behavior was the shyness of a bride-to-be. Our wedding is set for September." The reality of her plight sank in again, but this time she had no more tears; in fact, she was devoid of any emotion whatsoever. She felt dead inside.

Jordan reeled. She had thought the prospect of an engagement was firmly in Laura's past. Staggered that it had reasserted itself, especially now, she said, "You must go to your mother immediately, and if she will not listen, then you must tell Mr. Young that under no circumstances will you marry him."

Laura watched as Jordan paced, jaw set and firm. She wished she had her strength and determination. But then, Jordan did not have to deal constantly with Rachel St. Clair. "I'm afraid it's too late for that, Jordan," she said miserably. "It is my fate. If not him, then someone else would take his place."

Jordan strode forward, seized Laura by the shoulders and shook her roughly. "Laura, you must not give up. Stand up to your mother and tell her you cannot go forward with this marriage. If you wish, I'll come with you and help."

"And if she insists?" Laura asked, searching Jordan's eyes for something she was not certain even she knew. "I have nowhere to go and cannot live there forever. I would not be able to endure her wrath, which would surely be forthcoming. Even my father would disown me if I chose to disobey her. It is simply not possible, Jordan."

"Then run away," Jordan insisted. "I can help you."

Laura stared at her. "Help me? Help me to do what? I have no skills and I would not take charity from you, Jordan." Sounding harsh even to her own ears, she softened her tone. "Thank you, Jordan, truly. You are a very good friend. But I'm afraid that this is something I must endure alone."

Hearing the surrender in Laura's voice deflated Jordan. She could do nothing on her own if Laura was unwilling to act. Releasing her hold on Laura's shoulders, she sat wearily on the bed next to her, unable to look at her. Distraught, not just on Laura's account but also on her own, she stared at a snag in the rug at her feet.

When Laura saw the defeat in Jordan's body, she was all the more disheartened that she had caused it. Resting her hand on Jordan's thigh, she stared at the rug as well, hoping to find an answer in the swirl and mazes of the Oriental design.

They sat on the edge of the bed for some time, as the sun made its inescapable descent toward the horizon, draining light from the room. Jordan felt the searing heat of Laura's hand, and though she wanted to shift away from her, she held her breath, not wanting Laura to remove the source of this exquisite contact. Finally, as if by tacit agreement, Laura stood.

"I must go," she said in a voice leaden with sorrow. "I slipped out when Mother and Meg went shopping for our dinner party tomorrow evening. They'll be back soon."

"Of course." Jordan rose.

"Thank you for listening and for being such a good friend. I am certain that I would be mad by now were it not for your kind friendship."

Laura kissed Jordan on the cheek. She had been struggling for the longest time against doing so, but she thought that the cheek would be an innocent gesture. Drawing back slowly, she stopped when Jordan's gaze burned deeply into her. Her breath caught and she felt her heart hammering in her chest at Jordan's intent expression. She wanted to run from the room, afraid of what her heart felt but her mind refused to acknowledge. Jordan neared slowly and Laura felt herself drawn like a butterfly to a flower. When they were inches away from each other, her willpower deserted her and she once again felt Jordan's soft lips on her own.

Jordan marveled at the tenderness of Laura's lips, and the power of the physical and emotional sensations that assaulted her. She could not stop, could not help herself, but fell hopelessly into the abyss that had opened in her heart. After an eternity they separated, seeking in each other's eyes an explanation for what was happening.

Laura crossed the room as though in a dream and opened the door, then slowly pivoted and gazed longingly at Jordan.

"Good night, Jordan," she said, and closed the door behind her.

Jordan listened to the sound of Laura's footsteps receding down the hallway. She wanted to run to the door and fling it open, to beg Laura not to leave. Instead she sat as quietly as possible, straining to hear any sound of hope that Laura was not disappearing from her life forever.

Chapter Fifteen

Jordan took refuge in her mission. Kate Warne had asked her to assess the numbers of soldiers arriving in Richmond, so having no appetite for breakfast, she wandered down Broad Street in time to see the morning train from Hazel Run lumber heavily along the platform. Most of its occupants were soldiers, presumably arriving for the defense of Richmond. Still more soldiers boarded the train for unknown destinations. She kept a rough tally of those coming and going, depressed at the sight of numerous young men in a variety of uniforms including that of the Rebel army.

Since Davis's call for volunteers from the states of the Confederacy, she had hoped that the average citizen of the South would come to his senses and refuse to join. She was sadly disappointed at not only the large quantity of men flocking to the call, but also the enthusiasm with which they supported the cause. At the onset of the rebellion, she'd felt such confidence not only in the rightness of the Northern position, but also in their ability to defeat those in revolt. Seeing now how strongly the South felt, as evidenced by the number of soldiers before her, made her doubt the predicted brevity of war.

"Jordan!" A man approached her bench wearing the long gray frock coat of a cavalry officer. As he tipped his broad-brimmed hat, the black plume floated a little in the morning breeze.

"Ransom." Jordan started guiltily.

She felt transparent in her objectives, standing on a platform for no apparent reason. She was meeting no one and did not plan to travel. What was she supposed to say to explain her presence—that she enjoyed the grinding screech of train wheels and the smell of oil and hot iron?

Ransom didn't seem to notice as he kissed her gloved hand and asked the question she dreaded. "What brings you to the station? Are you returning to Washington?"

"No, I was simply taking a walk and decided to rest here awhile." She hoped her voice held a note of casual conviction. "My play opens tonight at the Marshall and I thought I'd clear my mind beforehand."

"Then I'll be delighted to escort you on your stroll," Ransom said cheerfully.

With a feeling of helpless gloom, Jordan took in the gauntlets tucked into his belt, his cavalry saber, and the Sharps carbine slung over his shoulder. He was ready for war, young and full of belief. Jordan could not beg him to go far away and have no part in this madness, so she said, "I don't mind my own company, and I'm sure your family will be thrilled to see you. I won't keep you from them a moment longer."

"Actually, my homecoming will be a surprise to them as I'm arriving a day early. At the last minute I was able to get a two-day pass, so there was no time to notify them. I can't wait to see their faces, and to get a home-cooked meal."

"Well, do please give your parents my regards and your sister my fond affection. I have enjoyed her company at rehearsals these past days." Her throat drying, she managed a farewell smile and started to walk away when Ransom came after her.

"Wait, Jordan, if you've nothing better to do, why don't you come along? We could take a carriage ride down by the river, invite Laura along and pack a picnic. Make a day out of it. What do you say?"

Jordan didn't know what to say. She knew it would be appropriate for her to decline. This was surely a difficult time and Jordan wanted to help Laura, not interfere in her life in such a way that she caused confusion and upset. She had a feeling her presence only made matters worse for Laura, making it harder for her to feel the necessary resolve in her decision to marry. Jordan had offered her an alternative, the possibility of a different future. But how realistic was it to imagine that Laura could become an actress and live independently? She had not been raised for such a life and perhaps Jordan had been wrong to suggest it. Perhaps her motivations had been more selfish than she'd admitted.

She desperately wanted to see Laura again, and she wanted to do the right thing for her. If that meant telling her to forget their conversation and accept her future as a wife to Mr. Young, then that was the duty of a good friend. Her mind leapt to their embrace in her hotel room, and she tried to reconcile the urges she'd felt with the affection of one friend for another. She wondered if Laura had felt the same urges and was now similarly perplexed. She wished she could discuss what had transpired between them with Laura. There was no one else she could confide in, and she was certain Laura would not dream of discussing that event with her mother or any other lady.

"Jordan?" Ransom's violet eyes held the same warmth and candor she'd so often seen in Laura's.

"I don't know. I don't know if I can." She tried to think of an excuse to decline, but her mind stubbornly refused to cooperate.

"Nonsense!" Ransom took her arm, slinging his haversack over his shoulder. "From the letters I've received from Laura, I can see she has grown fond of you. She would be furious with me if I did not invite you back to the house. What time do you need to be at the theatre?"

"About seven, but—"

"Perfect, plenty of time for a drive in the country, then. It's less than ten miles outside Richmond, so I should have you back long before you need to be there."

His pull on her arm, and the tug of her own yearnings, was irresistible and she fell into step with him.

❖

"She is a dreadful influence upon you," Rachel St. Clair rebuked her daughter as she threaded her needle. "It's improper for you to spend time with her, let alone be seen in public together. She is, after all, an actress, for heaven's sake, and, worse, she's a Yankee. I do not trust either. You're engaged to be married now and you would do well to consider your future husband's reputation. Reacquaint yourself with the young girls of Richmond society. You can avoid becoming the subject of gossip if you count yourself among them."

"Abigail Thornton says Miss Colfax has men visiting her dressing room at all hours of the day and night," Meg chimed in.

"That is a lie," Laura declared icily. "I must say I'm surprised that you have been taken in by Abigail Thornton's foolish fancies. The girl is a wretched little gossip who spreads evil rumors about innocent people."

"She's not the only one who has heard of Miss Colfax's wickedness," Meg said. "Emma Harper says she drinks whiskey with men in the saloon."

"Be careful what you say about others, Meg, as it can turn on you as well." Laura pinched her sister on the arm, earning a slap and howling protests in return.

"Stop it you two." Rachel lowered the gray homespun infantry jacket she was stitching. "Laura, I have heard the rumors as well. Do not discount them. Someone of Miss Colfax's profession would most likely find herself in such a position. It is not uncommon for those types of women to succumb to intemperance and the attentions of men with questionable character."

Laura's thoughts flew to Nell Tabor and to her own behavior in Jordan's hotel room. If her mother only knew, she would forever ban Laura from seeing Jordan again. Still, she refused to believe the gossip about men and whiskey. She returned to her sewing, seething at the attack on Jordan's reputation. Before she could calm down sufficiently to state her opinion, the door opened and Sarah showed Ransom into the parlor.

Laura threw down her needlework and leapt to her feet in delight, and the three St. Clair women flocked around him.

"Ransom, we didn't expect you today. What a marvelous surprise." Rachel kissed his cheek. "How long will you be staying?"

"Just two days, Mother. Then I must report to Colonel Stuart in the Valley."

Rachel stopped fussing like a hen, allowing Laura and Meg to greet their brother.

Throwing her arms about Ransom's neck and leaning her chin on his shoulder, Laura said, "You can't imagine how much I've longed to see you, darling Ransom. How I loathe this wretched war." She eased herself from his embrace and stepped back to study his appearance. "However, I must say you look very dashing in your uniform. Those hussars' bars make your chest look very broad."

She felt a pang at the change in him. He had seemed more of a boy when he left for West Point, and he was now suddenly a man.

"We shall have to keep him out of sight." Meg giggled. "Or he'll break the heart of every girl in the city."

"Silly creature," Rachel said, but the smile froze on her face.

Lurking in the doorway, trying to make herself as inconspicuous as possible as the family shared their delight in Ransom's return, Jordan managed a polite nod. Rachel St. Clair's disdain was evident, even from a distance.

Laura followed the direction of her mother's contemptuous stare and lifted a hand to her throat. Conflicting emotions darted across her face as quickly as a hummingbird amidst flowers in a garden. "Jordan," she said, her voice barely a whisper.

Jordan sidled in and closed the door behind her. "Good morning, Laura." She clamped her arms to her side, aching to reach out but waiting for an indication that it was all right to do so.

"I ran into her at the station," Ransom explained, "and forced her to accompany me. I knew you would be happy that I did so, Laura."

"Yes, very happy," Laura replied, unable to avert her eyes from Jordan. "Were you going somewhere?"

The uncertainty in Laura's voice nearly broke Jordan's determination not to touch her and she shook her head. "No, just out for a walk." she murmured. She hoped her expression conveyed reassurance and convinced Laura that she would not just leave without a word.

"Miss Colfax," Rachel said coldly. "You must forgive us, but my son is home for only a short time and there is much to discuss with him."

"Of course," Jordan replied. "Perhaps your man can drive me back to my hotel." She grasped the door handle.

"Wait!" Ransom objected. "Mother, I invited Jordan home. I thought it was such a beautiful day today that I might take her and my sisters on a picnic down by Drury's Bluff."

"Ransom, you are home only a short time and you wish to spend it away from your father and me?" Rachel was clearly hurt by this revelation.

"It would merely be for a few hours, since Jordan must be at the theatre before seven this evening for her performance. I promise to spend the rest of the time with you."

Rachel did not look happy, but it was clear that she could deny her son nothing. "I'll have the cook pack a lunch." With a sharp glance at Jordan, she swept from the room.

Meg flounced after her and stuck her head out the door, "Ruby!"

she commanded imperiously. "Bring me my parasol." To Jordan, she said, "I declare. Every time I need that worthless darkie for the simplest task, she is never to be found."

❖

Ransom guided the horses to a shaded area underneath an old spreading oak about thirty minutes' drive from Church Hill. Jordan waited for Meg and Laura to be helped from the carriage before taking Ransom's hand herself. They strolled along a path that led closer to the river where they found a comfortable spot beneath a pine. Spreading a blanket on the soft needles that had accumulated there, Laura unpacked the lunch while Meg took out sketching paper and a pencil. Ransom settled himself against the trunk of the tree and Jordan sat awkwardly next to Laura, studiously avoiding any inadvertent touch.

Oblivious to the tension surrounding him, Ransom regaled them on the life of a cavalry officer, briefly explaining everything from military tactics to what kind of food they had in camp. Laura only half listened, wishing she and Jordan could be alone so they could talk. She was so happy to see her, and every so often caught a glimpse of Jordan glancing her way. The look she gave her made Laura's heart flutter and she wanted nothing more than to press her fingers to Jordan's lips, to feel their softness on her mouth once again.

"I'm thirsty," Meg complained. "It's hot and there are ants crawling on my stockings. This was an awful idea, Ransom."

"You didn't have to come," he said, biting into a peach Laura passed him. After chewing contentedly for a few moments, he held the peach before him, admiring the juicy interior. "How I miss fresh fruits and vegetables. If we see a peach, it is only because a kind lady has brought a basket for her husband or son."

"They are scarce even here," Laura said. "The April storms damaged the trees. Mother says we have only half the usual crop."

Meg lowered the fashionable French outdoor sketching block Aunt Ann had given her for her last birthday. "I told Ruby to fetch me some peach cobbler yesterday and she said Martha had used up her stock of peaches. I thought she was lying again so she could avoid the walk." Laughing, she added, "I suppose I should not have beaten her."

"You most certainly should not," Laura said angrily. "It's for Mother to decide whether a servant is punished. I have a mind to tell her. It would do you a world of good to spend a few weeks without a maid to bully."

Having arranged the food to her liking, Laura removed her shoes and stockings.

"And perhaps I shall tell Mamma you bare your feet in public," Meg declared. "She would not approve at all. And Mr. Young. What about him? Do you think he would expect to see his future wife getting about like a field slave?"

"Neither Mother nor Mr. Young is here, are they, Meg? So you'll have to hope they believe tittle-tattle from a jealous younger sister."

"I don't know why that nice Mr. Young wants to marry you, anyway." Meg huffily returned to her drawing. "He should have chosen someone else and left you to be an old maid forever."

Laura had no desire to discuss Mr. Young and had had enough of Meg's petulance. She captured her hoops in one hand and used the other for balance as she got to her feet. "I think I'll take a walk over there." She pointed to a spot some distance from their picnic. "I see some lovely wildflowers that would look nice on our table this evening. Jordan, would you mind helping me?"

"Not at all." Jordan took the hand Ransom offered and rose, stepping away from the blanket.

She and Laura walked side by side in awkward silence, neither willing to begin the conversation that might lead to something they were unprepared to acknowledge. When they reached the wildflowers, Laura gathered her skirts and Jordan helped her down to sit among the tall grasses. Inhaling the loamy smell of earth and sweet clover, she found a spot across from her and they began picking blue violets, black-eyed Susans, pale pink columbines, and yellow lady's slippers, placing them in Laura's lap.

"It's a nice day, isn't it?" Laura decided to begin on neutral ground.

"Yes, very nice," Jordan responded quickly, eager to resume their relationship regardless of the form it took. She very much wanted to ask Laura about her mother and Mr. Young, and she also wanted to talk about what had happened between them, but she decided to be circumspect. She would allow Laura to guide their conversation as she chose.

"Jordan, I wanted to thank you for your aid and comfort the other day. I don't know what I would have done without you. Since my cousin Charlotte married, I've missed having a close friend to talk to, and sometimes life gives us more than we can bear alone."

Jordan sighed, thankful that Laura at least felt she could rely on her. "I only wish I could have done more. I feel as useless as an infant."

"On the contrary. You listened, and that was what I needed most. There is nothing I can do to change my destiny. I allowed myself to dream of a different possibility when you spoke of acting, but that's all it was. Just a daydream."

Jordan knew she should agree. Here was her opportunity to show her own calm acceptance of the inevitable, but her heart rebelled. Instead of voicing an appropriate sentiment, she said flatly, "So you are going to marry him, then?"

Laura could not see the pain so evident in Jordan's eyes and stay true to her course. Staring down at the plaid pattern of her dress, she whispered, "Yes." Her throat closed at the unhappy admission and she could not say another word.

Something deep inside Jordan shattered and she could no longer restrain herself. "How can you agree to marry someone whom you don't love? How can you accept your fate so meekly when I have offered you an alternative?"

"What alternative?" Laura demanded. "That I leave everything I've known, that I have been born to all my life, for something…I don't even know what to call it!"

"I don't know what to call it either," Jordan snapped. Her temper rose at Laura's careless dismissal of her affections. "But you cannot tell me that you feel for Mr. Young one ounce of what we feel for each other."

Laura gasped, completely unprepared for the open admission of what had occurred between them. Her heart wrenched painfully in her chest as she recognized the truth of Jordan's statement. She felt nothing for Preston Young, certainly not the fascination and ardor she felt for Jordan. But what did it all mean and what could she really do about it anyway?

"Laura! Jordan!" Ransom called. "Let's eat. I'm starving."

Laura gathered the hem of her skirt, creating a small bed for the flowers to lie upon. She stood slowly, glancing once more at Jordan, then headed back to the picnic area.

Jordan sat for a while longer, staring dully at the sea of color in front of her. She wanted to run after Laura, grab hold of her shoulders, and shake some sense into her. And kiss her. But what use would that be? Only Laura had the power to change her own life. Jordan was nothing more than a bystander. Holding back a fierce anger that threatened to erupt, she turned her back on the beauty in front of her and retraced her steps.

❖

Ransom stopped the carriage in front of the house on Church Hill as Edward St. Clair was climbing the steps to their front door. He was clearly surprised to see Ransom at the reins and welcomed him home with a delighted handshake.

The two men assisted the women down from the carriage. If the older St. Clair was surprised to see Jordan, he did not show it.

"Miss Colfax, you are looking well."

"Thank you, sir. Your son kindly invited me to join him and your daughters for a picnic."

"How long will you have with us, Ransom?" St. Clair asked.

"Long enough to empty the larder." Ransom grinned. "Two days, sir."

"Excellent. Then you will be here tomorrow for lunch. President Davis will be joining us and we may need your services."

"Sir?" Ransom was immediately alert.

Before his father could expand on what these "services" might entail, Meg swung her parasol up to shield her face, almost hitting Jordan as she did so. "The President," she breathed. "Someone will have to entertain the officers who ride with him, of course. I'll send word to Abigail. She *adores* officers."

"The President is not paying a social call, my dear." Her father's tone was long-suffering. "And his officers certainly won't have time to flirt with silly girls."

With a pout, Meg marched off into the house, all but throwing her parasol to Prissie as she barked a whiny instruction about wanting lavender water in her room. Jordan wanted to go after her and tell her that rude, trashy behavior to servants was beneath a refined lady, but she had more important concerns. St. Clair's comment had piqued her curiosity. The "services" alluded to could very well be something of significance to the Northern cause, and her mind raced at the possibilities.

"I've heard some very good things about your President, Mr. St. Clair," she remarked. "I sincerely hope that someone as wise as he will bring his full powers to bear on the tragedy that has befallen our country. Perhaps men of goodwill can prevent the bloodshed that others less sagacious clamor for in the houses of government as well as in the newspapers."

"Indeed." Edward seemed taken aback by her comments. Like most men, he was unaccustomed to women of her age speaking their minds frankly.

"Have you met President Davis?" Ransom asked her.

"No, I have not had the pleasure."

Jordan struggled to maintain her calm. With dismay, she realized she would now have to take her leave and perhaps not see the St. Clairs for quite some time, missing the opportunity to search St. Clair's desk. A desperate idea occurred to her and she did not have time to question its good sense. Calling upon her considerable acting skill, she cast a soppy look toward Ransom that would not be lost on his father. "I do hope your luncheon is successful. I must take my leave. Ransom has so little time to be with all of you, I can intrude no further."

She made sure to let her bosom rise and fall with the vehemence of her sigh, earning a look of blank puzzlement from Laura and a frown from Ransom. But her real audience was Edward St. Clair, a man old enough and experienced enough to recognize maidenly longing when he saw it.

Clapping his handsome son on the shoulder, Edward gallantly declared, "Miss Colfax, you are very thoughtful and I suspect Mrs. St. Clair will indeed want her son to herself today. However, we would be delighted to have your company tomorrow to dine with the President."

"Papa…" Laura blushed. "Why not arrange for Miss Colfax to join us on another occasion? After all, you'll have confidential information to discuss and we ladies will be in the parlor most of the time anyway."

Jordan tried to catch Laura's eye, but her friend made sure to look the other way. How much more plainly could she ask to be left alone?

St. Clair patted her hand. "Leave those considerations to me, my dear. We gentlemen will have ample occasion to make our decisions. A little gaiety first would be pleasant."

Jordan saw her opening and took it. "Oh, Mr. St. Clair. I would be delighted to join you." With a girlish flutter, she added. "I confess, I was quite desolate to think of Ransom leaving to do his duty so soon, with but a brief farewell."

Laura's expression almost made her laugh out loud. Even Ransom appeared bemused. But Edward St. Clair made up for his son's lack of perception. Taking Jordan's hand, he kissed it with the easy charm of a Southern gentleman.

"I'll send my driver for you tomorrow morning, Miss Colfax. May I wish you well for your performance tonight."

❖

Lunch the next day was a pleasant affair, partly because Jordan barely uttered a word throughout the meal. Laura was slightly puzzled by her behavior, but presumed that manners dictated respect for the President, even if she was a Yankee and disagreed with his politics. When the meal drew to an end, the ladies excused themselves, leaving Edward, Ransom, and President Davis at the dining table.

Jordan wished she could sneak back across the hall to listen in on their conversation. She only half-listened to what the women were talking about, pretending to be interested in a book laid out on her lap. Finally she could sit still no longer and excused herself on the pretext of washing her hands. As she neared the dining room, she slowed her pace and stepped as quietly as possible, straining to hear as much as she could in the time she had.

"…leave on the morning train and place it in the hands of General Beauregard and no one else. Should you be stopped, here is a note allowing you to pass through the line."

She couldn't see into the room, but she knew from the voice that it was Jefferson Davis speaking.

"Yes, sir," Ransom said. "Shall I wait for his reply, Mr. President?"

"No reply is necessary, Ransom. The general will know what to do."

Jordan heard someone approaching the door and stepped hastily back, bending as if to untangle her foot from a lace tear in her petticoat.

"Oh!" Ruby narrowly missed colliding with Jordan as she hurried into the hallway carrying a tray of dishes. "Beg your pardon, miss."

"That's quite all right, Ruby."

Jordan continued walking down the hall until she found the washroom. Pouring water into the basin, she kept the door ajar so that she could observe the hallway unobstructed. Within moments, Ransom left the dining room and climbed the stairs, a packet of papers in his hand. Jordan guessed he was on his way to his room and quickly trailed after him. Watching through the door he left ajar, she caught her breath as he slid the papers into a haversack lying at the foot of his bed. To avoid detection, she hurried along the upstairs hallway to Laura's room and waited until she heard his boots on the wooden stairs.

Her heart pounding, she returned to his room and withdrew the papers from his bag. Unfolding them, she was appalled to discover that they contained detailed plans of General McDowell's army. Most shocking of all was the date anticipated for his march toward Richmond and the route he would take to get there.

"What are you doing, Jordan?"

Jordan whirled to find Laura standing in the doorway. Her heart raced painfully from the surprise and fright, yet all she could do was stand there, clutching the papers she had rifled through Ransom's bag to obtain.

"Laura, I—"

"I don't understand." Laura crossed the room and removed the papers from Jordan's hand.

"It's nothing, Laura, really." Jordan thought quickly. "I was passing by and saw these lying on the floor. I assumed they fell out of Ransom's bag so I stopped to put them back."

Laura's confusion was evident in her expression. She shook her head slowly. "No, Jordan. I saw you remove them." She leafed through the documents. "Why are you in my brother's bedroom? What are you doing searching through his belongings?"

A bothersome thought struggled to make its way to the front of Laura's mind, but she shoved it back. It wasn't possible that Jordan, her friend, would lie to her. After yesterday, she'd started to wonder if Jordan was romantically interested in Ransom. The very idea seemed ridiculous, but then she'd overheard her parents arguing about the dreadful possibility of a Yankee daughter-in-law. Laura felt hurt that Jordan had not confided in her if she had developed feelings for Ransom, but her disapproval of Mr. Young and the forthcoming marriage had strained their friendship.

Laura frowned, trying to find evidence in Jordan's conduct of an attachment to Ransom. She could think of nothing, and with every passing moment, it slowly dawned on her that there was no attachment. Jordan had a very different reason for cultivating a connection with the St. Clairs.

"You're a spy." Laura was stunned. It was inconceivable what she had begun to believe. Images of the times she had spent with Jordan flashed through her mind. Yes, they had disagreed on the issues, but nothing had prepared her for this deception. She thought of their kisses and the indescribable feelings, both physical and emotional, that drew her to Jordan. "You've used me."

"No. Laura, listen to me," Jordan begged. "You are my friend and—"

"Friend! How dare you. Would a friend sneak into my family's home to steal from them?"

"No." Jordan was miserable. "Perhaps it started out that way, but then…everything changed."

"Yes," Laura whispered, the tears beginning to spill over. "Everything has changed."

How could she tell her parents what she had discovered? She was the one responsible for bringing a Yankee into their home. She had proven herself incapable of good judgment by making friends with a woman her mother disapproved of.

Jordan tried to embrace Laura but she stepped out of reach and placed the papers back in Ransom's haversack. Securing the strap, she said, "Get out."

The pain in her eyes made Jordan flinch. "Laura, wait, please give me a moment to explain."

Laura folded her arms across her chest. "All right then, proceed." Her tone was scathing.

Jordan was momentarily speechless, unprepared to explain the mess she found herself in, but she knew there could be no lies, not to Laura. "There's no excuse for my actions. But please believe this—I care for you very much."

"That doesn't explain why you are here, reading private documents."

"It's about Tyler," Jordan said, clutching at a half truth. "I'm terrified for him and he won't tell me anything."

"What does that have to do with my family and the papers you were reading?"

"Don't you want to know where Ransom will be and what danger he will be in?" Jordan begged. "I'm just trying to find out exactly the same information. We both love our brothers, Laura, and we are both loyal to our beliefs and this land we share. I know what you must think."

"Really?" Laura ran a hand across her damp brow. "You are not the one betrayed by a person who pretended to care for you."

"I never pretended," Jordan said starkly. "What happened between us…I don't know what it means, but I would like to have the time to understand. You cannot marry Preston Young, you simply cannot. Please convince your mother that it is wrong."

Laura did not move, her stance as firm as it was before, but her heart beat painfully. She felt her entire world collapsing around her—first her impending marriage, but even worse, Jordan's betrayal. "It is too late," she murmured. "Please leave. I won't speak to my father about this if you just go."

"Laura. Don't do this. I beg you."

"I said go!" Laura ran out of the room, colliding with Meg as she hurried down the hallway to her room.

Jordan slowly followed, her feet heavy as she moved as though in a fog, unseeing, uncaring. Meg spoke to her as she passed, but the words were incomprehensible to Jordan. She descended the stairs, opened the front door, and trudged out.

Chapter Sixteen

The small town of Manassas Junction lay some twenty-five miles south of Washington in northern Virginia. Here the Orange and Alexandria Railroad met the Manassas Gap Railroad, which led west to the Shenandoah Valley. It was a vital railroad junction, and whoever controlled the town controlled the best overland approach to Richmond. To this town Union General Irvin McDowell led 35,000 soldiers on a hot, humid July day on his way to the Confederate capital.

Confederate General P.G.T. Beauregard and 22,000 men were waiting for McDowell along the banks of a small stream called Bull Run. Searching for a way to outflank Beauregard, McDowell sent a division to pass by the Confederate right when they were drawn into battle at Blackburn's Ford. The Union forces withdrew to prepare for another day.

Lieutenant Ransom St. Clair arrived at Manassas Junction two days after this attack. As he rode into camp in search of Beauregard's headquarters, he was shocked by the number of wounded being transported to the rear. The gruesome sight of severed arms and legs collected in a pile outside the surgeon's tent nauseated him, as did the flies that had gathered, drawn by the stench. Farther on, he noticed how the graves of the dead, who were hastily buried under the hot July sun, stood out in stark contrast to the parched soil that covered most of the ground. However, despite their losses, the men were in excellent spirits.

Having delivered his message to General Beauregard, Ransom was about to return to his regiment in the Shenandoah Valley when he learned that his commander, Colonel Jeb Stuart, was on his way to Manassas Junction. Beauregard believed that the battle was not yet over and, knowing they were desperately outnumbered, he had summoned the nearly 10,000 forces under General Joseph Johnston in the Valley to reinforce him. Ransom therefore remained at headquarters to await the arrival of his regiment, acting as a messenger between the general and his brigade commanders in the meantime.

He was lying in his tent late that evening, writing a letter home to Laura, when the clatter of horses' hooves sounded outside.

"I am looking for Lieutenant St. Clair," a disembodied voice called out.

"Here!" Ransom exclaimed from inside his tent. He crawled out on his hands and knees, standing up once he was outside.

"Hello, Ransom!" Lieutenant Williams smiled upon finding him. "Sorry to rouse you so late, but Colonel Stuart sends his compliments and desires your presence at a staff meeting."

"Let me get my hat and I'll follow you." Ransom reentered his tent, donning his hat and slipping into his gray frock coat, then exited once again. Mounting his horse, he trailed behind his friend until they reached his regiment's encampment.

A small campfire outside Colonel Stuart's tent cast a soft light in the dark shadows from the surrounding woods. Stuart and several of his lieutenants were already seated around it, looking haggard from the long journey they'd undertaken in order to arrive as quickly as possible. They were wolfing down something from a pot that hung over the fire and laughing loudly. Ransom immediately recognized his commander by the peacock feather in the hat he always wore. At twenty-eight years of age, he was not much older than Ransom, and as fellow Virginians, they had much in common. But Stuart was not an untried soldier. Also a graduate of West Point, he was a veteran of Bleeding Kansas, where antislavery and proslavery border ruffians from Missouri clashed in disagreement over whether Kansas would enter the Union as a slave or free state. He had also fought in many of the Indian conflicts and had been wounded in one such battle on the frontier four years prior.

"Ransom, come join us," Stuart called upon seeing him. "Have you eaten?"

Ransom sat on a tree stump across the fire from him. "Yes sir, thank you, I have."

"Good, then let's begin."

Stuart outlined his orders and his expectations of them and the hundreds of men under his command. On a rock he laid out a hand-drawn map depicting the field of battle southwest of Bull Run, where the

Southern army was situated. Ransom had been there a full day longer than his regiment and pointed out the location of roads and landmarks.

"Here is the Warrenton Turnpike, which heads roughly east and west. A stone bridge crosses Bull Run there." He made a mark on the map. "There are other fords, here"—again he made several marks on the map—"but the main thrust is expected at Blackburn's Ford, where the Federals made their first attack. Over here is the Manassas-Sudley Road that heads north and south and intersects the turnpike here. There is a farmhouse near the intersection belonging to a widow, Mrs. Henry, and beyond the turnpike is a stone house."

"I take it these are defensible positions, if needed?" Stuart asked.

"Yes sir." Ransom marked other spots on the map as he descended Bull Run from north to south. "Troop dispositions are Evans, Cocke, Bonham, Longstreet, Jones, and Ewell. At least that's what I know as of this afternoon."

"Good work, Lieutenant." Stuart nodded appreciatively. "We'll hold back, awaiting results, then move to those areas that are hottest." He stood and stretched his lanky frame, then scratched his full dark beard as a yawn spread across his face. "Now I suggest we all get some sleep. Thirty-six hours in the saddle requires as much rest as possible, for us and the horses. Let's be prepared to ride at dawn."

Ransom returned to his tent and resumed the letter he had been writing to Laura. He had written to his parents the other day, but with Laura, he could confide his innermost feelings.

20 July 1861
Dearest Laura,

I remain at Manassas Junction for now as my regiment has been hurried forward in anticipation of battle. This will be my first engagement, and I must confess I am rather nervous about it. I have never shot a man before, but I know I must or else myself be shot.

The heat here is not to be believed! Not even a small breeze to rid the air of the smell of men and horses. I pity the Union soldier who must march in it, but if some should succumb to the climate, so much the better for us.

I have already seen my fill of wounded and dying and

it is a ghastly sight to behold. Dying on the battlefield is preferable to having wounds such as I have seen this day. To have one's arm or leg removed does not always guarantee one's recovery, and it is a terrible death indeed.

I was glad to have visited home one more time before this fight. To be able to see you, Mother, Father, and Meg was a blessing I shall keep foremost in my mind tomorrow. Only God knows what the outcome will be, but I am confident that when it is over, the South will be victorious and our new country will grow and prosper. Laura, if I am one of the soldiers destined not to return home, know that I have done my duty and am proud to serve my country.

Long live the Confederate States of America!

Your loving brother,
Ransom

He sealed the letter and placed it on top of his haversack, planning to hand it to the postmaster in the morning. Picking up his LeMat revolver, he lovingly cleaned it, knowing it would see its first use in battle soon. He was proud of this unique pistol and loaded nine .42 caliber bullets into the chamber, plus additional buckshot that discharged from the .63 caliber barrel below. A pivoting striker on the top of the hammer allowed him to alternate between the two. After verifying that his cartridge box was full and his saber ready, he was satisfied that all was ready for the morning. He was about to turn down the kerosene lamp resting on a wooden crate when he hesitated and found the Bible his mother had given him when he was a boy. Opening it to the book of Psalms, he settled back on his blanket and read well into the night.

❖

Tyler Colfax sat astride his horse and drank thirstily from his canteen. Checking his pocket watch, he noticed that it was a little after nine thirty in the morning. They were incredibly late due to hours of waiting for another division to get out of their way before they could march. They had heard the sole cannon blast earlier, the Union signal that the battle was to begin, but they had only now crossed Sudley Ford over Bull Run and were still at least a mile from their position. The men had broken ranks, running to the stream to drink during a humid morning with temperatures still climbing. No amount of cursing and threats could induce them to return to the line until they'd had their fill, causing further delay.

Now as they drew nearer, the sporadic sounds of the Union skirmish suggested the battle was already underway. Tyler fidgeted in the saddle, anxious to join in the melee he could see taking place farther down the hill. As he trotted slowly down the Manassas-Sudley Road, he could see a stone house where the road intersected with the Warrenton Turnpike. The head of his column had begun to turn east prior to reaching the turnpike and settled beside a creek known as Young's Branch. This was where they would make their stand.

He nudged his mount forward and it stumbled along, weary from hours of traveling without rest. Tyler felt sorry for the beast, but even more so for the men on foot. Almost all of them were raw recruits, those with seniority having scarcely a few months' drilling under their belt. Many had cast off their packs and other equipment during the three-day march to the field of battle, and Tyler worried about the amount of ammunition each man carried. He was also concerned about the state of their rations. Most had been issued a few days of rations and had already consumed the modest allocation of bread, salt pork, coffee, sugar, and salt each man received. Whether the commissary wagons would be able to reach them and resupply remained to be seen. So far the campaign had started badly, and Tyler hoped that the battle would go more smoothly than the march.

By ten-fifteen, he and his men had gotten into position when suddenly a force of Confederates hidden by the trees and brush attacked them. Taken completely by surprise, he rode hastily down the line firing at the attackers, emptying his Colt revolver into the oncoming mass of men. Shouted commands came from all around him, and it was unclear whether his own commander or the Rebels uttered them. The screams of men and horses, cannon and shot added more confusion to the chaos. He fired and reloaded, fired and reloaded, all the while his heart pounding from fear.

"Lieutenant Colfax, over here!"

Tyler dismounted and ran to his men, who were holding off a charge by a group of Confederate soldiers. Taking aim at a man coming up the hill, he fired, horrified as the bullet struck the man in the cheek and ripped open the side of his face as he tumbled backward down the hill. It was the first time Tyler had actually seen his gun cause harm to someone, and for a moment he could not move. But the bugle call for charge sounded, and he and his men flung themselves down the hill at the Confederates waiting below.

The variety of clothing that the soldiers wore made their allegiances confusing. Colors ranged from blue and gray to reds and greens and all manner of combinations. Tyler figured who ever attacked him or his men was the enemy and aimed at them. He and his men collided with the Rebels and, at close range, he drew his sword and began to slash away. He felt his sword make contact as it hit and sank into the fleshy part of a man's thigh, hitting bone. The soldier screamed and dropped to his knees, blood spurting from the wound. Terrified by the blood, the smell, and the bulging, glassy stare of the man, Tyler struck him with the hilt of his sword and sent him reeling.

Tyler stumbled ahead, seeing nothing but smoke and fire and men shooting and grappling with each other. The sounds were deafening as cannon exploded in his front and rear, shells striking everywhere. Men screamed, horses screamed, and still the fighting went on. It was as though he had already died and was experiencing what hell must certainly be like. It was impossible to conceive that human beings could inflict this kind of destruction on one another.

The battle raged for hours, and in the early afternoon an eerie, bloodcurdling cry went up from the Rebels as they surged forward into the Union line. Tyler's men broke, and he tried to stave off a rout by standing firm.

"Hold fast, men!" he shouted and stood in the way of those who were retreating. "We outnumber them and can still win the day."

"Get out of my way," a soldier shouted, shoving Tyler aside. "There's too many of them."

The man's head exploded in a fine mist of blood and brain matter that spattered Tyler's face and uniform. Tyler spun and fired desperately in the direction of the enemy and continued to fire until his gun was empty, then he reloaded again. His heart in his throat, he could scarcely breathe for the fear that gripped him. Union soldiers were now running headlong up the hill, and anyone who got in their way was brutally knocked aside. There was no stopping the flow, but still Tyler tried, screaming and cursing at them to stop.

He had glimpsed the brigade commander, Colonel Burnside, doing the same when he felt a sharp blow to the head. At first he felt severe pain, followed by a buzzing sound that became louder and louder. The noise of battle receded, the sound of cannon and men muted and indistinct. The field before him tilted and blurred, and for a dizzying moment he thought he might be ill. Mercifully, he was saved from sickness as he fell to the ground and his world went black.

❖

It was midafternoon when Ransom once again found himself chasing a remnant of Union soldiers up the Manassas-Sudley Road. The battle had gone badly for the South all morning, but now their luck was beginning to change. Reinforcements from General Johnston, who had been arriving by train from the valley all day, had been decisive in turning around a fight that might easily have gone the other way.

He rode close behind Colonel Stuart as he had throughout the day, sometimes fighting, other times collecting prisoners and escorting them to the rear. He was chasing a group of soldiers who were fleeing back to Sudley's Ford when a bullet struck his horse in midgallop, and Ransom tumbled over sideways.

"You all right?" Lieutenant Williams pulled up next to him.

"I'm fine." Ransom brushed the dust off his clothes. "Go on ahead. I'll find another horse and join you shortly."

He glanced around, watching as Jackson's men fought over several cannon near the Henry house. He stood entranced, as though at the theatre observing a scene from a play. It was completely unreal that so many men could be engaged in shooting and killing. At the whir of a bullet close to his head he threw himself to the ground and hugged the dirt. Casting a glance sideways, he came face-to-face with a headless body. It was the first time he had seen up close what cannon and shot could do to a man, and he vomited at the sight. Wiping his mouth with his sleeve, he finally stood up and saw a roan horse standing watch over an unmoving soldier, the reins dragging loosely on the ground. Ransom was thrilled to find a healthy animal so quickly and strode to its side, gathering up the reins from the dirt. He was about to mount when he noticed something familiar about the soldier whose hat had come off, exposing his face. Squatting beside him and rolling him over for a better look, Ransom was shocked to discover Tyler Colfax, bleeding profusely from a head injury.

"No!" he screamed.

His heart pounding, he put his ear to Tyler's chest, listening for any sign of life, but the noise of battle was too much. Blood poured from Tyler's forehead and Ransom removed his handkerchief and pressed it on the wound to stanch the flow. Glancing about, he saw a young oak tree nearby that provided a bit of shade, so half carrying Tyler, he dragged him to its shelter. Laying him in the shade, he tossed the blood-soaked handkerchief aside and reached around his waist to remove his sash. He lifted Tyler's head and wrapped the sash tightly around the wound. To cushion his friend's head, Ransom removed his own coat and folded it. As he lowered Tyler onto it, he nearly wept with relief at the sound of a moan. He then ripped open Tyler's coat, searching his body for signs of other wounds, pausing only when he heard footsteps approaching.

"You murdering Rebel thief!" a voice called out.

Ransom stood and turned around just as a bayonet was plunged deep into his midsection, twisting harshly. A rush of air blasted from his lungs as he grabbed the barrel of the rifle and held on. The look in his assailant's eyes was one of crazed glee as he shoved harder into Ransom, knocking his hands off the gun. Ransom slid slowly to the ground, collapsing atop Tyler as the soldier jerked the blade from his body. The soldier then spun around and resumed the battle, leaving Ransom to stare up at the clear blue sky, appalled by his change of fortune.

He was surprised that he felt no pain; everything was calm and peaceful. He smiled, thinking of his visit home and the apple pie that Martha had made especially for him. Images of home, of his father, mother, and sisters drifted in and out of his consciousness. For some reason, he remembered when, as a little boy, he and Laura played hide-and-seek with Ruby and Aaron among the tobacco plants. Always, after the game on a hot day, they ate juicy slices of watermelon in the garden off the kitchen walk. They were such happy times, and recalling them made him feel safe and loved.

It was his last thought as he drifted off into oblivion.

Chapter Seventeen

Jordan's performance that evening was not her finest, but she managed to stumble through it anyway. She felt that all of her performances the last few days had suffered. After the final bow, she returned to her dressing room, removed her stage makeup, and changed out of her costume into a green brocade dress. As she glanced in the mirror to fix her hair, she carried out some deep breathing exercises to settle her nerves. When that didn't work, she took a small silver flask and a crystal glass from the bottom drawer of her dressing table and poured a healthy shot of whiskey. After she took a sip, there was a soft rap on the door.

"Come in, Bill," she called, guessing her visitor's identity. Bill usually dropped by after a performance, once enough time had elapsed that she had washed and changed.

"You want a shot?" she offered. "It's good Irish whiskey."

"Since when do you go drinking whiskey straight out of the bottle?"

"Since the country has fallen into madness and my life has followed it." Jordan downed the whiskey and poured herself another. She held the flask up to him.

Bill sighed deeply. "You might as well pour me a large one."

She handed him his glass and moved to the settee. They sat in morose silence. Bill's grimace gave voice to his thoughts and Jordan surmised they were not much different from her own. The battle fought at Manassas Junction was a Rebel victory, and the mood in Richmond was one of near hysteria. The losses had been severe, and until the dead were numbered and identified every family was gripped with fear. Yet they had sent the Union army back to Washington in humiliating disarray.

"Have you heard from your father?"

Jordan set her glass down heavily. "There's not yet word of Tyler."

She knew her sick anxiety over Tyler's fate was affecting her acting. So, too, was her parting from Laura. Jordan was glad the short season of the play was about to end. She wanted to leave Richmond and never return.

Bill tossed the whiskey back and stood up. "I'll be packing up the costumes if you need me, then I'll see you to the hotel."

He closed the door, leaving Jordan alone with her thoughts and her drink. Presently she heard another knock, but this time louder and harder.

"What is it, Bill?" she called.

The door swung wide, admitting four soldiers—one sergeant and three privates. The sergeant was none other than George Lamont. "Well, well, Jordan. I told you I'd be seeing you again." He grinned, exposing his misshapen, tobacco-stained teeth.

"What do you want, George?" Puzzled and angry at being held up, Jordan stood, glass still in hand.

"Search the room, men."

The three privates entered the small room, crowding Jordan back against the settee, nearly colliding with Lamont.

"What do you think you're doing? You have no right, no authority to search my dressing room." She was angry, the alcohol giving her courage.

"On the contrary," George retorted. "You are in the South, and we don't take kindly to Yankee spies here."

Jordan felt her stomach lurch and her heart thud heavily. The urge to run was overwhelming, but the soldiers blocked her way.

"Found something, Sergeant."

Lamont strode to Jordan's dressing table where the private had rummaged through the discarded drafts of her notes to Kate Warne. She had not mastered the codes yet and drafted each communication several times so she could avoid sending information made useless by errors. She had intended to burn the drafts but became distracted in the chaos of the performance and the news of the battle.

Lamont scanned the papers and thrust them out to her. "What does it say?"

Jordan stared at him as it dawned on her that Laura must have reported her to the authorities. In shock, she sat back down on the settee, the glass in her hand forgotten. She had believed deep in her soul that Laura would not betray her; in fact, she had hoped that they would be able to reconcile. Laura had been hurt and angry, but Jordan felt sure that with time she could amend the situation. Now, all thoughts of reconciliation flew from her mind. A slow, roiling anger bubbled up from the pit of her stomach and she thought she might be ill. When Lamont repeated his question, she refused to answer.

"All right boys, we're taking her to Major Turner. Look smart! Guess we caught ourselves a regular lady spy."

Jordan wanted to wipe the smug look off his face but instead followed two of the soldiers as they led her out the door. Partway down the hall, she ran into Bill.

"Jordan! What the devil is going on? What are these damn Rebels doing with you?" When he attempted to take hold of her and pull her away from the soldiers, they pushed him roughly aside. His eyes grew wide when he saw George Lamont bringing up the rear.

"You!" Bill exclaimed, rushing to grab him but was blocked by the other soldiers.

"It's all right, Bill. I'm sure they'll be locking me up for awhile. Send word to my father if you would and I'll see you soon." She said this with more conviction than she felt.

Jordan was calm, the anger inside giving her the sustenance she needed to endure the consequences of her arrest. She put the image of Laura in the forefront of her mind, and the hatred she felt burned a path from her heart to her soul. The soldiers led her out into the alleyway and she went willingly, no longer caring whether she ever saw Laura again.

❖

"Where am I?" Jordan demanded. She sat at a table in the commandant's office and glanced about her. The only window looked out onto the street below, and even if she'd had any thoughts of escape, she was two floors up and would never have made it.

"Libby Prison, for the moment." The clean-shaven officer who'd just entered the room sat down in the chair opposite her. "We're trying to find other accommodations for you, as we do not normally house females here, but since all of our jails are full of Yankees, this will have to do for now. At least here we mostly hold officers, unlike other, less cheerful places."

He smiled pleasantly and Jordan took this for a cue to thank him. She remained silent, aware of George Lamont standing at attention a few feet away. He grinned evilly when she glanced his way.

"I'm Major Turner," the officer said. He set down the sheets of papers taken from Jordan's dressing room.

"I know my rights, Major, and I wish to see a lawyer." Jordan tried to sound forceful. What she really wanted was to go home, back to Washington, and forget that she had ever set foot in Richmond. The truth was hard to accept. Certainly she had come to Richmond at Kate Warne's behest, but her feelings for Laura St. Clair had played a role in her decision. Jordan did not know who she should feel more angry with: Laura for her betrayal or herself for her misguided devotion.

"It's most unfortunate that these documents were discovered in your dressing room," Major Turner said. "I fear that it does not bode well for you."

"I've never seen those papers before." Jordan said.

He raised an eyebrow. "That's not what we understand from the loyal citizen who claims you have knowledge of their contents."

Jordan grimaced as images of Laura rose unbidden to her mind. "Well, Major, you can't always believe the treachery of a Southern woman."

The major smiled indulgently. "If not for our Southern women, I wouldn't be here enjoying your company, Miss Colfax. Now, are you going to tell me what these say or aren't you?"

Jordan glanced at them as though they meant nothing to her. "As I said, Major, I don't know what you're talking about. If I've never seen those papers before, how would I know what they say?" She smiled disingenuously.

The major stood up from the chair. "I advise you to reconsider your position, Miss Colfax. If you refuse to cooperate, we will have to keep you here until we decide what to do with you. Sergeant, it's late. Take the prisoner to her cell. We'll continue this discussion in the morning."

"Be glad you're not going upstairs where most of the prisoners are," George remarked after his superior left. He escorted Jordan along a narrow hallway to a thick wooden door. "We sure have a bunch of Yankees crammed in up there. On this floor there are two smaller cells with only a few in each. At least you have your own room."

He unlocked the door and ushered Jordan past him into a small cell furnished only with a narrow cot, a stool, and a bucket, which she presumed to be her privy. The room smelled dank from the mildew on the walls and the musty scent of the blanket.

"It can get real cozy in here." George ran a finger down her arm, which she angrily shrugged off. Laughing, he closed the door behind him, and she listened to the jangle of the keys in the lock.

Alone and in the dark, Jordan felt her nerve leave her. Tears of frustration and fear welled up and she picked up the stool and crossed to the large bar-covered window. Standing on the child-size seat, she peered down into the empty street. There were no passersby due to the lateness of the hour and the rain, but by the light cast from the windows she could make out the two guards who patrolled on the street out front.

Resting her head against the wooden window ledge, she tried not to allow panic to set in. Her thoughts turned to Laura and she wondered how things had gone so wrong. Even now she wanted to see her, to talk to her, to try to reason with her and return things to the way they were between them. But the rift was too deep, the shock of her betrayal too profound. She might have been duplicitous in her own actions, but she would never have intentionally hurt Laura. And certainly she would never have placed Laura's life at risk. Deeply pained, she got off the stool and retreated to the miserable cot that would be her resting place tonight and for the immediate future. Jordan did not want to think about how many other heads had rested on the dirty pillow, how many tears had dried on the stiff cotton cover.

She would sleep and hope to think clearly tomorrow. If she was going to talk her way out of this situation, she would need more than a pretty face and a father with influence.

❖

Ruby put away the last dishes from her white folks' dinner and polished the silver. The clock in the hallway chimed once and she hurried to get finished. All night, while she was helping the young missies get ready for bed and cleaning the dining room to make ready for the next morning, she had nothing but freedom on her mind. Yankee soldiers in Virginia! Things were happening just like Tillie said. All the white men were leaving to join the army. There were slaves that went along with the ration wagons every week. They came back saying all hell had broke loose and this war was what colored folk had been waiting for. Problem was, no one knew what to expect. Should they wait for the Yankees to come or should they run north while their masters were busy with the fighting?

Ruby thought it was time to make a plan. She'd listened to President Davis and Marse Edward while they ate their roasted chicken and mashed yams. She didn't know where Manassas was but she'd heard enough to be sure that white folks had plenty else to think about right now. Marse Edward said he heard about slaves running away looking for Yankee soldiers. Ruby wondered if it was better to escape with a group or go by herself.

She ran her polishing cloth over the last fork, dropped it into the cutlery drawer, and left the big house. Too excited to return to her own cabin, she hurried to the kitchen.

Her ma was awake and sat up when Ruby crept in. "You late, girl."

Ruby got into bed next to her. "I's thinking, with the Yankees coming we should run off."

"You been talking to that meddlesome yaller again."

"Tillie got learning. She says after this war there won't be no masters and no slaves no more."

"Just 'cause she wish it, don't make it happen."

"I ain't staying," Ruby whispered. "Come with me, Ma. You a fine cook. White folks in the North, they pay for a cook as good as you. Tillie says colored lives in their own house on their own land."

"Sounds mighty fine, but I heard getting money sure has made fools of some highfalutin colored."

"You hears that talk from white trash," Ruby said. "They hates us worse'n quality white folks."

"Ain't that the truth." Her ma sighed. "Child, I ain't leaving Barrett Hall. This where I belong."

Ruby didn't understand. "You done complain 'bout how Marse Edward spoil you, but you want to stay?"

"I's born at Barrett Hall. I don't know nothing else, and the St. Clairs is good to us."

"They don't whip us nearly to death is all. They don't learn us to read and write. We don't have no church. And Marse Edward can sell us on the block any time he wants."

"Marse Edward won't never do that."

"Old missy, she hates you," Ruby said. "Only reason she don't sell us south is Marse Edward won't let her."

"Miss Rachel ain't never gonna sell us south." Her ma took a hold of her shoulder. "Don't be light in the head. If you run off, the paddy-rollers will catch you and there won't be nothing any of us can do."

"I'll hide, Ma."

Ruby lay down on her side. Her back ached, her feet were sore, and she was scared to death. But she smiled. One day she would have her own house and her own servant to fan the flies off the table. And when she left Barrett Hall, she was going to steal Miss Meg's hairbrush and use it for herself. She liked that idea. For all the bruises she had from being hit with that brush, she deserved to own it.

❖

Laura lit her lamp and turned the wick up. She couldn't sleep and was fed up with lying in the darkness thinking about Jordan.

The hurt was so fresh, Laura felt a pain in her chest with every breath she drew. She wished she had never gone upstairs, looking for Jordan after Meg mentioned seeing her going into Ransom's room. But she'd been driven by an emotion she recognized now as jealousy. She had wanted to know if there was a special affection between her brother and her best friend. The very idea made her corset feel unbearably tight and her body too heavy to move.

What else was it about Jordan that had her all aflutter one moment, then infuriated the next? She didn't know what to make of her mixed emotions and was exhausted by the effort of trying to understand why she couldn't just hate Jordan and resolve never to think of her again.

She picked up the book sitting atop a stack of volumes on her night table and opened it, hoping to escape from her futile thoughts. She had only read a line when she realized it was the book of poems by Browning and snapped it shut. Irritated, she got out of bed, padded over to her desk, and sat down to write in her diary.

25 July, 1861

I no longer know her. Everything I thought before about her, about us, is a lie. How can I go on? How can I have been so naïve and gullible? She says she is my friend, but how could she? How could she say that and then do what she did?

I can't help but care for her, for all that she is. I think I understand that she was trying to do what she thought was right, but if only she had told me. I would never have helped her, but I also would not have allowed her to use me to gain access to our government. I knew we disagreed, but why couldn't she have trusted me? If she was truly my friend, she would have done that.

Chewing thoughtfully on the end of her pen, she closed the entry with a final sentence.

I shall go to her in a few days' time, after I have had a chance to think. If nothing else, I must say good-bye. Our friendship is over.

CHAPTER EIGHTEEN

Laura sat in a chair by the window of her room trying to read but failing miserably. Not one word about the book would stay with her, so she finally snapped it closed and gazed at the street below. Just as she did, she saw her father descend from his carriage and a soldier dismount from his horse. They strode purposefully up the walk and entered the house. Puzzled by her father's arrival at home in the middle of the day, she left her room and entered the hallway where she ran into Meg.

A wail of inhuman proportions rose up from downstairs, and Laura and Meg froze for a moment then rapidly descended the stairs. Sarah and Ruby came running from the back of the house and they all entered the front parlor at the same time.

Edward St. Clair stood near the fireplace, a soldier in gray by his side, while Rachel sat on a chair nearby. Her head in her hands, she wept openly, something none of them had ever seen before.

"Papa, what is it?" Laura asked tremulously.

Edward's jaw muscle worked furiously and his eyes were so pained that Laura could not bear to look at them. "I'm afraid it's Ransom," he said between gritted teeth.

When he was unable to continue, the soldier said, "I regret to inform you, ma'am, that Lieutenant Ransom St. Clair was killed at Bull Run yesterday afternoon."

Laura stared at him. Her heart stopped beating and the breath left her. All sound stopped, and a rushing in her ears was the only sign that she was not dreaming. She wavered for a moment, catching hold of the corner of the settee.

"No!" Meg blurted. "It's not true! There must be a mistake. How do you know for certain?"

Finding his voice once more, Edward slowly sat on a chair opposite his wife. "A friend of his…a Lieutenant Williams…found him on the field. He brought his body back in an ambulance. I've seen him as well. The Lieutenant knew we would want to see that he was buried properly so I had him take Ransom to Bellevue Hospital. Dr. Bolton is watching over him until I can make arrangements."

The room began spinning and Laura shut her eyes to stop the nauseous motion. But when she opened them again, the room continued to swirl until everything went black.

❖

They were taking Ransom home. Many Richmond families decided to bury their fallen dead at Hollywood Cemetery, while soldiers without means or family remained on the fields of Manassas. However, as tradition dictated, the St. Clairs would bury Ransom at Barrett Hall. On a small knoll overlooking the James, many a Barrett ancestor had their final resting place on the plantation. Rachel's grandfather, who had fought in the Revolution, was buried alongside his wife and two of their children. And Rachel's father, Peter, who had survived the War of 1812 and later died of typhus, was buried there along with her mother Ruth and all of the siblings who had died during her childhood.

Now another war hero would be buried in the fertile Virginia soil, but this time, with no wife or progeny by his side to keep him company. Buildings were lined with black crepe and the somber mood followed the St. Clair carriage as it headed south out of town. A separate wagon carrying the coffin was driven by a slave whose nervousness at the proximity of a dead body translated itself through the reins to the jittery horses.

Laura sat in the back of the carriage next to Meg, who stared out the window. Edward and Rachel sat opposite them, Rachel's face barely visible beneath the black veil that she wore. Only conversation that was absolutely necessary took place between them, and Laura was relieved that her thoughts could wander uninterrupted.

She could not believe Ransom was gone. As the carriage rolled past tobacco fields, lush and green with growth, she recalled the times they had played hide-and-seek among the leafy plants. Meg had been too young to play then, but Laura and Ransom, Ruby, Aaron, and several other slave children would join in the game. Ransom, being the oldest and a boy, always seemed to find the best hiding places until with much practice they finally knew them all. As they grew older, their mother had told them that they were too old to play with slave children and that they needed to separate themselves from such familiar relationships. Laura had been hurt by the separation from Ruby, with whom she had become close, but Ransom had consoled her, even playing games with her when she knew he didn't want to. They had formed a close bond then, one which had never been broken.

The sun was beginning to set as they arrived at Barrett Hall. The horses, sensing they were home as well, picked up their pace, and they drew up to the house before anyone could come out to meet them. Several male slaves approached the wagon to help carry the coffin into the parlor where Ransom would rest overnight until burial the next day. Friends and family would be arriving around midday, and they had much to do to prepare for them.

Laura trudged tiredly upstairs, excusing herself from dinner, citing fatigue, and closed her bedroom door. She was weary, in body and soul, and her only outlet was to sit at her desk and write her thoughts in her diary. She changed clothes and readied herself for bed, then sat down to write.

27 July 1861

Oh, Ransom! How my heart aches for you. This morning I awoke and knew that another day had arrived, but there is no pleasure for me without you in it. I keep expecting to receive a letter from you, or see your face as it was the last time, so eager in the Southern cause. But no more shall I see that face, and the cause has yet to be fulfilled. There are so many dead young men on both sides, and still Mr. Lincoln calls for 400,000 more. Will it ever end?

Putting her thoughts down on paper did little to assuage Laura's pain. She was exhausted, from all that had happened and from the long journey from Richmond. She thought too about Jordan, where she was and what she was doing, and whether her brother had also been in the battle. Laura supposed with the end of the play that she had returned to Washington, never to return to Virginia. The thought of not seeing Jordan again, of talking with her, and touching her, left Laura feeling too depressed to continue in her diary. Writing had always been a comfort to her, but now she didn't wish to record what surely must be the saddest days of her life.

❖

The burial the next morning was a stressful and somber event, in keeping with the humid July day. A soft breeze rustled through the leaves, and the James shone brightly as it meandered by. Laura could not understand why the birds continued their singing when surely they ought to be respectful of the occasion. She felt removed from herself, as though she were watching the burial from somewhere other than where she was. Her emotions were spent. All she could do was stand dry-eyed beside the open pit, listening as the preacher spoke of ashes to ashes.

Charlotte had arrived with her husband Robert and stood next to Laura, holding her hand throughout the ceremony. Charlotte was six months pregnant with her first child, yet Laura's profound sadness destroyed her pleasure in this happy circumstance. She congratulated her cousin, of course, but the words sounded hollow even to her own ears. Still, having her there beside her helped somewhat, and she was grateful that Charlotte had made what must have been a very uncomfortable journey.

Preston Young had also arrived, and Laura was shocked to see him in uniform. He explained to her that while everyone had thought the battle of Manassas would decide the fate of the South, it appeared that things were going to continue. He felt he needed to do his part for the cause and had enlisted the day after the battle.

After the coffin was lowered, the mourners wound their way from the knoll back to the main house where Martha had prepared a large feast. Besides family and political associates of her father's, neighbors from nearby plantations had also come.

"Caleb Martin lost his son in the battle as well, and Jonah White lost an arm," Charlotte said as she walked beside Laura.

"Poor Mrs. Martin," Laura replied. "He was the only child left to her after the yellow fever took her little Jenny. I'll send her a note."

"Laura, may I have a word?" Preston motioned her toward the garden as the other guests entered the house.

Reluctantly, Laura followed him and they sat on a wooden bench in the shade of an apple tree.

"I know that I should have discussed the matter before enlisting," he said, "but it was my duty, and I knew you would not disagree."

"Oh, but I do," Laura replied fervently. "After what happened to Ransom, and all the other young men who were killed or injured, I must say that I disagree most vigorously. I do not want any more bloodshed. I have heard enough horror to last me the rest of my life."

Preston seemed taken aback, but spoke in the soothing tone of a parent to a confused child. "My dear Laura, of course you are repelled by the accounts of the battle. Every lady feels as you do. However, it is every man's duty to his country to fight for what is rightfully his. I will not be counted among the cowardly when the time comes. Can't you understand this?"

"All I know is that there are many women who will never see their sons, their husbands, or brothers again. What good are states' rights to the widow and the orphan?" Laura's eyes began to tear up. Whenever she thought that she had no more to shed, they burst forth in seeming endless supply. "Ransom was a soldier, but you are a landowner. What do you know of battle? Ransom was killed in the very first fight he engaged in. What makes you think that you will survive when others more trained and prepared did not? And what of your children?"

"My mother cares for my children, and they are well tended. As for survival, I can only do what is in my heart, and the rest is for God to decide."

He lifted one of Laura's hands from her lap and held it in his own. "And God knows, Laura, I wish nothing more than to return to you, healthy in body and mind, so that we may be married. I still hope to be here in September to fulfill our marital vows, but I leave in the morning for duty and I do not know where it will take me. Rest assured that if I can obtain leave, I will be here on our wedding day. But if not, I would hope that you will wait until I return."

Laura reeled at the news of his imminent departure. Her life seemed to have collapsed around her and although she took no pleasure in the prospect of their marriage, there was nothing else for her to do, and with Ransom's death, she knew her parents would feel desperate for a grandson. How could she deny them consolation? "You are leaving tomorrow?"

"I know it's sudden, but the army waits for no man. Please say you understand, and that you will wait for me." His eyes pleaded and he gripped her hands tightly, communicating his desire through touch.

Resigned to the inevitable and with no energy left to argue, Laura whispered, "Yes, Preston, I'll wait."

❖

The day the St. Clairs had left Richmond to bring Ransom home was shortly after Generals Bartow and Bee lay in state at the Capitol. Thousands lined Capitol Square for a chance to pay their respects to some of the first general officers to die in the war. The newspaper carried a full description of these events.

Rachel insisted on reading the full account to Laura and Meg. Stalwart in her grief, she had refused to allow them to take to their beds. They were receiving callers who had not been able to arrive in time for the funeral but who wanted to pay their respects. Between each visit, Rachel read the Bible or newspapers. Laura suspected her efforts were a means of avoiding more of the terrible sobs that had stunned the household since they first heard the dreadful news.

"And here is an article of interest to this family." Rachel rose from her chair in the parlor. "Female spy captured."

Laura gasped. "Let me see that."

"It's a disgrace that the woman was ever in our home. And to think that we took her to meet the President." Rachel handed the paper over with an air of satisfaction. "I was right about her all along."

Horrified, Laura read:

> *It has been brought to the attention of this newspaper that a female spy has been captured and confined in Libby Prison. Details of the arrest are as yet forthcoming, but the woman, identified as Miss Jordan Colfax of Washington City, is well known to Richmond society. An actress currently at the Marshall Theatre, she was performing in Romeo and Juliet, employment which surely complemented her questionable character. Citizens will do well to be on the qui vive for anyone who appears out of place or whose demeanor is suspect.*

"What will people think of us? The damage to your father's reputation may be irreparable." Rachel towered over Laura, her voice brimming with anger and disgust. "Have you nothing to say for yourself?"

Laura could not speak. Her throat was choked and dry, and the pain in her heart was unbearable.

"Well, all I can say is that we will have to think of some excuse as to how we came to know her and distance ourselves from her as much as possible. This family's reputation will not be sullied by that despicable creature."

"I must visit her," Laura murmured.

"You will do no such thing. No respectable young lady would ever think of going to that awful place, let alone to visit a spy. I forbid it." The sound of horses and a carriage out front drew her attention away from Laura. "That will be your father home for lunch. I do not want him to see you this way, but you will present yourself at dinner tonight. You will show no evidence of crying and you will acquit yourself at the table and participate in conversation like the rest of us."

As soon as she'd left the parlor, Laura broke down into tears. Why had Jordan stayed in Richmond after Laura had come upon her reading Ransom's papers? She should have fled then and given up her work for the Yankees.

"Why you are crying over a spy is beyond me," Meg said. "You should be glad she's locked away. Think of our brother."

Laura lifted her head angrily. "You're a spoiled child and know nothing about it. You know nothing about friendship, trust, and loyalty."

"And you do?" Meg asked scornfully. "Miss Colfax played you for the fool. You believed everything she told you and now see what it's gotten you. I shouldn't be surprised if she laughed the whole time she told you her lies. Well, look who has the last laugh now."

❖

Laura lay abed, listless and exhausted. She had cried for hours until she had no more tears to shed. Her eyes, swollen and puffy, throbbed painfully with the dull headache she had developed. She stared at the ceiling in her room, hearing household sounds as well as the occasional passing carriage on the street. But nothing distracted her thoughts.

A tap on the door was followed by Ruby, who placed a tray of tea and pastries by her bedside.

Laura lifted the damp cloth from her forehead. "I'm not hungry."

"Miss Laura, this ain't right. We's all sad 'bout Marse Ransom, for sure, but you can't have any tears left." Ruby rinsed the cloth and set it back on Laura's forehead. "You ain't got no fever again?"

"No, I'm well." Deciding she had nothing to lose by talking to Ruby, Laura told her about Jordan. "And now they've put her in prison for being a spy, and she thinks I'm the one who told the authorities!"

Ruby remained silent for a few seconds, but could not resist asking. "Well, did you, Miss Laura?"

"Heaven's sake, no. Jordan is my friend, I care deeply for her. I would never put her life in jeopardy. Even though I know what she did was wrong, I did not tell a soul."

Ruby was surprised at her confession. Miss Laura always talked about how good the South was and how bad them Yankees were for telling them what to do. That she would now say that she protected Miss Jordan for being a Yankee spy was mighty strange. Ruby didn't know what to make of it. "So, what you gonna' do, Miss Laura?"

Laura looked closely at Ruby, really looked at her for the first time. It had never occurred to her that a slave would be interested enough to ask such a question. She had always believed that Ruby disliked her, perhaps even hated her. To have her sympathy now was an unexpected kindness that made her see Ruby in a different light. They were in some ways alike, subject to the whims of those whose power was greater than their own.

Laura wiped a tear with the cloth on her forehead. "I don't know. All I know is that somehow I have to get her out of there. If Papa can't help, I would even consider helping her to escape myself. She would be able to head north to Manassas and reach the Union lines to safety."

Ruby nodded. If Yankee soldiers were near Manassas, that's where she had to go.

❖

A few hours later Ruby placed all her belongings in the small sack that she would carry with her on her escape north. Even though the Yankees had been whipped at Manassas, there was talk that the war would go on. Tillie had come with the Lewis family for Marse

Ransom's burial. She said she was making plans to escape with some of the Lewis colored and Ruby could run away with them. She had names of some people along the way that would help, including the preacher that traveled up and down the river preaching to the slaves.

Ruby hid the sack under a pile of rags in the corner of her cabin and made her way back to the big house to finish her chores. Once she was done, no one would look for her until the morning. She passed by Ransom's room on her way to clean the young missy's bedrooms and get their black dresses ready for the next day. Hearing sobs, she paused in the doorway and saw Miss Laura on the bed.

As she began to back away, Miss Laura saw her and said, "Don't go."

Ruby stopped in her tracks. Unsure whether to step further into the room, she stood still, waiting for instructions.

"Oh, Ruby, what shall I do? Ransom is gone, Jordan is gone, and now all that's left is my marriage to a man I do not love."

Ruby always thought she'd be glad to see Miss Laura miserable for one day of her spoiled life, as miserable as Ruby was ever since she was born. But now she felt pity. Miss Laura had lost people she loved, and Ruby understood how that felt. It seemed fair that if the first years of Miss Laura's life were filled with luxury and pleasure, she should pay some time for what God gave her. Ruby hoped God would be fair to her, as well. She had suffered, and now she could run away from that miserable life. She didn't expect to live like rich white folks, but she knew she could have a better life than the one she was leaving behind.

"Go to sleep, Miss Laura," she said. "Things is always better tomorrow."

Chapter Nineteen

Edward St. Clair sat at the breakfast table, reading the paper when Laura came down from upstairs.

"Good morning, Laura. You're up early."

"Good morning, Papa. I couldn't sleep. Where is everyone this morning?"

"Your mother is writing letters and Meg is probably still asleep."

Laura sat at the table while Sarah poured her a cup of tea. "Sarah, have you seen Ruby this morning?" she asked.

"No, Miss Laura. I 'spect she's sick or something. You want I should go fetch her?"

Laura shook her head. "No, not if she's ill. Leave her be. I have no need of her anyway." Not particularly hungry, she pushed her plate away and picked up a slice of bread and nibbled on it. "What time are we returning to Richmond?" she asked her father.

"Shortly. I have to meet with Mr. Humphreys this morning to go over some things." He paused to sip his coffee and continue reading.

"Anything of interest in the newspaper?" Laura asked halfheartedly.

"The *London Times* makes an interesting comment. 'So short-lived has been the American Union that men who saw it rise may live to see it fall.' We must increase our efforts in obtaining formal recognition from England. With the British in our camp, we are all but assured our independence."

Laura could not tolerate any more discussion about politics so she ate quickly. Kissing her father on the cheek, she wished him a good day and went outside to idle away some time until their departure. She walked aimlessly, with no particular destination in mind, but eventually found herself drawn to the path leading to Ransom's grave. She was still in disbelief, unable to clear her mind and calm her nerves. As the path wound among the trees and foliage, Laura could see to the clearing where the family cemetery was located. Kneeling alongside Ransom's freshly dug grave was a lone figure, placing fresh wildflowers against the stone and removing the wilting flowers that had been placed during the ceremony.

"Martha?"

Martha turned at the sound of Laura's voice, her striking beauty evident to Laura even from a distance. "Good morning, Miss Laura." She rose up from her position on the ground. "I was paying my respects."

"It's a beautiful place, isn't it?"

"Yes, Miss Laura." Martha breathed in deeply. "Mighty beautiful, and peaceful. The Lord sure done made Virginia a regular Garden of Eden. I 'spose now that Marse Ransom is gone, this here place will be yours someday."

Startled, Laura stopped to consider that fact. "Why, I guess you would be right about that, Martha. I hadn't thought about it until now."

The awareness that one day Barrett Hall would belong to her gave Laura a certain degree of comfort. All the people that she loved would be here, and she would be buried alongside them as well.

"'Course, you marrying Mr. Young and all, might be that you go live at his place. I reckon his kin is all buried there, and his children be there too."

Laura tried to imagine living somewhere other than Barrett Hall and could not picture it. The thought of moving away to be Mrs. Preston Young left her empty inside. They stood looking down at Ransom's grave for a while.

"Poor Marse Ransom," Martha whispered. "He done his duty and now he ain't never going to see what happens to the 'federacy."

Laura glanced at her, surprised at the wistful tone in her voice. She wondered what Martha, what all the slaves, thought about the war and the Confederacy. She debated with herself for a moment, as she always did before crossing the line when speaking frankly with a slave.

"They say that the North fights to free the slaves, Martha. If the Yankees win and you are set free, what will you do?"

Martha went very still. For a long moment, she neither moved nor spoke, and Laura could see the unrestrained maze of emotions swirl through the blue-green depths of her eyes. So many emotions that she could not begin to fathom them all.

"I would go find my children, Miss Laura," she said. "I would go find my children that been done sold off and then get down on my knees and praise God for letting me live to see the day. After that, if He done see fit to have me die, then that's fine by me. All I want in this here life is to see my children once more."

Laura had to look away, unable to maintain eye contact with Martha any longer. The depth of Martha's pain was something she could not look upon without shame. She struggled to keep the tears from spilling over, so she knelt at Ransom's grave and slowly brushed dead leaves and dirt from around the stone.

❖

Libby Prison was situated near the banks of the James River in Richmond, a short ride from the Marshall Theatre. Laura had paid a brief call at the theatre, and Bill O'Malley had mentioned a plan to contact Jordan's father. Perhaps they would be able to extricate her from prison. She could only hope. Descending from the carriage, she glanced up at the large, imposing brick structure, wondering in which room Jordan would be found. Although what Jordan had done was wrong, she could not bear to think of her locked away in that dreadful place. She approached the main entrance of the building and was met by the guard on duty.

"I'm here to see a prisoner," she said after greeting the man. "She was brought in several nights ago."

The soldier scrutinized her and scratched his head. "I'm not sure you want it known that she is a friend of yours. She's in a mess of trouble. Do you have authorization to see the prisoner, miss?"

Laura shook her head. "No, but I can get it. My father is Edward St. Clair, military advisor to President Davis." She hoped she wouldn't have to go to her father, but she wasn't above using his name to gain access to Jordan.

The guard summoned his sergeant, who asked, "Why would you want to see someone like that, ma'am?"

Laura took a deep breath. "She is a friend of mine."

"Well, if you insist." The sergeant held the door open for her, and Laura followed him into the commandant's room, where she was introduced to Major Turner.

"Sir," the officer reported, standing at attention, "Miss Laura St. Clair wishes to see the female spy."

"Miss St. Clair." The major took her hand and bowed. "May I ask why?"

"Miss Colfax and I have known each other since before the war. I understand she is being held here and I wish to see her."

The major nodded thoughtfully, his eyes never leaving her. "I don't see that it would do any harm. Sergeant, please bring the prisoner here."

When the soldier left, the major motioned to a chair and table alongside a window near the corner of the room. "Please, have a seat." Then he continued, "Miss St. Clair, it would be most helpful if you could get the prisoner to talk. We found documents in her dressing room written in code, and we must discover their meaning. Can you help us?"

Laura looked down at the table, uncomfortably aware of why she was allowed to see Jordan. She bit her lip, wondering how to respond.

"Miss St. Clair," the major said brusquely, "I don't think you appreciate the severity of the situation. The messages she has evidently been relaying north could have potentially grave consequences to our troops. I know of your father and your brother, God rest his soul. Surely your sympathies still lie with the South?"

Laura was indignant. "I am a Virginian, Major, and resent having my loyalty questioned. I would do nothing to jeopardize the South, and certainly not my own family."

"Then you should suffer no qualms about getting Miss Colfax to illuminate for us the meaning of her messages."

Laura returned her gaze to the surface of the table.

"We have searched the theatre and her hotel and have been unable to find the key to decipher these documents. If you could convince her that giving us that information would be in her best interests, we might be willing to let her go. We have not yet sent a woman to the gallows for this offense, Miss St. Clair, but we may be forced to make an example of Miss Colfax."

Laura gasped. "Surely you cannot mean that you would hang her, Major?"

"I am afraid the matter is out of my hands. A military tribunal is forming at this very moment to determine her fate. Once their decision has been made, it is final."

Laura felt ill, her heart pounded wildly, and her face and hands were cold and clammy. She felt like she was in a bad dream. The sergeant returned with Jordan, and when she looked at Laura, her hatred was so evident that Laura flinched.

"Miss St. Clair, you have ten minutes with the prisoner. I advise that you make the most of your time." The inference was obvious, and the soldiers exited the room, closing the door behind them.

Jordan's hair hung limply around her shoulders and her clothing was wrinkled and unkempt. Her eyes were hollow and rimmed with red from weeping. Shocked, Laura reached out to touch Jordan's face, but Jordan jerked away. "I…I never dreamed this would happen." Laura could not believe what she was seeing. How had it come to this?

"You never dreamed this would happen?" Jordan felt devoid of emotion. "What did you expect when you betrayed me?"

"Betrayed you? I did no such thing."

Jordan stared at her in disbelief. "Even now, to my face, you claim your innocence? I know you never really agreed with my political opinions, but do you think me a fool?"

"Jordan, please," Laura pleaded, "I care for you, you are my friend. I know that we have our political differences, but we should not let them come between us. I would never have said anything to place you in this situation. Please, Jordan, please, you must believe me."

"It's too late, Laura. Go away." Jordan was suddenly exhausted. Her heart hurt so much that she no longer cared whether she lived or died. Seeing Laura again was too much, caused her to feel too much, and those feelings warred within her, weakening her resolve.

The tears that Laura held in check spilled over and down her cheeks. The feeling of loss was so overpowering that, for a moment, she couldn't breathe. "Jordan," she choked, "I love you—"

"Love? Is this how you show your love?" Jordan stood abruptly, knocking her chair over. "Get out of my sight and never come here again."

"Jordan, don't say that—"

"I said leave. Guard!"

Shocked, Laura immediately rose from her chair, stumbling in her haste to leave the room. Sobbing, she reached the door and flung it open, only to run blindly into the back of the sergeant who stood blocking her exit.

She continued running down the hall to the main entrance of the prison and out into the street, desperately searching for her carriage that she had left waiting near the building. The driver stood watching the soldiers drilling in the open space near the prison. Laura yelled for the man and wrenched open the carriage door, wrestling with her skirts to gain entry unassisted.

"Damn you, Jordan," she choked out, as the driver rushed to earn his fare. "Damn you. Damn this war. Damn it all to hell."

❖

Abraham Lincoln sat at his desk with a dull headache. Reports kept pouring into the War Department as to the mismanagement and inexperience of the troops. At Bull Run, the soldiers had fled headlong back into Washington in panic, taking one day to return from the field that had taken three to get to. And all this despite the roads clogged by carriages of picnic-goers who had strolled out to the surrounding hillsides to watch the battle, as though going to a horse race. Those spectators who had strayed too close to the fight found themselves taken prisoner along with the fleeing soldiers. Among these was Congressman Alfred Ely of New York, who now found himself a guest at Libby Prison in Richmond.

The defeat had a sobering effect on the country, and Congress had given him the authority to call up as many as one million men for three-year enlistments. No one had ever dreamed that it would come to this, including Lincoln, who felt himself caught up in events that increasingly slipped beyond his control. The battle at Bull Run had resulted in the fearful loss of approximately three thousand men and led him to replace General McDowell with a much younger man, a man whose commanding presence and care for his men seemed to instill confidence in the soldiers. Thirty-four-year-old General George Brinton McClellan was one of only two Union generals to have achieved victory in the field so far in the war. While General Nathaniel Lyon had minor successes in Missouri, McClellan's victory in western Virginia had achieved two important goals: he prevented the rebels from severing the Baltimore and Ohio Railroad, Washington's link to the West, and he preserved the antisecessionist faction in that part of the state that was of paramount importance to Lincoln. As a result, the press hailed McClellan as the Young Napoleon, and indeed he carried that air of success about him. It appeared that the handsome, physically slight general believed his own press and considered himself to be the only man who could save the Union. As far as Lincoln was concerned, he would hold the man's horse if he would only bring victory to the Union.

Lincoln rubbed his temples vigorously, then ambled over to the table in his office where his chief military officer, General Winfield Scott, had laid out a map of his Anaconda Plan. The plan built on the blockade Lincoln had called just days after the attack on Fort Sumter. It set out a naval blockade of the entire 3,000 miles of the Southern coasts plus another 2,000 of inland waterways to prevent the exportation of cotton, tobacco, and other cash crops, as well as the importation of much-needed war supplies. The general also intended to control the Mississippi River to cut off the southeastern states from the West. Lincoln had accepted the plan and tasked the navy to implement the strategy as quickly as possible. However, Lincoln still wanted his army to be the major force in fighting this war, and he would use it to achieve the goal of "On to Richmond" called for by the press as well as the people.

As the country headed into the heat of August, McClellan insisted on rebuilding McDowell's army after the defeat at Bull Run and reinvigorating the morale that had almost bottomed out. While Lincoln could see the value in this, he worried that McClellan was procrastinating. The general seemed strangely reluctant to take the army forward into battle once again, and with the summer half over, Lincoln was impatient with the slow progress. A decisive victory was needed to boost the morale of the people. Lincoln wanted to see newspapers filled with splendid accounts of battlefield glory and predictions of imminent triumph over the Rebels. He feared that McClellan might allow winter to settle in with no movement at all. This, Lincoln could not afford.

He glanced down at the map and looked to western Virginia, an enclave of Union support that he hoped with time would prove to be of value. Richmond was the key to victory, and he knew he must devote all his energy and resources to finding a way to capture it. If McClellan didn't want to use his army, Lincoln just might borrow it for a while and use it himself. Chuckling at his own joke, he turned his attention to the plan once more. The success of the naval blockade would be essential if they were to win, and for Lincoln any other outcome was unacceptable.

❖

Bill O'Malley left the telegraph office and headed down Cary Street toward Libby Prison. When he reached the spot below Jordan's cell, he whistled the meadowlark birdcall, his signal that he was there. Within moments, Jordan appeared at her third-floor window and waved to him below. He jotted down a quick note and stuffed the message inside a rubber ball. Glancing around and seeing no one, he tossed the ball up to the window. This time she managed to catch it on the first attempt and quickly withdrew his note.

> *Your Pa is trying to get a pass to cross the lines to come here but no luck. They don't like his Lincoln newspaper here. He's asking some soldier friends if you can be exchanged for a Rebel prisoner. This might be the best way but will take time. Sad news. Tyler is missing. After the Manassas fight, nobody can find him. I'm sad to tell you this. Maybe he's a prisoner, just like you. So don't worry none.*

Jordan's hand flew to her chest and a sob escaped her lips. After all that had happened to her, Tyler's loss was almost too much. She knew it was possible that he was a prisoner, but she had also heard the Union men in the other cells talk about the battle. Many soldiers had been buried on the field because of the intense July heat. Since the North ran pell-mell from the scene, the Rebels were less interested in identifying Union dead, and some were even buried in mass graves. Trying to find Tyler, if he was dead, might be almost impossible, and the more time that passed, the less likely it would be. A desperate urge came over her to get out of her cell and travel to the battlefield as quickly as possible. If Tyler were alive, he could be wounded and in a Rebel field hospital. The possibility of his being injured and needing care was almost as bad as the alternative, that he was dead.

Using the stub of a pencil Bill had also inserted in the ball, Jordan quickly jotted her response:

> *Tell my father I'm well and have been treated decently, if not always kindly. I will wait to hear his progress on obtaining*

my exchange, but he must hurry. Please, Bill, find out what you can of Tyler and let me know as soon as possible.

She stuffed the pencil and note inside the ball and returned to the window. Peering onto the street below, she saw a prison guard speaking to Bill, who was gesturing wildly. She could hear them speaking but not what was being said, and she stepped away from the window so as not to be seen. Every time Bill came by, he was in jeopardy, and Jordan couldn't bear thinking about his fate if he was caught. After a while she heard the bird call again and threw the ball down to him. Depressed by his departure and the news about Tyler, she lay down on the cot, overcome with grief.

She had been in prison for more than a week, something she had not thought possible. But here she was, alone and powerless to help herself. She knew her father was doing all he could to get her out, but he was surely hampered by the tightening of borders between North and South. She did not know how much longer she would be in prison, nor how much longer she could tolerate it. Her entire world seemed to be crashing around her, and keeping her spirits up had been difficult at best.

Her thoughts wandered back to her arrest and Laura's betrayal. Her anger still simmered below the surface, but in moments of self-pity, she had begun to think about the reasons why Laura would have notified the authorities. When she set aside her anger and self-righteousness, she knew deep down that she'd intentionally deceived Laura and that Laura felt deeply hurt about being used. Ever since she began spying on Laura's father, Jordan had been besieged by guilt and torn loyalties. While it surprised her that Laura would expose her, she tried to think what she would do if their roles were reversed. If she'd discovered that Laura was using her to gain access to her own father in order to relay secrets to the South, wouldn't she have reported Laura? Wouldn't she feel angry and betrayed? But would she have turned Laura in to the authorities? Jordan was not sure. She knew it wrong of her to judge Laura so harshly for doing what she might have done herself, yet she wanted to believe that she would have made a different choice. She would have asked Laura to leave town and threatened to inform on her if she refused.

A nagging thought kept forcing its way to the front of her mind, insisting she acknowledge it. Jordan had been unable to forget the kiss she and Laura shared: two kisses, to be exact. She could no more disclaim the intense emotions those kisses aroused than deny her own heartbeat. No other kiss felt as those did. Nell's seductive lips against hers served only to prove that she enjoyed kissing a woman more than a man. Of course she had not kissed many men, but she doubted that kissing a hundred would turn up a single one who could inspire interest or excitement.

Despite everything that had gone wrong, she yearned to kiss Laura again.

The sound of a door closing along the hallway drew her to her own cell door. Peering through the small opening, she saw George Lamont leading a Union officer to one of the nearby cells. After locking the man in, he strolled in her direction and caught her watching him.

Leering as usual, he unlocked her cell with the arrogance of a man who knew his prisoner would not attempt to fight him. "You won't have heard the good news." He lounged casually against the door frame. "Word is we're going to be making prisoner exchanges soon."

Jordan lowered her gaze so he wouldn't see her hopes reflected in her eyes. Perhaps her father had convinced Union authorities to exchange someone for her. "I am glad that some poor mother will soon see her son. Keeping these boys prisoners does no one any good and requires too much of the South's resources."

"What do you care about the South's resources?" George spat, and a dribble of chewing tobacco slid down the corner of his mouth.

Jordan shrugged as if his news was of no concern to her. "I don't. It seems to me that the South would also want her own boys returned."

"Ha. There aren't that many, compared to the North." He ogled her again, as had become his habit, and left with a swagger. Peeking in through the small window in her door, he said, "Don't worry, the major says that there's no way in hell they would exchange you. Soldiers who fought bravely in battle are one thing, but a spy is quite another. I expect they'll make an example of you. Who knows? Perhaps they'll keep you here for a few years to make the Federals think twice about sending someone else to spy on us."

Even after he walked away, Jordan could hear his laughter for a long time.

❖

Laura sat in the parlor at Barrett Hall trying to read, but instead heard the ticking of the clock in the hall. The tedium of plantation life was broken only by the tasks associated with supplying soldiers with life's necessities. After weeks of such endeavors, Laura could not endure to sew another sleeve in a gray jacket or roll another length of bandages. Her hands were quite rough and red from tugging at wool and cotton and pricking herself with needles.

Then there was the listlessness she'd felt since Ransom's death. And despite her horror at the continuance of the war, she could not seem to stop reading the newspapers to find out about what was going on. An article in the *Richmond Dispatch* for Thursday the first of August, had caught her eye.

> *A Religious War—Harriet Beecher Stowe proposes that the present struggle between the North and South shall be designated "The Religious War." In this we are inclined to agree with the author of* Uncle Tom's Cabin. *It is a religious war. It is the Bible and pure Christianity against infidelity and God-dishonoring crimes, and we are glad to see that the churches of the South are alive to their responsibility in this regard. We learn that in two days during the present week 175,000 pages of religious tracts were sent from this city into the various encampments.*

The churches the St. Clairs attended, one in Charles City and the other in Richmond, preached that God intended Negroes to be slaves and that servitude to the white man was their lot in life as the inferior race. Laura had tried very hard to believe that, but the Bible seemed to be full of contradictions, particularly about Christian love. Laura conceded that she treated Martha, Ruby, and the slaves as inferior, yet she could not remember feeling that way as a child. She had played with Ruby and had thought of her as her best friend. However, everything had changed when she grew to adulthood.

Against her mother's wishes, she had read *Uncle Tom's Cabin* when she was sixteen and had wept at Simon Legree's treatment of Tom. She could not imagine anyone treating Martha or Ruby that way. But when she stumbled upon Mr. Humphreys and the stable boy that fateful day, she had discovered that the vicious abuse of helpless slaves not only happened, but occurred right under her own roof. Laura was ashamed that her parents continued to employ Mr. Humphreys, but when she raised the subject of his conduct her father told her it was not her place to question his decisions and that no slave was punished at Barrett Hall unless he deserved it. Laura had given up arguing with him some time ago and simply closed her eyes to the inhumane treatment, telling herself that there were worse masters than the St. Clairs and at least their slaves were well fed.

Laura tried to imagine the world the Yankees wanted to impose, a world where slaves were freed. In such a world, she supposed Negroes would have the right to complain to the authorities about their mistreatment, and the right to defend themselves when attacked. Men like Mr. Humphreys would be arrested and sent to jail, and men like her father would not believe themselves entitled to favors from their cooks. She wondered if such a change was even possible.

Refusing to think for another moment about what the future might bring, she turned the page of the newspaper and froze at what she saw.

FEMALE SPY TO BE SENTENCED

The female spy confined in Libby Prison is scheduled to be sentenced next Wednesday by a Court of Enquiry. Miss Jordan Colfax, lately of Washington City, was arrested at the Marshall Theatre upon suspicion of spying. The nature of the charges was not specified, but it is generally understood that they include the holding of treasonable correspondence with the enemy.

Laura jerked to her feet so abruptly, her skirt swung wide and knocked over the small table that held her teacup. Both crashed to the floor, and Sarah came running into the room, wringing her hands in her apron.

Rachel followed a moment later, demanding, "What in the world is all the commotion about?" When she saw the broken cup in Sarah's hands, she said, "Oh, Laura, one of my fine china cups. Even before the war it would have been expensive, but now, with the blockade? It may be irreplaceable."

"What happened?" Meg stepped around Sarah, who had knelt to sweep up the china fragments.

"I'm so sorry, Mother. It was clumsy of me." Keeping her face averted, Laura retrieved a shard that had escaped under her chair. She didn't want her mother to notice her panic and wonder if a smashed cup could possibly cause such despair.

"I'll write to Edward in Richmond and ask him to inquire of Mr. Sutton whether he still has this pattern in stock. If he doesn't, we'll have to order it from London. Even if one of the blockade runners can get through, it will come at a dear price."

"Richmond," Laura murmured, attracting an odd look from Meg. She stepped in front of the table Sarah had set back on its feet, hiding the newspaper from sight. "Mother, let me go and see if Mr. Sutton has a replacement. Why should Father have to bother himself when he is so busy with the war effort? And if Mr. Sutton doesn't have it, I could inquire of Angus and Byerly, Mr. Bulkley, Mr. Leroy, or any of the other shops."

"This family is in mourning and you wish to go about the streets of Richmond shopping?" Rachel glared at Laura as if she had taken leave of her senses. "What will everyone think?"

Meg sidled over to the table and plucked the newspaper aloft with a self-satisfied smile. "I see your Yankee friend will be on trial this week," she announced. "Perhaps you're planning to see her after you've finished looking for Mother's cup."

Laura's hand twitched at her side from the repressed desire to slap Meg's face.

"I hope you intend no such thing, Laura," Rachel said. "Your friendship with Miss Colfax has brought quite enough disgrace to this family, and we have distanced ourselves as far as possible. I forbid you to see that harlot again."

"Jordan is not a harlot! She is a warm, kind woman who nursed me when I was sick and slept on the floor near my bed to attend me."

"And had you come to Montgomery with us as I wished, your own family would have seen to your care."

"She's my friend," Laura insisted. She missed Jordan terribly and couldn't bear to think about the way they had last parted. She even dreamed about Jordan and woke up, longing to see her again. "I need to speak to her just once. Please Mother."

"She is a spy, and caught red-handed, from all appearances. She is due whatever punishment the court decides to give her."

"I have heard that they hang spies," Meg mused.

"Oh, be quiet, Meg! For once in your life keep quiet!" Laura snatched the paper from her sister's hands and rapidly left the room so that neither of them could see her distress.

Climbing the stairs to her bedroom, she thought her heart would break if she could not get to Richmond and see Jordan one more time.

❖

Laura searched everywhere for the fringed shawl she planned to wear outdoors but could not find it anywhere. Exasperated, she descended the stairs and out the front door to find Ruby, whom she was sure would know where she had put it last. She opened the kitchen door and found Martha making preparations for breakfast the next day.

"Good evening, Martha. Have you seen Ruby? I can't find my shawl and I've looked everywhere."

Martha did not turn around from her work at the table. "No, Miss Laura, I ain't seen her."

"Why, I haven't seen her for days." Laura stopped to consider this fact. "Prissie said she's ill. Should I call for the doctor, Martha?"

"I don't rightly know, Miss Laura."

"You don't know?" Laura was confused. She couldn't recall a time in her life when she hadn't seen Ruby for over a day. And surely her own mother would know her whereabouts or the state of her health. "Well, if she's still sick, I should think she would be in her cabin. I'll go find Auntie Quince and attend to her."

Puzzled by Martha's attitude, Laura headed down the path to Mr. Humphreys's house. After rousing him, and waiting for him to get to the end of his ingratiating greeting, she said, "I believe Ruby is ill, Mr. Humphreys, and I would like Auntie Quince to see to her."

"Sick? I was just down checking on the slaves, and she weren't in her cabin. I thought she was up with you at the big house."

"That's strange." Laura was completely befuddled. "I haven't seen her for several days."

Mr. Humphreys's expression changed in an instant from puzzled to alarmed. He took off on a run toward Ruby's cabin, with Laura close behind. He burst through the door and stood in the center of the tiny dwelling with his hands on his hips. Laura stared past him into the gloom. The cabin was empty, and meeting the overseer's eyes, she immediately understood what had happened.

"She's run off," he said.

Laura shrugged. "Let her go. We have more important things to think about than a useless servant."

As Humphreys stormed away muttering under his breath, she glanced once more into the cabin Ruby had abandoned and allowed herself a smile. She hoped her childhood friend would reach safety and the new life she was seeking.

Chapter Twenty

Ruby wiggled around, trying to get comfortable on a bed of pine needles. Her mind was too busy for sleep and her heart felt too big for her chest. That noisy, frightened beat was all she could hear except for the sounds of the night. She looked at Tillie, trying to figure out if she was sleeping yet. Her master had gone away with the army. He came back just before they escaped, and told Tillie the Yankees lost a big fight but President Lincoln was getting more men. Soon the Yankees would come back and there would be more fighting.

Ruby took a deep breath. She liked the smell of pine trees and soil. Any other time she would have fallen asleep. She hadn't stopped to rest properly since she left Barrett Hall. At first she hid some ways from the side of the road and waited for paddy-rollers to pass by with their dogs and their mean faces. Then, when she got to the Lewis plantation a day later, she acted like she had a pass from Miss Laura and wasn't going to tell no curious colored her young missy's business. She avoided the overseer and found Tillie. No one messed with Tillie because she was Marse Philip Lewis's favorite slave.

They'd waited until everyone was asleep, then she and Tillie and two field slaves, Joe and Tate, crept to the woods. They hurried away from the plantation all night hidden by the trees. When the sun rose they found a place no one riding by would see and slept for a while, taking turns to watch for any trouble. After they had some rest, they followed the river for a few days. Tillie said they had to look out for a traveling preacher name of Appleby. He was going to take them to Yorktown. His brother was a sailor on a fishing boat and they were going to be smuggled on board. Soon as they were out at sea, Tillie said they would force the captain to head north to freedom. If he refused, Joe and Tate would kill him.

Killing a white man was not something Ruby had figured on. She was terrified they would get caught. If they did they all knew what would happen. Ruby couldn't breathe for thinking about the terrible punishments white folks had for slaves who hit their master. What would they do if a white man was killed?

"Ruby, go to sleep," Tillie whispered.

"I's too afraid."

"You'll slow us down if you don't get any sleep. Close your eyes."

Ruby did as she was told and maybe she fell asleep for a few hours because when she opened her eyes, the sky was gray like a pigeon. She sat up and wrapped the fringed shawl she took from Miss Laura's room around her. Tillie was already awake. She and the men were eating bread and cheese that Ruby stole from the kitchen. They didn't speak to each other for fear that someone passing by would hear them.

The sound of footsteps crushing leaves brought them upright and ready to run. An owl hooted and they looked at each other. The sound didn't belong with the early-morning bird calls. Joe returned the call, and a few minutes later a short, wiry man appeared not far away on the riverbank. They all stood and the preacher led his horse toward them.

"I'm Reverend Appleby," he said.

"Yes, Marse sir." Joe was shaking so much Ruby thought he was going to fall on his knees.

"I'm not your master," the preacher said. "Only God has that distinction, and he is master of us all, black and white alike."

❖

Each day Jordan was allowed periods of exercise out of doors. From eight to nine in the morning, she strolled in the barren yard, then again for half an hour after lunch, and in the evening from six to seven prior to retiring for the night. She was never without a guard, whereas less important prisoners were sometimes allowed to wander on their own unattended. Returning to their cells was based on their word of honor, and besides, where would they go? There had been attempted escapes, some successful, some not. One or two had chosen suicide as a means of escape. They were always successful. But Jordan was too important a prisoner to be left alone. The fact that she was a spy and not a soldier in uniform made her all the more despised by Richmond society. A uniformed guard was as much for her own protection as to deter her from flight.

She exited the prison after lunch and was on her way along Cary Street to the exercise grounds with her guard when a parade of prisoners was led out of the building after her, escorted by several armed guards. Jordan counted about thirty men of varying age and sizes. Mostly officers, a few made an attempt to be as presentable as possible in public while several were disheveled and unkempt. It appeared that one or two of the soldiers had been wounded, as several of their comrades seemed to be holding them upright as they walked. Jordan longed to talk to them.

"Corporal." She turned to her guard. "May I have a few words with the prisoners? A few of them look injured or ill."

Eighteen-year-old Corporal Jake Dawson, the guard assigned to her on most days, had become somewhat of a friend to Jordan during her confinement. They passed time speaking of their childhood memories. "Well, I suppose it can't do no harm."

They strolled over to the group, which began to slow at her arrival. Those who still had caps removed them and greeted her politely.

With a bright smile, she said, "Good afternoon, gentlemen. I'm Miss Colfax. Is all well with you?" She tried to sound uplifting and encouraging.

"Excuse me, miss," a boyish soldier asked. "Are you the lady spy in the cell next to mine? I've never seen your face, but I have gone to sleep at night by the sound of your voice reciting poetry."

Jordan blushed, not realizing the men on her floor had heard her or paid any attention to her. She had found herself speaking aloud just to keep herself company. "Yes, that's me. And were it not for the treachery of a Rebel, I would this moment be sipping champagne on the Potomac."

They cheered her in unison, a response the sergeant didn't appreciate.

"All right, now, that's enough," he barked out harshly. "Do that again and I'm taking you back inside right now."

They hushed instantly, but the grins on their faces remained.

"Corporal, I should like to see the wounded, if I may. Perhaps there's something I can do to help."

"They've seen the doctor," the sergeant said. "And they'll live."

"Yes, I'm sure, Sergeant. But surely you can understand that a woman's sisterly care can be ever so much more than a physician's. I'm sure you would want this concern for your own wounded."

He eyed her speculatively and seemed to succumb to her prettiest smile. "Make it quick," he muttered grudgingly. "We don't have all day."

Walking down the line, she greeted each of the wounded individually, asking where they were from and inquiring as to their health. She implored them to write their families and reassure them they were alive and in Libby Prison. Toward the end of the line, a frail, sickly lieutenant seemed almost asleep, his head resting on the shoulder of a companion. A large bandage wrapped around his head was soiled and bloodstained, and she made note to have it replaced soon.

"Sergeant, this man needs more attention from a doctor. Look at him, he can barely stand unaided."

"The doc will be back on Friday," the sergeant said gruffly. "He's got more important things to do, like caring for our own sick and wounded."

"Well then, perhaps Major Turner will allow me to tend to the prisoners so as not to take up the doctor's precious time. There are several things I can do to help these men."

"Like what?" he asked.

"For example, this poor fellow right here. Captain, would you mind helping him to the ground?" She gestured to the officer holding the injured lieutenant and he laid the man down. "You see the bandage on his head? Why, all I need to do is—"

The breath was knocked out of her chest and her knees gave out. The men standing near her prevented her fall and she quickly collected herself. "Tyler?" Her throat was so dry she could barely speak. "Tyler, is it you?"

Tears flooded her eyes as the wounded man lifted his head. At first it seemed as though he didn't see her, but then his vision cleared and he stared at her for a long while. Jordan knelt down and clung to him with all her strength, promising herself that she would never let him from her sight again.

"Tyler, dear brother."

He struggled a little and mumbled something.

"I can't hear you," she managed between sobs. "Speak more loudly if you can."

"You're choking me," Tyler's voice seemed to break with difficulty from his lungs and she guessed he'd summoned all his strength.

A burst of laughter mixed with tears exploded from her and she released her stranglehold, but she could not let go entirely. The men standing around chuckled softly, and even the prison guards wiped a tear away. Jordan placed a hand against Tyler's cheek and realized he had a high fever.

"Please, help me get my brother inside. He is ill and needs to be in bed."

Several soldiers lifted Tyler from the ground and took him up to his cell, where they laid him on his pallet. Jordan knelt beside him on the wood floor and removed the bandage from around his head. A jagged crease along his scalp had become infected and pus oozed from the site.

"Here, Miss Colfax."

Jordan looked up to see Corporal Dawson standing over her, holding a bowl. He had fresh bandages draped over his arm. Jordan thanked him wholeheartedly, adding when he blushed, "Really, Corporal, I'm truly grateful."

Tyler shared his cell with three other men, who all sat with their backs against the wall, clearly trying to give Tyler some room. After Corporal Dawson left, Jordan dipped a cloth into the warm water and cleaned Tyler's wound, trying to remove as much infected material as possible. The task was difficult, as Tyler's shivering made her extremely anxious. Eventually, when she'd done all she could, she wrapped the bandages around his head and tied them off, feeling around the edges to ensure that they weren't too tight. One of the men in the cell brought a dipper of drinking water for Tyler. Introducing himself as Captain Brown from the Second Rhode Island Volunteers, he helped Tyler sip.

"How long has he been ill, Captain?" Jordan asked.

"More than a week, but he's been worse in the past two days."

"The doc here is pretty good, given the situation," a captain from Minnesota said. "But medicines are in short supply, even for the Johnnie Rebs. The blockade is working."

Jordan tore a piece from her petticoat and dabbed it in the remaining water. She washed Tyler's face and his neck around the collar, removing as much grime as she could. “We need to keep him warm. Can we get any extra blankets?”

“He can have mine,” Captain Brown said. “We don’t use them anyway. It’s too hot in here.”

They quickly wrapped Tyler in the wool blankets, and immediately his shivering dissipated. After a little while, Jordan could hear his breathing even out and she felt his body relax.

“Miss Colfax, Sergeant Lamont is coming.” Corporal Dawson warned. “The swine.”

“Please, everyone, I do not wish to draw attention to my brother. It might very well go hard on Tyler if Lamont takes an interest in him. If we could keep the sergeant away from him as much as possible, I would be grateful.” She spoke to her fellow prisoners, but her eyes remained on Dawson.

They all agreed while Jordan slipped out of the cell and the corporal locked her back in her own.

❖

“Laura, your father is home unexpectedly and we have a guest for dinner.” Rachel swept into the parlor with a benevolent smile.

“Mr. Young, what a delightful surprise,” Laura said halfheartedly.

Preston removed his cap and bowed. “Mrs. St. Clair, Meg.” He took Laura’s hand and kissed it gently. “Miss Laura, as always, it’s a pleasure to see you radiant as ever and a balm to these sore eyes.”

“I imagine you don’t get to see such sights in your regiment, now do you, Preston?” Edward joked.

“Edward!” Rachel admonished. “Don’t be ill-mannered. Won’t you come in, Mr. Young? We were about to sit down to dinner.”

“I would welcome a fine home-cooked meal, thank you.”

Once at the table, Edward told them he had returned to Barrett Hall to retrieve some needed papers from his study, papers he did not wish to be transported except by his own hand. He had met Preston, who was on leave and also on his way home to attend to business, and they had decided to travel together.

“How long will you be here?” Rachel asked him as dessert was served.

“I’m afraid I must return in the morning. Events in Missouri are developing rapidly and the President may need me to travel there. General McCullough appears to have his hands full outside of Springfield, but if he engages in battle and wins, the tenuous hold the Union has on Missouri might be shaken loose."

After dinner, Preston took his leave and, upon her mother's insistence, Laura reluctantly walked him to his carriage.

"It was wonderful to see you again so soon, Laura," he said. "Already I miss you terribly and yearn for the day when I may return to you and my children." He stepped closer until their bodies touched, and Laura resisted the urge to back away. "I hope you'll find it agreeable if I write to you? And I would be grateful if you would do me the honor of writing back."

"Of course, Preston, I would be most glad to. I would like to know where you go and what you do. While being in the military is terribly dangerous, I should think traveling to new places would be exciting as well."

"Yes, I suppose so," he said. "But when the war is over, I'll be happy to give it all up to stay at home the rest of my life, as long as you are there."

He leaned in and kissed her before climbing into his carriage. It was a chaste kiss and Laura dutifully received it, but she felt nothing except the scratch of his beard. As he drove away, she stood waving, then stared into the void until she could no longer hear the rattle of wheels or the hoofbeats of horses. She could just make out the shapes of the trees in the dark. It was an overcast night and the only light came from the house behind her.

"Are you all right, my dear?"

Laura turned around to find her father sitting on a cane chair on the veranda, smoking his pipe. The slight breeze caught the smoke, sending it twisting and turning up to the roof eaves. She trudged over to him, climbed onto his lap, and rested her head on his shoulder. She felt like a little girl once again, seeking solace from his strength.

"Oh, Papa," she sighed unhappily.

"Now, now, what is it, my girl?" He patted her on the back.

At the sound of his rich voice and the familiar consolation of his touch, she poured out her feelings. "I'm so unhappy, Papa. I know I am to marry Preston next month if he can take leave again. But I simply do not love him. He's a kind man and I suspect a wonderful father, all that a woman could ask. But I don't have the affection for him that he appears to have for me."

Her father rocked her slowly, absorbing her words before answering. "Sometimes marriage is less about love and more about companionship. Even if love does not flourish, becoming friends and enjoying each other's company can be vastly fulfilling. Life is a struggle, and through the pains and sorrows of life, an abiding respect and devotion to one another may get you through when love is not enough. Preston is all that you say and more. He is also intelligent and a respected member of this community. All of us planters see great things in him. Why, he could even become governor if he wished. His talents are limitless."

"I suppose," she sighed.

He puffed on his pipe. "There's something more?"

Laura lifted her head from his shoulder to look into his eyes. "How did you know?"

"Your mother told me you wish to go to Richmond."

"Yes, Papa, but as Mother said, I can't allow my association with Jordan to tarnish your position with President Davis."

"The accusations against her are quite serious," he said. "And people judge you by the company you keep."

"I'm not so selfish that I would forget myself again," Laura said bitterly.

"Indeed, we must all be cautious. Even the smallest appearance of sympathizing with Northern sentiments is unwise."

"Papa, everyone knows how I feel about Yankees. I'm a firm believer in states' rights. But Jordan is my friend, and she's in prison. Surely my visiting her would be seen as no more than an appropriate kindness from a Southern lady to an unfortunate lady who has fallen far and been very foolish."

"My dear child, your mother is right. Your good sense falls prey to that tender heart, but I can't find fault in you for the natural weakness of your sex."

Laura was certain she could detect a wavering in his resolve. "Jordan is all alone in that horrid prison with no one to care for her, and that thought is unbearable for me." She paused to gather her breath. "Please, Papa. Let me go with you tomorrow. I merely wish to see her one more time before her trial and tell her…" She paused, uncertain of exactly what it was she planned to say to Jordan. "I want to thank her for saving my life."

They sat together on the veranda for quite some time until Laura began to feel drowsy from the release of her pent-up frustration. After a while, her father released his hold and she got off his lap. He rose from his chair and cupped her chin with his strong hand. "Go pack a bag and get some sleep. We leave very early in the morning."

Mute with joy, she flung her arms around his neck. The tears she held inside finally spilled over and she wept openly. She was going to see Jordan. For now, that was enough.

❖

Tuesday dawned on another scorching August morning, the humidity already high at nine o'clock. Laura, usually a late riser, had gotten up early, not because of the heat, but in her excitement to see Jordan that day. She had obtained a pass from her father so that if anyone asked questions, it would clear the way. Rising so early, however, gave her too much time to wonder what she would say to Jordan once she saw her. The more she thought, the more her stomach twisted into knots. She wasn't even sure Jordan would want to see her, but she was determined to go to the prison.

Unable to keep still any longer, she climbed into their carriage and took the short drive from Church Hill to Cary Street. After showing her pass, she was ushered into the same room she was in the last time she saw Jordan, a familiarity that did little to calm her nerves. Soon, she heard footsteps outside and Jordan entered the room, followed by Sergeant Lamont.

Upon seeing Laura, Jordan froze, her heart pounding with mixed emotions, but her anger prevailed. "You can take me back to my cell now, George." She whirled around to go, but he blocked her way.

"That's Sergeant Lamont to you, Yankee spy," he growled.

Seeing Laura, however, he suddenly changed his demeanor. "Why, if it isn't Miss St. Clair. Whatever brings you to such an unladylike place as Libby Prison?"

The last time Laura had seen George Lamont was at the Governor's levee. A lifetime ago, it seemed. "Mr. Lamont or, I should say, Sergeant Lamont. I did not know you had enlisted."

Although she directed her conversation to him, she kept glancing back and forth at Jordan. Although a bit unkempt, she was as striking as ever, and Laura wanted nothing more than to embrace her. George continued talking, but when he stopped, she had not heard a word.

"Excuse me, Sergeant, but would it be all right if I spoke to Miss Colfax alone?"

"I said I wish to be returned to my cell, *Sergeant*," Jordan insisted.

"Of course, Miss St. Clair. Take as long as you need. I'll be right outside." Casting a smug grin at Jordan, he left the room.

Jordan sat down across from Laura in the only other chair in the room. She did not look at Laura, though, trying very hard to remain angry at her. But Jordan was overwhelmed by the sensations that enveloped her. Laura was so beautiful and it was so good to see her again that she almost wept. Had it not been for finding Tyler, she would easily have given up and thrown herself into Laura's arms, wanting nothing more than the comfort of someone who knew her. But reinvigorated by her love and trust in Tyler, she found the traces of anger still alive inside her.

"What is it you wish, Laura? You obviously have a captive audience."

Laura was disappointed. She had hoped that, with time, Jordan's feelings might have softened, as her own had. "I understand that your trial is tomorrow," she said, seeking strength in talking about the facts.

"Yes, what of it?"

"I wanted to be there, if I could, that is, if you wanted me to. If you needed someone to speak in your defense, I would be happy to help in any way that I could."

Jordan stared at her, not believing what she had heard. A heartbeat later, she giggled and then, unable to control herself, let it build into outright laughter. She laughed at the absurdity of her situation and Laura's offer.

Laura was concerned for Jordan's sanity when her laughter got out of control and wild. But a few minutes later, Jordan's laughter subsided and she dried her eyes on the edge of her sleeve.

"What a lovely offer, Laura. First you turn me in to the authorities, and now you wish to be a character witness. I'm sure that will go over well with the judges." Jordan giggled again, but she was so overwhelmed with sadness that she quickly stopped.

"Turned you in to the authorities? Jordan, I have no idea what you're talking about. I did no such thing. Yes, I was angry with you, but I would never…I love—"

"Why do you continue to deny it, Laura? No one else knew but you. To think that I trusted you," Jordan said disgustedly.

"Trust? *You* speak of trust?" Laura knew she was losing sight of the reasons she had wanted to come to Libby Prison, but she was tired of Jordan's narrow view of the facts.

Jordan looked away, unwilling to continue the same argument. She had not wanted the conversation to take this turn. She didn't want to argue with Laura. What she really wanted was to take her in her arms and kiss her the way she had before. Laura's lips were so soft, and the feeling was so intense that she forgot who and where she was. How did things get so far away from that? More importantly, how could they ever find their way back?

Laura stood to go, sick of Jordan's anger and unwillingness to reconcile. "I had hoped to tell you this under better circumstances, but I know you and your brother were friends with Ransom. He was killed at Manassas."

The words struck Jordan square in the chest. "Oh, no, Laura. I'm truly sorry."

There was no mistaking the pain in Jordan's eyes and her genuine grief. Laura softened immediately. This was the Jordan she remembered. "Do you want me to attend your trial or not?"

Jordan hesitated. She wanted Laura to be there. Despite everything, she loved her and missed her so much that she ached to be near her. She was confused by Laura's protestations of innocence and could see no other means by which the authorities could have discovered her. But what if she was wrong?

"I suppose I can't stop you," she said.

Exasperated, Laura almost lost her temper again. At this point, the grudging concession was probably all she would get from Jordan, so she accepted with a polite nod. "I'll see you tomorrow, then."

Jordan offered a dubious look. "As you wish."

As Laura left the cell, she heard Jordan speak again and paused, glancing back.

"I'm sorry about Ransom," Pain flashed across Jordan's beautiful features. "God rest him."

❖

The Court of Enquiry met in the commandant's office on the second floor of Libby Prison. The judges, three majors from the military, all of whom were lawyers, sat at a table in the room. Jordan had been appointed a defense attorney, also a lawyer and a captain of the militia. He deferred to the judges from the very beginning. She knew her case was hopeless, but the trappings of a trial and the desire for the truth to come out at least propelled her into concluding the farce. She only hoped that very soon her father would be able to make arrangements for her exchange and that she could take Tyler with her. The thought of home made her teary-eyed, but she refused to display weakness to the judges.

A couple of other officers were in the room, including the commandant himself, Major Turner, but Jordan quickly noticed Laura's absence. She had already decided that she did not want Laura to testify on her behalf, if Laura had been serious in the first place. She had done enough damage to the St. Clair family and it was unnecessary to further sully them. But Laura's nonattendance cut her deeply. She had taken Laura at her word, and the cruelty of the letdown deflated her.

However, as the trial was to begin, the door opened and Laura entered, breathless from her rush up the stairs. She had been held up at the door by a new guard who did not know who she was or the reason for her being there. It seemed to take an inordinate amount of time to get beyond him, but once she did, she almost literally flew up the stairs. As Laura found a seat, she briefly smiled at Jordan, trying to encourage her.

"This Court of Enquiry is now in session," one of the judges declared. "Has the evidence against the witness been submitted in writing?"

"Yes, Your Honor," Captain Harris, her lawyer, acknowledged. "But the defense has just now received it and I have not had time to read it."

"Neither have we, Captain," the judge admitted. "I suggest we take fifteen minutes to read over the document and then we can at least begin the examination."

While they read, Laura boldly moved up to sit behind Jordan and tapped her on the shoulder.

"Well, I see you made it after all." Jordan could not hide her relief.

Her slight smile was the first Laura had seen since the arrest, and it nearly broke her resolve not to cry. She let her hand rest on Jordan's shoulder, slowly rubbing it, wanting to comfort her. The connection was electric and they gazed at each other.

Try as Jordan might to remain angry, the physical proximity seemed to erase all feelings of animosity. In its place, a powerful surge of strength and love flooded through her and she reflexively placed her hand on top of Laura's. Tears filled Laura's eyes and they both almost laughed with a shared release of tension. Had it not been for the seriousness of the situation, Jordan knew Laura would have kissed her and the kiss would have been returned.

"I've finished reading the evidence, Your Honors," Captain Harris announced.

One of the judges was still reading while the other two conferred among themselves.

"We're almost there, Captain. A few more minutes and we'll be ready to proceed."

The captain glanced at Laura briefly, but then his gaze returned to Jordan, a puzzled expression crossing his face. He picked up the document again and flipped through a couple of pages until he found what he was looking for.

"Miss Colfax," he whispered.

Jordan let go of Laura's hand and turned in her seat.

"Yes, Captain?"

"Excuse my asking, but isn't that Miss St. Clair sitting behind you?" He kept his voice low.

"Yes, that is Miss St. Clair."

Silently, Captain Harris pushed the document over to her and indicated the paragraph he wanted her to read.

> *It is further avowed that on the 15th of July instant, that said perpetrator did enter the St. Clair dwelling on Church Hill and did stealthily enter the bedroom of Lieutenant Ransom St. Clair with the clear intent of searching said officer's room. Upon discovering documents of a sensitive military nature in the lieutenant's possession, said perpetrator did willfully*

and illegally appropriate the documents to her person, as attested to this court by affidavit of Miss St. Clair.

A cold so deep filled Jordan's heart that she felt as though Medusa had gazed upon her and turned her to stone. The court proceedings continued, and when she was asked to offer up her defense, Jordan sat motionless, unable to speak. When asked to present witnesses in her defense, again she remained silent. Laura sat forward and touched her arm, but the touch felt like Brutus's knife to Jordan, and she rose from her chair and walked away. A sentry at the door stopped her.

"Miss Colfax, have you nothing to say in your defense?" one of the judges inquired. "Silence will only serve as an indictment of your guilt."

Jordan glanced back at Laura, who looked confused and dazed. Ignoring Captain Harris's alarmed gesticulations, she said, "So be it."

After a brief hesitation, the first judge spoke again.

"It is the finding of this court that the accused, Miss Jordan Colfax, recently of Washington City, is guilty on all charges of espionage. It is the decision of this court that she shall serve a sentence of not more than five years nor less than three years."

CHAPTER TWENTY-ONE

"Gentlemen, what on earth have you been doing?" Jordan studied Tyler's cellmates. Several had dirt on their faces and hands, yet their clothes remained relatively clean. "You look as though you belong in a minstrel show."

The soldiers poured water from their wash bucket and began wiping the dirt off.

"How are you feeling, Lieutenant?" Captain Brown of Rhode Island asked, ignoring Jordan's question.

"Much better, thanks." Tyler sat up and leaned on his elbow. Just days ago he hadn't been able to do that unaided.

"Excellent, do you think you will be well enough soon to travel?"

"Well, yes, I think so, why?"

"We have almost finished digging a tunnel out of here," the captain replied in a low murmur. "If all goes well, we will be finished in a few days. I wouldn't want to leave you behind, Lieutenant."

Jordan and Tyler shared a surprised glance.

"A tunnel? But how?" Jordan asked.

"Captain Talbott down the hall is an engineer. He figured out how to do it. On the second floor, through the fireplace in the dining room, we've dug down into the cellar to the east side of the building. Between Libby and the next building is an open lot, about fifty feet wide. Our tunnel extends underneath this and we've almost reached a shed on the other side. From there, we can break through to the offices of the James River Trading Company building, which faces onto Canal Street. Once we've arrived there, we'll simply walk out the gates and make our escape."

Jordan was astonished that all this industrious digging had been going on undetected and that no rumor had made its way around the prison. She set down the book Corporal Dawson had brought in for her. At one time an escape into literature would have provided a welcome respite from her boredom in prison. But she felt crushed by her situation and could focus only on getting Tyler mobile, then finding a way back home. He was steadily improving. The color had returned to his face and the wound on his head had almost completely healed, although it would leave a long scar from his forehead into his scalp. He remained weak and bedridden, so news of the escape plan worried her almost as much as it thrilled her. Could she get him well enough in just a few days to leave with everyone else?

The lack of good, healthy food had slowed his progress. Food shortages throughout the city meant prisoners ate a steady diet of biscuits, bacon, and, if lucky, rotting vegetables. She made do with what they were able to get, and with George Lamont on leave to visit his ailing mother, Corporal Dawson had smuggled in better-quality meats and vegetables over the past few days. The entire South now faced shortages, he said, and while most everything was still available, prices were high.

"How have you managed to get in and out of here undetected to dig a tunnel?" Jordan asked, praying their guards were not just biding their time, waiting to catch the prisoners in an escape attempt.

"We have a key that gets us out of this cell. Captain Talbott stole it from a guard who was transferred to Manassas. From there, it's easy to slip downstairs to the dining room, especially at night. They post guards mostly on the outside, not on the inside of the building."

"Once we're out, how do we get back North?" Jordan asked. "How do we get through the lines?"

"I didn't say it was going to be easy," Captain Brown admitted. "We can't travel together because it would be too easy to get caught, so it will be every man for himself. But we've each had some time to think about how to get back. You should too."

Tyler's eyes gleamed in the dim light. "I feel much better. I'll be strong enough to take a walk tomorrow." He touched Jordan's hand and she bent low to hear him whisper, "Don't go without me."

Jordan's mind was already hard at work. She needed to get a message to Bill. If she could trust Laura St. Clair, she would be tempted to enlist her help. Laura had attempted to contact her, but Jordan instructed Corporal Dawson that she had no wish to see her and asked that he tell her so. She intended to close the door on that part of her life.

❖

In the parlor at Church Hill, Laura read in the newspaper of another battle at a place they were calling Oak Hills in far-off Missouri. On the banks of a small stream known as Wilson's Creek, it was another great Confederate victory, though again not without considerable loss on both sides. The Union general in charge, Nathaniel Lyon, had been killed, the first Union general to die in battle, leading ultimately to the Federals' abandonment of the field. Despite the excitement of yet another major Confederate win, the excitement was tempered by the actions of the Union commander out west, Major General John C. Frémont. The general imposed martial law in Missouri after the Union defeat, confiscated secessionist property, and emancipated the slaves in the state. The Confederate response was outrage at his actions.

Laura supposed she should take the carriage out and visit friends to celebrate the victory with them. She could work up little interest in socializing. Out of respect for her mourning, most people didn't pester her with questions about her friendship with the Yankee spy, but Laura could sense the speculation every time she entered a room.

She was still hurt and confused by Jordan's behavior at the trial several days ago. Their friendship had appeared to be on the mend, and when they touched just after Laura arrived in the commandant's office, the feeling was so intense that nothing else seemed to matter. Laura knew Jordan had shared that powerful connection; how could she deny it just minutes later, treating Laura as though she had suddenly contracted leprosy? Laura had visited the prison to see her the next day, needing an explanation, or even just a decent good-bye if that's what Jordan wanted. But she was rebuffed at the door and informed Miss Colfax did not wish to see her.

Laura tossed the newspaper aside and stepped out into the hallway, looking for a servant. Since Ruby's departure, she had become more independent. Prissie was a hopeless body servant who could not create a hairstyle of any distinction and forgot most of her responsibilities as a replacement for Ruby.

In frustration, Laura wandered through the house. Why had

the foolish girl decided to run off as well? It seemed every day the newspaper was filled with advertisements for runaways. Teams of men scoured the roads every day, finding slaves and returning them to their masters in exchange for substantial rewards. Some severe punishments were meted out so that all understood that talk of freedom was just a Yankee stratagem to unsettle the Negro and disrupt production.

Laura had asked her father to ignore Ruby's escape, but he said that would set a dangerous example and within days the St. Clairs would have no slaves left. He had offered a fifty-dollar reward for her safe return. Laura hoped they would never have cause to pay it.

When she finally found a servant, Laura said, "Please have the carriage brought around."

She intended to make one final attempt to visit Jordan, then she would go home. Go home to Barrett Hall. Go home and plan a wedding. Go home and plan a life she had never wanted for herself but knew was her fate. And she would try very hard to be happy. And try even harder to forget.

❖

Jordan and Tyler, along with many of the prisoners, took their exercise on the open lot. She couldn't help but think of the tunnel beneath her feet, and her pulse raced at the idea that they would soon crawl through it on their way to freedom. Every day brought improvement to Tyler and she was confident now that he would be able to make the escape after nightfall. They had reached the far side of the lot when Jordan saw Laura standing at the opposite end. She was surprised at the mildness of her response to the sight of her. She was still angry, though the feeling was a small flame compared to the once-raging blaze. For the most part, she felt only emptiness, and sadness for her misplaced trust and her belief that something special existed between them. When she looked at Laura now, she could still see the beautiful woman she'd once considered intelligent and kind. But she also saw a sad, desperate woman willing to do anything for her cause. She had once thought she loved Laura, but those feelings had withered.

"Tyler, stay here and rest, I'll be right back." Jordan headed in Laura's direction.

Laura's heart fluttered each time she saw Jordan, and this time was no different. She wanted nothing more than to run to her, to embrace her and know that all was well between them and there was some future for their friendship. The mere fact that Jordan was coming over to talk to her gave her hope, and she smiled tentatively.

"What is it you wish, Laura?" Jordan asked tiredly. She could see the uncertainty in Laura's expression, and a part of her wanted to reassure her, to make it easier. But the time for such compromise had passed. Laura no longer deserved her consideration.

Laura felt her smile disappear. The disappointment was so overwhelming that the dull ache in the pit of her stomach turned into a tight knot. She gazed longingly at Jordan's beautiful face, searching for some sign of what had been there in the past.

Jordan's hazel green eyes regarded her with listless disinterest. "Whatever it is you need to say, please do so and we can end this farce of friendship."

Shocked to be spoken to so callously, Laura said, "I wanted to say how sorry I am for your sentence." Laura could hear the misery in her own voice. "I want you to know I'm going to ask my father to send a pardon for you from President Davis. You would be allowed to go home, but not to return to Virginia."

Jordan smiled grimly. "Why would I ever want to return to Virginia?"

The sharp pain at the implication cut Laura deeply, and her throat closed. She turned her head away, hiding the tears that had already begun to form. After a moment, she found her voice again. "Obviously you don't, and I'm truly sorry for that. However, I shall always cherish the memory of happier times. I'm grateful to you for having cared for me during my illness. And I'm grateful to you for—" At this her voice caught. "For giving me something…I shall never forget."

Jordan was about to say good-bye and walk away, but she could not go without asking the one question that kept her awake even now. "Laura, why did you betray me?"

"I didn't betray you," Laura denied hotly. "How can you believe such a thing of me?"

"I saw the evidence myself," Jordan said, disgusted that Laura was still determined to lie. Clearly she felt guilty that her decision had consequences. She had knowingly sent a "friend" to prison.

"What evidence?" Laura's cheeks were as white as the daisies wilting under the mid-August sun.

"During a trial, the defense attorney sees the evidence brought against the accused," Jordan said coldly. "Your name was there as the informant against me."

Laura gasped. "That can't be possible."

"I suppose you were told you could remain anonymous." Jordan shook the dust from her grimy skirt and prepared to leave.

"I was told no such thing because I never spoke to any of those people. Jordan, I didn't give you up. I'm telling the truth."

She was so convincing, for a moment Jordan almost believed her. She smothered an urge to confide in her and seek help for the escape. Her poor judgment of Laura's character had cost her dearly in the past and with Tyler to consider, she was not going to take another risk. She watched Laura's beautiful mouth form words, but stopped listening. After a moment, Laura fell silent and they stared at one another.

"I'm sure you have regrets," Jordan said generously, wanting to let her know any grudge she bore was in the past. "These are difficult times for all of us and we make the decisions we feel we must. If it will make you feel any better, I forgive you."

"*You* forgive *me*?" Laura's breathing was uneven. "Well, I do not forgive you. I do not forgive you for tricking your way into my home and my affections. And I do not forgive you for refusing to listen to me now, or believe me, after all that has passed between us."

Her black kid gloves caught at her skirts and she angled her head back. Beneath the black bonnet she looked incredibly fair and her welling eyes were the bright aqua of a far ocean.

"Good-bye, Jordan," she said.

"Good-bye, Laura."

It was only when Laura crossed toward the street and summoned her carriage that Jordan knew she was telling the truth. Whatever the explanation for the paperwork, however Laura's name had arrived on that document, Laura had not betrayed her.

Panic and guilt set Jordan in motion. She stumbled across the rough open ground as the driver tapped his horses with the whip. "Laura!" she called.

But the wheels turned and a gloved hand tugged the curtains closed. As Jordan watched the carriage speed down Cary Street, her tears gushed and she roughly brushed them away. She did not want to feel. She did not want to care. But she knew that she did.

❖

"Lovely night for a stroll, darlin'." Bill O'Malley grasped Jordan's elbow as she and Tyler hurried east along Canal Street.

"Tyler, this is Bill O'Malley, my stage manager," she said.

Tyler grasped the man's hand firmly. "Mr. O'Malley, I was never so honored to make a new acquaintance."

"Aye, the honor is mine, Mr. Colfax." He slowed his walk, compelling them to keep to his leisurely pace. "Let's not appear to be in great haste," he said calmly. "Now, tell me about your escape."

"It was brilliantly executed," Tyler said.

"And extremely filthy." Jordan brushed dirt from her hands and wondered where everyone was now.

They'd slipped from their cells at one o'clock in the morning. Captain Brown led Jordan and Tyler downstairs to the dining room and removed the bricks from the back of the fireplace before summoning them into the gaping hole. Jordan had already removed her hoop from beneath her skirt, and slid down the shaft until she found footing on a ladder against the wall, and the captain assisted her into a dimly lit cellar. In no time, Tyler had descended, followed by more men. As the cellar filled, Captain Brown pushed aside a barrel that blocked the entrance to the tunnel, and picked up a lantern sitting on top. Lighting the wick, he crouched down on his hands and knees and crawled into the tunnel. Jordan and Tyler squatted and followed him inside.

The ground was relatively even and they made quick progress in the damp, dank cavity. Coaxed on by the smell of fresh earth, the sound of dripping water, and the fear of collapse, Jordan didn't slow when her knee hit a rock. She glanced back to check on Tyler and saw a long line of crawling men behind them. The sight was like something out of a nightmare and she shivered in fear, anticipating a company of soldiers waiting at the other end of the tunnel, even shooting them.

After a few minutes, the tunnel took a dip, then rose rapidly. Dirt and debris fell from above as everyone scrambled up toward the light. Emerging from the tunnel, they'd found themselves in a small shed stocked with crates and farming implements. The captain led them through a door and into the James River Trading Company building, where they scuttled toward the side that faced Canal Street. Pulling back a bolt on the large gate from the inside, Captain Brown slowly opened the door a crack. When he signaled the route was clear, he wished everyone luck and instructed them to spread out into the city and find their way north.

"Don't travel in groups," he warned.

Jordan hugged him tightly. "Thank you, and good luck to you too. I hope we see you again soon."

Even now, with the prison a few blocks behind them and no sign of an alarm, she wanted to run. At Twenty-First Street, Bill turned them toward the canal and increased their pace to a brisk walk.

When they came to a long flatbed boat moored alongside a low-lying dock, he stopped and said, "Welcome aboard my little pleasure craft."

Jordan smiled as Bill helped her and Tyler down onto the deck; it felt so good to be free again. They had a long way to go and the risk of capture would be high until they reached the Maryland border or a company of Union soldiers, whichever came first. But nothing could dampen her spirits.

"We're going home," she breathed, planting a kiss on Tyler's cheek.

Their advantage was in heading south, a direction the authorities wouldn't expect. Jordan trusted Bill's judgment on this choice. He said that no one would look for them if they headed that way, plus Fort Monroe at the tip of the Virginia peninsula where the James met the Chesapeake was still in Union hands. If they made it to the fort, the rest of the way home would be simple.

"Set yourselves down and get comfortable," Bill said. "We're going to be here for a bit."

Jordan and Tyler sat on a board positioned across the sides and in the middle section of the long boat. Elsewhere onboard, piles of tobacco were strewn across the floor.

"Are we to ride this thing all the way to Washington?" Tyler sounded skeptical.

Bill pushed hard on the pole, moving them along the waterway. "This *thing* is what they call a bateau, and don't you say nothing unkind about her. She's going to get us to our next stop."

They had only gone a short distance when a clamor arose from the direction of the prison. Lights were being lit inside the prison, and presently they heard the crack of a rifle. Jordan's heart rate picked up and she began to fidget.

"Now don' go capsizing us, darlin'." Bill's movements remained steady and relaxed "All's well."

He chewed on his cigar and began to hum. Jordan didn't know the tune, but recognized it as one she had heard from him before. Oddly, the song comforted her and she calmed from the music as well as from the rhythmic suck of the pole being lifted from the water with each push toward freedom. They passed buildings and shops, and after a while entered the James River, where Bill caught the current and was able to relax on the pole except to guide the boat.

They meandered downriver for several miles before Jordan felt reasonably comfortable that they'd escaped. The gentle rocking of the boat and the tumbling sound of the James lulled Tyler to sleep and Jordan dozed against him. When she woke fully, the sky had changed from black to the blue-gray of impending dawn.

"That's the mouth of the Appomattox River ahead," Bill said, studying a map. "Up ahead is City Point, and over yonder on the port side down a ways is Charles City. Pretty soon we're going to need to find a place to spend the day so we can avoid the Rebel patrols. We can only travel at night."

"How much farther do we have to go?" Jordan asked.

"Another night should do it, and we can get an earlier start tomorrow evening. The current is swift, but we can't make it tonight."

Jordan scanned the shoreline, knowing that Barrett Hall lay nearby somewhere. She peered intently into the darkness for several minutes, when she glimpsed a light shining intermittently between the trees and foliage.

"There!" She pointed. "Guide the boat over there, Bill."

He dipped the pole cautiously. "Are you sure?"

"Yes." She was drawn to the light like a beacon. Somehow she just knew they were meant to follow it.

Chapter Twenty-two

Laura wandered aimlessly from room to room in the Church Hill house, dreading the arrival of the first afternoon callers. Upon hearing of the daring escape from Libby Prison, Rachel St. Clair had promptly arrived in Richmond, determined to salvage the family's reputation. For reasons Laura couldn't fathom she seemed to think the escape provided the ideal opportunity. The family was to rally around the cause and show themselves to be just as angry and shocked as the rest of the city. By now people would be ready to accept that Laura had seen the error of her ways and was suitably chastened. It was time for her to don sackcloth and ashes and present herself as the grieving sister of a fallen hero and future wife of another fine Confederate officer. Rachel felt with the right overtures to the right dowagers, the social embarrassment of Laura's friendship with the Yankee spy would soon be forgotten. She only hoped that it wasn't too late to ensure that all was not lost with respect to Preston Young and the impending wedding.

Rachel's campaign to return to the bosom of feminine society in Richmond was to commence with a sewing party to which every lady would bring items of uniform and they would all drink tea together. She had assumed a martyred demeanor upon her return to Richmond, declaring herself to be mindful of the cause and willing to sacrifice herself even when she was in deep mourning.

Meg was thrilled. She had done nothing but complain bitterly about the personal price she had to pay because her older sister had consorted with "that soiled dove." Laura paused at the door to Meg's room and saw her bewailing Prissie's attempts to copy an elaborate coronet braid from a copy of *Harper's Weekly.* They kept the journal out of sight because of its Northern sentiments.

Noticing Laura in the doorway, she said, "That no-good Ruby

stole my hairbrush. Where am I going to get another good one? Mamma gave me this old thing." She knocked the brush from Prissie's hand, then cried, "What are you waiting for, girl? Pick that up."

Laura pointed to the lavender dress laid out on the bed. "Are you wearing that?"

"Why shouldn't I?" Meg indicated the black crepe collar and cuffs sitting on her dressing table and said, "The bows on my hairnet are black also."

"Ransom has only been dead for three weeks. You can't change to half-mourning. Mother wants us to make the right impression."

"No one cares what I wear," Meg said. "It's you they'll find fault with. You're the one who visited that Yankee in prison."

Laura stared down at her black bombazine dress. If her mourning clothing were any more somber and her veils any heavier, she would be mistaken for a widow. She would have to wear the same black dresses for six months before she could consider a change to lavender or black and white. Their mother would be in full mourning for a year.

"I will not apologize to anyone for acting as my moral conscience dictates, least of all to nincompoops like Emma Harper and Abigail Thornton."

"Moral conscience!" Meg twittered. "You should not be lecturing me about conscience. I know what you did."

"What are you talking about?" Laura didn't like the smug expression on Meg's face. She marched into the room and bent over her sister. "Explain yourself."

"I shall do no such thing. You're a traitor who consorts with spies."

"How dare you!" Laura grabbed a handful of Meg's hair.

Meg squealed. "Let go of me." She tore at the cuff around Laura's wrist, trying to pull her hand away. "Prissie, quick. Fetch my mamma."

"Stay where you are," Laura commanded the terrified servant. "Don't you set a foot out that door."

She shook her sister's coiffure loose, yelling, "Tell me what you think you *know*, you horrid creature."

"Mamma, help." Meg wailed shrilly, making a grab for Laura's new latticed cap. As she caught hold of it, she lost her balance and tumbled backward off her stool, drawing Laura down onto the floor with her.

At the sight of the two of them wrestling in a sea of petticoats,

Prissie covered her face with her hands, crying, "Stop it. Stop it. Oh, Miss Laura."

"Silence!" Rachel St. Clair swept into the room. "For shame. Get up off that floor."

"I done told her not to mess up that hair, Miss Rachel," Prissie said.

Laura and Meg scrambled upright.

"I will not have you debasing yourselves in this manner," Rachel said grimly. "It's after two o'clock and you look like strumpets in a public saloon. Prissie, see to them immediately. And if you are not sitting with me in the parlor before the chime of three, you'll all feel the whip."

❖

"This ginger cake is excellent." Mrs. Dunne nibbled diligently. "Of course, you make your own butter, do you not?"

"Why, yes." Rachel smiled at her guests. "And if any of you would enjoy some Barrett Hall butter and produce, I've prepared hampers for each of you as gifts. You'll find them in your carriages when you are ready to depart."

Laura stared down at her boots, stifling an urge to giggle. Rachel never gave away so much as a slice of ham if she thought it could be sold.

Their guests positively glowed with delight. No one would turn down such gifts in these times, even with the taint of scandal hanging over each heavy basket.

"It's quite wretched that you cannot attend Mrs. President Davis's party next week," Mrs. Wilson said. "Especially for poor dear Meg. With so many of our young men gone to war, eligible dance partners are in scarce supply."

"Indeed, the girls may yet attend with a relative, but mourning prohibits me, of course."

"Oh, what a river of tears you must have wept these past weeks." Mrs. Dunne dabbed at the corners of her own eyes. "Such a tragic loss and such trying disappointments…close to home."

Laura stitched meekly as Mrs. Wilson picked up the litany.

"The disappearance of that worthless darkie…the scandal…and now…Why, I simply cannot believe it. A tunnel, no less."

"Disgraceful," Meg said.

"Is it true that you actually visited that Yankee in the prison?" Abigail Thornton asked Laura.

Keeping her mother's words in mind, Laura said, "Alas, I did so." She was aware of the steady regard of each woman in the room. Almost choking, she said, "I regret most dreadfully that my thoughtlessness caused anguish to my dear parents."

"The trial too," Abigail remarked. "You must have been very devoted to her."

"I was." Such terrible sorrow welled in her that she could not prevent her tears. Hoping they would be interpreted as remorse for her conduct, she stammered, "Sadly, my loyalty was not returned."

Mrs. Wilson seemed to take pity on her. "Abigail," she said, deftly changing the subject. "Is that India shawl new?"

"It is." Abigail shrugged the handsome garment a little higher and lifted a corner to display the rich pattern. "Papa complained, of course. He said for the same price he could have bought himself a good breeding slave."

The ladies oohed. A shawl like that must have cost at least a thousand dollars, Laura thought. Letting the conversation swirl around her, she gazed out the window but saw nothing. The rain continued to pour on the muddy streets of Richmond, and only those who had no choice ventured out. Laura listened to the clock ticking on the mantel. Her mind swirled with a hodgepodge of thoughts that ranged from Jordan and their kiss to their cold parting near the prison. Where was Jordan now? Laura prayed she hadn't been caught.

At the sound of carriage wheels and horses' hooves, the conversation ceased and several of the ladies craned to see who had arrived. Not Emma Harper. That paragon of virtue couldn't stoop to sip tea with the St. Clairs. Laura's father descended the carriage steps as the driver held an umbrella over him. Two other men followed him toward the house. One was the family lawyer, Mr. Burton, the other was unknown to her. Her father walked slowly through the downpour, seemingly in no hurry. Laura felt the weight in her heart grow heavier, fearing that his reluctant step indicated bad news. A few seconds after their arrival, Sarah entered the parlor and whispered to Laura that her father wished to speak with her in his study.

Puzzled but not completely surprised, Laura excused herself and joined the three grim-faced men standing in front of the fireplace. They waited for her to take the chair her father indicated before being seated themselves.

"I suppose you're here about the escape at Libby Prison," Laura said.

Her father's jaw muscles tightened and flexed. "Mr. Atwater is a prosecuting attorney for the government. He's here to ask you some questions, and I want you to be completely truthful and tell him whatever he wants to know. Mr. Burton can give you advice if you are confused."

Laura regarded each man in turn. "I don't understand."

"Are you aware that your friend Miss Colfax was among the escapees?" Atwood asked.

"Yes, it was reported in the newspaper. Has she been caught?"

"Why do you ask?" Mr. Atwood was a pinched, officious man, and Laura sensed he had taken an instant dislike to her.

She gave the response she knew her mother would have appreciated. "I ask because I would hope that anyone found to be an enemy of my country serves the prison sentences handed down."

"Several of the escapees have been recaptured," Mr. Atwood said. "But many are still at large, she and her brother among them."

Laura was careful to disguise her reaction to this news with a disinterested shrug. "Then it seems you have more important things to do than call upon me, Mr. Atwood."

Her father gave her a wry warning look. "Laura, a guard at Libby Prison has alleged that you were instrumental in helping the prisoners escape."

"That is absurd! Who makes such an allegation? Surely you do not believe this, Papa."

His gaze softened. "No, sweetheart. I do not."

"If you assisted Miss Colfax in any way, it's called giving comfort to the enemy." Mr. Atwater said.

"She wasn't the enemy to me, sir," Laura said indignantly. "She was…*is* my friend."

"Would you say Miss Colfax was your confidante?" Mr. Atwater asked.

"In some matters, perhaps."

"Did she ever mention that she'd been in Mr. St. Clair's room during a visit to your home?"

Laura pondered the question, knowing only too well how the truth would look. The palms of her hands felt damp and perspiration formed on her brow and top lip. Reluctantly, she said, "I saw her there."

Mr. Atwood was obviously pleased with himself. "And yet you did not inform the authorities, or your father, brother, or President Davis, who were sitting downstairs in the dining room at that moment?"

Laura uttered a vehement, "Of course not."

The prosecutor seemed nonplussed. "Why not, Miss St. Clair?"

Blushing, Laura said, "Is it not obvious?" Making a show of her discomfort with the topic, she stirred in her seat, then turned a pleading stare on her father. "This is very embarrassing, Papa. The impropriety… How can I be expected to besmirch the memory of my dear brother?"

Color flooded her father's face, "Are you saying—"

"Please." Laura clasped a hand to her heaving bosom. "Don't tell Mamma. Imagine how this would affect her."

The three men exchanged embarrassed stares.

Mr. Atwood was bold enough to ask, "Miss St. Clair, did you actually see your brother and Miss Colfax…together?"

Feigning outrage, Laura rose from her chair, prompting the three men to leap to their feet. "I cannot bear to speak of this vile matter any further. I declare, it is most ungallant of you to embarrass me this way." Swaying slightly, she clutched her father's arm, intent on living up to each man's cherished idea of feminine virtue. "Papa, I feel faint."

"Calm yourself, my dear." Her father glowered at Mr. Atwood. "If you'll excuse us, sir, my daughter needs the attention of her maid."

With a curt nod and a bow in Laura's direction, Mr. Atwood conceded defeat. But before they could take a step toward the door, he asked, "St. Clair, did you have any notion of this?"

Edward paused. "I harbored suspicions." He didn't conceal his annoyance. "Mr. Atwood, I take it these unseemly questions are at an end and my daughter can return to sewing uniforms for men of courage?"

"Papa." Laura raised a trembling hand to her father's chest. "Mr. Atwood is only doing his duty." She smiled sweetly at each of the gentlemen visitors.

Mr. Burton's periwinkle eyes held a gleam of admiration. In the future, Laura suspected, he would not speak to her as if she were a brainless child.

❖

Laura didn't return to the parlor when she heard the men depart. She strolled down the hallway to Ransom's room. Everything was as he had left it when he rode off to Manassas Junction that fateful day. She sat on the bed and glanced around, her eyes resting on a tiny tin soldier on the nightstand beside the bed. It was a replica of George Washington, the soldier Ransom most admired and tried to emulate. A Virginian, a soldier, a planter, and the first President of the United States, Washington embodied all that a Southern gentleman would wish to be in life. Ransom had played so often with the toy that she could see the places where his fingers had rubbed or chipped off some of the paint. Not having noticed the damage to the little toy before, she clutched the small soldier to her breast and lay down across the bed. After a minute, she began to sob quietly into the bedcovers.

❖

Jordan bolted upright from a dead sleep and for a moment she was disoriented, trying to clear her head and remember where she was.

Auntie Quince stood over her, holding a tray of food. "Martha made this special just for you." She placed a tray on the floor beside Jordan.

Jordan remembered the three of them stumbling through the woods in the dark and coming upon the slave quarters of the St. Clair plantation. She recalled her visit among them during the winter. They remembered her attention to their illnesses, offered shelter in an empty cabin, and provided them with blankets and hot food. Martha's cooking, as always, was delicious.

Tyler and Bill were still asleep, so she rose quietly, taking the tray to a corner of the cabin.

"You can go outside and eat if you want," Auntie Quince whispered. "Mr. Humphreys done gone to Charles City for supplies and won't be back till late. Folks up at the big house don't never come down here."

"Thank you." Jordan smiled and went out the door of the cabin.

Martha had prepared fresh eggs, ham, spoon bread, and gravy, and Jordan ate at a wooden table in the shade of an oak tree. When she finished, she decided to take a stroll to clear her mind. A slave named Isaiah pointed to a dirt path near the river and she briskly walked along the winding shore.

It was a beautiful day on the river and she watched as the boats traveled easily downstream. She made sure to keep well into the trees, although there was little likelihood of anyone seeing, let alone recognizing her. She'd been walking for nearly twenty minutes when she crested a small knoll and she realized she'd reached the family cemetery. She slowed her pace at the sight of a recently dug grave. *Oh, Ransom.* A sharp pain almost brought her to her knees and she cried, softly at first; then, with the weight of all that had happened to her, she collapsed to the ground and sobbed. She wished she could turn back the clock and begin all over again. She wished she had never met Kate Warne and Allan Pinkerton. She wished the Confederates had never started this awful war. But most of all, she wanted Laura back.

She cried for a long time, sifting the dirt of Ransom's grave through her fingers, feeling the richness of the soil. She recalled the first time she'd met Ransom, and how kind he had been to her, even defending her against one of his own kind. After a while, spent and exhausted, she got up and followed the trail back to the slave quarters. Tyler and Bill were eating breakfast at the table beneath the oak tree.

She greeted them pleasantly and asked Bill, "When will we leave?"

"We'll move on downstream tonight. Once we reach Hampton Roads, we'll be home free."

Jordan didn't ask for details. The less she knew about Bill's contacts and his routes north, the better.

"See that fella over there, the big one?" Bill pointed to Isaiah, the slave who had showed her the path. "He wants to come along."

"I'm not so sure that's a good idea," Jordan said. "If we were captured, he'd be convicted for aiding escaped prisoners. I think the Rebels would be more callous to him than they would be to us."

"Darlin', if we get caught, we'll all hang together." Bill slouched against the trunk of a tree. "I don't mind telling you that a big strapping man like that could sure help to handle the boat. No disrespect to you, but Tyler's still weak. Besides, Isaiah knows the river. Says he was sold to the St. Clairs from a plantation near Williamsburg. If we have trouble, he could be a help."

"Well, you've gotten us this far, Bill," Jordan said. "Whatever you say is fine with us."

❖

The sun set around seven thirty that evening, and the four of them climbed into the bateau and pushed off from shore. They traveled for hours under heavy cloud cover that threatened rain but protected them from being seen. Bill and Isaiah each had poles to push them along, but for the most part they simply let the current take them. Tyler insisted on taking a turn but found, to his chagrin, that he was too weak for the task.

"What river is that, Isaiah?" Bill asked as they reached the mouth of a river that emptied into the James.

"That there's the Chickahominy," Isaiah said. "Few more miles and we close to Williamsburg and my ole marse's house." He gazed longingly in the direction. "That's where my kinfolk be…and my wife and children. I ain't seen them near six years."

No one spoke as they glided silently by the river mouth, pressing on more rapidly. Shortly before dawn they approached Hampton Roads, which led into the Chesapeake Bay. They hugged the north shore of the James and were rounding a point when they spotted the outline of a Rebel patrol boat anchored nearby. Bill and Isaiah quickly guided the bateau into an overhanging tree and stopped to consider what to do. The darkness was beginning to lift, and if they passed the patrol boat they would surely be seen.

"Whaddya think, Isaiah?" Bill chewed his cigar.

"If'n it was just you and me," Isaiah pondered, "I'd say you my marse and I's your nigger. But ain't no white ladies on bateau."

"And Tyler ain't exactly a Southern boy neither," Bill said. After a few moments of thought, he smiled. "I got an idea."

The sun began to rise when a lookout on the deck of the patrol boat hailed them. Several other soldiers came to the bow to see what was passing by, and an officer onboard called, "You there! Come aside our bow and let me see you."

Bill and Isaiah guided the bateau over to the larger vessel and drew alongside. The captain of the ship peered over the side.

"Where you going so early in the morning, sir?"

"Me an ole' Isaiah, is taking this tobacco up to Mill Creek."

"That's quite a ways from here. What're you doing so far from home?"

"Ain't that far," Bill drawled. "And the distance seems a mite short when you got a girl over in Warwick County." He grinned and winked, chewing his cigar roughly.

The captain returned the grin. "Yeah. I got me a girl over in Newport News myself."

"And you got a faster boat than me, you lucky devil."

The captain laughed. "That I do. All right, be on your way, then. And watch yourself. There's Yankee sloops out there blockading the roads."

"Don't I know it. Damn Yankees. I had two slaves that done run off to Fort Monroe. I'm still trying to get 'em back."

Bill and Isaiah pushed off from the patrol boat and let the current move them away. A few soldiers on deck watched them move away until he could not see them anymore.

"All's clear," he said.

The mounds of dried tobacco leaf rustled and lifted away, revealing Jordan and Tyler buried beneath.

"Keep your heads down," Bill cautioned. "I don't think the Rebels will come out this far 'cause of the Yankees and Fort Monroe being so close and all. But we need to be careful."

By now Bill and Isaiah were exhausted, the tension of the trip the primary cause, but suddenly the walls of Fort Monroe came into view. The six-sided stone structure, which had remained in Federal hands since the firing on Fort Sumter and had been reinforced to keep it there, was their final destination. Bill and Isaiah pulled the bateau into shore and let her ground. As the four of them climbed out, several armed Union soldiers approached.

"You can't stop here, this is Federal property," one called. They surrounded Jordan's party. "Identify yourselves and state your business."

Tyler stepped forward and tried to make his dirty, torn uniform presentable. "I'm Lieutenant Tyler Colfax, US Second Cavalry, and this is my sister, Jordan Colfax. We escaped from Libby Prison two days ago with the help of this man here." He gestured toward Bill.

The sergeant didn't seem surprised by the claim. "I read about that in the newspaper." He glanced toward Isaiah. "And who might you be, ole' Jim?"

"My name ain't Jim, sir. I's Isaiah, Isaiah Curry. And I's contraband." He gave a toothy grin. After a lifetime of slavery, he'd finally reached freedom.

CHAPTER TWENTY-THREE

Ruby had given up swatting mosquitoes. The Reverend said they were east of Williamsburg and once they got there, they would head overland to the York River and then continue to Yorktown. There they would get on a boat and sail up the Chesapeake to Havre de Grace. But first they had to walk across the worst swamp she'd ever seen with mosquitoes so thick she had to cover her eyes and mouth to stop them flying in. She was hot and tired, and wanted to stop and rest awhile. But she didn't complain. She just kept right on walking so she would not be left behind. Sometimes she thought about going back, but everyone would be looking for her by now. She wondered how much Marse Edward was offering for the reward. It was a hundred dollars for John. Maybe she'd bring half of that. She was young and Miss Rachel had learned her house manners.

Ruby switched her sack to her other shoulder and praised the Lord that they were almost into the woods. She wished she had some of Auntie Quince's castor oil for all the bites itching her skin. She didn't scratch because scratching caused bleeding and mosquitoes smelled blood and then they bit even more. She had bites on her ears and one of her eyelids was swollen. They probably bit her there too.

Ruby stepped over an old rotting tree trunk and froze at the sound of a dog barking. No one moved. Tillie's green eyes lit up in fear.

"Run!" Joe yelled at them.

He disappeared into the woods. Tillie grabbed Ruby's hand and they ran after him, with Tate a ways behind.

"We got to get to the river." Tillie stumbled and fell against a tree. Ruby took hold of her hand and pulled her along down the embankment toward the river.

They could hear several dogs, now, along with horses' hooves and the voices of men. Ruby could scarcely breathe from running and her legs felt so heavy she was dragging them. Ahead of them, Joe jumped into the James with a loud splash. Ruby didn't know how to swim. Terrified, she stopped at the water's edge. She didn't know how to go forward or how to go back, and if she got lost, she didn't know what she would do.

"I can't get across that river. Oh, Lord help us."

"Stay with me," Tillie said.

Ruby followed, keeping her eyes on Tillie's back. A thicket of briars blocked their way but Tillie didn't stop. The thorns cut Ruby's skin and caught at her skirt. She felt like they were trapped in a sea of molasses. Everything was dragging her down. The thorns, the mud, the weight of her fear.

Tillie pushed her down as they heard the crack of a rifle, and they both crouched behind a tree, covering their mouths to stop the noise of their panting. Ruby looked back and saw three white men standing at the river's edge, with their rifles aimed. Joe was still in the water, struggling against the current, tired from running. His head bobbed on the surface like he was resting, then the air was filled with the sound of gunfire and smoke rose from where the white men stood. Joe went under but came up again, waving his arms and trying to float. There was more gunfire. Ruby knew she and Tillie should be running while the men were laughing and yelling, but she couldn't move.

"He dead," she whispered.

Joe's body rose in the water and the river carried it along. Ruby watched as it collided with a floating log, spun around, then went under.

Tillie shook her arm and they got up, ready to run again. But a man on horseback stood before them, his rifle resting in his lap. He smiled.

❖

The trip home from Fort Monroe had been quick and comfortable. When the military forces there had informed Washington of the arrival of the escapees, the USS *Pawnee*, a light-draft steam sloop of war, was diverted on its way to the North Carolina coast to take them home. The three men slept in their berths below, still recovering from the journey down the James. Jordan walked the deck, trying to stay out of the way of the crew.

A squall had arisen before sunset, and an officer approached her to recommend that she go below deck to get out of the rain. Jordan politely thanked him, but preferred the feel of the warm rain and the cold spray against her face. The awnings that hung across the deck provided shelter from the elements for both her and the sailors, and they shared the space peacefully. Every now and then a sailor would gaze longingly at her, and she smiled at him, knowing that each had probably not been home for some time. Their ship had been heading to Hatteras Inlet off the coast of North Carolina for a possible engagement and would be returning as soon as they delivered her and her party to Washington. It was possible that some of the men would never return, and if a smile or a hello from a woman made them happy, she was willing to oblige.

A helpful sailor, trying to engage her in conversation, told her she was standing at the forecastle of the ship, on the starboard side. She asked about a large cannon they were standing next to, as it was the only one of its kind among the other cannon that made up the ship's battery.

He was proud to show off his knowledge of the ship. "These smaller cannon are nine-inch Dahlgren shell guns, while that there big one is a hundred-pounder Parrot rifle." He would have continued but for a stern glance from a nearby officer.

"I guess I better be getting back to work, miss." He grinned, and Jordan realized that she was interfering with the running of the ship.

Waves battered the sides of the vessel and it dipped and rose. The storm clouds were dark and angry and matched Jordan's mood. She felt a kindred spirit with the ship and the storm, that they were destined to be together during the tumultuous ride home. Finding a seat out of the storm aft of the ship, she watched the swells of dark gray sea where it met the lighter gray sky on the horizon. She wished that instead of going home, the ship would alter its course and head out into the vast emptiness of the ocean. She wanted to forget everything that had happened to her, all her memories of being in prison and of Laura.

No matter where she was, what she was doing, or what she was feeling, her mind was never really free of Laura. It would seem that Laura had indelibly marked herself on Jordan's heart, like a scar that held no pain, but constantly reminded her of the injury. Unfortunately the wound had yet to heal and every time she recalled it to memory the pain was as sharp as the initial cut. It was, she realized, the memory that kept the wound open, and she determined that henceforth she would do all that she could to erase it from her mind as well as her heart.

❖

The *Pawnee* steamed up the Potomac, then headed onto the Eastern Branch before docking at the Navy Yard on the north bank of the river. They had no sooner disembarked than the *Pawnee* shoved off to return to its mission at Hatteras Inlet, and they waved to the sailors on deck as they departed.

"I'm going to introduce Isaiah here to some friends of mine," Bill said, "and then I'm going to find me a big steak and a pint of this town's best. After that I plan to sleep for a week." He shifted the cigar from one corner of his mouth to the other. Watching Jordan carefully, he went on. "Then I'll be heading to Ford's to see what's what there. Hopefully Mr. Ford still has some work for me."

"You're the best in the business, and I'll be sure to let him know all that has transpired since we left. I will not have you alone on our first night back. You're coming to dinner, seven o'clock sharp, and don't be late." She glanced at Tyler. "I for one want to go home and see Father, and sleep in my own bed. Then I shall burn these clothes."

They shared a carriage and dropped Bill and Isaiah at Bill's room near the theatre and continued home. When they arrived and entered the house, Joshua Colfax was not home, but the housekeeper, Mrs. Johnson, was in the kitchen.

"Oh, my babies! My little babies! Oh, look at you! What have they done to you? Come here, come here." She threw her arms about them, hugging and kissing them until she nearly smothered them. They laughed and cried and when she finally believed they were really home, she let them go.

"Now you go upstairs right now and change clothes and wash up. I'm going to make an apple pie and a peach pie right this minute, and you each get half. Then you are going to tell me what you want for supper, and if you each want something different, then I'll make both dishes. When you're done up there, I want you to come down here and tell me all that has happened to you since you left."

She bustled into the kitchen, still laughing and crying.

That evening at dinner, Jordan, Tyler, and Bill regaled Mr. Colfax and Mrs. Johnson with their tales. Jordan began with her meeting with Kate Warne and eventually Allan Pinkerton. She told of how she had agreed to spy on behalf of the North and how she had been captured, sentenced, and imprisoned in Richmond. Mrs. Johnson gasped, and Joshua glared harshly at her.

"Why didn't you tell me you were performing such a dangerous task on behalf of our government? I would have done all in my power to dissuade you of such foolish notions."

"I would have done the same," Tyler chimed in.

"Which is why I couldn't tell you, either of you," Jordan said earnestly. "Father, you had so much on your mind then, and Tyler, you were going off to war. The last thing I wanted to do was have you worry about me."

"And see how well that turned out," Joshua muttered.

"Yes, but look how I found Tyler. For all we know, with the lack of medical care, he might not have survived in prison. Certainly he would not have been well enough to make the escape."

Jordan and Tyler then told them of the tunnel that had been constructed out of Libby Prison and of their trip down the James. She told of the slave Isaiah who had helped get them safely to Fort Monroe where the *Pawnee* finally brought them home.

"If it had not been for Bill, we most likely would never have made it out of Richmond, let alone Virginia."

"Mr. O'Malley," Joshua said, his eyes misting over, "I cannot ever thank you enough for what you have done for my son and daughter. I cannot conceive of how I may ever repay you for risking your life to save theirs."

"You are a most welcome guest in this house for as long as you wish," Tyler continued.

"And you must tell me what your favorite dish is so that the next time you come I will make it for you," Mrs. Johnson added, smiling shyly at him.

Bill reddened with embarrassment from the attention and praise directed at him. But glancing at Mrs. Johnson, his eyes danced and he winked at her.

"It weren't nothing, Mr. Colfax," Bill said, brushing the praise away. "What I done for Jordan was not even close to all she's done for me since I've known her. Shoot, she's like my own daughter, she is."

Joshua saw the affection in their eyes, as Jordan and Bill smiled at each other. He knew that what Bill had said contained more truth than he wished to hear, and he looked away.

"I bet those Rebels are still poring over those documents they found in my dressing room that night, trying to make sense of all the signs and symbols on the pages." Jordan laughed at the image. "What I don't understand is that I know they searched my hotel room. Surely they must have found my bag containing the code book."

Bill snapped his fingers. "I knew there was something I was forgetting." He reached into his coat pocket and withdrew the book, handing it to Jordan with a flourish.

"However on earth did you get this?" she asked, astonished.

"Well, I wasn't sure you was really a spy, but I thought I'd play it safe and go to your hotel room myself. Seems I got there ahead of the soldiers. I found the book and got out before they got there. I ain't looked at it none, but I figured what was in it."

"Thank you, Bill." She was thrilled to know that it hadn't fallen into Rebel hands.

"A toast." Tyler raised his glass and the others followed suit. "To Bill O'Malley, for all that he has done for the Colfax family, and of which he is now an honorary member."

"Hear, hear," Joshua concurred, clinking his glass against the others.

Bill drained the rest of his wine and stood. "Seeing as how the hour is late and I can't take no more of this backslapping, I best be getting on home to bed. Thank you all for including me tonight, and Mrs. Johnson, thank you for the lovely meal. It was fine."

Mrs. Johnson blushed and giggled.

"I'll see you out, Bill." Jordan placed her napkin by her plate.

In the entryway, Bill paused and whispered to Jordan. "That Mrs. Johnson o' yourn, she be married, right?"

Jordan smiled knowingly. "She's the Widow Johnson. Her husband passed on some years ago and that's when she came to work for my family."

"Aw, 'tis a shame it is, a downright shame." He grinned and winked.

Jordan opened the door and he descended the steps. As he strolled out into the night, he hummed that same tune again, the one that he'd hummed the night of their escape. Jordan tried to remember it so she could ask him what it was the next time she saw him. After he'd disappeared around a corner, she remained on the steps outside the Colfax home, gazing across Lafayette Park to the White House. It seemed ages since she had dined there. So much had happened since that happier time, so much of her life had changed that she almost didn't recognize herself anymore. In a matter of months, she had gone from a simple actress with a promising career to an imprisoned spy, and back again. In between she had managed to fall in love, with a woman. A woman who might not return her love, who might in fact even hate her with all that had happened.

Jordan could not shut out the memory of Laura closing the curtains in her carriage and driving out of her life. Soon she would be married, but the world around her was changing. Would she even live the life she imagined, on a plantation with a husband and children? Would Preston Young survive the war? Jordan contemplated a life in which she would never see Laura again. The thought was unbearable, and there could be no point in trying to renew their brief friendship. She had deeply wounded Laura, first through her deceit, then in her determined belief that Laura was lying about betraying her to the authorities.

Jordan gazed sightlessly across the army tents in the park as her instincts vied with the facts. She was all but convinced now that Laura was telling the truth; she had nothing to gain by lying to her the last time they spoke. Their friendship was already in tatters. Yet Jordan knew what she'd seen in the commandant's office at Libby Prison. How would Laura's name have ended up on that document if she wasn't the informant? Could someone else have claimed to have suspicions and named Laura as a source? Jordan frowned. There had to be some way she could get to the truth in this matter. Going back to Richmond to make her own enquiries was out of the question. She would need to find someone who could do it for her, if it mattered that much.

It did matter, Jordan thought; she needed to know for certain who had betrayed her. But it could wait. Events had overtaken the lesser concerns of men and women, and she felt the need to get her bearings once more. She sighed. She felt old beyond her years, old and tired. And she wasn't sure whether she would ever feel any other way again.

❖

Early one afternoon in late August, Jordan narrowly escaped one of Nell Tabor's warm-lipped embraces and returned home from a visit to Ford's Theatre where John Ford and the stage workers were happy to see her. He had assured her that he wanted her to consider a role in an upcoming production, but that she would no longer need to go to Richmond. Since the war started, it had become harder and harder to cross through the lines to Virginia anyway, so he had decided to postpone any touring productions in that theatre.

Although pleased that her life had returned to normal, Jordan felt a simmering unease that she shoved down. Richmond and the Marshall Theatre had always been part of her routine, part of the rhythm of her performance schedule. Not performing there was one more thing that had changed in her life, and she wondered when it would ever be the same again.

When she entered the house and walked past the parlor, she glanced in. Her father and Tyler sat stiffly inside, and when Tyler saw her, he was clearly relieved and stood up. She was surprised to see him dressed in an entirely new uniform, everything sharply creased and his boots mirror-polished. He looked almost exactly as he had the last time she had seen him before going off to war except for the bright red scar that creased his forehead.

"Jordan, I'm so glad you are here. Please, you must convince Father that I must return to my regiment."

"What?" Jordan felt as though he had hit her in the stomach. "What are you talking about?"

"There's a new general in charge, George McClellan, and from all accounts he is whipping this army into shape. He has reorganized it, renamed it the Army of the Potomac, and morale is finally improving. The cavalry will play a more important role than it has, and I have sent word to my commanding officer of my return to and fitness for duty. He has requested my presence as soon as possible."

Jordan was dazed and looked to her father, who sat stonily in his chair by the fireplace.

"But, Tyler, you have been home only a week. You have yet to recover all your strength."

"I'm fine, truly I am. I have had plenty of rest and plenty to eat. As a matter of fact, I have gained a few pounds already because of Mrs. Johnson. Remember, too, I am in the cavalry, not the infantry. It is not as though I must march everywhere I go."

"But haven't you done enough already? You fought bravely and have been wounded in the service of your country. Surely you have done your duty." Jordan was insistent, not wanting to lose Tyler so soon after she had found him.

"I fought one battle and was wounded, yes. But had I not been taken prisoner, I would surely have recovered nicely in a Union hospital and would have been returned to duty immediately. As it is, I have had far more time for relaxation than most of my comrades who have suffered worse wounds than I. Besides, I must do what I know Ransom would do. I can expect no less of myself."

"I have tried talking sense into him, Jordan," Joshua spoke tiredly, "but he is as stubborn as you are."

"Tyler, please, think of what we have all been through. You have done enough."

"I have done nothing!" Tyler's voice rose in protest. "I was in one battle, then sat in prison. The war continues and I will fulfill my obligation as I swore an oath to do, as Ransom and I both swore an oath to do. I leave in the morning," he said. "I hope you wish me well."

He made his way out into the hallway and upstairs to his room. Jordan looked to her father, who also sat expressionless.

"I suppose there is no stopping him," Joshua finally said.

"No."

He got up slowly, and Jordan thought that he had aged tremendously since they had returned home, so much so that for the first time, she felt as though she should assist him. She even took a step forward, but he waved her off. He headed toward his study across the hall and closed the door, leaving her alone with her thoughts.

Chapter Twenty-four

Ward Lamon paused before entering the office of the President, watching as Lincoln paced from his desk to the window, his arms clasped firmly behind his back. Periodically he would clutch at his hair in frustration and mumble incoherently about his generals. Upon seeing Lamon in the doorway, he bade him enter, and Lamon closed the door behind him.

"I have one general who is immovable and another who won't stop," Lincoln despaired.

"Sir?"

"General McClellan insists that the troops need to be whipped into shape. I understand that, but he cannot see that the rebels are also doing the same. The next time they meet, both sides will be equally whipped into shape and will cause more injury and death than Bull Run. I'm telling you, Ward, the people won't stand for that many dead and wounded again."

"The people will understand that battles must be fought and won," Lamon soothed. "I understand that the men respect and even love him. They call him 'Little Mac.' He has cleared all the bars and hotel lobbies of stragglers and demands officers and men alike have passes authorizing their absence from duty. He is restoring order and securing the defenses of the capital."

"So I hear," Lincoln said. "And that is most welcome news. But aside from the general's constant drilling and preparations for defense, there is no movement south. The only indication of action is when he is astride his horse accompanied by his staff of counts, princes, and dukes. He even has John Jacob Astor as an aide, served by his own valet, steward, and chef."

Lincoln flopped down in the chair at his desk, his head flung back and his eyes closed.

"Out in Missouri General Frémont is not much better with Hungarians and Italians on his staff. He issues orders and demands more troops to send hither and yon for God knows what purpose. And all we have to show for these past four months is Manassas and Wilson's Creek."

Lamon stood quietly, not knowing what to say to assuage the President's gloom.

"At least our navy is having some initial success," Lincoln continued. "But we cannot afford to have our army encamp for the winter on the banks of the Potomac. We need to act, and we need to act now. The people and the Congress clamor for it."

He pushed himself out of his chair and returned to the window, looking out at the troops drilling outside.

"We must move on to Richmond, Ward, and end this war quickly. The country will not endure another year of fighting."

❖

The closing days of August were gray and rainy in Richmond, and the nights were unseasonably cool. Laura sat at her desk with her mind on Preston Young and his farewell kiss. How she wished she could feel something for him. But when she compared that kiss to those she had shared with Jordan, she could not explain the overwhelming difference. How was it possible to feel so much with her and to feel nothing with Preston? Even being with Jordan was so much more pleasurable and exciting than the company of men.

Laura gave up trying to write a diary entry and returned to bed. Thinking about Preston or Jordan did no good as she had started to believe she would never see either of them again. Jordan was gone from her forever, and Preston could be killed on the battlefield. Her family provided little consolation.

Meg had not spoken to her since their fight. Her mother only bothered to speak to her about the wedding, a topic she detested. Her father's mind was elsewhere. Charlotte had taken to her bed to rest before the birth of her baby.

Oh, if only Ransom were still alive. Laura could remember the day of their picnic at Drury's Bluff as if it was only yesterday. She could see him sitting across from her boasting about the life he would have as a cavalry officer. The war had seemed like a great adventure then. Laura almost laughed at the thought. Staring up at the dark ceiling, she listened to the rain and resigned herself to returning tomorrow to Barrett Hall and to the future she couldn't bear to think about. Finally, she closed her eyes and let the tears fall as they had every night for weeks. She had grown so accustomed to sorrow's nightly visit, the dark imaginings it brought along had become her only companions. Eventually they lulled her into a dreamless sleep where she thought no more about Jordan or the cold lump in her chest where a heart was supposed to beat.

❖

After kissing Mrs. Johnson's cheek, Tyler and Jordan left the house. They crossed Lafayette Park and the grounds of the White House, observing the soldiers who stood guard or relaxed off-duty. It seemed as though they were on holiday rather than in the midst of a great war, but the lesser-rank men saluted Tyler sharply as they passed. Approaching Pennsylvania Avenue, they hopped onto the streetcar that had arrived and the horses pulled away at a slow pace. The Capitol Building, its unfinished dome still under construction despite the war, loomed in the distance, and they marveled at its size and grandeur.

When they arrived at Matthew Brady's studio, they found there was no wait to have Tyler's photograph taken. Jordan recommended a full portrait, and for five dollars, Tyler received twenty-five cards.

As they left the studio and stepped back onto Pennsylvania Avenue, he handed her a card. "I want you to have this. You will have it to remember me by, in case anything should happen. If I do not return this time, it will be all I have to offer."

A lump formed in Jordan's throat, but she determined not to have Tyler's departure be a sad affair. "I'll look at it every day and think of you. Write often, and I shall do the same." She couldn't bear to think of not hearing from him.

"I'll do my best, but know that there will be times when the mail may be difficult to come by where I am. However, somehow I'll get word to you."

"Where do you go now?"

"I am to meet a fellow officer at the Smithsonian. He has a carriage and from there we cross the Long Bridge to Alexandria. I shall be issued another horse when I arrive."

"Well, then..." She sighed.

He smiled and embraced her. "Thank you for taking care of me in prison, but please, this time, try to stay out of trouble."

After their farewell embrace, Jordan stood on the street for a long time. Army wagons rumbled by and pedestrians moved around her, oblivious. She wanted the world to stop, to notice her sorrow. First the loss of Laura, and now losing Tyler again. Surely someone other than herself should take note of this heartbreaking moment. But life went on. People had their own troubles to worry about, and she was merely another one in the crowd.

Rather than head back up Pennsylvania Avenue toward the theatre, she walked in the opposite direction toward the Capitol Building. President Lincoln had determined that the work on the building would continue and that it and the nation would survive. When she approached the building, she rambled among the large blocks of marble that lay upon the ground, running her hand over the smooth surfaces. She was about to leave when a group of men descended the Capitol steps, heading in her direction. President Lincoln was among them, his height and top hat placing him a good foot taller than his companions. Following close behind was Allan Pinkerton wearing a bowler hat, his clear blue eyes scanning everyone in his path. They had almost passed her when the President stopped.

"Why, Miss Colfax." His face was almost handsome as a smile transformed it. "I am so glad to see you safely back home. I hope you didn't suffer greatly in your recent confinement?"

"No, sir," Jordan replied. "I'm quite well, thank you."

"Sir." An extremely short man peered up at the President. "I must be on my way. I'll call upon you again for a decision on the matter we discussed."

The man tipped his hat and strode away up Pennsylvania Avenue with purpose.

Lincoln shook his head. "That man can compress the most words into the smallest ideas of any man I ever met." Returning his gaze to Jordan, he asked, "Your brother was wounded wasn't he?"

"Yes, at Bull Run. But he is recovered and has just this morning left to return to his regiment in Alexandria."

"That is excellent news. I am very glad for his recovery and grateful for his service to the country. Please tell him so from me."

As Jordan thanked the President for his concern, she became aware of Allan Pinkerton's steady scrutiny. "Miss Colfax," he inquired.

"Will you be able to continue with the theatre now that you are unable to return to Richmond?"

"Yes, Mr. Ford has been exceedingly kind. I'll be performing here in Washington and in Baltimore. He's arranged for a local actress to perform my role in Richmond. It is just as well. I've no desire to return to the place."

"I can imagine," Pinkerton said.

Jordan hesitated as an idea took shape in her mind. "Mr. President, I wonder if I might detain Mr. Pinkerton for a moment."

"Certainly." Lincoln excused himself and joined the other men waiting on the stairs below.

"I have a favor to ask, Mr. Pinkerton." At his nod, she said, "I wonder if you have an agent in Richmond who could investigate a matter for me."

Pinkerton's mild grin was indulgent. "After your services to my agency, there is no need for you to pay a fee. I'll gladly obtain the information you seek, if I can."

"It's related to my arrest," Jordan said. "I'm aware from reading the evidence documents that Laura St. Clair reported me to the authorities. However—"

"I think you're in error." Pinkerton's brow drew together. "I'm not aware of any statement in your case from Miss Laura St. Clair."

Jordan was intrigued that Pinkerton had knowledge of the evidence against her. It was his business to know such things, she supposed. If charges were brought against one of his spies, Pinkerton might fear being implicated. "My attorney showed me the court documents," she said. "I saw the name entered into the record, with her statement."

"There was a statement made by Laura St. Clair?" Pinkerton continued to seem puzzled. "Do you recall the content of that statement?"

"Yes, it was the reason I was convicted. She said that I entered her brother's room to steal the documents."

"Ah, yes. I recall the statement now." Pinkerton said. "Miss Colfax, what you saw was correct. It was a Miss St. Clair who informed the authorities. Miss Margaret St. Clair."

"Meg?" Jordan's entire world turned upside down. "How can you be certain of this, sir?"

"Our operative at the Confederate White House, Mary Bowser,

whom you know, overheard a conversation between Mr. St. Clair and Jeff Davis about Margaret St. Clair's claims."

"Margaret St. Clair," Jordan repeated dully.

With each breath, she could hear the wild pounding of her heart. Laura had not betrayed her. Like a blind fool, Jordan had seen only the name "St. Clair" and had not added together the obvious clues. Meg detested her and had never bothered to conceal the fact. She must have passed Ransom's room before Laura did. The possibility hadn't occurred to Jordan.

Every deeply held emotion she had tried to crush rose within her along with a deep, racking sob.

"Miss Colfax, are you all right?" Pinkerton asked with consternation.

Unable to speak, she held her sides.

"We can discuss the inquiries you want made at another time," Pinkerton said.

"No, that won't be necessary," Jordan managed a halting reply. "You've just provided the information I need."

She desperately needed to get away, to run as far and as fast as possible. She needed to get to Richmond, but how? How would she get through the lines? Even if she could get there, she would be recognized and returned to prison. But she had to see Laura, even if it meant exchanging her freedom for Laura's peace of mind. Oh Laura, the innocent one, who had done nothing to deserve unkindness and who had stood by Jordan throughout, risking her own reputation and enduring reproach and contempt from her family and friends for doing so.

Jordan had denied her, had turned her back on her, even knowing that underneath all her anger, she loved Laura. Her heart shattered at the thought. She could not remain silent and allow Laura to marry and go on with her life. She had to know if Laura loved her, too.

❖

"Are you insane?" Joshua Colfax nearly shouted, something he never did.

"I must go," Jordan said determinedly.

"You are an escaped prisoner, convicted of spying," her father said. "The Rebels will surely be glad to have you walk right into their midst where they will promptly lock you up and this time never let you go. And all will be for naught."

Jordan closed the clasps on her carpet bag. "I do not intend to walk right into their midst and announce myself. I'm an actress, Father. If I can convince an audience of intelligent people that I'm an Italian nobleman in love with Juliet, I can persuade a few gullible Southern men that I am not a dangerous spy but something else entirely."

Joshua looked dubious. "And after you have managed this feat, what do you hope to accomplish speaking with Miss St. Clair?"

"Well…I haven't quite worked that out yet, but I will."

Joshua planted himself in front of her bedroom door as if to prevent her departure. "Jordan, I must insist that you not go. In fact, I forbid it."

Jordan sighed, not really angry at her father, but she knew nothing in this world would keep her from seeing Laura, no matter what the consequences.

"Father, I know you're worried, but I promise, I'll be very careful. I'll be back before you know it."

"And if you're not?"

She paused to look at him kindly. In that moment, she knew she had to be as honest as she could, because she might not see him again. "Then you will know that I have tried to do what was right and honorable. You should expect no less from me than you do from Tyler."

❖

"Thank you for coming," Jordan placed a kiss on Bill's cheek as he let them into the theatre.

"I'm drawn to mad acts and foolhardy enterprise," he said dryly.

They spent an hour selecting and then discarding different costumes, wigs, and stage makeup until Jordan finally decided upon what she needed. She packed all of it into her bag and they left the theatre and headed to Riggs Bank, where Jordan emptied her account of funds.

"What're you going to do with all that money?" Bill asked when they exited the bank.

"Well, I need to purchase a horse and carriage, and the rest I suspect I can use as bribes if need be."

"Save your money, darlin'. I can let you have one for nothing."

The Haymarket, south of Pennsylvania Avenue on Seventh Street, was the place to buy hay and feed, as well as to hire a hack for transport about the city. Bill boarded a horse at one of the many stalls nearby and also kept a phaeton in storage. After he had the horse and rigging attached to the carriage, he helped Jordan climb up onto the seat.

"You ever driven one of these before?" he asked.

"Many times," Jordan assured him, "don't worry. But if anything should happen, I promise to replace them."

He waved the offer aside. "That's not what I want returned to me." He looked at her, a sad expression on his face.

"Thank you, Bill. You'll be seeing me soon."

"So what are your plans?"

"Well, right now I'm going to drive across town to the Long Bridge into Alexandria. It is there that I will make my transition from a Yankee to a Rebel. I know the area well enough to pretend to be from there. I hope to convince anyone that should ask that I am a refugee from Alexandria, on my way to Richmond to stay with relatives. So many have already left the area to destinations farther south that I think it utterly believable."

"And what'll you do when you get to that godforsaken Rebel city?" Bill squinted up at her through the swirl of tobacco smoke.

"I'm still working that out, but I'll think of something."

"In that case, you better take this." He reached into his coat, withdrew a Colt derringer, and handed it to her. "This is for just in case."

Jordan hesitated, but took the weapon, slipping it into her bag.

Bill added a box of bullets. "You sure I can't come along?" he asked for the hundredth time. "I sure hate to miss out on all the fun."

Jordan smiled down at him.

"Not this time, but thank you anyway. Good-bye, Bill. I'll see you soon."

"Good-bye, darlin'." His voice caught at the end.

Jordan snapped the reins and the horse took off, heading south to Long Bridge and into Virginia.

❖

Jordan had no sooner crossed the Potomac when a group of soldiers guarding access onto the bridge and the road leading into Alexandria hailed her. She pulled the carriage to a halt and waited for them to approach. A corporal approached the side of the carriage and asked for her pass.

"A pass?" Jordan was surprised. "What do you mean, a pass? I don't know what you're talking about."

"Well, then, I guess you can't go on, ma'am. You can only get to the troops billeted over yonder with a pass."

"Oh, but I don't wish to go to where the troops are." A fleeting thought of Tyler rushed to mind.

"Well, where are you going then, ma'am?" he asked, obviously confused.

"I intend to go to Richmond," Jordan said matter-of-factly.

"Yes, ma'am," the corporal said earnestly. "That's what we aim to do as well. And General McClellan is fixing it so that we'll get there real soon."

He and his companions laughed at Jordan's presumptuousness.

"Corporal, clearly you do not understand my situation." Jordan did her best to sound charming instead of furious, but she knew her cheeks must be bright red with anger. "I must get to Richmond. It's important."

She lifted the reins to continue on her way, but one of the soldiers held the horse's bridle. The others lifted their rifles, although they did not point them at her.

"Now, ma'am," the corporal said in the tone men used when they were trying to calm a troubled horse, "you can't get through the lines without a pass, General's orders. My advice is, forget about the no-good gentleman you're trying to see. Ladies like you come by every day, always for the same reason."

"Oh, for goodness' sake." Jordan's eyes burned. Refusing to let the men see her weakness, she turned the carriage around and fled back over Long Bridge into Washington City.

❖

Jordan sat in the anteroom of the War Department, where she had been waiting impatiently for the past two hours. Men had come and gone during that time, and she knew that not all of them had appointments, but she was determined that before the day was out, she would see Secretary of War Simon Cameron. And she would not leave empty-handed. After inquiring at several departments as to how she could obtain a pass to travel through the lines into Virginia, she had learned that the only person who could clear her through the military was the Secretary of War.

When the last man who had been seen left his office, Jordan was finally ushered into the War Secretary's office by his assistant, who closed the door gently behind him. The gray-haired, clean-shaven War Secretary sat behind his desk, seemingly absorbed in paperwork. With a self-important air, he ignored Jordan's presence. After another interminable wait, she cleared her throat and he looked up as if surprised that she was still there.

"Yes?" he said. "What is it that you want?"

Flabbergasted at his incivility and the lack of introduction, Jordan came quickly to the point. "Mr. Secretary, I need a pass to travel through the lines into Virginia."

"What is this all about, Miss…?"

"Colfax. Jordan Colfax. You might know my name, sir. I was spying on behalf of the Union, and escaped from Libby Prison two weeks ago."

At this disclosure his demeanor altered slightly, but Jordan was not sure if the change was due to disapproval or reluctant respect for a woman who had proven her value to the Union. "And now, having enjoyed the hospitality of our Southern brethren, you wish to return?"

"It's an unusual request, sir, I do not deny it." Jordan fidgeted. "But I beg you, I need that pass by which to travel."

The War Secretary shook his head. "I'm sorry, Miss Colfax, but I cannot authorize your traveling through dangerous territory. Even if I were to issue a pass and you were able to get beyond our pickets, you would never be allowed to pass through the lines of the Rebels. They are still entrenched around Manassas, and their cavalry regularly patrols the outlying areas."

Jordan tried to remain calm. "I wish that you would accept that I can take care of myself beyond our lines. The Rebels will not harm a lady. I simply need to get to Richmond."

Cameron shuffled through his paperwork, making it plain that she had wasted enough of his time. "I'm sorry, but I cannot see how a pass will help you achieve your objective. And I hesitate to be the man responsible for sending a local heroine to an unknown fate at the hands of our enemy. Good day to you, Miss Colfax."

Jordan wanted to reach across his desk and shake him. Furious at her helplessness, she bade him a sharp good-bye and slammed his door as she left.

Fleeing the War Department, Jordan stormed past the tents and soldiers encamped near the White House, not even noticing the appreciative glances cast her way. She was angry and frustrated and unable to think of an alternative solution to leave the city and reach Richmond. She felt almost as helpless as she had when she was imprisoned at Libby. Stopping to catch her breath in the heat of the day, she gazed up at the White House and happened to see the President standing at a window upstairs. As soon as she saw him, any hesitation about intruding upon his time vanished and she headed for the door.

She was ushered into the President's office where she found him with his head resting heavily in the palm of his hand. It appeared to Jordan that he was writing a document of some sort and had stopped to collect his thoughts before proceeding. While Lincoln was aware that Jordan sat only a few feet away, unlike Secretary Cameron, who ignored her, Lincoln was lost in his own world, unintentionally leaving her to her thoughts.

"What do you think of slavery, Miss Colfax?" Lincoln asked suddenly.

Taken aback by the abruptness of the comment, Jordan responded immediately. "It is the scourge of the earth, Mr. Lincoln, and should be brought to an end as quickly as possible."

He pondered her response for a few moments. "And then what? What do you do with millions of slaves who have nowhere to go and no means to be self-sufficient? And what happens to the white families who have depended upon their labor for generations, who also will be thrust into poverty with no means of caring for themselves? An entire way of life has come crashing to an end and neither party may be able to recover from it." He rubbed his hand across his forehead, obviously trying to clear his thoughts.

Unsure what the President wanted from her, Jordan offered another approach. "The Rebels say that it is asserted in the Bible that the black man is destined to a life of slavery, that God has ordained it so."

Lincoln laughed. "Whenever I hear anyone arguing for slavery, I feel a strong impulse to see it tried on him personally." He laid his pen down beside the ink bottle and swiveled in his chair to face her. "I am sorry, Miss Colfax, the subject has been weighing heavily upon me of late. What can I do for you?"

Lincoln heard her out, then returned to his desk where he picked up his pen and dipped it into the inkwell. He quickly wrote a note on a piece of paper, let it dry, and handed it to her. "I hope this will assist you," he murmured.

Jordan read the note:

Please allow Miss Jordan Colfax to pass between the lines.

A. Lincoln

Tears of gratitude welled up in her eyes. "Thank you, sir," she whispered, unsure of her voice.

Lincoln patted her shoulder gently. "You must be careful, my dear," he said. "If you are captured again, I fear I can do nothing to help you."

"I understand, thank you again."

Jordan left the room, glancing over her shoulder one last time as she saw the President return to the document at his desk. John Hay, one of the President's secretaries, walked her out, and she climbed into the buggy and headed south toward Long Bridge.

Chapter Twenty-five

The white men from the Lewis plantation stared at Ruby.

"Reckon we got us that Barrett Hall nigger, too," one of them said. "Fifty dollars' reward ain't it, Jake?"

The man he was talking to yanked Ruby's head up by the hair. "Edward St. Clair your master, girl?"

Ruby's teeth were locked with fright. She could only make a small grunting sound.

The man let go of her hair and tied a rope around her wrists. "They want you back real bad. Humphreys been looking all over for you." He tied the other end of the rope to his horse.

One of the other men took a turn whipping Tate's bleeding back. After a few lashes, he raised the cowhide over Tillie, then let it fall to his side, laughing like a fool. "Five hundred dollars for the quadroon but only if there ain't a mark on her." He prodded Tillie in the back with the whip. "Get walking."

The rope jerked her arms out before her and Ruby almost fell. She was so tired she couldn't think except to put one foot in front of the other. It was dusk by the time they arrived at the plantation. Mr. Humphreys met them in front of his cabin, arms folded across his chest. Slaves coming in from the fields watched in silence as Ruby fell to the ground.

"I brought you your nigger, Humphreys." The man leaned over his horse and spat.

Humphreys sauntered over to Ruby. "Well, now, I sure am glad to see you home. Mr. St. Clair might just give me a big reward for getting you back, seeing as how you're so valuable to him and all." He laughed. "But first, I'm gonna have to make an example of you to the other niggers."

Humphreys took the rope from Jake and dragged Ruby into the

stables. She fell into a stall lined with filthy straw and dried horse dung. As she huddled, trembling and begging for mercy, Mr. Humphreys took down one of the riding crops mounted around the stables. Without warning, he cut Ruby hard across the face, knocking her against the wall.

Ruby was dazed. Just as her head cleared, another blow took her by surprise. Then the blows came, across her shoulders, her back, buttocks, and legs. She tried to protect her head, but the blows rained down and her pleas only seemed to drive him on. Her head buzzed and her mind went numb. With no idea where the next blow would fall, she could not even tense her body to prepare for them. Blood trickled down her sides and her clothes were shredded from her body. The burning pain was so intense she couldn't breathe. Just when she thought she would black out, the beating stopped.

Humphreys backed away, panting. Sweat poured off his forehead. "Damn, it's a hot one today, ain't it, Jake?"

"I sure hope it rains tomorrow and cools things off."

"Yeah." Humphreys wiped his brow with his sleeve. "Listen, I gotta sit down. I'm already tired from flogging a couple of other niggers today, and I've been all over trying to find out where this one went. Mind taking a turn?"

Jake slid down off the wall and took the proffered whip. "Sure. Maybe later we can get a drink over at Whitley's."

Ruby had started to relax and thought she might survive when the crack on her shoulder brought her back to reality. Her entire body was soon nothing but pain and she floated away, becoming part of it.

Jake was much bigger and stronger than Humphreys and he put all he had into the whipping. After a while, he staggered to the corner and dropped down onto a bale of hay, breathing heavily. As if from far away, with her head below water, Ruby heard him speak.

"That's it, that's all I can do. I'm all in."

Humphreys rolled her onto her back with the toe of his boot. When she didn't move, he knelt beside her. "Aw, shit, Jake. She's dead. You killed her."

"Hell, I beat the niggers at the Lewises a lot harder than this one. What you got here, Humphreys, weak niggers?"

"Mr. St. Clair ain't gonna be happy about this," Humphreys grumbled. "And we never got to have any fun with her, neither."

They stopped talking then, or Ruby just stopped hearing. There was nothing. Even the sound of her heart in her ears seemed far, far away.

❖

Laura sat on a blanket alongside Ransom's grave, pulling weeds and clearing debris. A shadow passed over her shoulder and she glanced up to see Martha standing next to her. The stricken expression on her face made Laura's heart stop.

"Martha? What's happened?"

"It's Ruby."

Laura could see that even those two words were more than Martha could bear to speak. "Ruby's home?" she whispered.

At Martha's mute nod, she rose and brushed some earth from her skirts. Ruby must have found the outside world terrifying and fled for the safety of Barrett Hall. Martha was plainly afraid of the punishment her daughter would face and was seeking her help. No doubt she had Ruby concealed somewhere out of sight until she could be confident all would be well.

"You did the right thing, coming to me," Laura said as Martha led her toward the barn. "I'll see to this, don't worry. I'll talk to Papa." Upon entering the darkened interior of the barn, she allowed her eyes to adjust for a moment. "Where is she?"

Martha pointed to a corner stall, but all Laura could see was a pile of rags that had been dumped on the straw. Laura approached the stall, peering into the gloom, and her heart began to thud heavily in her chest. Sticking out of the pile of rags was a pale hand. A leg. Light honey hair, matted and wet looking. Laura knelt. A cold sweat overtook her as she dragged some filthy straw aside. Ruby's dress clung in torn shreds to a body so bruised and battered, she was almost unrecognizable. Blood seeped from deep gashes on her face, arms, and back, soaking the hay around her. Laura could see bone where her flesh had been torn open as if by wild animals.

"Oh, Ruby. My God. Who did this to you?" Turning toward Martha, she begged, "Tell me who's responsible for this…this despicable outrage."

Hot, angry tears gushed from her. Shaking with horror, she gathered Ruby into her arms. Ruby moaned, a sound coming from so far away Laura thought she imagined it. Ruby's eyes fluttered open and though her gaze was directed at Laura, Ruby seemed to look through her, to something else beyond.

Laura bent low and asked gently, “Ruby, who did this to you?”

“All’s I wanted was to be free, Miss Laura,” Ruby choked, and blood spilled from her mouth and down her cheek.

Laura dabbed it away with the hem of her skirt.

“Ma?” Ruby murmured.

Martha knelt down and Laura moved aside to give her room, holding Ruby’s head in her lap. Martha’s tears fell bright and shiny against her light brown skin.

“I’s sorry, Ma.”

“Shh, hush now, Ruby,” Martha whispered, stroking the matted hair. “The Lord is with you and so is me and Miss Laura. Ain’t nobody gonna hurt you again, child.”

“I ain’t afraid.” A thin breath wheezed from Ruby’s chest.

“Nothin’ to be afraid of,” Martha said.

Ruby smiled, and Laura heard a strange soft gurgle like the whisper of a stream. Then Ruby was still. Martha continued stroking her hair, her tears dropping onto Ruby’s face, mixing with the blood. She laid her head down on Ruby’s chest and wrapped her arms protectively around the broken body. In between sobs, she began to hum. It was a song Laura had never heard before but it pierced her heart and she looked away. Her gaze fell on a riding crop covered in blood, lying half buried in the straw. The sight filled her with rage so deep and so intense that for a moment she could not see. She blinked to focus and then picked up the whip and got to her feet.

She didn’t know how she got to the door of Albert Humphreys’s cabin, but she found herself shoving it open without a knock and walking in. The overseer sat at a table, dirty dishes piled on top along with a bottle and half-filled glass of amber liquid. His shirt was filthy and the room reeked of sweat and stale cooking odors.

“Miss Laura,” Humphreys drawled, taking a drink from the glass and wiping his mouth with the back of his hand. “I wasn’t expecting company.”

He stood, swaying slightly, and grabbed hold of the table to steady himself.

“You’re drunk,” Laura spat.

“It’s my day off.” He grinned.

“Did you beat Ruby?”

"Why, yes, Miss Laura, I needed to make an example of her to—"

Laura took three steps and was upon him, striking him across the face with the whip, and when his arms flew up in defense she hit them as well. He shouted her name and stumbled back, tripping over his chair. As he fell to the floor, she hit his head, his arms, his back, his legs—anything that was him, she hit. She didn't think; she didn't feel anything but a hatred so deep it took over her body, and she let it.

Humphreys was crying and begging her to stop, but she went on, switching the crop to her other hand when her arm became tired. When both arms were drained of strength, she kicked him again and again. She was about to return to the whip when a hand stopped hers and she spun around to face Martha.

"Enough, Miss Laura." She gently removed the whip from Laura's hand. "They's been enough whippin' here today."

Laura let Martha guide her out of Humphreys's cabin and lead her back to the kitchen. She was dazed and disoriented. So tired she couldn't speak. When she thought of Ruby she felt numb; she was incapable of feeling anything else.

❖

Jordan had passed easily through the Union lines with the help of the note from President Lincoln and joined a caravan of northern Virginians heading south, away from the source of conflict. Dressed in black, she had donned a wig and a deeply veiled bonnet, pretending to be the widow of a Confederate soldier lost at Manassas. No one questioned her, and she drew quite a bit of sympathy from the refugees. There were many like her, only their losses were real, and many were fleeing to relatives' homes or friends who lived elsewhere in Virginia.

During her time alone in her carriage she thought about Laura. All those days she had been angry with her had been a waste. Laura had been true to her, but Jordan had not believed her. She was ashamed of herself and sick at heart for not trusting her and believing her. Laura had risked her own reputation by coming to her trial and even offered to be a character witness, but Jordan had thrown it all away and, instead, accused her of treachery and betrayal. Hot tears slid down her cheeks and she ignored them. She wanted to feel them, wanted to feel the pain that gnawed at her heart, because she could understand the pain that Laura must be feeling about her at this very moment.

Jordan determined that when she finally saw Laura she would beg forgiveness and confess her love, for that was surely what it must be. She knew what she felt for her was more than friendship, yet she did not know how that could be. She was afraid of her own emotions, afraid of Laura's reaction to them, and more importantly, she did not know what Laura's feelings for her might be. Laura had risked everything to come to her defense. Was that only because of their friendship? Would she be appalled at Jordan's emotions for her? Was there something wrong that Jordan felt the way she did?

As she rode along she pondered these confusing thoughts and finally decided that no matter what, she would tell Laura everything. If she and Laura both survived, she would never keep anything from her again. Life was too capricious to allow things to pass unsaid between them anymore. She loved Laura, and even if nothing came of it, even if Laura rejected her and told her she never wanted to see her again, she would at least have told her the truth.

She was amazed at how easily she was able to move along with the group with barely a notice from Confederate soldiers who constantly passed them. After a few days on the road, they approached the outskirts of Richmond, and Jordan's anxiety increased with every mile they drew nearer. She still did not know how she would get Laura to agree to see her, but she was at least determined to try. She had so much to say to her, so much to apologize for. Somehow, later, she would figure out a plan for her return to Washington.

Those traveling with her who did not turn off for other locales entered Richmond with Jordan via the Deep Run Turnpike. The road eventually merged with the Richmond, Fredericksburg, and Potomac Railroad, then became Broad Street. But this time, Jordan did not take her usual route from the train depot to the Broad Street Hotel. Rather, she turned right at Third Street, avoiding places where she had normally gone. While her costume and makeup disguised her somewhat, she did not want to take any chances of being recognized. At Main Street she turned left and, after a half mile, she glimpsed the Capitol in between the buildings on her left. She continued another half mile to the Exchange Hotel, where she checked in under the name Jane Tyler.

Chapter Twenty-six

Two men lowered the plain pine box into the freshly dug grave and then stood back so the preacher could say the last rites. He sprinkled a handful of dirt on top of wood, making a dull clattering sound that chilled Laura. All the slaves who were allowed to attend the funeral were there, the rest either working the fields or up at the main house. Laura's was the only white face among the mourners. She stood with her arm around Martha, still numb from the rage she had felt at Ruby's death the day before, and from the horror of seeing the results of what such a brutal beating could do to a human being.

While Martha wept softly at her side, Laura was appalled at her own inability to shed a tear. She had never before felt such emptiness, such desolation at what had happened within her own family. How was it possible that such a thing could occur at Barrett Hall?

When the preacher finished, each slave approached Martha and embraced her, offering words of condolence. They had only been given a brief respite to attend the funeral and most had to hurry back to their work. The two men who had lowered the box into the ground stood at a distance with shovels, waiting for Martha and Laura to depart.

"Good-bye, Ruby," Martha whispered. "You's free now."

She stepped to the edge of the grave and bent down to grab some dirt. Laura watched as she slowly released a few grains at a time, her tears falling onto the coffin along with the soil. Something about the way she cast the earth reminded Laura of how her own mother had stood over Ransom's grave doing the same. Back then, Laura had stood to her mother's right as she did now with Martha. The sun filtered through the trees, casting a dappled pattern across Martha's face, and Laura again admired her features.

As she observed Martha, a sense of familiarity pressed insistently into her mind. She felt as though she had forgotten something that she was supposed to remember, something about Martha, and she stared at her, wondering what it was. Her face was decidedly that of a woman of mixed race. Her nose was slender and sharp, her eyes a beautiful blue-green. She looked like someone who did not belong in the kitchen but rather in one of the plantation homes along the James.

Laura even had the odd sense that she'd seen Martha in such surroundings, wearing a beautiful dress and dancing with a handsome man. Her face, her nose, even her smile seemed imprinted from another familiar face, as if she were a portrait painted from memory, her features not quite the same as the living person, but similar enough that she could be recognized. Laura stared and saw the imprint of her very own family. The thought hit her with the force of a summer storm and she rocked backward, nearly stumbling, as she realized that Martha looked very much like Rachel St. Clair. In fact, Martha and her mother could be sisters.

Martha finally turned away from the grave. "Miss Laura, is you all right? You looks poorly all of a sudden."

Laura did feel ill, and she had difficulty speaking. "No, I'm fine, Martha."

"You best get out of the sun, you being such a sickly child and all."

Laura could only nod. She felt faint and wanted to hide her face in shame. Martha motioned to the men to begin their work and stood by silently as they began to fill Ruby's grave. Laura could not bear to watch and found herself heading in the direction of Ransom. She practically ran to the clearing near the house and dropped to the ground by his stone. Her tears finally came, falling hotly down her cheeks.

Oh, Ransom. She wanted to tell him, speak with him about what she now knew. That Martha was their aunt, an aunt who was a slave at Barrett Hall and who had cooked their meals every day of their lives. And what was worse, Ruby was their cousin. Ruby, who had cleaned Laura's room, dressed her and fixed her hair, and who now lay dead, beaten to death by their overseer. They were part of the St. Clair family, yet they were slaves.

Laura wept for the loss—the loss of Ransom and being unable to talk to him now; the loss of Ruby, who was as much a part of their family as Meg; and the loss of Jordan, whom she loved. Oh, if Jordan were only here now, she would beg forgiveness for all the times she defended this ugly institution. Laura could see now what Jordan had surely seen herself. How could she have been so blind to all that had happened at Barrett Hall? She knew her father frequently visited Martha; surely her grandfather had done the same with Martha's mother.

The more Laura thought about the situation, the more her tears dried and her anger increased. She understood now why Jordan abhorred slavery, and why so many others wished to see it abolished. Slavery did unspeakable things to human beings, things that no one should ever have to endure. And yet the Barretts and the St. Clairs committed these acts against their own family. How she wished she could talk to Jordan, just be with her and be held by her.

She stood up from the ground and brushed the dirt from her dress. With a strength of conviction she had never known she could feel, she knew that she had to leave Barrett Hall. She could not lead this kind of life, knowing what she knew, and she could not marry a man only to continue it. She strode away from Ransom's grave and returned to Ruby's.

"Martha, may I speak with you a moment?"

Dutifully, Martha left her child's graveside. "Yes, Miss Laura?"

"Martha, I am leaving Barrett Hall."

Confusion in her eyes, Martha said, "Yes, you is getting married to Mr. Young."

"No." Laura shook her head. "No, I am not marrying Mr. Young. I'm leaving Barrett Hall forever, and I want you to come with me."

"Miss Laura, what do you mean?"

"I'm going north, where Miss Colfax lives. And if you come with me, I'll set you free. I'll sign whatever manumission papers are necessary, and you can either continue to live with me or go anywhere you wish."

Martha's hand flew to her mouth and her eyes registered shock. "You can't mean it. What would your mamma say, and Marse Edward?"

"I don't care anymore. My life is my own and I no longer believe that you, or anyone else, should be a slave. Please, Martha, come with me. I'll set you free."

Martha stepped back, as though burned by Laura's words. She glanced over to the men shoveling dirt on her daughter's coffin, and then up the path toward the big house.

"I can't Miss Laura. I can't go with you. I's born here, and I 'spect I'll die here. I can't go north 'cause Ruby's here. And someday I want to rest next to her. I don't know where my other children are, but at least I knows where she is."

Laura saw the determination in Martha's face and the set of her jaw and knew she would be unable to convince her otherwise.

"I love you, Martha, and I'll miss you. But most of all, I'm sorry."

Martha gazed into Laura's eyes and after several heart beats, placed her hand to Laura's cheek.

"Good-bye, Miss Laura."

❖

Jordan sat in the hotel dining room eating breakfast. Richmond was a busy place since it had become the capital of the Confederacy. Hotels were full, restaurants were packed, and people and soldiers were abundant.

"I tell you, it's outrageous," a matron sitting at a table nearby exclaimed. "I paid one dollar and fifty cents for a pound of coffee just yesterday. It's robbery, I say, pure and simple."

"Well, that's nothing," a woman sitting across from her commented. "Seventy-five cents for butter. Can you imagine? Seventy-five cents! I have half a mind to take this to the door of President Davis. He must know the shopkeepers in town are making immense profits because of the war. It's a disgrace."

Jordan finished her breakfast and left the dining room. Crossing Franklin Street, she entered the post office and dropped off a letter to Mrs. Johnson, letting her know all was well. She addressed the letter to the Colfax housekeeper because she was afraid her father's name might be recognized. Northern papers were still available, and Virginians read his with disdain. Leaving the post office, she strolled up Franklin, admiring the fall foliage and the cooler temperatures September had brought. It was still somewhat warm, but the wind carried a hint of change and the weather would soon grow colder.

Approaching an open park, she saw a group of children playing, mostly boys, but a few girls as well. She stopped briefly to watch and realized after a time that they were playing at war. The little boys were soldiers, riding imaginary horses and dashing about the park, while the little girls were nurses, bandaging the wounded. One boy even hopped about using a stick as a crutch, his knee bent in imitation of an amputee. Jordan looked away.

Halfway up the street was St. John's Episcopal Church, and she stopped before it, contemplating entering it. She needed time to think, to clear her head, and she had nowhere else to go. Climbing the few steps to the large oak doors, she opened them slowly and stepped inside. The interior of the church was brightly lit in various shades of blues, reds, and yellows as the morning sun streamed through the stained-glass windows. She walked down the main aisle and slid into a pew several rows back from the altar. The church was empty except for a few old women interspersed in aisles throughout the church. A caretaker was polishing the brass candlesticks and collection plate, but otherwise, no one paid her any attention.

Jordan sat and contemplated how she might persuade Laura to talk to her. She hoped that being in the church would somehow provide divine inspiration. A Southern church or not, God had to be listening. She had a vague notion of how she would escape to safety after she'd said the words she needed to say, but finding her way up north was another thing entirely. Jordan slid to her knees and folded her hands in prayer, resting them on the pew back in front of her.

Please, God, give me the strength to spirit us away to safety. I know the Rebels pray to You in this church, just as we pray to You in our churches up north. But as President Lincoln says, even you cannot be for and against something at the same time. Please let Laura see me and hear what I have to say. Please let her know that I love her.

❖

Laura carelessly stuffed clothing into a large carpet bag and slipped in the jewelry that her grandmother had left to her. She might need to sell some of the pieces to have enough money to live on until she could find gainful employment.

"Where are you going?" Meg asked from the doorway.

Laura didn't bother to turn around or stop packing. "Richmond, for now. I refuse to live in a place where a defenseless woman can be beaten to death for no reason."

"Mr. Humphreys had every reason to whip that ungrateful nigger."

Laura spun around, her rage still simmering just below the surface. "Ungrateful! Ungrateful that she was a slave and could not call a moment her own? Ungrateful that she could be taken advantage of by any man who took a fancy, or worse, beaten for refusing the advance?"

"Oh, Laura, don't speak such foolishness. It's a slave's lot in life. Just as an ox pulls the plow, the slave is another animal given to us to do the work. We take good care of ours."

Appalled, Laura had to restrain herself from slapping Meg across the face. "You are a heartless, soulless child, Meg. It was you who turned Jordan in to the authorities. It was you who told me she was in Ransom's room that day. It could only have been you."

Meg tilted her head defiantly. "And I would gladly do it again. She was a spy and deserved what she got. Everyone said so, except for you. Too bad she escaped."

"Sometimes I don't even think I know you." Laura stared at her, bewildered. "It's as though we're from two different families."

"I wish we were," Meg huffed. "You certainly don't act like a Barrett, running around with Yankee spies and such."

"'Scuse me, Miss Laura," Prissie interrupted, "There's a lady here to see you."

"Me?" Laura was not expecting any lady to call on her at Barrett Hall. "Who is it, Prissie?"

"She didn't say. Just said it's about Marse Ransom."

Immediately Laura stopped packing and headed to the stairway with Meg following behind. They entered the parlor to find a woman in widow's mourning standing near the fireplace, a heavy veil concealing her face.

"May I help you?" Laura asked.

Jordan's heart leapt at the sight of her and her arms lifted of their own volition, seeking the embrace she ached for. She quickly dropped them to her sides and concentrated on the tone and Georgia accent that formed part of her disguise.

"Miss St. Clair, I have information regarding your brother, Lieutenant St. Clair."

"Please, won't you sit down, Mrs…?"

Jordan glanced at Meg. "Tyler. Mrs. Tyler. My brother was at

Manassas and knew your brother. In fact, he was at his side when he was most cruelly taken from this world."

Laura gasped. "Meg, Mother will want to hear this. Quickly, go get her. She's down by Ransom."

"Why do I have to go? Get Prissie to go."

"Prissie is doing the work of two now. Go and get Mother, hurry."

"Oh, all right," Meg grudgingly agreed. Casting a curious look at their visitor, she left the room with a hint of foot-stamping.

As soon as the door closed behind her, Jordan drew the veil over her head and said, "Laura, it's me."

"I know." Laura didn't hesitate. She ran to her, desperate for the strong comfort of her arms. "Oh, thank God you're here," she sobbed.

"Laura, oh, my love." Jordan kissed Laura's forehead and cheek. It felt so wonderful holding her, she swore to herself they would never again be parted by anyone or anything.

Laura was barely able to compose herself. "What are you doing here? If you're caught, they'll send you to prison. You must leave now."

"I'm not going anywhere without you," Jordan said firmly. "I love you, Laura. I love you and want to be with you always."

The adoration in her gaze weakened Laura's knees and she pressed her body against Jordan's, trying with all her strength to convey how much she loved her in return.

Jordan nearly crushed her. "I have come to get you and take you back with me where you belong. You can't marry Preston Young. You don't love him, and I can't bear to see you unhappy. I know I cannot give you some of the things that he can, but I'll do everything in my power to make you happy. Don't worry about how you will live. I'll take care of us and provide for us, and somehow we will manage. Just say you'll come with me."

Laura cried and laughed and brushed away her tears. "Oh, Jordan. I love you so much that words can never express what I feel. Yes, yes I will come with you. I never want to be away from you again. I don't care about Preston and I don't care about the life that awaits me here. I only know that I want to be with you. I was just now packing my bags to leave for Richmond."

Consumed with relief that Laura did not hate her and ecstatic over her declaration of love, Jordan kissed her. The kiss was not gentle, but forceful, filled with passion and a need so great she thought she might hurt Laura. Drawing back, shaking and breathless, she marveled that Laura loved her too.

"We could stay here this evening and leave first thing in the morning," Laura said excitedly. "Then, when we reach Richmond, we can spend the night at our house on Church Hill."

"No," Jordan said. "We must leave here as soon as possible, and we can stay the night in Richmond, but not on Church Hill."

"But why?" Laura asked.

"Because someone will recognize me and I'll be arrested. Do you trust me, Laura?"

Laura looked up into Jordan's pleading eyes and saw concern, as well as so much more. She had never received such a look from anyone before. "Yes, Jordan, I trust you," she whispered.

Tears filled Jordan's eyes at Laura's belief in her. Overwhelmed with love, she kissed Laura's lips softly, sweetly, and gently. She prayed that she would always be worthy of her trust.

"I am so happy you are here and that we are friends again," Laura whispered.

"Friends?" Jordan mused. "No, we're much more than that. I love you, Laura."

"As I love you." Laura caressed Jordan's cheek with the back of her hand.

Jordan let herself savor the touch for only a second; then, with an urgent glance toward the door, she invited, "Come, let's run away together."

❖

The time passed quickly as they drove to Richmond. When Laura told Jordan about Ruby and about her realization that her family had made slaves of their own relatives, Jordan slowed the phaeton and they cried and held each other. Jordan wished she could turn back the clock and start over again, but knew they could only go forward. She still couldn't believe Laura was sitting beside her and was determined to travel north with her. God must have been listening to her prayers earlier that day.

It was dusk when they arrived, and the city was as congested as Jordan had ever seen it. Her appearance did not attract the stares she had expected. A widow deep in mourning and shrouded in veils could drive a phaeton herself these days without inviting shock or derision, it seemed. Jordan found she was unable to resist driving past Libby Prison.

"What are you doing?" Laura demanded. "People will see you."

"Laura, your sister didn't recognize me and we've dined together."

She reined the horse in as a troop of soldiers crossed the street in front of them at a brisk march. A few looked their way, but without suspicion.

"Please, let's get away from here," Laura pleaded.

Jordan immediately felt guilty for causing the anxious note in her voice, and turned into Nineteenth Street. As they approached the corner of Main Street, they were faced with a scene of chaos. A supply wagon had overturned after colliding with a buggy. Several soldiers had been injured and were lying on the ground, assisted by others. Richmond residents swarmed the spilled supplies, fighting over bags of flour, bacon, and salt. Additional soldiers poured in from the surrounding streets, trying to restore order. Meantime, the road ahead was blocked. A gunshot failed to disperse the mob and startled the horse. Jordan climbed down and patted the skittish mare. She had decided to lead her by the bridle, when a soldier stopped a few feet away.

"Good evening, ladies. May I be of assistance?"

He gazed up at Laura and took a step closer. "Why, Miss St. Clair. What an unexpected pleasure."

Laura looked to Jordan, the fear in her eyes evident even in the dark. Jordan, her heart pounding, hurried to think of a way out of their dilemma before George recognized her. She could run, but not without Laura.

"I do not believe we've been introduced, Mrs…?" George stepped forward, trying to see Jordan beneath her heavy veils.

"Tyler," she said.

The startled expression on his face told her she was not anonymous to an actor she'd worked with closely.

"Well, well, well. If it isn't my old friend Jordan Colfax. I cannot believe my good fortune this evening. I may very well be in line for promotion, capturing an escaped spy." He laughed.

"George," Jordan thought quickly. "I can give you quite a sum of money if you let us go."

George's eyes glittered. "How much?"

"All that I have, almost one thousand dollars."

"Yankee or Confederate money?"

"Northern currency, and gold coin," she said, taking note that the way was now clear.

"Let me see it." George was all but licking his lips.

"It's in the carriage." Jordan climbed into the back and opened her bag, withdrawing the money and the derringer Bill had given her. Slipping the gun into her waistband, she jumped down and handed the money to him. George greedily opened the bag and fondled the money inside, chuckling and jingling a few gold coins in his hand.

"All right, you've got your money." Jordan steered Laura toward the carriage. "Now we'll be on our way."

"Not so fast." He drew closer, resting his hand on the horse's bridle. "I thank you for the money, but I can't let you go."

"You have the money, George," Jordan retorted, angry at his deception. "Now let us go, before it is too late."

"Too late for you, you mean." He grabbed hold of Jordan's arm, yanking her into him.

"Jordan!" Laura cried out.

She tried to pull Jordan away from him, but the fabric of Jordan's dress slipped through her fingers. George gave Laura a shove and she fell hard against the carriage. As Jordan struggled, George slapped her harshly across the face. Somehow she managed to hang on, digging her fingernails into his eyes. He cursed and pushed her hands away, hitting her hard in the stomach, then flinging her to the ground. The derringer flew out of Jordan's waistband and landed in the dirt, but neither of them saw it. Jordan tried to reach into her waistband, but George was on her, tugging at her wrists and trying to pin her to the ground. Finally he managed to climb on top of her, his weight trapping her beneath him. He clamped his hands down on her throat and Jordan hit his shoulders and chest, but he managed to keep his face away from her flailing punches.

She was choking and couldn't breathe, her vision blurred, and her strength seeped out of her. In that moment she knew that she was going to die and her thoughts went to Laura and what would happen to her. She had failed.

Suddenly, a loud bang released George's grip around her throat, and for the first time in what seemed like forever Jordan was able to catch her breath. George fell sideways off her and she gasped and coughed, trying desperately to breathe in the fresh air. Feeling her throat, she began rubbing the pain away and soothing the tension that had been there moments before. She sat up, curious why George had stopped and why he was lying next to her clutching his stomach and moaning.

With a look of utter horror on her face, Laura stood motionless, her arms still extended holding the gun.

"Laura?" Jordan scrambled up off the ground. "Laura, it's all right." She stepped carefully toward her, took hold of the gun, and removed it from Laura's hands. "We have to go now." Glancing about, she noticed several soldiers beginning to take interest in them.

She retrieved her money and led Laura, who moved as though in a trance, up into the phaeton, then climbed in next to her. Taking hold of the reins, she slapped the horse's back. Shopkeepers, hearing the carriage clatter down the alleyway, rushed out to see what the commotion was about, and she nearly ran them over. She could hear the shouts and cries of the people behind them as they sped off into the night.

❖

Jordan turned the corner at Grace Street, thinking hard about where she was headed. She thought she could hear a carriage behind them, and she gave the horse free rein. This was not the way she had anticipated slipping off into the night with Laura, but it was too late now, and she knew what she had to do. They weren't far from Church Hill, and not far from their initial destination on their escape. Jordan glanced over at Laura, who was clinging to the carriage seat trying to hang on.

Passing Twenty-third Street, Jordan risked a quick look over her shoulder and drove another block. Seeing the house she sought ahead of her, she pulled off into the dirt and drove around to the back to hide the carriage from view. The six white pillars of the mansion stood out in the dark night, identifying it as their safe haven. At the sound of the horse and carriage, the door opened and a matron holding a lantern came out to meet them, followed by a powerfully built black man.

"Jordan, whatever are we doing at Elizabeth Van Lew's house?" Laura whispered, afraid she would be heard.

"You'll soon see." Jordan helped her down from the carriage, and kept an arm about her waist as they walked toward the house. "Mrs. Van Lew?"

"I am, and who might you be?" the woman with the lantern asked.

"Jordan Colfax. Kate Warne said that if ever I was in trouble, I should seek you out. Well, ma'am, I am most certainly in trouble and we desperately need your help."

"Kate, hmm?" Elizabeth smiled. "I suppose you must have done something to upset the Rebels, then."

"You might say that. Please, may we come in? I believe the authorities are close. Will you help us?"

"Anderson," Elizabeth instructed, "take the horse and buggy into the carriage house and out of sight." She gestured up the steps. "Please follow me, Miss Colfax."

She led Jordan and Laura into the house and up the back staircase, climbing several floors until they reached the top. Walking down a long passage, she opened an unseen door in the wall and showed them into a hidden space under the eaves of the roof. They had to bend down to enter, the sloping roof only five feet at its highest point.

"You must stay here for now," Elizabeth told them, leaving the lantern on a small wooden crate. "I will not know for how long until things quiet down and it is safe to move you. I will have Anderson bring up your bags and some blankets. Are you hungry?"

"No, thank you, Mrs. Van Lew, merely tired." Laura's legs felt shaky from the shock of their encounter with Sergeant Lamont. She was thankful when Jordan helped her sit on a crate.

Elizabeth stared at Laura for a minute, then stepped closer. "Why, aren't you Rachel St. Clair's child, the one accused of consorting with the Yankee spy?"

Embarrassed to be recognized in such a way, Laura whispered, "Yes."

Elizabeth laughed heartily. "Well, it is truly an honor to have you in my home. I only wish I could tell your mother to her face that I have helped your friend flee the city. Rachel has always looked disdainfully upon me. I wonder what she would say now."

She laughed again as Anderson entered the room, placed their bags on the floor, and left a pile of blankets and pillows on top.

"If you ladies need anything, tap on the floor. Someone will hear you eventually. I will bring you breakfast in the morning, but you are not to leave here unless I come for you. There is a chamber pot over there." She pointed to a corner of the attic. "If you require medicine, let me know that in the morning as well."

"Thank you, Mrs. Van Lew," Jordan said. "We're both very grateful to you."

Elizabeth waved her away. "Think nothing of it, my dear. I do this all the time, mostly for runaway slaves, but also for prisoners escaping Libby Prison. Sleep well." She crawled out through the opening in the wall and closed the door behind her.

Jordan still had her arms around Laura and they remained that way for a while, adjusting to where they were and to the shock of what had happened. Then Jordan spread the blankets and pillows on the floor and helped Laura lie down. Removing her shoes, Jordan lay down next to her and they stared at their own shadows cast against the wall by the lantern.

Laura could not help but feel sick to her stomach. She had shot and possibly killed a man. It was unbelievable, yet she replayed the scene again and again in her mind. At the time, she hadn't hesitated to pull the trigger of the little gun. She had never fired a pistol before, and the loud noise had startled her, as though someone else had caused it. She thought again of Lamont with his hands clenched tightly around Jordan's throat, and shuddered as panic set in. Jordan felt the shudder pass through Laura's body and wondered if she had done the right thing in bringing Laura with her. She worried about what Laura was feeling, both physically and emotionally, and knew that Laura had to address the latest events before they could continue. She rolled on her side to face Laura, propping her head in her hand.

"Laura, are you all right?" She spoke softly, not wanting to add to Laura's stress.

Seeing the compassion in Jordan's eyes was her undoing. Sobbing loudly, she flung herself into Jordan's waiting arms and clung to her, crying and heaving while Jordan simply held and soothed her. It felt so good to be held by Jordan again, to feel her strength and know that they were no longer estranged. Laura wasn't sure what had changed to cause Jordan to return to her; she would ask her about that later. For now she wanted to lose herself in the safety of Jordan's warm embrace. She cried for all that had happened and for the loss of what she could no longer return to. What would she do without Barrett Hall and her family? Where would she go and what would she do? She was a fugitive from justice and a possible murderer, and she was terrified.

Jordan ran her fingers through Laura's golden tresses, marveling at the softness. She rubbed Laura's back and stroked her face, telling her everything would be all right even though she wasn't sure what was going to happen. All she knew was that she had been determined to get Laura away from Preston Young, and she had succeeded. What they would do now was something she needed to think about. Laura's shooting of Lamont had definitely complicated matters, but she could do nothing about it until morning. She would have to find out through Mrs. Van Lew what was going on and how dangerous it would be for them to travel. She needed time to think, and she hoped Mrs. Van Lew would allow them to stay until she came up with a plan.

After a while, Laura settled down, her tears spent and her strength all but gone. She dozed in Jordan's arms while Jordan rocked her. When she felt Laura relax and breathe deeply, she turned the lantern wick down until the flame extinguished, leaving them in the dark.

Chapter Twenty-seven

The door in the wall opened softly and the light from the hallway bled into the darkened attic room. Jordan was instantly awake and reached for the derringer by her pillow.

"It's only me," Elizabeth Van Lew whispered. "I've brought some breakfast."

She climbed into the hole in the wall with a tray while Jordan lit the lantern. Laura was still asleep, her hands tucked childlike beneath her cheek.

"I'll leave the tray here for when she awakes," Elizabeth said, placing the tray on the wooden crate. "How is she feeling?"

"Exhausted, I'm sure." Jordan gazed down at Laura's pale face. "I hope yesterday's events have not destroyed her confidence in our plan. Have you heard anything about last night?"

"Have I?" The matron chuckled. "The news of your return is everywhere and they've closed off the city. They're fairly certain you haven't left yet, so all the roads leading out of town are blocked. The river is also being watched. It would appear that they want your return badly."

"Any word of Sergeant Lamont?" Jordan asked.

"He has been wounded but will recover. I know of this man, and his acting skills alone were worth shooting him for. You did the town a service."

"It was not I but Laura. She shot him to save my life."

Elizabeth's eyebrows rose in surprise.

"I did not intend to put you in jeopardy, Mrs. Van Lew. But don't worry, we shan't stay long."

"Hush now. I do not abide guests in my home telling me what I can and cannot worry about. Listen to me, you will do exactly as I say and I shall get you both north where you belong. Of course, you will need to stay here a few days, until all the excitement abates. By then they will be convinced that you have slipped through their hands yet again. After that you should travel only at night."

Elizabeth poured a cup of tea and handed it to Jordan. "I'll bring up a washbasin in a bit, and then if you like, you can stroll about the upper floor of the house. But if anyone comes, you must return to this hideaway quickly." As she retreated into the hallway, she left the door open.

Jordan sipped her tea and ate her breakfast absently, not tasting any of it. She watched as Laura slept, worried that she would not be strong enough to endure the rigors of what lay ahead. But she had to, and Jordan vowed that if they made it north, she would take care of Laura and never let anything happen to her again. She had caused her sufficient pain and sorrow, and now, despite Laura's claims that she wanted to leave Barrett Hall forever, Jordan was taking her away from the only place she had ever called home. How would she ever be able to make up for that?

Laura stirred under the blanket, the light from the hall penetrating her closed eyelids and the smell of breakfast bringing her awake. Slowly she sat up.

"Good morning, Laura." Jordan smiled. "How are you feeling?"

"Better, thank you." Laura managed a weak smile. "Are we safe?"

"Of course. Elizabeth Van Lew has done this sort of thing before. I think we should take her advice."

Laura ate hungrily and later, after Mrs. Van Lew had brought the washbasin, she bathed and felt almost herself again. They left the cramped crawl space in the attic and sat in a small room with windows facing the street. They avoided standing in front of the windows, but it was a relief to be in the sunlight once again. The weather had turned cooler and Laura sat in a chair wrapped in a blanket, dozing intermittently.

"What are we going to do, Jordan?"

"I don't know."

They fell silent at the sound of pounding on the front door, followed by footsteps running up the stairs.

Anderson burst into the room where they were sitting. "Get in the attic!" he ordered. "It's soldiers at the door."

Jordan took Laura by the arm and they rushed to the safety of the hiding place. Anderson sealed the door behind them and then all was quiet. In the dark, they could hear the muffled sound of voices that grew louder and more distinct as booted feet climbed the stairs.

"Everyone in Richmond knows you're a Yankee sympathizer, Mrs. Van Lew," a man's voice said.

"And what of it, Captain? Can I help it if the entire South has gone mad? It still gives you no right to enter my house, and I again ask that you and your men leave."

"Not until we have searched it thoroughly. If you are hiding any Yankees or even runaways here, you will be arrested, you understand?"

Jordan gripped the derringer in one hand and held Laura's hand in the other. She didn't know if she would actually use the gun, but knowing it was there was a comfort. A crash sounded in a room down the hall from them, and they could hear Elizabeth cursing the men for breaking something. They held their breath as they heard footsteps approach their hiding place.

"...you nursing Yankee wounded in town," he said. "It's bad enough we got plenty of our own sick and wounded, and there you are caring for the enemy. You ought to be ashamed."

"The only thing I am ashamed of, Captain, is to be a Virginian in this hour of our nation's greatest need."

"This is the top floor and there's nothing above, is that right?" he asked.

"See for yourself if you don't believe me. Now, will you please leave my house? I shall not suffer this ignominy much longer. I will speak to Mr. Davis if I must."

"I'm sure he will welcome you with open arms," he said patronizingly. "All right, boys, let's go, but rest assured, Mrs. Van Lew, we shall return again if need be."

"And I shall be waiting, Captain."

Laura and Jordan heard the footsteps descend the stairs, more muffled conversation, and then the closing of the front door. Laura sighed and leaned heavily against Jordan, who held her tightly.

"It's all over," Jordan whispered, kissing Laura's forehead.

The kiss brought them both to a halt. Laura tensed, then relaxed into Jordan's embrace. It had been so long since she'd felt affection from anyone other than her father that it was almost foreign to be treated so kindly. Only Jordan had ever reached out to her, had felt comfortable and at ease in her presence, unafraid to show her emotions. Ransom had been that way with her, but recalling him caused too much pain and she quickly suppressed the memory.

"You shouldn't have come back to see me, Jordan," Laura whispered.

Jordan gripped her more firmly. "Don't speak that way. Of course I had to come back. I abused your trust and then was arrogant enough to claim that you had betrayed me! What a fool I was."

The bitterness and self-recrimination were harsh, and Laura wanted to soothe her upset away. She placed the palm of her hand against Jordan's cheek, and when the touch brought Jordan's gaze to her, she searched Jordan's eyes for a reply to the emotion brimming inside her. Without hesitating, she brought her lips to Jordan's and kissed her. The surge of feeling rushed from her heart to her stomach and in places she had never known could feel such passion. Pulling away, she linked Jordan's hand in hers and smiled.

The door to the hiding space opened and Elizabeth Van Lew leaned in. "Those damn Rebels broke my mother's spinning wheel. I don't use it anymore, but it was hers." Her eyes glittered in the light from the hall. "Oh, well, they can suspect all they want about me, but they haven't caught me."

"Have they gone?" Jordan asked.

"They're out back, so you must stay put a while longer. There's nothing to identify you in the carriage, is there, Miss Colfax?"

"No, everything is here and the phaeton is like any other, as is the horse."

"Good. If anyone should ask, it's mine."

"I'm sorry we have caused you so much trouble," Laura said.

"Oh, Miss St. Clair." She laughed. "I have been dealt worse at the hands of the Confederates. They are an unruly mob who follow no law but one of their own making. They will not rest until this war is over and every last one of them is dead. It's the only way to stop them."

Laura cringed. Ransom wasn't so single-minded and blind in his loyalties, and neither was she. They had believed in the right of the South to throw off their oppressors, end unfair taxation, and be left alone to decide for themselves what was right for them and for their way of life. And Laura believed in the rule of law, wishing that somehow conflict could have been avoided. But in the long run, war had been the only choice left to the South. If it meant freedom and a chance to begin a new country, then so be it. She had never dreamed of what it would do to Ransom. She wondered if Jordan agreed with Mrs. Van Lew's assessment of Southern folk.

"Once they've gone, I'll bring you supper," Elizabeth said. "But I think it best that you stay inside this room for the rest of the evening. They might return, hoping to surprise us. Now I must go and see what destruction they are causing to my carriage house."

"Are you all right?" Jordan asked.

"Yes, fine," Laura reassured her. "Jordan, do you think Mrs. Van Lew is right, that the only way to end this war is when all the Southern soldiers are dead?"

Jordan grasped Laura's hand in both of hers. "Laura, many soldiers have died in this war, and many more have yet to die. I'm so sorry Ransom was one of them, and Tyler may yet meet his fate upon the battlefield as well. One day the war will end, and I hope the Union will be the victor because I believe deeply in the rightness of her cause. Slavery must be brought to an end once and for all because we cannot continue half-slave and half-free in this country any longer. After that, we must somehow try to get along and resolve the animosity that began this war in the first place. I hope North and South can once again become the one country it was destined to be."

Laura pondered all that Jordan had said long after supper and well into the night. She wondered about her own beliefs and where they fit in. How would she ever reconcile with her family, especially when she felt so disillusioned? But more importantly, would she ever even see them again? She could not return home, and yet she had nowhere else to go. In a land now of two countries, she belonged to neither.

Laura thought she would go mad if she did not get out into the fresh air soon. So she was relieved after three days of confinement to learn they would be leaving that night. Where they were going she did not know, but as long as it was somewhere other than the oppressive attic she did not care. She did know they were headed north, a prospect that both intrigued and terrified her. A whole new way of life would begin, and while she had certainly complained of Barrett Hall and the expectations of her, it was her home. Knowing where she fit in and the life she was meant to live had comforted her. She had known where her next meal would come from. The future now held nothing but uncertainty for her, and she was afraid. She shivered slightly.

They had spent the day preparing for their departure. Mrs. Van Lew had cooked several days of rations for them on the road. It would not be enough, but people along the way were prepared to receive and feed them before they proceeded to the next stop on the Underground Railroad. They had spent the afternoon resting and sleeping, knowing they would be up all night. Laura had recovered from the shooting incident, but still feared that they would be recognized once they left the safety of their hostess. Still, they couldn't postpone the trip, as many people had to make plans to accommodate them. And spending another night in the attic was not particularly appealing.

Sundown had come and gone, and after supper, Jordan and Laura finally came downstairs for the first time since their arrival. They sat in the dining room in the dark with Mrs. Van Lew and Anderson, waiting for a knock on the door. As the minutes passed, Laura nodded off until a soft tapping alerted everyone in the room. Mrs. Van Lew swiftly moved to the back door and admitted someone into the house. When the person removed the hood from their head, Laura saw it was a Negro woman, her eyes shining brightly even in the dark. She was thin and wiry, moved gracefully like a cat, and had obvious inner strength.

"This is Esther Stark," Mrs. Van Lew said. "And Esther, this is Jordan Colfax and Laura St. Clair."

The woman did not step any closer. "Are you ready to go?" She didn't waste time.

Jordan and Laura looked at one another. This was it.

"Yes," Jordan answered for them both.

"You will do everything I say, when I say it. Anything else may get us all killed. Do you understand?"

Laura swallowed her fear. "Yes."

"Then let's go now." Esther turned back to the door.

"Good-bye, child." Mrs. Van Lew hugged Laura, then Jordan. "Do all that she says and you will arrive safely. Send me a letter one day telling me how you are, but do not use your real names, as I always find my mail opened when I receive it."

"Thank you for everything." Laura's eyes welled up. "I can never repay you for your kindness."

"Do unto others, child." She cupped Laura's cheek and smiled.

"Good-bye," Jordan whispered.

They followed Esther out the door and into their future.

After leaving the Van Lew house, they darted in and out of shadows on foot for about a mile until they reached the First African Church near the Capitol. Although the church was dark, Esther led them around to the back where a man sat on a tree stump, apparently waiting for them. He was massive, his shoulders broad and his neck thick under his large head.

"Howdy, Esther," he said.

"Good evening, Samuel."

Jordan and Laura were not introduced and nothing further was said. Esther and Samuel moved about the grounds as though they had done this many times before. Samuel took them to a team of horses hitched to a wagon, and Jordan and Laura climbed in the back under blankets and other household items.

"We have to get across the bridge at Fourteenth Street and outside the city before curfew," Esther told them as the wagon moved forward.

"What time is that?" Jordan asked, her voice muffled under the blankets.

"Nine o'clock, but even now, it's dangerous to move about the countryside. Slaves are not allowed to be out at all without being accompanied by a white person. But we cannot afford to show your faces because of the wanted posters everywhere. So we'll stop for the night at a farmhouse a couple of hours from here. The further away from Richmond we get, the easier it will be to travel during the day."

"Where are we heading?" Laura supposed it really didn't make that much difference to her, but wanted to at least have some idea.

"West," Esther said, "through Charlottesville and on to Rockfish Gap. And from there north along the Blue Ridge."

"That seems to be quite out of our way," Jordan objected. "It'll take us at least a week, perhaps longer. Why not simply head north?"

"Because due north is where the entire Confederate Army of the Potomac is encamped, and we can't pass through them. Besides, the mountains give us protection and places to hide. We also have friends there who will help us. We have to avoid the cities. They're not safe."

"What is our final destination?" Laura asked.

"Pennsylvania."

"Pennsylvania? My father is in Washington. I supposed that was where we were going. I thought you knew."

"There are too many spies in Washington," Esther said. "You could be retaken at any time and returned to Richmond. There's a reward for your capture and return, and I advise you to remain out of the Rebels' reach until it is safe. Once we are there you can get word to your father."

Though their circuitous route surprised Jordan, she supposed she and Laura had no choice. They were in the hands of these strangers and would be helpless on their own.

❖

After an uneventful ride of nearly two hours, Laura peeked out from underneath their blankets to find they were no longer in the city. The trees cast menacing shadows along the road, but the sky was bright and full of stars. Presently the wagon turned off the road and came to a halt.

"Inside, quickly!" Esther called to them.

Jordan and Laura scrambled out from the wagon and into a small farmhouse surrounded by yellowed stalks of corn. Once inside, they met Samuel's wife, Virginia, who held a lantern and showed them to a ladder up to a loft above the main room.

"You sleep up there." She pointed.

Jordan, Laura, and Esther climbed the ladder to where several pallets lay on the floor. Next to one of them was a lit candle, and once in bed, Esther blew it out. Laura sensed that just like her, the others were too anxious to sleep.

"Esther, whatever possessed you to engage in such perilous activities?" Laura asked. She was sure that she could never do anything remotely as hazardous.

"Both my parents were freeborn in Pennsylvania, and that means I'm freeborn too. My mother worked and saved from when I was a baby, then sent me to school in Philadelphia where I learned to read and write. I wanted to open a school back home for black children to teach them everything I knew, but one day some white men came to our house. They claimed that my father was a runaway, and even though we showed them the papers that proved he was free, they took him away in chains."

"How awful!" Laura whispered.

"My mother and I never saw him again. And from that day forward, I determined to do all I could to help runaways escape north to freedom. So as you can see, Miss Colfax, even in Pennsylvania a free person can be abducted and taken south. Nowhere near the slave states is safe."

Laura was shocked. The only aspect of the Southern way of life she had ever questioned was slavery. It had done unspeakable things to her family and to the lives of their slaves: her father's infidelity, the whipping of the stable boy, and the loss of Ruby, all because of the color of their skin. She hated the institution and what her people had done to the Negro. Would a war truly end it all?

After a while, Jordan could hear Esther's deep breathing, and assuming she was asleep, she thought about what Esther had said and pondered what it would mean for both her and Laura. Being unable to return to her father's house or to communicate with him would be difficult. She didn't know how to earn a living or support herself, let alone Laura too. Without the theatre as a source of income, how would they survive? Jordan rolled over onto her side and faced Laura, who she could tell, even in the dark, was looking back at her.

"You must be exhausted," Jordan whispered.

"I'm tired, yes, but I have so much on my mind." Laura shifted on the hard pallet. "I don't even know where to begin with what has become of my life. I'm going to live in the North, a foreign land to me, with no family or roots, and with no means of support. I shall have to find some type of work to earn my way, but I don't know how to do anything worthwhile."

"Please, don't think about any of that now." Jordan placed her hand over Laura's. "Don't forget, I'm in this with you. I won't let anything happen to you now. We've managed to avoid arrest and escape from the city, so finding gainful employment cannot be anywhere near as difficult."

Laura smiled. "You use the art of understatement well, Jordan."

Jordan returned the smile, her fingers involuntarily stroking the soft skin of Laura's hand. She was trying to comfort Laura, but the motion soothed *her* as well.

"If not for you, Jordan, I would be marrying Mr. Young very soon and be doomed to a life of unhappiness." She lifted Jordan's hand and kissed it softly.

"Well, I can't promise you happiness, either," Jordan said. "It's not too late for you to leave. You can go to Church Hill and deny all knowledge of me."

"I shot George Lamont," Laura said. "I don't think my prospects in Richmond are worth staying for." She shook her head. "Besides, being with you has always made me happier than I've ever been."

She watched Jordan's expression change from earnest concern to an entirely different emotion. Laura had seen that intense, yearning stare before, when they were in Jordan's hotel room. How she felt now was pleasant, yet so terrifying to contemplate that she pushed it down to examine later. In her journals she had always been able to sort out her feelings, and she missed being able to write in them. Perhaps at some point she would be able to acquire another book and record her thoughts again.

Jordan marveled at the rush of feeling that washed over her simply because of that small kiss on her hand. She wanted to take Laura into her arms and cast away all her fears and anxiety. She wanted to take care of her, to protect her and, yes, love her, but she was unsure how to talk to Laura about her desires. She was certain Laura felt as she did, and shared the odd tight feeling in her stomach. Very soon they would have that talk.

❖

They were on the road at daylight, not needing the cover of darkness out in the country where Jordan's and Laura's faces were not as well recognized. Occasionally they were stopped by guards at crossroads who questioned them as to where they were going. Since they were headed west, they encountered less suspicion than if they had been heading north. Their story was that they were attending a wedding in Charlottesville and Esther and Samuel were their slaves. They were seldom held up for more than a few minutes.

Arriving in Charlottesville late in the day, they approached a neat little farm on the western edge of town, and Samuel stopped the horses out front. Immediately an elderly white couple emerged, smiling to welcome them to their home. Clarence and Eliza Dutton were Quakers who had only recently moved to Charlottesville from northern Virginia and had quickly offered their home to runaway slaves. The travelers were led into a small kitchen where a simple but filling meal awaited them, and afterward, Jordan and Laura decided to take a walk in the waning light of day. It was the first time they were able to do so, and the freedom felt wonderful.

If it were not for the seriousness of her situation, Laura would have felt giddy as they strolled along a creek that ran across the Dutton property. The early evening air was crisp and the leaves were beginning to turn the valley into an impressive show of harvest colors. Fall was Laura's favorite time of year, and being with Jordan was occasion to feel peaceful and content. She sighed when she thought of the reasons that brought her there, and the anxiety that never quite left her reasserted itself.

"What is it, Laura?" Jordan asked.

"I was thinking what a beautiful place this is and how I wish we could be here under more pleasant circumstances. Back at Barrett Hall, September is a wonderful time. The harvest is over and we're preparing for an autumn celebration. Martha makes a lovely cider and an apple brown Betty that is sublime…" She trailed off at the memory. It was no use thinking about such things any longer, as she would never see them again.

"We'll make new memories, Laura, I promise. I'm not much of a cook, but when I can I'll write to our housekeeper and ask her for the recipe. Running from the Confederates will seem as child's play compared to my cooking."

Laura laughed and was pleased to see Jordan's eyes sparkle. She had become so accustomed to Jordan's sad countenance that she had almost forgotten the delight of her smile. She thought about all the hardships that Jordan was enduring because of her and decided she would do what she could to make the journey more bearable. Instead of burdening Jordan with her troubles, she would keep them to herself and present a cheerful countenance. Jordan deserved that much from her, and more.

"We'd better go back," Jordan said. "It will soon be dark and I don't think we should be outside much longer. I don't want you to catch a chill, nor do I wish to worry our hosts."

Though disappointed at having to return so soon, Laura knew Jordan was right. When they approached the house, she could see

Esther in the window watching them as they walked arm in arm. For some reason she pulled away from Jordan and they entered the warm house.

❖

They turned north early the next morning and entered the Blue Ridge Mountains, traveling a route regularly patrolled by the Confederate army. Their new driver, Ethan, was a member of the Duttons' meeting house. He was to get them halfway to Front Royal, where they would be handed over to the next station along the way. After several hours on the road, they came to a small town and stopped to enable Ethan to purchase some oats for the horses. Jordan and Laura followed him into the dry-goods store to stretch their legs and browse the few items for sale. Laura admired a bound leather journal but had no money to purchase it.

"That's a beautiful journal," Jordan said.

"Yes, unfortunately, I had to leave mine behind in Richmond," Laura said wistfully. "One day I'll buy another and begin writing again."

Ethan strolled over as she set the handsome book down. "I have what I need for the horses, but take your time. We'll let them rest a bit before moving on."

Jordan and Laura continued to browse for a few minutes when they heard horses' hooves rapidly approaching. Outside the store, a cavalry company halted and the riders dismounted. Jordan walked to the window and observed the riders cautiously. When a familiar face caught her eye, she called Laura over and pointed out a young man tying his horse to the hitching post.

"Isn't that Lieutenant Kincaid, Ransom's friend?"

In a panic, Laura nodded. "We can't let him see us."

Not wanting to alert the shopkeeper by exiting hastily, Jordan asked if they could use his privy. He pointed to a back door, and they casually exited as the lieutenant entered. They ran to the side of the building and Jordan peeked around the corner, trying to catch the attention of Esther and Ethan. Eventually Esther saw her and strolled unhurriedly toward them.

Jordan could feel her heart pounding and thought that surely they could hear it too. "Esther, we both know the lieutenant who just entered the shop."

Esther glanced around the town, which consisted of a single dirt road with four shops and a few homes. She pointed to the forest a short distance away. "Hide in the woods and I will come for you when they've gone."

Jordan and Laura hurried down the hill and into the pines and oaks that surrounded the small village. They stumbled into a shallow ravine and slid to the bottom, dry leaves noisily breaking their fall. They lay still, side by side, holding their breath. After a few moments when they realized no one was coming after them, they exhaled and panted. Jordan tried to roll onto her stomach and moaned in pain.

"Are you hurt?" Laura whispered urgently.

"It's my ankle." Jordan grimaced. "I think I twisted it."

Laura slid closer, lifting Jordan's skirt to examine her ankle. "Which one?"

"The right one." Jordan winced when Laura probed the ankle, and she quickly withdrew her hand.

"It's all right," Jordan said through gritted teeth. "But if the soldiers come, you must run and hide. They'll capture me and think I'm alone. I know Esther and Ethan won't give you away."

"I will do no such thing," Laura said. "I will not allow you to be returned to prison while I'm free. We're in this together, Jordan, and I won't leave you."

The determination in Laura's face surprised Jordan. She'd always assumed that Laura was delicate and frail. Certainly Laura had been physically weakened as a result of past illnesses, but her inner strength was something Jordan had seldom glimpsed until now. Laura's dedication moved her immensely.

"Hey!" Esther called to them.

"The soldiers are gone, you can come up now."

"Jordan is hurt," Laura shouted. "We need to help her up the ravine."

Presently Ethan and Esther slid down to where they were and half carried her up the hill. Esther examined the ankle and pronounced that it was not broken and that in time she could walk on it again.

"Do nothing in the next two days to injure the ankle further," Esther instructed. "You must be healed sufficiently to travel on foot in a couple of days. Do you think you can do that?"

Jordan glanced at her foot and tried to wiggle it around, stopping instantly when it sent a searing pain up her calf. "I suppose I must," she replied.

Chapter Twenty-eight

Lincoln leaned out the upstairs window of his son Willie's bedroom and observed the soldiers bivouacked below. Their campfires guttered, the evening meal consumed and the embers slowly dying. Somewhere a soldier played a fiddle, the melancholy tune drifting up to him, increasing his already sad mood. He thought about going to them, sitting among them and talking about their thoughts and fears. But Willie had been feverish and had now finally fallen asleep. Lincoln didn't want to leave his side in case he woke up and needed him.

The end of the summer seemed to bring more bad news than good, and he felt as though nothing he did went right. The Battle of Wilson's Creek near Springfield, Missouri, had been another resounding Confederate victory, and in the weeks since that disaster he'd despaired of the Union ever being able to win this war. His popularity was plummeting rapidly, though he had not been all that popular to begin with. But in order to help pay for the war, the government had issued the first income tax, which had not helped reverse the trend. The only promising note on the horizon was the fact that Confederate General Leonidas Polk had invaded neutral Kentucky, the state of Lincoln's birth, and the Kentucky legislature asked the Union for assistance in removing him. It was a small thing, really, but losing Kentucky would be tantamount to losing the entire game, he felt, and anything he could do to assist her would serve to keep him in her good graces.

But the realization that the war was continuing when everyone believed that Bull Run would be the beginning and end of it caused him to be restless. The Union loss had only caused the Northern people to become more steadfast in their determination to see the Rebels punished, and he was obliged to keep the conflict going. How long it would last he could not begin to guess, perhaps another year, maybe more. However, he did not know how long the people would remain resolute when the casualties were unlike anything the country had ever seen.

The sound of laughter below drew his gaze to a group of soldiers playing cards. They seemed to live a carefree life, despite knowing he could determine their fate in an instant. Still, he almost wished he could join them, wished he could avoid the complex burdens that weighed upon him night after night. He almost preferred the singular burden of possible death in battle to his never-ending concerns.

A cough drew him away from the window, and he returned to Willie's bedside and stroked his cheek to quiet him. As he gazed down at the angelic face, he wondered which of the men out in the yard also had sons. And he wondered how many of them might never return home to see the faces of their children again.

❖

The wagon creaked along slowly, the passengers arriving much later than expected due to a broken wheel that took Ethan two hours to fix. The sun was setting and a light rain had begun to fall, covering the wagon in a light mist. Laura was tired and hungry, and while she was covered by an oilcloth to keep out the damp, the cold seeped through. Neither of them had clothing warm enough for the rapidly cooling mountain temperatures. Wishing she could climb down and walk a while, Laura shifted yet again to try to find a more comfortable position on the lumpy wagon bed. She knew that walking would further delay their arrival, but her back was aching and her foot had fallen asleep, a painful reminder of her inactivity.

Her gaze settled on Jordan, who dozed fitfully in her lap. Each time the wagon hit a bump she would jerk awake briefly until she once again resumed her nap. Laura noticed the weariness in Jordan's face and the tight lines that had formed in response to the pain in her ankle. While the ankle was not broken, it had swollen noticeably, and keeping it elevated kept her from sleeping peacefully. Laura wished she could do something to alleviate Jordan's pain. She covered Jordan's face with an oilcloth while she slept, and occasionally stroked Jordan's shoulder comfortingly. Despite their dangerous circumstances, Laura felt oddly at peace holding Jordan in her lap.

Finally Ethan turned off the main road and onto a rutted trail that led farther up into the mountains. After another half hour of deeply rutted road and dense woods, the trail opened up into a clearing where a small wooden shack nestled among a grove of pines. A lantern shone invitingly in the front window and a trail of smoke swirled up from the chimney, dissipating into the darkening sky. Nearby were a hog pen and chicken coop, while farther back a barn also had a lantern shining on a barrel outside. Ethan pulled the wagon up to the barn and swung down from his seat. He walked to the barn door and pulled it open wide, then unhitched the horses.

Esther hopped down as well, followed by Laura, and they assisted Jordan to the ground gently. Laura was grabbing their bag when she noticed movement coming from the house. A Negro man strode toward them while his wife and two children approached hesitantly. The man walked over to speak with Ethan and Esther, while Laura watched as the two children observed her curiously.

"Hello." She smiled at them.

Both children shrank back to the safety of their mother, hiding behind her skirt.

"Y'all are welcome to spend the night in the barn," the man said. "My wife's fixed some vittles for you. It ain't much, but it's hot."

"We are most grateful, Mr. Washington." Ethan nodded.

Mr. Washington picked up the lantern and led the way into the barn. A small corn crib sat against the back wall, but most of the barn was taken up by blacksmith equipment. A bellows, anvil, hammer, and other necessities lay about as though temporarily at rest, waiting for their master's return. The forge was still hot and warmed the barn nicely, keeping the dampness away. A ladder led up to a hay-covered loft.

While Jordan sat on a chair to rest her ankle, Ethan and Esther went to the house to fetch their dinner. Laura walked about the barn, shocked they would be spending the night in such a place. She climbed the ladder to the loft and saw the dreary, dirty hay, then noticed the rain trickling in through a hole in the roof. A stack of moth-eaten patched quilts sat on the floor awaiting them, and she shuddered to think of covering herself with them. She backed down the ladder as Ethan and Esther entered carrying a cast-iron pot and eating utensils. They sat wherever they could find a place and Esther spooned the contents of the pot into the wooden bowls. Laura ate a mouthful and almost gagged. Corn mush with bits of gristly bacon was not something she was accustomed to, and while she tried to eat it, she simply couldn't, so she placed the bowl on the anvil next to her.

Esther had an angry expression when she placed her dish to the side. "What's the matter, Laura?"

"Oh, nothing, I guess I'm not hungry." Laura took a sip of water to rid herself of the unpleasant aftertaste.

"You're not feeling ill again, are you?" Jordan asked worriedly.

"I think it's the food and not her health that's bothering her, isn't that right?" Esther retorted.

Stung by the rebuff but mostly embarrassed, Laura lost her temper. "I am unaccustomed for anyone to speak to me in such manner, Miss Stark. I should be glad for you to keep such opinions to yourself."

"Laura—" Jordan began.

"You will eat the food that has been offered you so graciously," Esther replied. "It's what they eat every day, and if it's good enough for them it's good enough for you."

"I warn you, Miss Stark," Laura said through clenched teeth, "I shall not stand for your impertinence."

"Or else, Miss St. Clair? Or else you shall have me taken out back and whipped?" Esther trembled, obviously angry.

"How dare you!" Laura stood, knocking her bowl over and spilling the contents on the ground.

Everyone stared in silence at the upturned bowl. Embarrassed by the scene she had caused, Laura flushed and fled from the barn.

When Esther caught up with her on a rutted trail leading back to the main road, she said, "You'd best return to the barn, Miss St. Clair. We cannot afford to have you catch your death."

"I would think that would be most satisfactory to you, Miss Stark," Laura said bitterly. She stopped walking and abruptly faced her. "Have I done something to offend you, Miss Stark? For the life of me, I cannot think of anything I may have said to cause you to treat me so harshly."

Esther replied in kind. "You are accustomed to a way of life that scorns that of the Washingtons. I could see it in your eyes. Unlike you, they cannot afford the creature comforts, and it makes me angry to see you disparage the food they could ill afford to spare."

Laura's blood was up and she could feel her face grow hot. "Well, Miss Stark, I find myself trying to join the ranks of the Washingtons as I am even more destitute than they. I have nowhere to go and no means to provide for myself. I suppose that someday I will regret not having a meal such as the one provided this evening. But forgive me if I require more time to adapt to my present condition."

As Laura pushed past her on her way to the barn and Esther watched her go, Laura wondered if Esther regretted that she had agreed to undertake this particular rescue.

❖

The next morning they were subdued while they prepared to depart. Mr. Washington added wood to the fire in the forge and got it going early. He was going to construct a permanent replacement pin for the wheel axle that Ethan had temporarily fixed the day before. Mrs. Washington brought them breakfast and Laura dutifully ate it all, avoiding Esther's occasional glances. After breakfast the Washington children, a girl and boy, emboldened by the light of day, overcame their fear of white people and approached cautiously. They had never seen such a white person as Laura, her golden hair an oddity for them, and they reached out to touch it to see if it was real.

"You leave that lady alone!" Mrs. Washington yelled at them.

They obediently retracted their hands, placing them shyly behind their backs. The boy ran off to be with his father, but the little girl stayed close.

Laura looked the child over, noticing that she had a twisted foot she dragged as she walked. She wondered at the reason for it, but did not wish to embarrass the girl.

"My daddy's gonna take you on the Underground Railroad." She smiled, her top front teeth missing.

"He is?" Laura glanced back to him in the barn. He had already worked up a sweat as he hammered with powerful forearms at a piece of hot iron. She guessed that they had arrived at the halfway point where Ethan was to turn back and Mr. Washington assisted them on their way.

"Uh-huh." The little girl nodded. "My pa is smart. He knows how to get hisself home in the dark. He say to me and my brother Jack if'n we's ever run away, to follow the drinking gourd and we find freedom."

Laura was puzzled. "The drinking gourd? Whatever do you mean, child?"

"Why, everybody know the drinking gourd, miss." The child stared at her as though Laura was a simpleton. She pointed upward and spoke slowly so that Laura could understand. "In the sky in the nighttime, the stars what looks like a drinking gourd."

Laura automatically looked up to the sky and realized the girl meant the Big Dipper with its bowl pointing toward the North Star. She glanced back at the little girl as she began to sing.

"I thought I heard the angels say,
Follow the drinkin' gourd.
The stars in the heaven gonna show you the way,
Follow the drinkin' gourd."

She stopped singing and smiled shyly at Laura. Taking Laura's silence as lack of comprehension, the girl smiled patiently at her.

"It's okay. My pa will teach you that song so's you can't get lost. Just ask 'em. So long as you know that song you ain't never gonna be lost again."

Unbidden tears came to Laura's eyes and she pulled the child to her bosom and hugged her tightly.

"Laura?" Jordan approached behind her and at her arrival the little girl ran off.

She sat next to Laura, putting her arm around her shoulder when she saw the tears in her eyes. She wanted to ask her what was wrong, but was unsure of Laura's emotions lately. She knew Laura's outburst last night was due to the stress of their situation. And they still needed to sort out the immediate future, but for now, Jordan didn't want to add to Laura's delicate frame of mind.

Laura sniffled and rested her head on Jordan's shoulder. "I'm sorry." Laura sighed. "I'll be all right, truly I will. I'm just so tired. Sometime soon perhaps we could stop and rest awhile. I cannot seem to think clearly in the back of that wagon, my mind rattles so."

"Tonight we stop in Front Royal," Jordan soothed. "What would you say if we spent the night in a nice hotel where you can have a hot bath and a feather bed?"

Laura smiled through her tears. "Oh, Jordan, you're so kind." She grasped Jordan's hand and squeezed it tightly. "But you must save your money and not squander it on my foolishness."

"But what else is the money for if not to use it when we need it? We also need to purchase coats since what we have is insufficient. Besides, I do believe Miss Stark could use a break from us as well."

Laura laughed. "I'm quite sure she's had her fill of me, and I cannot say as I blame her. I've behaved like a petulant child, and I must be stoic at least until our journey's end. Then I suppose she will be glad to part ways with me."

Jordan drew Laura closer, feeling the warmth between them and taking strength from simply being together. All that mattered was that they had each other, and once they crossed the Potomac they would be safe from the Confederate army. After that, nothing could compare to the hardships they had endured during their escape. Jordan vowed silently that never again would Laura suffer the privations they had on this journey. She would protect her from all adversity, whether real or imagined.

The skies threatened all day as they traveled. Ethan had returned home by donkey while the wagon was driven by Mr. Washington. Occasionally a flash of lightning could be seen followed by the deep rumbling of thunder that echoed through the mountainous terrain. They were fortunate that the weather held until they entered the town of Front Royal, when the dark clouds finally opened and the rain fell in sheets. Told of their desire to spend the night in a hotel, Mr. Washington took Jordan and Laura to a respectable establishment in the center of town. But when Jordan realized that neither he nor Esther would be able to stay in the hotel, she immediately withdrew the suggestion.

"No," Esther objected. "Appearances would allow for you two to stay here. Mr. Washington and I shall spend the night at our usual place. We will come for you in the morning."

They drove off in the rain as Jordan and Laura entered the hotel and obtained a room. The hotel had a dining room, and while a bath was being prepared in their room, they went in to supper. They ordered roast chicken with yams and cornbread and a bottle of red wine. Laura ate ravenously, thoroughly enjoying every bite. Jordan watched with amusement as it took a full five minutes before Laura even said a word.

"It has been ages since I've eaten like this," Laura admitted, taking a sip of wine, savoring every drop.

"What, the meal or the speed with which you have consumed it?" Jordan teased.

Laura blushed, realizing that indeed she had eaten half the contents of her plate. She gazed at Jordan, happy to see the sparkle back in her eyes, although fine lines still tinged her brow. The swelling in Jordan's ankle had gone down, but it was still larger than the other, and she favored the swollen one as she walked. She made a mental note to ask the desk clerk if they had an icehouse nearby.

"The meal is delicious, thank you," Laura replied sarcastically. "But I'm really looking forward to the bath and a chance to wash some of my clothing. I know I shall feel much better to be clean again."

"As shall I," Jordan said innocently.

"Jordan! Surely I am no worse than you!" Laura complained.

Jordan laughed and Laura was reminded of the first time she had heard the sound. A warm feeling overcame her and she laughed as well.

"I meant," Jordan managed between chuckles, "that I shall be glad to be clean as well."

"Oh." Laura blushed again.

Jordan loved the way the color rose in Laura's cheeks. It gave her pale complexion a healthy glow, and it pleased her to see Laura regaining her strength. She was again struck by Laura's delicate beauty, and her pulse raced at the thought of kissing her again.

They finished the meal and when they arrived in their room, a tub filled with steaming water had been placed in front of a crackling fire. Besides the fire, the only other sound was the booming distant thunder and the rain that pelted the windows.

"You go first," Jordan spoke softly, suddenly shy, "then while you're in the bath, I shall take our clothes and wash them out."

Laura undressed while Jordan busied herself at the washstand near the window. Waiting until she heard Laura sink down into the tub and groan with pleasure, Jordan finally turned around and gathered up Laura's things. She scrubbed Laura's clothes with a bar of soap, rinsed them, then hung them over a chair by the fire to dry.

"I'm finished." Laura rose out of the tub.

Jordan quickly turned around and waited until Laura had dressed in her last clean nightdress. Then, hobbling over to the bath, Jordan undressed, placing her clothes on the floor. Trying to climb into the tub with only one good foot, she nearly fell and had to grab the sides. Laura was instantly at her side, grasping Jordan around the waist to steady her. Jordan flushed hotly, embarrassed by her incapacity as well as by the nearness of Laura to her nakedness. For a moment, they stood transfixed, aware of each other's bodies for the first time. Jordan finally got into the bath and, with Laura's help, slowly lowered herself into the still-warm water.

"Thank you," Jordan said.

"You must not be afraid to ask for help, Jordan," Laura said. "You have been very brave, and I should have known better than to allow you to attempt the bath without me."

Laura returned to the washbasin, her inner turmoil at odds with her outward calm. She had not wanted to exacerbate Jordan's obvious discomfort, so she had feigned indifference to Jordan's body. Yet her own body seemed to hum with the contact and she put extra effort into a particularly stubborn stain.

Jordan tried to relax in the warm water, feeling it soothe her aching body as she lay back and closed her eyes. But the bath had the opposite effect on her, stimulating her senses into wakefulness. Rather than wait for it to turn cold, she washed quickly and then squeezed the excess water out of her hair. She tried to rise on her own but realized she again would need Laura's assistance and she sat back again, delaying the inevitable. Finally, knowing she could wait no longer, she cleared her throat.

Laura had placed the damp clothes near the fire to dry when Jordan called out to her. "I'm sorry, Laura, but…" Jordan gestured at her predicament.

"Oh! Yes, of course." Laura came swiftly to the side of the tub, bringing a soft towel.

She helped Jordan up, then quickly wrapped her body. Jordan leaned on her shoulder while she climbed out of the bath. Trying to get out and stand on her own, Jordan accidentally lost the towel and nearly fell as she lunged to catch it.

Laura caught her again, and as she bent to pick up the towel, her gaze fell on Jordan's wet body, glistening from the glow of the fire. Enchanted by the sight, Laura could not help but comment. "You are so very lovely, Jordan," she murmured softly.

Jordan stood very still, not wanting to break the spell that seemed to have fallen over them. Her body grew warm under Laura's gaze and she felt that familiar ache once again in the pit of her stomach. They stood there for what seemed like a very long time until, hesitantly, they moved toward each other, stopping short of touching.

"I…thank you," Jordan stuttered, unsure what to say.

Laura marveled at the way Jordan's clavicle stood out prominently, and without thinking she traced a finger from her throat to her shoulder. She was surprised to feel Jordan tremble beneath her touch.

"Are you cold?" she asked.

"No," Jordan managed. She didn't say that she thought she could no longer stand. Laura's touch had left her weak but definitely not cold.

They did not move, still standing and facing one another, inches away from contact. Laura recognized Jordan's look. She had seen it before, that first time on a picnic so long ago that it seemed like a lifetime. She wanted to recapture that moment, the carefree feeling, the warm sun and the fragrant dogwood blossoms. Memories of the past spilled into the present, suffusing her body with the same sensations she'd experienced all those months ago.

Jordan drew Laura to her. She tilted her head as her lips met Laura's. The kiss was everything she remembered and more. The softness of Laura's lips, the dizzy, heady feeling was clear and unmistakable. Her mind closed to all things but Laura, here and now, how she felt and tasted. It was familiar and comfortable, yet new and exciting. As the kiss deepened, Jordan's passion overtook her, calling out to her, to something timeless and permanent buried deep within. It awakened that dormant part of her that she had largely ignored until now, and she welcomed her unexplored self as though she had come home.

With trembling hands, she removed Laura's nightdress, marveling at the translucent perfection of her skin. This time, when their bodies pressed together, Jordan groaned from the intensity of the feeling. Understanding now what it all meant, she took Laura by the hand and led her into bed. They lay facing each other, mere inches separating them from pressing forward, never to return. Jordan saw only acceptance, love, and desire in Laura's gaze. It was all she needed.

Laura felt a little shy, but the way Jordan consumed her with her eyes, the heat and the desire between them only intensified. Jordan was stunning, her breasts firm and her chestnut hair falling loosely about her shoulders; she looked like a goddess Laura had seen in a painting in a museum. She couldn't help herself; she wanted to know what it would feel like to touch Jordan's breasts, and before she realized it, her hand cupped and fondled one. It was so incredibly soft, and when her fingers stroked the nipple, it stiffened under her touch. She was amazed to discover the power she had over Jordan's body, and the idea caused the ache in her center to ignite and burn swiftly.

"Oh, dearest Laura." Jordan could bear it no longer. Pulling Laura on top of her provided the sweet relief she had been craving. A mighty power overtook them and they kissed, at first gently and inquiringly, but soon with an almost ferocious appetite. Their mouths opened and their tongues sought to discover what their bodies had been seeking. And then their hands. No longer tentative or doubtful, they stroked each other's sides, hips, and stomachs, but still avoided the last intimacy left to them. Knowing that they could not turn back if they were to explore the most private of womanly places, they waited reverently for the moment when that too would cease to be a barrier between them.

Jordan was almost insane with desire and she gently rolled Laura over onto her back. With a boldness she didn't know she possessed, she kissed Laura's neck and shoulders and then, wanting so much to taste her skin, she licked a path between her breasts, tracing the curve underneath. Without stopping, she found her way to Laura's nipple, coaxing and sucking and drawing it into her mouth, tasting the warm flesh and the scent that was all Laura. She wanted to consume her, to imprint her body in her memory forever, so that if this was the only moment she would ever have with her, she would never forget it as long as she lived.

Laura moaned and grasped Jordan's head, caressing her hair and face, encouraging her onward, needing more and now knowing what that meant. She spread her legs to allow Jordan to nestle between them and when she did, she was astounded at the wetness she felt there. Nearly out of her mind, she pushed her center up into Jordan's body, intuitively knowing that she could find relief if she could rid herself of the ache that demanded attention. As she rocked into Jordan, Jordan's hand found its way to the base of her curls. Laura held her breath, a little afraid of what would come next.

Ever so delicately, Jordan slipped her finger into Laura's silky center and nearly wept with joy. She was so hot, wet, and incredibly beautiful, Jordan knew this was what was meant by making love. This was what she wanted, and this she would protect with all that was in her. She stroked the swollen, prominent peak at the apex of Laura's folds and heard her cry out. Afraid she had hurt her, she glanced up to see Laura's head flung back on the pillow, her eyes closed and her mouth open. She was glorious and Jordan wanted this moment to last forever. Returning her mouth to the nipple, she sucked while she continued stroking Laura's wet center until she could feel Laura's body tense beneath her own. Laura cried out one last time, then shuddered repeatedly, holding onto Jordan until nothing was left, and then she was still.

Jordan lay beside her, one arm underneath her head, the other encircling her waist. She could hear the rapid thumping of Laura's heart and was astonished at what had happened. She did not know that this was what women spoke of euphemistically when out of earshot of their men. No one had ever told her what it would be like to make love. Since her mother had died so young, she and her father had only discussed politics and business, but never would he have imparted any knowledge of this to her. She gave a silent prayer of thanks that she had lived to see this day and vowed that she would never take such a thing for granted again.

Chapter Twenty-nine

Laura stretched on the soft down mattress, feeling rested and more alive than she could ever remember. Every sound, every smell, every touch seemed more acute to her, and she luxuriated in her newfound well-being. Rolling onto her side, she found Jordan asleep, her chestnut tresses cascading about her on the pillow. Memories of the previous night washed over her and she gazed at Jordan in wonder. How was it that something she had been dreading with Mr. Young had felt so natural with Jordan? She had cringed whenever he touched her and yet with Jordan, even a knowing smile was exhilarating.

She watched as the dawn gradually spread across the quilted coverlet on the bed. Jordan was cast in shadow and light while she slept, dappled patterns forming over her face and hair, mimicking the patchwork on the bed. In the tranquility of the morning, Laura could almost believe they were not running for their lives and instead were on some kind of holiday. She wished desperately that it were so, and that her forced exile from her family and Barrett Hall would not be permanent.

Jordan's eyelids fluttered and she gazed up at Laura as if she had crept inside her thoughts. Touching Laura's cheek, she asked, "Are you all right?"

"I am more than all right, Jordan." Laura caressed a strand of Jordan's hair. "I am happy. Perhaps for the first time in my life I am truly happy."

Despite the words, her tone was melancholic. Jordan searched Laura's eyes for any glimmer of doubt. She felt like laughing and dancing wildly about the room at the thought of what they had discovered in one another's arms.

A knock on their door was followed by the announcement that it was seven o'clock, the hour they had asked to be awakened. Laura slid into Jordan's waiting embrace and they held each other in the sanctuary of the bed.

Laura looked deeply into Jordan's eyes, searching for the answers she knew were never easy. "We are North and South, Jordan. We may never agree on the issues facing our country."

Jordan leaned in until Laura's face was mere inches from her own. "We have something North and South do not have."

"What is that?" Laura asked.

"Love."

They kissed warmly and Jordan could feel Laura's passion rise as quickly as her own, but time was not on their side. Reluctantly, she rose from the bed and they dressed before descending the stairs to the dining room.

After breakfast, they found Esther and Mr. Washington with the wagon waiting for them out front.

"Mr. Washington will take us to Martinsburg before nightfall," Esther informed them. "After that, we're on our own. I hope your ankle is sufficiently healed, Jordan, as we'll be walking for quite a distance."

"Have no fear, Esther. I won't slow us down."

Esther nodded. "We'll cross the Potomac tonight while we can move unseen. Every bridge is guarded by Rebel pickets."

"But you've done this before, haven't you?" Jordan felt her nervousness increase at the prospect before them. Intuitively she knew that this would be the most dangerous part of their journey, aside from their initial escape from Richmond. She worried about Laura's safety and wanted reassurance that all would be well.

"I have done this many times," Esther said. "We must be vigilant, however, as descriptions of you both are being circulated."

"No one is going to catch us," Jordan said in a show of confidence for Laura's benefit.

A rare smile crossed Esther's face. "I can tell you this, ladies. It's infinitely more perilous to take a band of slaves, including children, across the Potomac than to take two white women."

Mr. Washington laughed, gave the reins a snap, and the horses picked up speed.

❖

The day was chilly and the winds swirled through the autumn leaves. But the sun was warm and the sky was a bright azure, and Jordan and Laura sat comfortably but restlessly in the back of the wagon. They held hands almost the entire trip and exchanged fleeting, reassuring smiles at the prospect ahead of them. They were nearing the end of their journey, and the thought of being no longer on the run filled them with hope. Yet they were also aware of the impending danger and that knowledge kept them on edge.

The trip seemed to pass more quickly than usual, even though by the time they reached Martinsburg the sun had already set. By now everyone in the wagon was on alert, listening and watching for anything out of the ordinary. They continued until they could see the flowing waters of the Potomac as it wound its way through the valley. In the distance they could see the bridge that crossed the river, as well as the Confederate pickets encamped on the Virginia side. At this point, Mr. Washington turned off the main road and followed the river upstream for approximately a mile. A small house on the hillside with a lantern glowing in the window signaled yet another safe house on the Underground Railroad. He brought the wagon to a halt and they quickly climbed down.

Laura stood next to Jordan, taking her hand for reassurance. The water looked black and the current moved swiftly, but here and there she could see patches of dry land as though stepping stones had been placed within the river. On the other side was Maryland and the nearness of it caused Laura's heart to beat wildly. It was so close, and yet just beyond their reach. If they could not cross via the bridge, she was loath to contemplate a crossing by swimming. Since Laura did not know how to swim, she was exceedingly concerned.

A Negro man came out of the house, shook hands with Mr. Washington, and hugged Esther, who gave a fleeting smile.

"Them Rebels been up and down the river all night long," the man said. "They looking for somebody but I don't know who. Maybe you folks or maybe somebody else. I don't know."

Laura glanced at Jordan.

"It will be all right," Jordan reassured her. "No one knows we are here, but we must be careful. Esther will know what to do."

Overhearing them, Esther moved closer.

"Do you think we should wait for another night?" Laura asked her uncertainly.

Esther shook her head. “Whether it is tonight or another is all the same. The Rebels are always watching the Potomac, just as on the other side the Federals are doing likewise. When crossing the river, we always have to be cautious. We can ill afford any mistakes, and now is when you must do precisely as I tell you.”

“How is the river tonight, Arly?” Esther asked the man.

“Rains have made it deep in places, but up aways there’s spots that can be crossed. My boat won’t do no good tonight. It’ll bottom out and get stuck. You’ll have to swim over in places, but most of it’s dry.”

Laura’s heart pounded and she took deep breaths to calm herself. Jordan squeezed her hand and she squeezed back, trying to be brave.

“How far up?” Esther asked.

“Come on, I’ll show you,” he said, and Esther motioned to Laura and Jordan to remain behind.

Mr. Washington leaned against the side of the wagon and lit a pipe, puffing thoughtfully on the stem. He looked for all the world as unconcerned as though he was on a simple outing in the country, and it amazed Laura to see his apparent calm. Of course, he did not have to cross the river, she thought ruefully.

“So when will you be returning home, Mr. Washington?” Laura asked, wanting to fill the time with anything but silence.

“I ’spect soon,” he puffed. “Soon as Esther says you’s gonna cross the river, I be on my way.”

“Why do you and your family not go north as well?” Laura was curious.

“Maybe someday we will,” he replied. “And maybe someday we won’t have to. But for now, during these troublous times, we have a heap ’o folks such as yourself needing our help. If’n we didn’t help you, who would?”

Laura was dumbstruck by his response. “But why? You risk so much for people you don’t even know. If you knew me, and knew my family, I am sure you would hate us, for what we are and what we represent.”

She could see him shrug even in the dark.

“So why is you escaping, then?”

“Well…the authorities suspect me of shooting a Confederate soldier and being a Yankee sympathizer.” She glanced away, barely able to say it aloud.

“Is you?” he asked.

"I…" She searched out Jordan's hand in the dark and intertwined their fingers. She did not know how to answer him. She was confused as to what she truly believed and what she wanted to see happen to her country. It would take a long time for her to come to terms with who she was and what she would become.

"If'n you have to think about it, s'all the same to me." He tapped his pipe on the side of the wagon. "I don't 'spect white folks know themselves what they's for and what they's agin'. Us black folk, we never know day to day what folks to trust. Me? I take 'em one at a time." He blew into the bowl of the pipe to empty the last vestiges of used tobacco and then put it in his pocket. "I hope you figure it out someday, miss, but I 'spect you's on the right track."

Esther and Arly returned to the group and they went into the house to get warm. Arly made a pot of tea for them and they gratefully sipped the hot brew.

"There is a place we can cross that doesn't appear to be too dangerous. Arly says there are two deep spots that we will need to swim, but they are only for short distances. The rest is dry. However, the dry places are where we are most vulnerable to being seen. We have to hurry across at those points."

"It is fairly cold and I worry about Laura getting chilled," Jordan said. "When we reach the other side, what then?"

Esther motioned them to the window facing the river. On the other side of the river in the distance a faint light shone on the hillside.

"Do you see that light?" Esther pointed to it. "That is where we may stop and collect ourselves. However, we will also use the oilcloths to wrap a change of clothes to take with us, to prevent them from getting wet."

"I can't swim," Laura said.

"What?" Jordan asked, unsure she heard her correctly.

"I never learned how to swim," Laura repeated, glancing from Jordan to Esther to gauge their reactions.

"We'll keep you between us," Esther said. "The distance is not great, and if you float on your back and do as I say, you'll get across safely."

Esther's confidence calmed Laura's doubts and she relaxed slightly. She knew they had no other choice, so she determined to be as helpful as she could.

"Are you ready?" Esther asked them.

"Now?" Laura asked.

"Yes." Jordan took Laura's hand and held it tightly. "We're ready."

❖

They said their good-byes to Mr. Washington, who climbed up into the wagon and drove away without looking back. The four of them continued on up river until they reached the spot that Arly had selected for them to cross. Although he would not accompany them, he promised to stand vigil on the riverbank should any mishap occur. Esther and Jordan each carried an oilcloth with their belongings, while Laura was left unencumbered. Esther led the way down to the river's edge, stepping into ankle-deep water with Jordan and Laura following closely behind. They had gone no more than thirty yards when a shout from the riverbank made them all jump. Within moments, three Confederate soldiers came running from downstream, each carrying a rifle pointed at them. Jordan was relieved to see Arly fade into the brush. She did not want to see him punished for his role in their escape.

"Halt or we shoot!" one of the soldiers called out to them.

All three of the women stood still, knowing that trying to make their way across now would be futile.

"Don't make me come get you," the same soldier said, his rifle aimed at Esther.

The three of them retraced their steps. Laura thought she might be ill over their near escape. They were almost there. She could see the light in the woods on the other side, beckoning them to safety. She was near tears at the thought, but more importantly, she wondered what would happen to them now. They reached the shore where the soldiers stood waiting and climbed back up the hillside.

"Who are you?"

The soldier who was doing all the talking appeared to be in charge. They could tell by his uniform that he was a sergeant and the others were privates. No one replied to his question and he became angry at their defiance. Extending his rifle with bayonet toward Jordan, he repeated his question. Laura glanced nervously at Jordan and then to Esther, wondering what she would do. Esther stared at the soldier, her eyes conveying the hatred she felt for the man.

"All right, then," he said. "Seeing as how you look to be crossing the river without a pass, and with a nigger, I expect you was aiding in the escape of a runaway slave."

Jordan, realizing that Esther was no longer in charge in this particular situation, took matters into her own hands. Knowing the only excuse was the obvious one, she sought to at least take responsibility for the lesser charge. Perhaps with bribes, they could still get across.

"Yes, Sergeant," she confessed, "we are heading to the other side without a pass and with a runaway slave." She caught Esther staring at her, but she continued. "My sister-in-law and I are returning this slave to her master, my father, in Maryland. She ran away a week ago, but we were unable to obtain a pass to cross through Confederate lines due to the war. So we decided to make our way on our own."

Laura was amazed at Jordan's ability to make up such a story on the spur of the moment. Then she realized that Jordan was playing a role, as she so often did in the theatre. Their very lives depended upon the scene she was acting out, and Laura had to support her the best she could. Turning on her best Southern charm, Laura stepped into her own character.

"Why, Sergeant," she flirted shamelessly, "surely you do not think ladies of our breeding would condescend to such behavior were it not for the simple explanation my dear sister-in-law has given. We simply desire to get this ungrateful darkie back where she belongs."

At that moment, Jordan wanted nothing more than to throw her arms around Laura and kiss her.

The sergeant glanced nervously at his men and proceeded cautiously. "Why, ma'am, I can see that you are an upright, God-fearing, Southern lady of high standing. But you must consider that I have to report you to my superior officer."

"Sergeant," Laura stepped a little closer to him so that he lowered his weapon, "my uncle, the colonel, would be most angry should I and my dear, sweet sister-in-law shame the family name so grievously by our thoughtless actions. Surely there is some way we can come to an understanding, you and I, so as to avoid any embarrassment."

"I would be more than happy to compensate you for the inconvenience we may have caused you and your men, Sergeant." Jordan withdrew several gold coins from the pouch she kept for safekeeping in the waistband of her dress.

All three soldiers gaped at the sight of real gold coins. Jordan could see their minds working as to all the luxuries they could buy, and when she withdrew a few more, she knew she had them hooked.

A soldier on horseback thudded noisily to a halt on the slope above them. "Sergeant! What is the meaning of this?"

The sergeant and his men snapped to attention. "Sir! We came upon these two ladies and their slave attempting to cross the river. We ordered them back to this side to question them."

The soldier dismounted and slid down the hill to where they stood. "And what did they tell you, Sergeant?"

"They were retrieving their runaway, sir." The sergeant informed his superior of the details he'd gleaned, leaving out the part about the bribe.

The officer studiously inspected the three women, concentrating his attention on Jordan's face, then Laura's. "Lieutenant Osborne, at your service." He gave a brief bow.

Jordan sized up the officer and understood immediately that he could not be handled in the same manner as the three soldiers. "Lieutenant, this has been a long evening, and we do so wish to get home before it gets much later."

"What is your name, miss?" The lieutenant stood stiffly before her.

Jordan was at a momentary loss. She thought of the pseudonym she had used previously. "Tyler, Lieutenant, and this is my sister-in-law, Laura Tyler."

His smile held no warmth. "Why, that is indeed a surprise." He reached into his tunic and withdrew a piece of paper, which he proceeded to unfold. "It says here that you are the spy Jordan Colfax and this is your accomplice, Laura St. Clair, a lady sought for the attempted murder of a sergeant in this army."

Laura's heart stopped beating and she thought she might faint. The three soldiers raised their rifles. The only sound was the rushing of the Potomac that grew louder in Laura's ears with each passing moment.

"Sergeant, gather these women and their nigger together," the lieutenant ordered, "and escort them to the captain for further interrogation. I suspect the government will reward us handsomely for their capture and return."

He returned to his horse while the men surrounded the women and led them back to their outpost.

"I am sorry about this," Jordan said to Esther.

"It was bound to happen sooner or later." Esther shrugged. "I've managed to help save many lives. If God wills it now that I should give mine in exchange for theirs, I do so willingly."

Laura stared at Esther, in awe of her selflessness and resilience in the face of certain death. How could people like Esther, Samuel, and the Washingtons risk their lives for her, a member of a slave-owning family? She raised her hand to her face and could see it trembling. She wondered if she would be able to survive this event only to face long imprisonment for the crime of shooting that vile wretch Lamont. As she felt Jordan's warm hand slip into her own, she started to weep. She was grateful they were together but devastated that the same fate had befallen them both. She tried to express all the love she had for Jordan through the squeeze of her hand and knew Jordan understood.

When they reached the Rebel outpost situated next to the bridge crossing the Potomac, the lieutenant told them to wait outside while he went in to inform the captain of their capture. A moment later he called. "Bring them in."

The sergeant and his men immediately complied, and after they presented the prisoners, they quickly retreated, closing the door behind them. The captain stood in front of a fire with his back to them. When he finally turned around, Laura gasped. The officer before them was Preston Young.

❖

"Hello, Laura." Preston had grown thinner since the last time she saw him. The lines on his face had deepened as well, and his careworn expression filled her with pity.

Embarrassed by the circumstances that brought them together again, she struggled to think of something to say. "Hello, Preston."

"Miss Colfax." Preston nodded toward Jordan.

She helplessly dipped a polite curtsey, trying to determine whether it was positive or negative that Laura's fiancé was their captor.

"It would seem that you are in a great deal of trouble," he said sadly.

"So it would seem," Laura replied. "I'm sorry, Preston. I never meant to hurt you."

He nodded. "I believe you. Won't you sit down?"

He gestured toward a wooden table covered with papers, a map of the Potomac spread out on top. The only other piece of furniture in the room was a small cot against the wall farthest from the door. Esther hung back slightly, eyes downcast as Laura and Jordan sat. Jordan tried to reassure her with a gentle pat on the hand.

"You've placed me in a most indelicate position." Preston paced in front of the fireplace, his gaze focused on the floor. "If I return you to Richmond, I suppose I shall be regarded a hero of my country. Not to mention receiving the sizable reward for your capture. And while the money means nothing to me, I'm sure my boys outside have already determined how they shall spend their share." He stopped pacing and regarded Laura. "Yet how can I consign the woman I love to certain imprisonment?"

Laura swallowed, her heart beating so hard in her chest she thought it must surely break this time. She tried to think, but her mind was such a jumble that she felt as though she were dreaming and nothing she was experiencing could possibly be real. Their lives were at stake and perhaps she was the only one now who could save them.

"She has done nothing," Jordan spoke up. "I deceived her so as to purloin documents from her father and his associates. She was loyal to me as the most tender of friends, and the shooting of which she is now accused is a slander. The derringer is my weapon and I can prove it." While Jordan spoke, Preston's eyes never left Laura. It was almost as though he did not hear her words or even notice the presence of anyone other than Laura. Jordan noted that Laura's eyes remained on him as well and she fell silent.

He stepped closer to Laura and squatted at her feet, his hand resting on the arm of her chair. "Why are you assisting this spy, Laura? Why did you keep silent about her activities when you must have known?"

Laura could not control her shaking. She felt Jordan tense next to her and wished she could hold her and be held. She didn't know if she was strong enough to endure this test, and had she been alone, she knew she could not have. But she drew strength from Jordan and faced Preston with determination.

"Because she is my friend, Preston. Our political views are not the same, it is true. But I have found that there is more to a relationship than that. There is more than the fact that she is a Northerner and I a Southerner. Our two countries may be at war, but we are not. We are only human and we have our weaknesses. We argue and disagree, and I must confess that at times I thought we might come to blows. But in the end, it is love that binds us and makes us stronger. I fervently pray that someday our two countries can find that it is what we have in common that makes us one people, instead of being torn apart by our differences." Laura took a deep breath, hoping she was getting her heartfelt meaning across. "Betraying Jordan to the authorities was not possible, Preston, because it would have been a betrayal to myself. I could not betray someone I love, no matter my political persuasion."

Laura stopped speaking and her tears fell in earnest. Jordan took her hand, and it was all she could do not to collapse into her arms. Come what may, she had committed them to her fate.

Preston slowly rose. With a single long stare at Laura's face, he returned to his former place in front of the fire, his back to them once more. He was quiet for a very long time. Finally, without turning, he said in a voice heavy with sorrow, "I only wish it were that simple, Laura. While I love you, duty to my country prevents me from doing that which I know to be wrong. I wish I could help you, but I cannot. In the morning I'll have to remand you to the authorities in Richmond. I suspect you and your friend will be imprisoned and perhaps even hang for your crimes. I wish it were not so, but I have no choice in the matter."

He faced them once again and his eyes were immediately drawn to Jordan, who pointed the derringer at his head. He blanched and shifted his glance uneasily to Laura.

"I am sorry too, Preston," Laura whispered, barely able to speak. "I know you to be a good, kind man and a wonderful father to your children. I wish you all the happiness in the world. And someday I hope you will understand why I have made the choices that I have."

The three women rose from the table, and while Jordan held the gun on him, Esther removed the sheet from the cot and tore it into strips. They bound Preston quickly and Laura shoved a strip of cloth into his mouth, then tied another around his head to keep the gag in place. When she'd finished, they stared down at him.

"Good-bye, Preston," Laura said.

"We'll leave through the back window," Esther said. "Hopefully we'll have enough time before he is discovered."

She silently opened the window to the crisp air and climbed out, dropping softly to the ground below. Jordan helped Laura out next, and then with a last glance back at Preston, who helplessly watched them, she ducked through the window, closing it behind her.

Esther was already running toward the bridge, leading them in and out of shadows and underbrush until they were behind the pickets who sat huddled around a fire. "If we stay close to the sides of the bridge and in the shadows they won't see us," Esther whispered. "Come on."

Crouching and walking single file, they stepped onto the bridge and hugged the beams that formed the sides. Trying to remain as quiet as possible and yet move as quickly as they could, they hurried toward the Maryland side. They were halfway across the bridge when they heard shouting and cursing. Glancing over her shoulder, Jordan could see a couple of soldiers mount horses while several others on foot ran onto the bridge.

"There they are!" a soldier called out and a rifle went off, striking a beam nearby.

Reflexively, all three women ducked and ran in a crouched position. Jordan paused, pointed her derringer, and fired. The shot had the intended effect. Under fire, the men on horseback pulled hard on their reins, the horses rearing and whirling about. The men on foot dropped to the ground, surprised they were being fired upon.

"Run!" Jordan urged.

Her ankle throbbed with each step, but she blocked the pain from her mind. She didn't know what would happen once they reached the other side. Would the soldiers follow them into Maryland and try to recapture them, invading Northern territory as they did so? The thought horrified her. As they reached the other side, she paused to catch her breath, crouching behind a beam at the end of the bridge.

"Jordan! What are you doing? Come quick!" Laura cried.

"You two go on!" Jordan shouted. "I'll try to slow them down."

To reinforce her words, she fired the derringer down the bridge. A man's yelp informed her that she had hit something and she smiled grimly. Quickly she reloaded the pistol, took aim, and fired again. The soldiers halted their advance, unsure whether to proceed or retreat. Jordan kept the gun pointed at them when she heard footsteps and Laura promptly squatted beside her.

"Laura, go. Get away. You and Esther have a chance to escape. They won't follow as long as they know I'll shoot them."

Before she could say another word, Esther stumbled against them and sat down roughly on the ground. Panting hard, she leaned heavily against Laura. "What's wrong with you white women?" she wheezed. "Are you mad?"

"Esther, take Laura and run," Jordan insisted. She saw movement down the bridge and fired another shot.

"Esther, you go, I'll stay with Jordan," Laura commanded.

"Don't you go ordering me around, Missy," Esther said angrily. "I'm not your slave."

"Would you both just go?" Jordan was exasperated.

"How many bullets do you have left?" Laura demanded. "How long do you think you will last before you have fired the last shot and they are upon you?"

Jordan did not answer. She looked down at the bag of bullets in her lap and counted two more rounds. It would not be enough to kill all the soldiers in pursuit of them. If Laura and Esther were to leave now, she could hold them off for a while longer. Then she would save the last bullet for herself.

A lone soldier made a dash for their end of the bridge and Jordan fired. He clutched at his chest, collapsed on the bridge, and was still. She reloaded again.

"Please, Laura, Esther, go now, I beg you." Jordan was desperate.

"No, Jordan, your destiny is mine. We shall face it together, whatever it may be."

Laura touched Jordan's cheek and for a moment it was only the two of them, alone in the midst of the chaos churning about them. Laura met Jordan's lips, kissing her with all the love she could convey in that one simple act. When they drew apart, the world came crashing in upon them.

Angered by the loss of one of their men and infuriated that only a single gun fired by a woman prevented their advance, the soldiers charged. Grabbing Laura's hand, Jordan leapt up and started running alongside Esther. Gunfire erupted and ricocheted off the rocks they had climbed onto in their flight, impelling them onward. The jagged outcropping was unanticipated and slowed them down. Jordan's ankle gave out and she stumbled.

From up the trail, rifle fire sounded and minié balls whizzed overhead. Laura glanced up to see Federal cavalry riding toward them, firing at the Rebels as they advanced toward the bridge. The Confederate soldiers halted, fired a few uncertain shots in the direction of the Union men, then turned and ran back onto the bridge. Within moments, Federal troops surrounded the women and a soldier leapt from his horse to the ground before his horse had even come to a full stop. He appeared surprised to find three women lying in the dirt and rushed to their side.

"I'm Lieutenant Wilson T. McClain, U.S. Second Cavalry, at your service." He bowed.

Esther flung herself into the astonished man's arms and kissed him roughly on the cheek. Tears streamed down her face as she laughed hysterically. Quickly recovering, she assisted Laura in helping Jordan to stand.

"Lieutenant," Jordan said, "we owe you our lives."

"What is going on?" he asked.

"It is a very long story." Jordan laughed. "And we shall tell you all about it, if you wish. But by way of introduction, I'm Jordan Colfax, this is Laura St. Clair, and this is Esther Stark. You may know my brother, Lieutenant Tyler Colfax, also of the Second Cavalry."

"You're the spy." The lieutenant's face lit up in recognition. "I read about you and Miss St. Clair in the newspaper. The Rebels were most anxious for your return." A slow grin spread across his face. "But I guess Southern men are accustomed to having ladies keep them waiting, so they can wait a little longer."

Chapter Thirty

The three women, resting comfortably in the back of a wagon, were escorted into Hagerstown, Maryland, by five members of the Second Cavalry, compliments of their commanding officer. They were exhausted, both from the physical demands of their escape and the extreme tension of nearly being caught. When they pulled up to the house on their next stop, an elderly farmer and his wife came out to greet them. They directed them to their rooms in the upper level of the farmhouse, and bade them good night.

They slept late into the morning and rose only when hunger drove them from their beds in search of food. After they'd enjoyed a full country breakfast, the farmer hitched a team of horses to his wagon and, with a picnic basket provided by his wife, they headed north toward Chambersburg, Pennsylvania. It was the final destination on their seemingly endless journey and they sat quietly in the back of the wagon, each absorbed in her own thoughts.

Jordan was the first to speak. "If we were to head southeast from here, we would soon be in Frederick and from there on to Washington. It would be nice to see my father and have one of Mrs. Johnson's apple pies. I'm quite sure I could eat an entire one by myself."

"Jordan, there's nothing preventing you from going home," Laura said. "I could go on to Chambersburg with Esther, and you could write or visit when you wish."

Jordan stared at her, unsure what she was saying. Guessing that she was simply being unselfish, she took Laura's hand and kissed it softly. "As you said on the bridge, your destiny is mine and we'll face it together, whatever it may be."

Laura let her gaze rest on Jordan's strong features, enjoying the way the sun shone brightly on her hair. She thought about the strength of this woman, and how she managed to survive because of it. And she thought about the future, their destiny, as they had decided to call it. She did not know what it would bring, and they had much to think about. What they would do with themselves and how they would support themselves was always in the back of her mind. But more importantly, what did their relationship portend? What exactly were these feelings she had for Jordan? The physical intimacy they'd shared in Front Royal was the most wonderful experience of her life, yet she couldn't help but wonder how such passion would fit into the world they shared.

She also thought about her parents and what she had left behind in Virginia. She wondered if it would ever be possible for her to see them and her sister Meg, who would, in a few years, be ready for marriage herself. And finally, she thought about Ransom, buried deep within the soil of Barrett Hall. Had it been worth it for him? Had his devotion to Virginia and the Confederacy been worth the loss of his life? He had died doing his duty, and she knew that above all else that was important to him. He would not have wished it any other way.

She sighed, wishing she had her journal so she could write down her thoughts. She had too many ideas flitting around in her head to sort them all out clearly, and she knew it would be a long time before she would be able to record them.

"By the way, I just remembered. I bought you a present." Jordan rummaged around in her bag until she found what she was looking for. Withdrawing the leather-bound journal that Laura had seen in the shop outside Charlottesville, she handed it to her. "I know how much your journals meant to you, and I'm sorry you had to leave them behind. Perhaps you can begin the next chapter of your life with this one."

Tears formed in Laura's eyes, but this time, they were tears of happiness. "Oh, Jordan," was all she could manage.

The journal was the greatest gift anyone could have given her, and Laura knew definitively that Jordan understood her heart. She opened the first page to find a pencil inside, picked it up, and began to write.

8 October 1861

I have lived to see another day when I did not think it possible, but someone in my life made it so. I had another journal before this one. It seems so long ago now that I wrote Jordan was my friend, and yet so much more if only I knew.

Now I do. I have found that someone who truly makes me feel something, and I now know that it is love.

She paused for a moment, placing the tip of the pencil to her lips, then wrote once more.

The sun may darken, heaven be bowed
But still unchanged shall be,
Here in my soul, that moonlit cloud,
To which I looked with thee!

The wagon continued north to Pennsylvania and the small town they would call home until the day it might be safe to return to Washington. Until then, Laura knew that while life would not be as she had known it at Barrett Hall, she had found a new home in Jordan.

Author's Note

House of Clouds is a novel, first and foremost. The story takes place from late 1860 to late 1861, and for narrative purposes I've taken certain liberties with the historical timeline. Ford's Athenaeum, now Ford's Theatre, did not open its doors until December 1861, whereas I have it in use earlier in the year. And the tunnel out of Libby Prison in Richmond, leading to the escape of over one hundred Union prisoners of war, was not dug until February 1864. Any fiction author approaches the representation of historical figures with trepidation, for we are in the business of storytelling, not biography. The written record and eyewitness accounts provide a source of dialogue attributed to Lincoln, and I have drawn from these where I could. Sometimes conversations appear in my narrative prior to or after the actual event. I hope the reader will indulge my occasional manipulation of historical detail to serve the requirements of my story.

About the Author

KI Thompson began her writing career when her first short story, "The Blue Line," was included in the Lambda Literary Award–winning anthology *Erotic Interludes 2: Stolen Moments* from Bold Strokes Books. She also has selections in the subsequent anthologies, *Erotic Interludes* 3, 4 (IPPY Award Silver Medal, Goldie Award), and 5, a story in *Best Lesbian Romance 2007* (Cleis Press), as well as one in *Fantasy: Untrue Stories of Lesbian Passion* (Bella Books). Her second novel, *Heart of the Matter*, is forthcoming from Bold Strokes Books in 2008.

Books Available From Bold Strokes Books

House of Clouds by KI Thompson. A sweeping saga of an impassioned romance between a Northern spy and a Southern sympathizer, set amidst the upheaval of a nation under siege. (978-1-933110-94-3)

Winds of Fortune by Radclyffe. Provincetown local Deo Camara agrees to rehab Dr. Bonita Burgoyne's historic home, but she never said anything about mending her heart. (978-1-933110-93-6)

Focus of Desire by Kim Baldwin. Isabel Sterling is surprised when she wins a photography contest, but no more than photographer Natasha Kashnikova. Their promo tour becomes a ticket to romance. (978-1-933110-92-9)

Blind Leap by Diane and Jacob Anderson-Minshall. A Golden Gate Bridge suicide becomes suspect when a filmmaker's camera shows a different story. Yoshi Yakamota and the Blind Eye Detective Agency uncover evidence that could be worth killing for. (978-1-933110-91-2)

Wall of Silence, 2nd ed. by Gabrielle Goldsby. Life takes a dangerous turn when jaded police detective Foster Everett meets Riley Medeiros, a woman who isn't afraid to discover the truth no matter the cost. (978-1-933110-90-5)

Mistress of the Runes by Andrews & Austin. Passion ignites between two women with ties to ancient secrets, contemporary mysteries, and a shared quest for the meaning of life. (978-1-933110-89-9)

Sheridan's Fate by Gun Brooke. A dynamic, erotic romance between physiotherapist Lark Mitchell and businesswoman Sheridan Ward set in the scorching hot days and humid, steamy nights of San Antonio. (978-1-933110-88-2)

Vulture's Kiss by Justine Saracen. Archeologist Valerie Foret, heir to a terrifying task, returns in a powerful desert adventure set in Egypt and Jerusalem. (978-1-933110-87-5)

Rising Storm by JLee Meyer. The sequel to *First Instinct* takes our heroines on a dangerous journey instead of the honeymoon they'd planned. (978-1-933110-86-8)

Not Single Enough by Grace Lennox. A funny, sexy modern romance about two lonely women who bond over the unexpected and fall in love along the way. (978-1-933110-85-1)

Such a Pretty Face by Gabrielle Goldsby. A sexy, sometimes humorous, sometimes biting contemporary romance that gently exposes the damage to heart and soul when we fail to look beneath the surface for what truly matters. (978-1-933110-84-4)

Second Season by Ali Vali. A romance set in New Orleans amidst betrayal, Hurricane Katrina, and the new beginnings hardship and heartbreak sometimes make possible. (978-1-933110-83-7)

Hearts Aflame by Ronica Black. A poignant, erotic romance between a hard-driving businesswoman and a solitary vet. Packed with adventure and set in the harsh beauty of the Arizona countryside. (978-1-933110-82-0)

Red Light by JD Glass. Tori forges her path as an EMT in the New York City 911 system while discovering what matters most to herself and the woman she loves. (978-1-933110-81-3)

Honor Under Siege by Radclyffe. Secret Service agent Cameron Roberts struggles to protect her lover while searching for a traitor who just may be another woman with a claim on her heart. (978-1-933110-80-6)

Dark Valentine by Jennifer Fulton. Danger and desire fuel a high-stakes cat-and-mouse game when an attorney and an endangered witness team up to thwart a killer. (978-1-933110-79-0)

Sequestered Hearts by Erin Dutton. A popular artist suddenly goes into seclusion, a reluctant reporter wants to know why, and a heart locked away yearns to be set free. (978-1-933110-78-3)

Erotic Interludes 5: Road Games, ed. by Radclyffe and Stacia Seaman. Adventure, "sport," and sex on the road—hot stories of travel adventures and games of seduction. (978-1-933110-77-6)

The Spanish Pearl by Catherine Friend. On a trip to Spain, Kate Vincent is accidentally transported back in time—an epic saga spiced with humor, lust, and danger. (978-1-933110-76-9)

Lady Knight by L-J Baker. Loyalty and honor clash with love and ambition in a medieval world of magic when female knight Riannon meets Lady Eleanor. (978-1-933110-75-2)

Dark Dreamer by Jennifer Fulton. Best-selling horror author Rowe Devlin falls under the spell of psychic Phoebe Temple. A Dark Vista romance. (978-1-933110-74-5)

Come and Get Me by Julie Cannon. Elliott Foster isn't used to pursuing women, but alluring attorney Lauren Collier makes her change her mind. (978-1-933110-73-8)

Dynasty of Rogues by Jane Fletcher. It's hate at first sight for Ranger Riki Sadiq and her new patrol corporal, Tanya Coppelli—except for their undeniable attraction. (978-1-933110-71-4)

Running With the Wind by Nell Stark. Sailing instructor Corrie Marsten has signed off on love until she meets Quinn Davies—one woman she can't ignore. (978-1-933110-70-7)

When Dreams Tremble by Radclyffe. Two women whose lives turned out far differently than they'd once imagined discover that sometimes the shape of the future can only be found in the past. (1-933110-64-3)

Burning Dreams by Susan Smith. The chronicle of the challenges faced by a young drag king and an older woman who share a love "outside the bounds." (1-933110-62-7)

Fresh Tracks by Georgia Beers. Seven women, seven days. A lot can happen when old friends, lovers, and a new girl in town get together in the mountains. (1-933110-63-5)

Tristaine Rises by Cate Culpepper. Brenna, Jesstin, and the Amazons of Tristaine face their greatest challenge for survival. (1-933110-50-3)

Unexpected Ties by Gina L. Dartt. With death before dessert, Kate Shannon and Nikki Harris are swept up in another tale of danger and romance. (1-933110-56-2)

Passion's Bright Fury by Radclyffe. When a trauma surgeon and a filmmaker become reluctant allies on the battleground between life and death, passion strikes without warning. (1-933110-54-6)

Sweet Creek by Lee Lynch. A celebration of the enduring nature of love, friendship, and community in the quirky, heart-warming lesbian community of Waterfall Falls. (1-933110-29-5)

Sword of the Guardian by Merry Shannon. Princess Shasta's bold new bodyguard has a secret that could change both of their lives. *He* is actually a *she*. A passionate romance filled with courtly intrigue, chivalry, and devotion. (1-933110-36-8)

Turn Back Time by Radclyffe. Pearce Rifkin and Wynter Thompson have nothing in common but a shared passion for surgery. They clash at every opportunity, especially when matters of the heart are suddenly at stake. (1-933110-34-1)

Promising Hearts by Radclyffe. Dr. Vance Phelps lost everything in the War Between the States and arrives in New Hope, Montana, with no hope of happiness and no desire for anything except forgetting—until she meets Mae, a frontier madam. (1-933110-44-9)

Innocent Hearts by Radclyffe. In a wild and unforgiving land, two women learn about love, passion, and the wonders of the heart. (1-933110-21-X)

Justice Served by Radclyffe. Lieutenant Rebecca Frye and her lover, Dr. Catherine Rawlings, embark on a deadly game of hide-and-seek with an underworld kingpin who traffics in human souls. (1-933110-15-5)

Justice in the Shadows by Radclyffe. In a shadow world of secrets and lies, Detective Sergeant Rebecca Frye and her lover, Dr. Catherine Rawlings, join forces in the elusive search for justice. (1-933110-03-1)

A Matter of Trust by Radclyffe. JT Sloan is a cybersleuth who doesn't like attachments. Michael Lassiter is leaving her husband, and she needs Sloan's expertise to safeguard her company. It should just be business—but it turns into much more. (1-933110-33-3)

Storms of Change by Radclyffe. In the continuing saga of the Provincetown Tales, duty and love are at odds as Reese and Tory face their greatest challenge. (1-933110-57-0)

Distant Shores, Silent Thunder by Radclyffe. Dr. Tory King—along with the women who love her—is forced to examine the boundaries of love, friendship, and the ties that transcend time. (1-933110-08-2)

Beyond the Breakwater by Radclyffe. One Provincetown summer, three women learn the true meaning of love, friendship, and family. (1-933110-06-6)

Safe Harbor by Radclyffe. A mysterious newcomer, a reclusive doctor, and a troubled gay teenager learn about love, friendship, and trust during one tumultuous summer in Provincetown. (1-933110-13-9)

shadowland by Radclyffe. In a world on the far edge of desire, two women are drawn together by power, passion, and dark pleasures. An erotic romance. (1-933110-11-2)

Love's Masquerade by Radclyffe. Plunged into the indistinguishable realms of fiction, fantasy, and hidden desires, Auden Frost is forced to question all she believes about the nature of love. (1-933110-14-7)

Honor Reclaimed by Radclyffe. In the aftermath of 9/11, Secret Service Agent Cameron Roberts and Blair Powell close ranks with a trusted few to find the would-be assassins who nearly claimed Blair's life. (1-933110-18-X)

Honor Guards by Radclyffe. In a wild flight for their lives, the president's daughter and those who are sworn to protect her wage a desperate struggle for survival. (1-933110-01-5)

Love & Honor by Radclyffe. The president's daughter and her lover are faced with difficult choices as they battle a tangled web of Washington intrigue for…love and honor. (1-933110-10-4)

Honor Bound by Radclyffe. Secret Service Agent Cameron Roberts and Blair Powell face political intrigue, a clandestine threat to Blair's safety, and the seemingly irreconcilable personal differences that force them ever farther apart. (1-933110-20-1)

Above All, Honor by Radclyffe. Secret Service Agent Cameron Roberts fights her desire for the one woman she can't have—Blair Powell, the daughter of the president of the United States. (1-933110-04-X)